Queen Bee
Goes Home Again

Also by Haywood Smith

Queen Bee
Goes Home Again

HAYWOOD SMITH

St. Martin's Press

New York

QUEEN BEE GOES HOME AGAIN. Copyright © 2014 by Haywood Smith. All rights reserved. Printed in the United States of America. For information, address St. Martin's Press, 175 Fifth Avenue, New York, N.Y. 10010.

www.stmartins.com

Designed by Kathryn Parise

THE LIBRARY OF CONGRESS CATALOGING-IN-PUBLICATION DATA
IS AVAILABLE UPON REQUEST.

ISBN 978-1-250-00351-5 (hardcover)
ISBN 978-1-4668-6453-5 (e-book)

St. Martin's Press books may be purchased for educational, business, or promotional use. For information on bulk purchases, please contact Macmillan Corporate and Premium Sales Department at 1-800-221-7945, extension 5442, or write specialmarkets@macmillan.com.

First Edition: September 2014

10 9 8 7 6 5 4 3 2 1

*This book is dedicated to my precious friend and confidante,
Willow Heart Catron, who has been a model of grace,
patience, and faith both in living and in dying.
And to all my precious friends who have gone to heaven before me:
Kappy and Roslyn and Bess and Cindy and Gracie and Vera,
to name a few. We will meet again in the presence of Christ,
but I sure do miss them now.*

Acknowledgments

First, thanks goes to Dr. Donald Dennis of Atlanta, allergist, surgeon, and ENT, whose research and regimen have helped me live without pain or inflammation for more than seven years. God bless you!

I also give thanks daily for my precious sister Elise for being Christ's hands and heart in my life, showing me what true perseverance, agape love, and acceptance look like, even in the face of her own physical and emotional challenges. What a joy and privilege it is to have you as my sister by blood and in Christ. And thanks to my sisters Susan and Betsy, who have done the same. I love you so much.

I also love my brother James Hill Pritchett, on his terms, but no less deeply.

And thanks to my son and daughter-in-law, for making sure I don't go without health insurance. God bless you for your help and generosity. And to Blackshear Place Baptist Church for being such a wonderful community of God and generous helper.

Thanks also to my wonderful editor, Jennifer Enderlin, for her guidance and help in making this book a reality. What would I do without you? And to my agent, Mel Berger, for helping put food on my table and much-needed prescriptions in my medicine chest. And to my wonderful copy editor, Ragnhild Hagen, who catches my mistakes and errors in continuity.

And thanks, too, to my wonderful friends and the Red Hat Club. What love and acceptance I always find from you.

Thanks, also, more than I can say, to all the readers and friends who have prayed for my granddaughter, who has a rare form of epilepsy, and supported legislation in the Georgia State House to allow cannabadiol (a nonintoxicating natural marijuana extract for treating seizures) to be used in our state. At this writing, the bill passed the Georgia House, but was made unpassable in the Georgia Senate Health committee, so we are packing to go to Colorado to see if the Charlotte's Web extract helps.

And to all my readers who let me know they enjoy my books: Your wonderful e-mails never fail to lift my spirits, no matter what challenges I face. That is why I write what I do, to encourage and bring laughter to you all.

To those of you who don't like something, please be merciful and keep it to yourselves. Neither I nor my books are perfect, no matter how hard we try. Fortunately, books are like food: Everybody likes something different.

I also owe thanks to Hayes Chrysler Plymouth for putting Queenie back together after a deer hit us. And to Maaco in Lawrenceville, Georgia, for always doing such a great job with Queenie's dents and scrapes. The older I get, the more there are.

My life has never been a dull one, so I am thankful to God for all the material He gives me. And for the 12-step enabler's program that got me outside of myself and showed me a better way to live, a way devoid of judgment that starts every day with gratitude instead of worry, helping me live with joy, no matter what. Between that and my Bible, I'm doing great. And there are more books in me yet.

Queen Bee
Goes Home Again

One

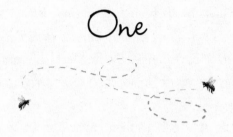

Don't you just hate it when God hits the replay button on the tough stuff in your life? I sure do, and when He hit it in my life a year ago, it was a biggie.

A lot has happened in the year since that day: wars were fought, disasters raged, great things began, and great things were lost, but I was too caught up in the minor miracles and tragedies of my own little life to notice. (I *did* vote, though; happily on the local level, but when it came to Washington, I had to choose the lesser of the evils, which I am seriously sick of, but I voted anyway. Use it or lose it.)

On that blazing July seventh a year ago, I took the long way back to my mother's (Miss Mamie to everyone, including my brother Tommy and me) at 1431 Green Street in Mimosa Branch, Georgia.

Despite all my efforts, there I was, moving back to my mother's domain. Again.

The phantom umbilicus that connected me to my mother had turned into the string on a yo-yo.

Ten years older than I was the first time I'd had to move back home. Ten years tireder. Branded as the local scarlet woman for something I didn't do. And really, really ticked off.

Anger was the only energy I had left.

Through all the tribulations I've endured—and there have been a few—my prayer has always been *Please, God, let me pass this test the first time, because I sure don't want to have to take it again.*

Apparently, I must have flunked the first test ten years ago when I'd had to move in with my "eccentric" (read: crazy) Southern family in the town I'd married to escape.

I hadn't had any other options then, either. My straight-arrow CPA husband of thirty years had gotten engaged to a stripper and supposedly spent all our money (including what we owed the IRS), so I'd lost everything but what I could carry and the furniture I'd squirreled away with friends in Buckhead who'd promptly dropped me after the divorce.

This time around, I had the economy to blame. After years of working twenty-four/seven selling houses during the building boom, I'd finally managed to buy my own little brick ranch ten miles from town, then disappeared into the blessed anonymity of exurbia. My own little Fortress of Solitude.

Boy, was that a relief after being under constant scrutiny in Mimosa Branch.

But when the real estate bubble blew, plunging the economy into a depression, I was once again reduced to penury, upside down in my mortgage.

So on that hot, fateful July seventh a year ago, I'd signed over my house in a short sale for a fraction of its true worth and finally given in to Miss Mamie's pleas to come home and help her with the house, now that the General and Uncle B were roommates in the Alzheimer's wing of the Home, as the local nursing facility was known by one and all in Mimosa Branch.

Everybody but Tommy and I called my daddy the General—not because he'd been one in the military, but because of his dictatorial personality and the fact that he'd been the premier general contractor in Mimosa Branch for fifty years, till age and Alzheimer's caught up with him.

Heading for my mother's from the lawyer's office, I tried my best to be grateful that I could move into the garage apartment again. I couldn't even scrape up a deposit for lodgings elsewhere, much less commit to paying rent. At least I wasn't in a shelter, which definitely wouldn't have fit my small-town aristocratic sensibilities, or my mother's.

Which left me right back where I'd started a decade before: not-so-instant replay, on a cosmic level.

Give thanks in all things, the Bible says, but I wasn't doing very well with that one under the circumstances.

As I had in my divorce, I climbed up in the Almighty Creator of the Universe's lap, beat on His chest, and asked Him why this was happening. Again.

And cussed about it, but only in my mind. Not as bad as I had cussed ten years ago, mind you. Back then, I'd been so hurt that vulgarities I'd never even *thought,* much less said, became my mantra for almost a year. My very prim Christian marriage counselor/psychiatrist at the time had told me that if cussing was all I did, I was doing great, all things considered.

Ever since, I'd done my best to clean up my act, but my thoughts were still rebellious. I'd replaced the cussing with *shoot* and *rats*—and in extreme cases, *antidisestablishmentarianism,* backward—but God knew what I really wanted to say. Yet He is still steeped in grace, putting His arms around me in comfort, not in condemnation.

So there I was, towing a crammed U-Haul trailer behind my crammed 2009 Chrysler Town and Country minivan (paid for when I was selling houses hand over fist, thank the good Lord). I turned onto Main Street from South Roberts, only to find myself the last in a long line of stationary traffic.

Traffic, in olde towne Mimosa Branch! (The merchant's association had tacked on the extra *e*s at the height of the building boome.)

About ten cars ahead of me, a restaurant delivery truck was blocking all of my lane and half the other at our local upscale bistro, Terra Sol, which was probably a major traffic violation, since there was a perfectly good alley in the back. Definitely wretched timing, unloading during the lunch rush.

Not that I was in any hurry to finish moving into the garage apartment I'd renovated on the first go-round, but I've always been a face-the-music-and-get-it-over-with kind of person.

Taking advantage of the traffic backup, I punched in the previous calls screen on my Walmart prepaid cell phone, then scrolled down to my best friend Tricia's number and pressed the green receiver button to call her. I heard a nanosecond of dial tone, then the phone beeped out her number in Alexandria, Virginia. After four rings I was about to hang up when she picked up the phone, breathless.

"Sorry," she panted out, "I was out deadheading my roses."

Thank goodness she was there. I really needed to vent. "Well, I'm headed back to Miss Mamie's from the lawyer's office with the last of my earthly goods, and I feel like throwing up."

"Poor baby, poor baby, poor baby," she commiserated, one short of the four *poor baby*s I felt the situation merited. "I don't blame you for feeling sick," she soothed. "So the house closed?"

"Finally." An ache the size of Stone Mountain squashed my heart. "So this is it. Back to Miss Mamie's turf. Back to having my every move evaluated and criticized by the whole town."

Thanks to Miss Mamie's prayer chains, both Baptist and Methodist, who saw me as the sum total of every mistake I'd ever made and every sin—real or imagined—I'd ever committed.

I went on, "I *hate* losing my privacy. And the awful thing is, I don't think I have the energy left to escape again." I inched forward as the line of SUVs and pickups condensed. "I am too *old* to start over."

"Speak for yourself," she said.

Oh, sure. Easy to say when all you have to worry about is deadheading your rose garden. Tricia had scored big in her divorce.

I'd gotten zip.

Oh, Phil had signed the divorce decree granting me decent alimony. Then he'd promptly quit his job and disappeared. I'd gotten several contempt-of-court convictions on him before I realized I was just wasting time and money.

It was up to our son David—furious at his father—to inform me that friends had bumped into his dad living high on the hog on St. Bart's with his "fiancée" Bambi Bottoms (she'd legally changed it to that) on the money he'd squirreled away offshore. And bragging about it.

Humiliated and furious, David had promptly called and told me.

Thank you so much. Like I needed more reason to resent his father. I mean, really.

At least David had his great job and his great wife Barb in Charlotte to distract him, plus my precious grandbabies—Callista (what were they thinking?), four, and sunny-bunny Barrett, two. But after my only child had told me about his dad, David had become oddly distant, so I hadn't nagged him about not calling me. Yet I sure missed hearing about his job and his family. I'd tried calling them, but they politely blew me off. So I left them alone, hoping things would work out some time before I died.

All I had to distract me were bills and useless contempt citations.

Considering my destitution, I wondered if I'd get a percentage if I ratted Phil out to the IRS. The trouble was, I had no idea exactly where he was.

"Are you still there?" Tricia asked.

"Sorry." I rescued myself from useless resentments and vowed to stay in the present. "My mind wandered. It does that a lot lately."

"Stress," she diagnosed.

Then she promptly ignored the rules of our Poor Baby Club and lapsed into *it could be worse,* with, "At least the apartment is air-conditioned this time around."

I wasn't in the mood. "Why did God let this happen to me? Again," I demanded for the jillionth time.

Tricia let out a brisk sigh. "God didn't do this. Your crooked ex and the crooked banks and subprime lenders and the politicians did. Everybody's taken a hit."

Except Tricia's ex, who did high-security alternative-power backup systems for the Fed.

When I didn't reply, she said, "Anyway, you've been praying that God would bring America back to its knees, whatever it took."

"Yeah, but I didn't think that would mean *I'd* be driven to poverty. And have to move back home. Again."

Gratitude, my inner Puritan scolded. *At least you have a place to go, with people who love you.*

Love me too much, I mentally retorted. At sixty years of age, I did *not* need to be mothered. Or constantly evaluated, no matter how subtly.

I looked up at the traffic. Rats. The blasted delivery truck was still there. "I've repented and cleaned up my act since Grant Owens." My one disastrous fling. "God knows, I have. So why am I having to repeat this purgatory?"

"Honey, you're the best person I know," Tricia told me, and I knew she believed it, but compared to the politicians and government contractors she still hung out with, anybody half decent looked like a saint. "Bad things do happen to good people."

Surely Jehovah God, Author of All Things (including me), wouldn't punish me with destitution just for mentally cussing Him out when nobody else was around. Well, maybe not mentally all the time, but it was my sole remaining vice.

"Are you still there?" Tricia asked.

"Yes. I'm thinking."

God bless her, she let me.

Other than cussing in my brain, I did my best to live a good Christian life. I went to see God at His house most Sundays and tithed, and I tried to be compassionate with everybody—well, except my ex. (Not that I'd had the chance. He'd been out of the country for ten years.)

I'd forgiven Phil long ago as an act of obedience and spiritual self-preservation, but my emotions hadn't quite gotten the memo. Especially since I'd found out he was still screwing me over, and in the Caribbean.

Not that I hated Phil—I didn't have that in me—but I'd love a chance to give him a good sheet-beating till he coughed up some cash. Wishful thinking, but I didn't encourage it. Life goes on.

As my Granny Beth always said, "Being bitter is like drinking poison and expecting it to kill the other person. It only hurts you."

I wasn't bitter. At least, not till the bottom of my life had dropped out. Again.

"I just don't understand why a criminal like Phil can break all the rules," I complained to Tricia, "and end up in the catbird seat, but I'm the one who's homeless and destitute."

Tricia sighed and quoted scripture. " 'Why do the evil prosper?' "

"So the question isn't a new one," I griped. "I still want to know why."

"Remember what your Granny Beth always used to say," Tricia reminded me. " '*Why* doesn't matter. It's the devil's most destructive distraction. What matters is how you deal with it.' "

"I did not call for logic or solutions, missy," I scolded. Our Poor Baby Club expressly prohibited logic or solutions. Only sympathy allowed. "Or *it could be worse*. And this is definitely a four, not a three."

"Poor baby, poor baby, poor baby, poor baby," she corrected. "Now, whine away."

So I did, till both of us had had a crawful.

Disgusted with myself for going on so long, I ended with, "Sorry I dumped my pity party on you. Next time I call, I promise to be more positive."

Tricia chuckled. "You can dump on me all you want. Anytime. Lord knows, I dumped on you a lot more when I got divorced. So you still have a serious whine credit with me."

"Thanks," I said. "Bye."

"Bye."

I always felt better after talking to Tricia, but nothing could make this day any easier.

I, Linwood Breedlove Scott, was officially returning to the Mimosa Branch Hall of Shame.

Two

I looked ahead and saw the deliveryman load up his dolly, *again,* with flat boxes that let off cold fog in the heat, then he headed back to the front door of Terra Sol, one of three remaining upscale restaurants in town. Four other establishments had bitten the dust when the depression hit.

If I had to wait in the heat much longer, I'd have to turn off the AC, and maybe the car, to keep the motor from conking in the hot sun.

Frustrated, I distracted myself by looking at the stores on either side of Main Street. I hadn't been back "downtown" in the three years since I'd moved to my much-mourned little brick ranch Fortress of Solitude house near Sunshine Springs. At least the few surviving restaurants here seemed to be doing well, evidenced by the traffic and resulting lack of parking spaces.

But all the New Age artists' studios were gone now, much to the relief of the churchgoing ladies of Mimosa Branch, Miss Mamie among them. FOR SALE or FOR RENT signs replaced the nude paintings and sculptures (even *males!*) that had so alarmed the locals when downtown was invaded by the coven of modern artists (or *mod-run,* as many of the churchwomen carefully pronounced it) more than a decade ago.

My wonderful, free-spirited glass sculptor friend's gallery had only lasted ten months in ultraconservative Mimosa Branch, and even the County Art Center had refused to exhibit her work. So she and her partner had moved to Asheville, a lesbian Mecca in the mountains.

The recession, combined with the local evangelicals' efforts to "save" those "weirdo" artists, had finally run the rest of the modrun artists back to California where they belonged. The few remaining local "boats and barns" artists and sculptors had retreated, rent-free, to the old mill warehouse, now vacant and for sale, where they rattled around like beer cans in the bed of an old pickup truck, hot in the summer and freezing in the winter.

Miss Mamie had kept me up on all the gossip by phone, whether I wanted to hear it or not (mostly not).

I knew better than to hope she'd lay off, now that we'd be seeing each other so much. Miss Mamie was Miss Mamie, and at ninety, I knew there was no chance that she'd quit gossiping, so it was up to me to ignore the irritations and focus on her good parts, which were many. (I had my church psychologist and 12-step enabler's group to thank for that revelation.)

Still, a wave of psychosomatic nausea brought me back to the present just as the delivery truck finally pulled away, only to have a car back out of the fifteen-minute parking in front of the drugstore.

Chief Parker's—so named through a succession of five owners—was now Mason's Hometown Drugs, retaining its defiant mid-sixties appearance, if not its name. Old Doc Owens's NEVER CLOSED TO THE SICK sign was missing from the plate-glass storefront, along with the pharmacist's home phone number—a casualty, no doubt, of the twenty-four-hour pharmacy in the new Kroger over by the huge mall at the Interstate.

Megamall or not, though, downtown Mimosa Branch was still Mimosa Branch, despite the suburban transplants who'd overrun it and the new sidewalks with brick inserts lit by replicas of antique Victorian streetlights.

At last, the car ahead of me got going.

Passing the drugstore's plate-glass windows, I flashed on Grant Owens, and the nausea spiked. Can we say, Mr. Wrong?

But it hadn't been his fault. All the signs had been there that he was totally incapable of relationships, but I had deluded myself into thinking I could have a fling with him, no harm done, and he was worthy of my attentions.

Not, on all counts.

I'd repented at leisure and knew God had forgiven me, but that didn't make it any less shameful, a fact that Mary Lou Perkins—the first and foremost of Mimosa Branch's self-righteous pot-stirrers—continued to drag up in a "serves her right" tone whenever anything bad happened to me, like losing my home. Never mind that plenty of good, hardworking Christians had lost their houses, too.

Mary Lou controlled the women's programs at First Baptist and was dead set on preventing "pollution" in the church. Totally negative and judgmental, she was clueless that she'd been seduced by the dark side of the Force. Poor baby.

Thanks to a decade in my 12-step enabler's group, I'd finally realized I couldn't control what people said or thought about me. I could only control my responses.

Which at the moment included the distinct possibility of hurling in my car.

Finally exiting the business district, I eased my minivan and U-Haul past the old cotton mill, where a Mexican butcher's and a *supermercado* were the sole remaining tenants, evidence of the continued influx of illegals who now did all our yard work and had taken all the entry-level jobs at the poultry plant.

Leaving olde towne behind at last, I passed First Methodist, then the old brick Presbyterian church that was now the newest First Baptist. (The *previous* new, giant metal First Baptist across the highway had gone back to the bank after the real estate bust and ensuing depression had halted growth and decimated tithes.)

Then came "silk stocking lane," railroad tracks on the left, big houses on the right. Gone were the tall, sparsely leafed-out elm trunks that had lined the sidewalk in my youth, leaving the houses unshaded to bake in the setting sun. I'd long known that there was no hope for the elms since Dutch elm disease had swept across the country, but now that all evidence of them had been erased, I felt a tug of grief, as if those stubborn trees had stood for my own determination to survive.

The new sidewalks, shiny metal benches, streetlights, and wispy, twelve-foot replacement trees looked very nice, but the houses were left exposed, stripped of their buffer.

The first big house I passed was the handsome old brick First Method-ist manse (sold off years ago to help pay for repairs to the historic church). Next, I passed the same gorgeous white house that was still a law office, one of the few left in town. Next came the hundred-year-old Greek revival replica of a plantation house I'd always loved.

Beyond that, at a right angle facing town, sat the youngest of the Breed-love mansions, built in the 1920s, a brick Italianate whose pretentious exte-rior and life-sized cement lions had always looked out of place in Mimosa Branch.

Lately, the house had been converted from a bed-and-breakfast to a "Christian Family Retreat" by an African-American televangelist who'd bought it and moved in with his family, stirring remnants of residual preju-dice deep below the surface in the local white racists, but nothing in the open.

The biggest change was in front of those old mansions. Taking advan-tage of the boom before the bust, the city had extended the sidewalks and streetlights all the way to the railroad crossing three blocks past Miss Mamie's. Then they'd done away with the dogleg in front of the "Christian Family Retreat," where Main Street had become Green Street, filling the resulting triangle with a new park that sported an open-air amphitheater that faced away from the tracks (for logical reasons).

The city had rerouted all the traffic between the tracks and the back of the amphitheater's wall, making the whole thing look backwards to me, so I'd immediately dubbed it Backwards Park. And sure enough, there it was, presenting its bare curved brick wall to me as I passed, all the trees and flowers on the other side, a disturbing metaphor for my life.

Almost home.

Four more restored houses/offices sported FOR SALE or FOR LEASE signs, even Mrs. Duckett's fancifully redone Victorian. The bank had taken it over from the developer who'd done a green-stick restoration, updating the wiring, plumbing, and insulation. Poor guy. He'd spent so much restoring it, yet ended up with *nada*.

Across the side street from Mrs. Duckett's, our house loomed ahead, unchanged, at 1431 Green Street, one of the few remaining residences amid the commercially zoned houses that faced our side of the tracks. The verandah still anchored the sides and front of our sturdy foursquare Victorian colonial revival.

Miss Mamie's porch, all eighty feet of it, was her claim to fame. That, and her shoulder-high hedge of pale pink gumpos that bloomed all summer, to the envy and bafflement of the entire garden club and the county extension agent.

Miss Mamie's claim to infamy still sat by the front door as it had for the past twenty years: a cast-iron bathtub painted deep purple on the outside, perched on gilded ball-and-claw feet, and brimming with dark pink dragon-wing begonias, our shiny brass house numbers glued to the side.

It still reminded me of an ancient belle in her underwear, stretched out on a swooning couch for all to see, but I filed my opinions away in the *Let go and let God* drawer.

Tommy and I had long since given up trying to get our parents to have somebody haul the bathtub away for scrap. Daddy had protested that it would end up costing too much money, but that was before metal salvage paid so much.

Now that Daddy was in the Home, I think Miss Mamie held on to the tub out of misplaced loyalty for him, too guilty about having him committed to get rid of it.

When I looked closer, I saw that my childhood home was showing its age, and I couldn't help wondering what it cost Miss Mamie to keep it up. Had to be a small fortune.

The neglect was a disturbing clue that my mother might be hard up financially. But she'd never allowed us to discuss her finances, and at ninety, I doubted she would surrender that final bastion of control without a fight.

Miss Mamie wouldn't even tell us what it cost to keep Daddy in the Alzheimer's wing at the Home. Had to be at least three thousand a month, a major financial hemorrhage.

Not your business, the voice of my 12-step enabler's group chided. *You've got enough problems of your own to deal with.*

Not my business. For the moment, anyway.

Still, as I passed the historical marker that declared the accomplishments of our Breedlove ancestors, I felt a sudden spike of panic, and my arms refused to turn in at either entrance of our crushed-gravel circular drive.

I just couldn't do it.

So I deflected the inevitable by going to see Daddy at the Home, something I'd put off for months.

You've got to know it's bad when you'd rather go to a nursing home to see your crazy father than officially announce another failure by moving back in with your mother. Again.

Three

I took the crossing gently, hearing a few ominous clinks from my cargo and clanks from the U-Haul as I did.

Shoot. Shoot, shoot, shoot. Did I break anything?

I pulled past the taqueria and the Exxon station to the light, then turned left on the highway for half a block before entering the sizzling parking lot of the Home.

Of course, the only place I could park with the trailer was half a block from the door, and thanks to the heat inversion, the air was hazy with pollution. I locked my car, then hiked inside to be met by the odor of urine, stale sweat, overcooked food, and despair.

As usual, they kept the thermostat at eighty-five. I breathed through my mouth and tried not to think what germs Daddy and Uncle Bedford were exposed to daily from the overbooked, underpaid nursing assistants.

The Home had remained perpetually understaffed through four owners, and it didn't take a genius to know why. With only a few exceptions, they'd never paid the aides enough to keep anybody decent, so turnover was brisk, and most of the ones they hired came from the dregs of the work pool.

And as usual, there was nobody at the nurses' station when I passed it on the way to Daddy and Uncle Bedford's room in the Alzheimer's wing. At the security door to the wing, I punched in the daily access code written on a Post-it note stuck to the wall above the keypad, then went inside.

Halfway down the hall, I found Daddy's door slightly ajar, so I knocked softly as I opened it. "Hey. It's Lin."

What I found inside took me aback. Clothes and bed linens had been hurled every which way. Uncle Bedford's bare mattress was on the floor (the bed frame wasn't even in the room), and he and Daddy were lying on their exposed plastic mattresses, butt naked except for the sheets that covered them!

Daddy looked awful, but Uncle Bedford was a waxy yellow and didn't even seem to be breathing. Alarmed, I went over and shook him, hard. "Uncle Bedford," I shouted. "Wake up!"

He didn't budge. "Uncle Bedford!" I yelled into his ear.

Of course, he was stone deaf without his hearing aids, as was Daddy. The two of them carried on totally separate demented conversations at the top of their lungs all the time, but Uncle Bedford now gave off an unfamiliar sour smell and still didn't respond to my vigorous shaking.

As pitiful as their lives had become, I panicked at the thought that either of them might be dead. I'd prayed for God to take them both from their misery, but that didn't mean I was ready for it to happen that day.

To my relief, Daddy let out a rasping gasp, his jaw dropping, then started sawing logs, which at least told me he was still alive.

I grabbed the call button from his bed and punched it again and again, but nobody answered.

Frantic, I hurried out into the hall, where I spotted one of the few long-time nursing assistants emerging at a snail's pace from the Alzheimer's dining area at the far end of the corridor. "Shalayne!" I called to her. "Hurry! Something's wrong with Uncle Bedford."

"Hold yer horses," she said, clearly unimpressed. Her progress didn't speed up one whit. "I'm a-comin'. These blessed bunions is killin' me. Just hang on. It's all good."

Frustrated beyond endurance, I went back into Daddy's room and tried to rouse Uncle Bedford again, with no success.

My Aunt Glory would never forgive me if I simply stood there and did nothing. She felt guilty enough as it was, for finally throwing in the towel and committing him.

The General hadn't been in the Home for two weeks before Aunt Glory gave in to Uncle B's constant agitated demands that we find his brother. So she'd had her husband of fifty-seven years declared incompetent (duh!), then committed him to the Home on the condition that Uncle B and Daddy could be roommates, bless her heart.

Free at last, she'd fled Mimosa Branch in Uncle Bedford's red Corvette, to live with my cousin Susan in Alpharetta, where she had central air-conditioning, her own bathroom, peace and quiet, and mahjong groups aplenty.

My cousins Susan and Laura took turns coming up to check on Uncle Bedford, but only once a week.

Not that I could throw stones. I'd been avoiding the Home for months, since Daddy had stopped recognizing me.

I looked down at my uncle, who lay there like a corpse.

Should I do CPR? Mouth-to-mouth?

Would that even work, without his teeth?

Oh, *yuk*!

Should I just stand there and let him go?

Sensible though that was, I couldn't, so I started chest compressions.

Why didn't that woman *hurry*?

Shalayne finally shuffled in. "Now, Miz Scott, you can quit that CPR. They's no cause to go gittin' so upset. Last night yer daddy and yer uncle took off all they clothes and was packin' to leave. All night, hollerin' away at each other the whole time, as usual." She cracked a broken-toothed grin. "They was havin' such a good time, we just left 'em to it. They didn't git to sleep till an hour ago, so I'm not surprised you cain't rouse 'em." She smiled again. "We just covered them as they lay, for modesty, don't you know."

Uncle Bedford finally let out a strangled snore.

I wanted to be stern with Shalayne, but the picture she conjured made me laugh instead, washing away my fear.

I was grateful that the staff had let Daddy and Uncle Bedford keep doing what they'd been doing as long as they were having a good time.

When I collected myself, I asked her, "What happened to Uncle Bedford's hospital bed?"

Shalayne shook her head, exhaling. "He kept climbin' out of it and fallin', so we just put the mattress on the floor. Safer, and a lot less trouble than restraints."

She pursed her lips with a knowing nod. "We tried restrainin' him once, and he like to tore the whole bed apart. I's afraid he'd break his wrists, fightin' like he was." She leaned closer. "They's strong as a WWE rassler with 'roid rage when they have them psychotic spells, don't you know."

She looked back down at my uncle. "So far, puttin' Mr. B's mattress on the floor seems to work just fine."

Uncle Bedford took a long, blessed breath, then blasted out a barely intelligible hunk of vitriol on the exhale, still asleep.

His prejudices had come back to haunt him in the form of an armless little black man who bit him on the knees (unless you sprayed him away with Windex), phantom Japanese soldiers who sat on the furniture unless he covered it with sheets, and his wife Aunt Glory, who had turned into "that gay guy" who'd kept "stealing" his shoes (probably to put them where they belonged).

That gay guy. Please. My father and all three of his brothers had grown up so homophobic, they were probably repressed gays themselves.

As usual when confronted by the bizarre Southern gothic elements of my family, I tried to laugh it off.

Lying there, Daddy and Uncle B looked so frail and harmless.

As if she'd read my mind, Shalayne frowned. "Mr. Bedford's dangerous, don't you know? Coldcocked that new boy we hired last week. Thought he was gay, when all the boy was doin' was trying to git Mr. B's unmentionables clean in the shower."

Shalayne went on in her monotone with, "We had to give Mr. B a hypo of Haldol ta git him settled down, and that new boy quit right there on the spot. But that's all past, now we went back to lettin' the women bathe 'em both."

Nothing like a woman with a warm, soapy rag in the shower, regardless of what she looked like.

Men. I mean, really.

Shalayne pulled the sheet over Daddy's feet. "They seem to like that." She crossed her thin arms at her waist in satisfaction. "I tell ya, these old men is still randy, even when they cain't hardly breathe."

But looking at the two of them lying there, wasted and helpless, my heart broke for my sole surviving uncle and my father. And their genes within me.

Please, God, I beg you not to let me get to this state. Take me home now, if you have to, but don't let me come to this.

Then I flashed on the two of them, naked and hollering and flinging clothes and sheets, and I chuckled in spite of myself.

The only positive thing about visiting the nursing home was, it certainly gave me a proper sense of perspective.

At least I had my mind, and so did Miss Mamie.

I could start over, as long as I had my mind.

Heck, I might even go back and finish college, so I could get a decent job teaching. That sounded like a plan. I loved teaching things, and the vacations would be great. All I had to do was figure out how to pay for my degree.

"C'mon, Miss Lin." Shalayne beckoned me to the door. "They's out cold. You go home and come back another time, when they's better."

Better was definitely a relative term, pun intended.

So I went back out into the searing parking lot, then headed home to face the music, Lord help me.

Four

Turning in at the crushed-granite drive of my childhood home, I decided to park in the shade of the porte cochere beside the dining room, then hunt for my brother Tommy to help me unload and carry my stuff up the rickety stairway to the tiny apartment that had once housed the full-time gardener.

But Tommy's truck wasn't in the garage beneath the apartment, nor anywhere on the grounds. As usual, he'd managed to be elsewhere when he was needed.

I was unbuckling my seat belt when I heard the screen door to the dining room *skreek* open, then slam. I looked that way to see Miss Mamie's lower legs march out onto the smoke-gray floorboards of the verandah, half a flight above me.

"Oh, my Lins-a-pin, you're finally back home where you belong!" my mother declared, finishing with a self-satisfied, "I knew you'd come. I need you. Things have been so hard since your Aunt Glory flew the coop."

Leaving Miss Mamie alone and lonely.

My fingers locking on the steering wheel, I closed my eyes and bent my forehead to the rim. My life was Cinderella, in reverse. *Again.*

Help me do this. Please.

"Yoo-hoo, Lin," Miss Mamie called again, bending down so low to see me that her hem grazed her swollen ankles and sensible, lace-up Clarks. "Are you all right?"

No. I was a total failure, and ticked, ticked, ticked about the whole thing.

It didn't matter that the entire country was in a depression (except those lucky ducks who got unemployment), I took this personally.

I mean, how else can you take it?

The papers said things were getting better, but nobody had ever talked to the subcontractors and self-employed. We were still ruined.

So much for a meek and teachable spirit. But never mind that.

"Come inside," the Mame instructed, still looking years younger than her nine decades, despite her now snow-white weekly Queen Elizabeth "do" that she'd had since I was a teenager, along with her pleasingly plump physique.

She'd always told me that being plump was good when you get old, because the fat fills out most of the wrinkles, but now I noted deep brackets flanking her mouth, and a new weariness around her eyes.

She motioned me to get out. "I've made a nice pitcher of iced tea to cool us off."

Iced tea sounded good. I hoped the through-the-wall, high-efficiency air conditioners I'd had installed in her kitchen could make a dent in the heat.

The house had central heat and air, but running them cost almost a thousand dollars a month to achieve barely discernible results, so compartmentalization had definitely been in order. Still, in this heat, the power bills had to be enormous.

Thank goodness I'd put the AC units in the garage apartment with my first real estate commission. After I'd paid Miss Mamie back for my training course and license fees, of course.

At least I wouldn't bake myself alive out there the way I had right after my divorce.

Determined to start over—again—I finally forced myself to get out and climbed the stairs to the verandah. I caught a sidelong glimpse of the blasted bathtub by the front door, but relegated that to the dead-issue file and topped the stairs to face the latest ordeal of my life.

Her face flushed from heat and anticipation, Miss Mamie opened her arms to draw me in. *Jus' like a spider,* the voice of Mammy from *Gone with the Wind* whispered in my brain. Déjà vu, all over again.

I loved my mother, but this definitely hadn't been my plan for life at sixty. Till my world fell apart, I'd always imagined my husband and I would retire and travel. Phil was traveling, all right, but with a blond ex-stripper half his age, and all our money, half of which was legally mine. But what is, is. My ex was a crook, and may have been all along.

Move on, my twelve steps prodded. *Let go and let God.*

I forced the anger down with a mental mantra: I forgive him, I forgive him, I forgive him. *Forgive us our sins as we forgive those who sin against us.* No way around that one.

One day, I'd mean it when I said so. For now, I "acted as if" and kept praying it into being.

Shifting my attention to the present, I gave the Mame a brief squeeze, then escaped to hold open the screen door for her. "Where's Tommy?"

"Gone to one of his meetings," she said cheerfully as she shepherded me through the hot, stuffy grand dining room into the much cooler kitchen. "It was a special one—a birthday party, I think."

Somebody would get their one-year-sober chip. Or their twenty-first.

The kitchen smelled of everything wonderful and edible from my childhood, fried chicken foremost. My stomach rumbled, but quietly enough not to set Mama off.

She smiled. "Thank God for AA. Your brother hasn't had a drink or drugged in seven years."

For which I was truly grateful, but the twelve steps hadn't cured his laziness. He'd known when I was coming home and wasn't there. Nor had he been there the day before, when my broker and childhood friend, Julia Tankersley, had rented a small moving truck for the day, then drafted her family into bringing what was left of my good furniture into the garage apartment.

Typical Tommy.

Seeing the criticism in my expression, Miss Mamie took the tea out of the icebox as she defended, "He'll be back directly, I'm sure." Pouring the cold brew over ice in a quart glass, she aimed some motherly judgment my way. "Your brother has been a big help to me, keeping up the house since your daddy got sick," she scolded. "Give him credit for that, at least, Lin."

She refrained from listing the things I *hadn't* done to help her since I'd escaped to my little Fortress of Solitude ten miles away.

Shamed, I nodded. "I know. You're right."

That last sentence had taken me five years of intensive therapy to master, along with several weekly meetings in my 12-step enabler's group.

Miss Mamie handed me my tea as if it were a prize for agreeing with her. "Tommy's takin' care of the outside the best he can. Now that you're here to help me with the inside, we'll all be just fine."

I did my best to conceal the panic that rose afresh at the thought of being trapped as a maid, at Miss Mamie's beck and call, for the rest of my life.

Visions of *Psycho* flashed in my mind.

I took a sip of tea to calm myself and my eyes watered, teeth curling at the syrupy sweetness.

Sweet tea was one thing. This would induce diabetic coma.

"Goodness," I sputtered out. "I must have forgotten to tell you that I can't have sugar anymore."

Contrary to rumor and Dr. Oz, Splenda hadn't made my taste buds any less susceptible to real sugar. The cloying sweetness lingered on my tongue, and my teeth ached.

My mother's eyes widened, her hand dramatically splayed across her chest. "Oh, no. Don't tell me you're diabetic."

"No," I temporized, "but the doctor doesn't want me to be, so he said I should avoid sugar." Which was true. But the truer truth was, I couldn't afford new clothes, so I had to lay down some strict dietary boundaries right away, before my mother could use her favorite weapon—guilt—to fatten me right up with her Southern cooking. Then I'd have no chance of ever finding a decent man.

Not that there were many good men loose out there, as far as I could tell. The good ones were either still married to the wives of their youth, or snapped up so fast I didn't even know they'd been divorced or widowed.

The truth was, sex had been great, but I wasn't sure I was willing to put up with what I'd have to do to get it anymore. And as I'd learned from my one disastrous effort at a casual fling with Grant Owens ten years ago, I was anything but casual about sex.

I'd tried to find someone online, but there were no takers within driving distance, even though my digital photo showed that I still had good skin, a pretty face, and a good figure (when I wore foundation garments).

In my experience over the past ten years, commitment had gone the way of the dodo. So both times I'd pursued a relationship with darling Christian men, they'd dropped me like a hot lug nut when they realized I wouldn't sleep with them outside of marriage.

I mean, after a decade of single and celibate, I figured I was a virgin again by the statute of limitations.

But noooo. They just wanted me to sleep with them, and when I wouldn't, poof! They were gone.

Christian men!

As my Granny Beth always said, *"If all Christianity had going for it was the people who belonged to it, it wouldn't have lasted five minutes. Fortunately, it offers us more than ourselves."*

My mother smiled. "You look so thin, sweetie. Are you all right? I really think you could stand to gain a little."

So much for boundaries.

My new thinner self was the reward for working seventy hours a week on two meals a day, but I didn't tell Miss Mamie the truth, because she'd smother me for sure and insist I eat something fried, on the spot. I noted the wide basket on the counter heaped up and lumpy under a bunch of Mama's starched tea towels. Fried chicken!

For generations, Miss Mamie had been ignoring sanitation standards by keeping the chicken she'd fried just before lunch covered on a platter at the counter till dinner, but so far, nobody had gotten sick.

Yet.

It was a chance I gladly took for the perfection of her fried chicken.

"Thanks for the tea," I deflected, "but I need to get started unpacking." I got up. "I'm going to turn on the air conditioners in the apartment and unload."

Mama seemed to shrink a little, and for the first time in history, didn't offer to help. "Mmmm." Suddenly she looked very old and alone.

"Why don't you get some rest?" I suggested, worried. Was she sick? "I'm sure Tommy will be home soon to help." Not.

Miss Mamie didn't protest. "I think I will try to take a little nap." Her verve evaporated. "I'm not much for stairs anymore, especially when I'm carrying things. Ten flights a day is my maximum, and I'm almost there."

"You don't need to worry about my stuff, in the first place," I said. I'd always thought of my mother as immortal and indomitable, but I could see now that she was neither. My parents had drawn strength from their constant bickering, and Miss Mamie had always looked and acted twenty years younger than she was.

Maybe not having my father around to fight with accounted for her weariness. At the Home, Daddy had Uncle Bedford to keep his juices flowing, but Mama had been left in sudden silence, and it had definitely taken its toll.

It hit me that she needed to take care of someone and always had. "Mama, do you miss Daddy?"

She looked to me with gratitude. "Believe it or not, I do. But I couldn't keep him here after he started trying to kill me at night."

I grasped her hand. "Mama! You never told me."

Her other hand covered mine like a protective shell. "Your plate was full enough without knowing that."

"But I want to know. You can tell me anything."

She straightened in her chair. "Thanks. I may take you up on that, but not today. I need a nap."

"Rest," I told her. "I'll come back when I'm done."

My mother rose, brightening. "I fixed all your favorites for dinner. Fried chicken, butter peas, stewed corn, homemade potato salad, fresh tomatoes from the garden, fresh pole beans, rice and gravy, pickled peaches and my green tomato pickles, and homemade peach ice cream. I cooked all yesterday, but the chicken's fresh this morning."

That explained the aromas. All my very favorite foods. My stomach growled again, audible all the way across the room.

Maybe I'd set those boundaries tomorrow. "Wow. I'll be there. What time?"

"Seven-thirty," she said. Miss Mamie thought it was absolutely uncivilized to eat any earlier, which set her apart from most of the elderly I knew.

"Great." I ducked out and fled before my body could drag me to that platter for a piece of pan-fried chicken.

Four hours, one side salad from Wendy's, and fifty-six trips up the garage stairs later (not counting the downs), my brother strolled into the apartment. "Hey, sis."

I looked at Tommy and suddenly realized he looked way older than his fifty-seven years. Still lanky and muscular as a long-distance runner, he had gone white at the temples, which just made him look distinguished. But decades of sun, booze, and cigarettes had etched their consequences deeply into his face, never mind that he'd quit smoking and drinking seven years before.

His grin, though, still looked like a boy's. "Why didn't you wait till I got here? I told the Mame I'd help you unload."

We both knew perfectly well that I was constitutionally incapable of waiting for anything if I could help it. "I got it."

Tommy grinned. "Well, I'm here now. What's left?"

"Nothing. Julia"—my broker and high-school friend—"and her family helped me move the big pieces yesterday, after the bank finally confirmed the closing." I refrained from reminding him that he hadn't been there to help then, either.

He shrugged, his eyes narrowing. "If you choose to be mad at me because I wasn't here when you wanted help, that's your prerogative. All you had to do was call me ahead of time and schedule this when I could come. The fact that you didn't was your choice."

I hated it when he went all 12-step on me. "I didn't know for certain till yesterday at noon, and I left you a message. The closing had already been postponed four times."

I straightened. "And anyway, I told Miss Mamie when I would be here today," I shot back. "You could have come sooner."

Tommy didn't take the bait. "You didn't tell *me*. I'm not a mind reader, Lin," he said with maddening calm. "Sorry I didn't get your message, but I was booked solid till now," he said, peering at me without judgment. "I chaired three meetings today, so I couldn't leave them in the lurch."

So he'd left *me* in the lurch, instead.

All he'd done for the past ten years was AA. And working on the big house, which, I had to admit, was pretty much a full-time job.

Tommy must have read my mind. He shook his head with a wry smile. "Welcome home, sis. Maybe you'll be able to relax and regroup, now that you're here."

That struck a nerve.

Relax, my fanny! The last thing I'd wanted was to move back home, but even after selling everything I could part with, I still didn't have but a few hundred dollars left after the short sale.

I needed a job that wouldn't make me want to commit suicide.

Thanks to the economy, real estate was out. The whole area was glutted with foreclosures and short sales, so in the past five years, I'd had to work three times harder for a fourth of the money. Julia had only kept me on because we'd gone to high school together. When I realized I was just a drag on her, I'd quit.

Tommy swung around a white leather side chair, then straddled it. "So, what's the plan?"

My knees aching, I settled in the club chair facing the sofa. "There is no plan. Not yet. I finally got the mortgage off my back. That was my main objective."

He nodded. "Kudos for that. Moving anything in this market is a miracle."

I appreciated the thought, but still had a horrible taste in my mouth about the whole thing.

Tommy eyed me with assessment. "So maybe we could knock around a few possibilities."

He wanted to advise *me* about life choices? AA or no AA, no way. "Maybe another time."

"No time like the present." When he saw my stubborn frown, he shifted gears. "Want to go fishing with me tomorrow? It's very calming."

"Have you forgotten the last time?" I reminded him. I'd caught a bass worthy of a lifetime on my first try, much to Tommy's chagrin. Since all I could do was go downhill from there, I hadn't gone back. Not to mention the fact that I'm terrible at sitting still and keeping my mouth shut, so fishing definitely wasn't the sport for me.

"That was just beginner's luck." My brother didn't know when to take a hint. "Wear your bathing suit. We can swim when it gets hot."

No way was I going to put on a bathing suit. I'd tortured myself enough for the time being. "Sorry, but I've got plans."

"And what would those be?" he asked archly.

I rubbed my aching knees. "Sleep. Lots of it. And plenty of Advil. I probably won't be able to move tomorrow."

I hated not being able to do what I wanted without ending up in bed with the heating pad. Hated it.

"Sleep is good," he agreed. "Take a few days. Rest. Consider your possibilities."

I couldn't help smiling. "So now *you're* the guru, huh?"

Tommy actually blushed beneath his fisherman's tan. "You live, you learn. It's progress, not perfection."

Maybe he would know about the Mame's finances. "Tommy, do you know how Mama's doing financially? Paying for Daddy must be costing a fortune."

His brows lifted. "I thought the same thing, but when I try to get her to talk money, she reacts very negatively. I think she sees it as losing control over that one last responsibility." He shook his head. "I tried to make her understand that I only wanted to help, but it was like trying to get a pit bull to let loose of a wild boar. Ain't gonna happen."

Just as I'd feared. "We really need to find out where she stands. I don't want all three of us to end up homeless." There I went again, mothering, martyring, and managing. And projecting the worst. But I came by it honestly.

Tommy leveled an open expression my way. "I know this is the last place you want to be, Lin, but it's good to have you back. It'll be nice to have somebody to talk to about the General and Miss Mamie. We're losing them by daily degrees, and that's hard to face alone."

It dawned on me how selfish I'd been to run away from my family, only calling Tommy when I needed something fixed, never just to talk, so immersed in my work that I'd never offered to take some of the load with my parents. "Boy, I really left you holding the bag, didn't I?"

He nodded, but his smile didn't falter. "You did the best you could. That's all any of us can do."

How often had I felt the same thing about him? Never.

Maybe it was time. Maybe there *was* some divine providence in this particular replay.

"I'm here now," I told him. "What can I do to help?"

Tommy brightened. "Go see the General and Uncle Bedford with me, as soon as you're all slept out."

"I can do that." I was too tired to tell him about what I'd found in their room that morning. Later.

He sobered. "And talk to me. I'm your brother. It's safe, I promise."

That was a new one. Tommy, asking me to talk to him?

"I can do that, too," I said with less conviction, remembering when the drunk Tommy had blabbed my secrets, but wanting to believe he could keep them now that he was sober.

I saw him looking around and suddenly I realized . . . "Oh, Tommy. You were living out here, weren't you? I didn't mean to put you out of—"

He shook his head with a look of contentment. "It's okay. Miss Mamie needs somebody in the house now that Daddy's gone. I'd already decided to move back before you sold your house. Miss Mamie needs somebody she can take care of. " He grinned. "Frankly, I don't mind being waited on one little bit."

He had a point.

You should be the one helping your mother, not Tommy! my inner Puritan fussed. *You need to make up for all that neglect.*

But my inner hedonist countered immediately with, *Hey! We can still help out from here. We need some peace, space, and air-conditioning to get through this.*

A guilty "Are you sure it's okay for me to live here?" escaped me.

"Yep." Tommy stood. "Place looks good. All I had out here was a blow-up bed."

I got up yawning, then gave him a hug. "*Bed* looks good."

"Hit the hay. I'll tell the Mame you can't make supper."

I gripped his upper arm. "Oh, now, don't do that," I hastened to say. "I'll sleep much better on a full stomach." I'd swear off all the fat and carbs *after* my welcome-home dinner.

Tommy crooked his fingers like outspread talons. "Nya-ha-ha! The fried chicken." He laughed, then imitated Al Pacino in *The Godfather* movies. "Just when you think you've gotten out, they pull you back in."

I pushed him toward the door and the tiny stoop beyond. "Get out of here so I can take a shower."

When he was gone, I locked the door, then turned to the tiny apartment and sighed. "Welcome home again, Lin Breedlove Scott. We're in for a mighty bumpy ride."

But not before I hid in my bed for a few days with the covers pulled over my head.

First, I needed a shower. Then a nap. Then food. Lots of fried chicken and corn and pole beans and rice and gravy. Yum. Then I could face the future.

I kicked off my shoes, flopped onto my white plissé blanket cover just to rest for a few seconds, and fell sound asleep.

Five

Maybe it was the aroma from the kitchen, but I woke just in time for a quick shower before supper.

The meal turned out to be fun. The three of us laughed and sated ourselves, swapping stories about Daddy and his brothers from our childhoods, and Miss Mamie definitely perked up.

Our funny recollections had brought Daddy and Uncle B to the table in spirit, if not in body, and I could see that it helped my mother. I resolved to apply the same therapy on a regular basis.

Then, stuffed with my mother's country cooking, I took home the two huge bags of leftovers Miss Mamie had forced on me. Time to sleep off my exhaustion and all those carbohydrates.

It took three days, but it sure felt good.

Shaded by the giant oak above it, the air-conditioned garage apartment was cool and comfy, as was the fancy, cool-engineered space-foam mattress I'd splurged on during the building boom.

The only times I got out of bed were to go to the bathroom or eat leftovers. Yum. I didn't even raise the shades. But the food was eventually gone, and I finally grew weary of hiding from my life.

We type As don't do well with leisure for long. So when I found myself awake and ready to get up at seven A.M. on day four, I punched the button on the side of my recharged prepaid cell phone and croaked out, "Call Tommy." My eyes were bleary from too much sleep.

"Call Tommy mobile?" the automated female phone voice asked.

"Yes," I answered, dragging out the *s* so she would understand me.

Apparently, I dragged it out too long. "Call Tommy mobile two?" she chirped.

There wasn't a Tommy mobile two in there, and she knew it!

"No," I corrected, "call Tommy home."

I had a serious love-hate relationship with technology.

But the recording was already saying, "No listing for Tommy mobile two."

Annoyed, I hit hang up, but pressing a button did nothing to express my frustration.

I looked around the room for my reading glasses, but didn't see them. So I tried the voice-dial again with better results, and Tommy answered in a surprisingly chipper voice. "Hey. I was beginning to wonder if you were still alive in there."

"Alive and ready to stop running away from my life," I said in a gravelly voice, then yawned.

"Throw some clothes on," Tommy instructed. "I'll take you to the diner for breakfast. My treat."

"Sure." The diner. How long had it been?

Not since I'd gotten my house near Braselton.

The Mame had told me "the Koreans" had bought the diner, so I wondered if it was still the same place as of old.

My little house had been closer to Pappy Jack's out on Sunshine Springs, so I'd been going there for my daily fix of eggs and caffeine till I couldn't afford it anymore.

"Pick you up in fifteen," Tommy offered.

I could do that. Pull my Shy Fawn blonded hair back with combs, cover the deep circles under my eyes. Rub some bronzer on my cheeks. Mascara, lipstick, and I'd look decent enough not to scare the children.

Not that I was dressing up to impress anybody.

After my last dating fiasco, I'd given up. A crumby social life quickly pales in the face of bankruptcy and destitution.

The really ironic thing was, Legal Aid doesn't do bankruptcies, and the lawyers who do wanted thousands to represent me. What's wrong with this picture?

But I digress.

Tommy picked me up exactly when he'd said he would, and five minutes after that, he pulled his pickup into the last available space among the SUVs, minivans, panel trucks, and other pickups at the Mimosa Branch Diner.

On rainy days, you couldn't get in with a crowbar for the tradespeople, but this morning was a fine one, though already in the mid-eighties.

I got out, reading the same old signs on the brick exterior: WE MAY LOOK FULL ON THE OUTSIDE, BUT THERE'S PLENTY OF ROOM INSIDE. NO SHOES, NO SHIRT, NO SERVICE. CASH ONLY. "Just like it used to be," I told Tommy.

"Pretty much." He held open the door. Inside, the stools at the soda bar had been re-covered in green vinyl instead of red, but the rest of the place looked just the same as it had when we were kids, except for the Asian staff.

Conversation lagged as all the regulars immediately zeroed in on me.

A somber, middle-aged Korean woman said from behind the register, "Ged morning, Tommih, wecome to dinah."

I didn't recognize any of the men taking up all the stools at the long brick lunch bar, but my gaze caught on a pair of aluminum Sheetrockers' stilts, then shot upward to find them attached to a full-busted midget (correction: little person) in tight jeans and a low-cut top, all bosoms, with way too much makeup and a saucy blond ponytail.

As if she'd felt my stare, she turned and gave me a haughty look. "What?" she demanded, prompting a wave of protective defensiveness from the men at the bar. "Haven't you ever seen a little person before?"

Flustered, I glanced to Tommy for help, but he was talking to a guy at one of the single tables and doing his best to avoid the woman.

"Sorry," I told the tiny tart, "I just haven't met one who was so ingenious."

The tradesmen at the bar roared with laughter, and so did the midget/little person. "All right," she said, giving the plumber next to her a high five, then laughing my way. "You're okay."

Tommy tugged at my elbow. "Let's go to the back. It's too hot in here." As always in the summer, the biscuit ovens in the front overwhelmed the ancient air conditioner.

In the back room, the same old zinc-coated ductwork dragon alternately blew the place too cold with great noise, or fell silent and let the place get too hot, in maddeningly irregular rotation.

We took the sole remaining table at the far end of the room, our progress inspected just as thoroughly by the backroom regulars as it had been by the ones up front.

Mimosa Branch was still enough of a small town for everybody at the diner to think everybody else's business was grist for the mill.

A young waitress I didn't recognize slapped two bagged setups on the plastic place mats covered with local ads. She went all flirty with my brother. "Git y'all somethin' to drink?"

"Unsweet tea for me," I said, happy to see that they had Splenda on the table. That was a welcome innovation.

"Coffee," Tommy told her.

The waitress leaned closer to him, displaying her cleavage in the sleeveless V-necked T-shirt blazoned with MIMOSA BRANCH DINER over her D cups. "You havin' the usual?"

Tommy cocked her a winsome grin. "Yep." Then he turned to me. "What'll you have, sis? Or do you need more time?"

When he called me sis, whispered conversations erupted among the regulars, doubtless about my recent reverses. Or was I just being paranoid? Or an egomaniac?

Ears burning, I focused on the waitress. "I'll have three over medium and bacon, flat and crisp. No sides." Atkins, here I come. "And please make sure the whites of the eggs are done, and the yolks are creamy, not runny." I shivered. "Runny whites make me gag."

The waitress didn't write a thing, her eyes still glued to Tommy. "I'll tell her." Then she went for our drinks.

Once we had them, Tommy settled back to chat. "If it's okay with you, I'd like to go by the nursing home on the way home."

I'd meant to tell him about my visit, but dared not do it there. Everybody in town would hear about it before lunch. "Sure."

Tommy nodded. "Uncle Bedford and the General are usually a lot better in the morning, but by the end of the day, there's not really any point in going."

How well I knew. "They call that sundowning, don't they?" Right after the General had moved into the Home, I'd gone to see him at four in the afternoon, and he hadn't even known me. Same thing happened the next day. And the next. Seeing how much that upset me, the nurse had explained that it would be better to visit before lunch.

But instead of going back earlier in the day, I'd copped out and stayed away for months, telling myself Daddy wouldn't know the difference, and Tommy would be there.

What a coward. Never mind that I'd been working night and day in an effort to keep my home. As usual, I'd let myself get caught up in the urgent and neglected the important.

"I should have gone to see him a lot more," I confessed.

Miss Mamie was so guilt-ridden about having him committed that she hadn't been able to make herself go see him, even once.

I went on making my excuses. "But the smell was so awful there, and he looked so bad. They never shave him properly." My father had always been meticulous about his grooming.

"He wouldn't sit still," Tommy explained. "Kept getting cut. So I bought an electric razor and started doing it myself, first thing after breakfast. He holds still for me."

Guilt surged. "Every day?"

Tommy smiled. "Not every. But most." Except for that morning I'd gone to find them out cold and naked. "It's such a small thing to do," my brother said with absolute sincerity, "but he really appreciates it."

Maybe Tommy *had* become the life guru.

Internally, I heard that still, small voice mimic the one on my GPS. *Redirecting. Redirecting.*

The better part of me vowed to open my eyes to the needs of my family instead of being so obsessed with my own problems, but to be honest, the rest of me would rather have headed for the hills, far and fast.

Would that I could, but blood's thicker than my mother's sawmill gravy. She and Tommy needed me. And so did Daddy. He might be homicidal and crazy as a rabid raccoon, but he was still my father.

I had thought of moving back home as a penance, but it just might be my chance at redemption.

The waitress brought our food, and I was surprised to see the diner's signature smooth, flat brown biscuit—with lots of flaky crust around its shallow, fluffy insides—beside Tommy's scrambled eggs and grits.

I'd caught a glimpse of the cook on the way back, and she was definitely Asian. "How could she make that biscuit?" I challenged my brother. "I've tried to make biscuits like that all my life, and they come out like hockey pucks. With freckles."

"Estell, the old cook," Tommy said, "taught the new owner's sister how to do it before she retired."

Miss Mamie had tried to teach me, but even when we worked side by side with the same ingredients and the same oven, mine had flopped, while hers rose high and light as they always did.

Maybe it was my electromagnetic field.

I bowed my head and murmured the blessing over the food. Then, with perfectly acceptable diner etiquette, I cut up my fried eggs and mixed them well to coat the whites with thick, creamy yolks—perfectly over medium.

A lot of people had been upset when the previous American owner had sold out to the current "foreigners," but our breakfasts proved that a good cook's a good cook, the world around.

To my chagrin, I heard my voice say, "I saw Daddy and Uncle B the morning I moved in."

Tommy stopped eating. "How were they?"

Ears pricked up all over. I leaned closer to my brother. "I'll tell you when we get to the truck."

Clearly annoyed that I'd brought it up only to put him off, he frowned.

"Sorry," I whispered. "I shouldn't have brought it up. It's private. But I feel like I'm on display here."

He regarded me with assessment. "Only till they get used to you. They're good people." He grinned. "For the most part. We always have a sprinkling of scoundrels, just to keep things interesting."

I leaned forward again to ask, "Do you know anybody in here?" I scanned the room. "I don't recognize anybody."

Tommy smiled and nodded toward a nice-looking couple sitting side by side in the far corner, facing a white-haired guy with a sunny expression beside a mountain of a middle-aged man. "That couple's the Dotsons. He's retired military, slightly to the right of Attila the Hun. Bought a house in town and restored it. She runs a flower shop and doesn't put up with any of his guff."

He took a sip of coffee, then wiped his mouth with a paper napkin from the dispenser on the table, never looking at the people about whom he spoke. "Guy with the white hair retired from being a lineman at the GM plant in Doraville, when there still was one. Wife told him he'd have to get out of the house at least half the day to keep from driving her nuts, so he comes here, then goes to the old men's club at Hardee's. Fella beside him owns all kinds of stuff, including rental property and land all around here."

The players had changed, but the place was still the same.

I wondered how long it would take me to reacquaint myself with the town's occupants—not the thousands of exurbanites out by the mall, just the townies.

When I'd first moved back to Mimosa Branch ten years before, it had been a small town of about six thousand, expanded from three. Now it had sprawled across the interstate to take in the new mall and scads of apartments, over sixteen thousand households in all, mostly people from other places.

Tommy stirred his grits. "Did you hear? Donnie West isn't going to run for mayor again next year."

A major item Miss Mamie had neglected to mention. "Why not?"

Ever since we'd overthrown our corrupt mayor ten years before in favor of Donnie West—the most down-to-earth, honest Gospel preacher we'd ever known—things at City Hall had straightened up and stayed that way.

Who knew what would happen here without him?

Tommy exhaled. "Said the Lord was calling him to a church in Pittsburgh, so how can you argue with that?"

"You can't." If Donnie said so, it must be true.

Hamm Stubbs, Donnie's crooked predecessor, had gone to jail for racketeering and laundering drug money, so we were safe from him, but I had no idea who could replace a man as good as Donnie. There'd be plenty of politicking going on in town, for sure, so at least the gossip at the diner would be interesting.

And as Tommy had said, there were always a few scoundrels in the mix.

I sent up an arrow prayer: *Lord, keep us from some wolf in sheep's clothing. Things are hard enough as it is.*

I sure would hate to see things at City Hall go downhill. Especially since we now had an *olde towne* district to take care of.

Tommy broke my concentration by asking, "So, what do you have on tap for this afternoon, after we see Dad?"

Convinced I wouldn't get it, I confessed, "I thought I'd go over to Ocee U. to get an application and find out if it's too late to get in. Assuming I can get a scholarship."

Tommy cocked back, dubious. "You're serious about that?"

"I know. I'm old. But real estate is out, for obvious reasons, and I'm not really fit for anything else. I can't touch-type or do anything complicated on a computer, and my knees are so bad, I can't work on my feet. Education is one field where my age won't work against me. I was thinking of teaching high school English."

My brother's expression screwed up. "High school English? Are you crazy? Have you seen the teenagers out there?"

"Yes, and I have a perverse affection for them. Don't ask me why, but I do." I stared at him, flat-mouthed. "At least I'd have some benefits till I qualify for Medicare." Assuming I got my certificate in three years, going full-time. "Plus, the vacations are great."

"I think you've lost your mind," he whispered, leaning forward. "Haven't you heard all the jokes about having an English degree and not being able to find work? Google it. And what happens if you spend all that time and money to get a teaching certificate, and nobody wants to hire you?"

"I'll deal with that when it happens," I told him calmly, my resolve stiffening against his rejection. "But this is my plan." My impulse, actually, but he didn't need to know that.

Tommy cocked an eyebrow. "I think you might want to consider a plan B. Like another job."

I leaned forward to whisper, "I *tried* to find another job, but nobody wants a sixty-year-old high school graduate with bad knees, who can't touch-type or use Excel, or work an electronic cash register, or balance a checkbook. The only openings I could find were collection agencies, straight commission sales for pyramid companies, phone sex, and telemarketers, but you have to draw the line somewhere."

Tommy shot me a smug expression. "I don't know; what does the phone sex pay?"

"Very funny." Why couldn't he at least be a little supportive about my going to college? "Never mind," I concluded. Since both of us were finished, I picked up my purse as I rose. "Let's go see Daddy."

As he looked up at me, Tommy's face reflected a twinge of regret. "I'm sorry. I was wrong to be so negative. I know you're just doing the best you can." Which was AA-speak for doing things that were hurtful or unwise.

"Why don't you go back for a degree, too?" I challenged. "Or technical school. Who knows? Maybe you could graduate with me."

Tommy barked a laugh. "No way. I long ago drank away too many gray cells." He grabbed the check, then threw a generous three-dollar tip on the table. "And anyway, I *have* a job, fixing things for hire and looking after the Mame and the house. And the General." He got up, then followed me to the front. "You're the smart one. You'll do fine, I know it."

"But first," I told him as we reached the register, "I have to get a scholarship."

After we checked out, we drove to the Home. On the way, I told Tommy what had happened there the day I'd moved home, and both of us ended up hilarious.

As luck would have it, we came in to find Daddy and Uncle Bedford decently dressed in flannel pajama pants and matching VFW T-shirts. Daddy immediately strode over to give Tommy a back-clapping man-hug, but it took Uncle Bedford time to recognize me.

"Are you that boy?" he grumbled. "That gay guy?"

Ignoring my sore knees, I crouched in front of his wheelchair and gently stroked his hair away from his face. "No, sweetie. It's Lins-a-pin, your niece."

Daddy's geriatric psychiatrist had said that even if they were deaf, people with Alzheimer's were highly sensitive to touch, tone, and expression, so I did my best to act calm and reassuring. I smiled up at him despite the tears that stung the backs of my eyes when I thought of the lively, laughing man he'd once been.

His expression cleared, and for a moment he looked like himself again. "Hey there, little girl. You come back home?"

I nodded. "Yep. I've come back home." .

The question was, would I ever escape again?

The odds were against it, but maybe that wouldn't be the end of the world.

"Lin!" Daddy hollered. "Get over here and tell your brother to quit mumblin'. I cain't hear a bleemin' thing he says."

I gave Uncle Bedford a pat, then rose to face the General with a purposeful smile on my face. "He's not mumbling, Daddy," I said distinctly into his better ear. "If you want to hear people, let us get you some hearing aids."

Tommy started laughing.

"What?" I asked.

"We got him some. Twice." Tommy gave Daddy a sidelong hug, then sat him aslant on the bottom corner of the bed and stepped behind him, massaging our father's sloping shoulders, which Daddy seemed to enjoy.

Out of the General's line of sight, Tommy explained quietly, "He wouldn't—or couldn't—adjust to them, so he kept taking them out and hiding them to get us to stop trying to make him wear them."

He shook his head. "When they disappeared, we got new ones with the insurance, but the insurer said they would only replace them once in four years. I explained it to the General, but the next thing you know, he'd chewed the replacements to pieces and swallowed them with his chili, so that was that. Sayonara, six-thousand-dollar state-of-the-art hearing aids, plus a trip to the emergency room to have the pieces fished out of his stomach."

Tommy hadn't told me about any of that. Or the Mame. Apparently, the sane members of my family had cut me out of the loop.

I scowled. "He chewed them up?" Yuk.

"Yep."

I gave Daddy a bear hug. "You sweet, silly old fella," I said softly into his ear. "I love you."

My father wrapped his long, sun-freckled arms around me and murmured back, sweet as could be, "I love you too, Lin. Always have. Always will."

For that precious moment, I had my daddy back, and the world was put to rights.

Until I got to Ocee University.

Six

Twenty minutes north of Mimosa Branch, I found the campus of Ocee University sparsely inhabited by summer-quarter students, most of whom looked too young to drive. The one-story brick buildings were attractive, but far spread, and the grassy quadrangle had been burned to tan by the drought. Beyond the library, I noted a gym and a new humanities building with five stories.

Nice, but lots of steps between classes.

I followed the directionals to the registrar's office (as far from where I'd parked as you could get), then signed in behind two girls who were decked out in major slut, with large tattoos on their upper arms and multiple piercings, both of them glued to their smartphones, one texting and the other playing games.

God forgive me, but I judged them. I know it was wrong, but I mean, isn't that the whole point of how people present themselves: to show the world what kind of person they are? The message from these two was, *cheap, easy,* and *phone-obsessed.*

The girls sat down on opposite sides of the room while I filled in the "purpose for your visit" blank with *I want to go back for my degree on scholarship,* then sat down without even a brief glance from the girls.

So much for the chance to ask them how they liked it there.

If you ask me, "smart" phones and electronic tablets will be the death of real human communication. At the first opportunity, kids dive into their world of games and texts, remaining isolated from any real relationships and hiding behind their user names. Not to mention causing car wrecks.

Bossy as I am, I couldn't resist asking them in a loud voice, "Hi. When y'all go out, do you just text your dates, or actually talk?"

Both girls briefly glared at me as if I were dog-doo, then resumed what they were doing without comment.

"I thought so."

Half an hour into the hour I waited, the receptionist rose to tell me, "Miz Scott, if you'll please follow me, you can fill out our application on our computer and the FAFSA before Miz Brady sees you."

I approached her, leaning close to her to whisper, "I'm sorry, but what's a FAFSA?"

"It's the form all students have to fill out to apply for assistance," she blared out cheerily for anyone and everyone to hear.

Scalded by embarrassment, I straightened to my full height and looked down my nose at her. "I thought such things were confidential," I said softly. "Would you please lower your voice?"

"Sorry," she said without feeling, then led me to a hall alcove with a computer. "Let me just pull this up for you." Standing, she typed away at blazing speed with her black, acrylic talons, going through several screens till the registration form came up. "Just fill in the blanks. If you make a mistake, you can go back and correct it. Until you hit the 'completed' button, so don't hit that till it's ready to go."

She stepped back, and I sat with trepidation. I knew how to do basic word processing and e-mails and Facebook; that was it. But I'd croak before I bared my ignorance by asking that *chiquitita* for help.

It was a good thing I had to wait so long, because it took every minute for me to complete the registration form. I mean, who the heck remembers when they "graduated" from elementary school? I hadn't thought of that since I'd filled out an application for the temp service when I'd first moved back home ten years ago. As it had then, it took some serious mental math for me to come up with the dates they were asking for. I knew when I'd graduated from high school (1968) and the year I'd been at Sandford College: from fall of 1968 to May of 1969, when I'd met and then married my ex, Phil.

And as for my job history, I'd had nine menial jobs in my teens and first two years of marriage before I got serious about infertility therapy and finally gave birth to David four years later. I knew how many jobs because Phil had needled me about it forever, but I could only remember four of them: Teen Board; sales associate at Baker's Department Store in Mimosa Branch; receptionist and tester for a temporary service; and being a very bored private secretary for one of my father's surveyor friends. So I put those down and spread the dates to cover the whole time, despite a gasp of horror from my inner Puritan.

It wasn't as if they could check the dates. All three companies were long since out of business, something I had nothing to do with, I swear.

My Puritan hopped to my shoulder and scolded me for not being completely honest, but my Practical Self gave her the raspberry.

I mean, it wasn't a lie if I couldn't remember, was it? And I definitely didn't think a big question mark would impress the admissions committee, so there you are.

Oh, gosh. Could it be the beginnings of Alzheimer's that I couldn't remember?

I shuddered, stuffed the idea into a mental cubbyhole and slammed the door, and went on.

I filled the next twenty-eight-year span with "homemaker and mother." Last, but by no means least, I listed my career selling and appraising residential real estate, then added my professional degrees and qualifications.

Then I filled in the rest of the form.

I had just reread it, then clicked the "completed" button, setting off the printer beside me, when the loudmouthed receptionist snuck up behind me and blared, "Miz Brady is ready to see you, now."

I jumped half out of my skin. "I'm just old, not deaf," I grumbled as I stood.

Unfazed, the girl handed me the now printed application. "It's the last door at the end of the hall." She pulled a yellow handout from the stack file on the wall. "I see you didn't get to the FAFSA, so here's one you can take home and fill out."

One? I made a mental note to pick up several more on my way out, just in case I made mistakes, which I always did when filling out forms—a perverse bit of masochism that sprang from I knew not where.

Inside the office at the end of the hall, a kind-looking black woman (correction: African American) rose behind her desk with a welcoming smile, then closed the door behind me.

Good. I didn't want my business spread all over campus.

"Hi." Her smile was warm and open. "I take it you're the 'mean woman' who insulted my two previous appointments," she said with wry humor. "They told me what you said."

Heat pulsed up my neck to bloom in my cheeks. "Guilty as charged."

She grinned, extending her hand in greeting. "Good for you. Welcome to Ocee. I'm Pam Brady."

I shook, finding her grip firm and dry. "I'm Lin Breedlove Scott. Thanks for seeing me without an appointment."

"Things are a little slow in the summer, so we could fit you in," Pam Brady explained as she sat. "Please have a seat, and we'll go over your application." She scanned the printout as I perched nervously in the chair facing her.

I was relieved that she didn't snort or laugh in derision while she read.

When she finished inspecting the registration form, she leaned back with an affable, "It's too late for fall semester, but you're right on time for winter/spring applications. That quarter starts in January, the sixth. You can finish filling out the FAFSA at home and bring it back, along with an active passport or official copy of your birth certificate, your driver's license, and a copy of the last year of your tax returns."

She glanced at the printout again, then turned her attention back to me. "To give me a better idea of your qualifications for aid, would you mind my asking you a few financial questions? Strictly confidential, of course."

She must have seen that I was skeptical, because she told me, "All our information is confidential and accessible only to qualified staff, not student aides."

"Thanks. That's a relief." I relaxed a bit. "What would you like to know?"

"What was your AGI for last year?"

"I beg your pardon?"

"Sorry," she said. "We get so used to the acronyms around here. Your adjusted gross income from your tax return."

"Oh." I thought for a minute, picturing the screens of my online tax prep program. "I'm an independent contractor, so I have lots of expenses and health insurance to write off." My mind finally got to the AGI screen. "To the best of my recollection, the AGI would be about twenty-six thousand. But my taxable income was only twelve."

She nodded and jotted that down on a notepad on her desk.

"And this year, to date?" she asked. "Just a ballpark estimate will be fine for now."

I sighed, the figure sticking in my throat. I knew exactly how little I'd made in the seven months since New Year's Day. "Three thousand, seven hundred, twenty-two dollars. Gross. With no prospects pending for more."

Her brows shot up. "Hard year for everybody." She wrote it down. "Any assets?"

"Just my 2009 minivan. I lost my house to a short sale. My credit rating's trashed, and I'm broke, except for two hundred dollars in my checking account." Shoot. Would that be enough for the registration fee?

She brightened. "So you're homeless?"

That was good news?

"Actually," I said, "I moved back into my ninety-year-old mother's because I didn't have the deposit for an apartment."

She lifted an index finger. "We have special funds for the homeless, but I'll have to check to see if your situation qualifies. Is your mother receiving any income beyond Social Security?"

"Not that I know of." I'd have to ask her. For all my mother's gossipy phone calls, what I didn't know about Miss Mamie was a *lot*.

Maybe that was why she liked to talk about everybody else so much; it kept the focus off her.

Pam Brady made a note in the margin. "Based on what you've told me, I think you'll qualify for a Pell Grant. But things are so crazy in this economy, not to mention the whole undocumented student situation, that there's fierce competition for the assistance we have left."

My face must have fallen, because she was quick to say, "But don't get discouraged. Since you're an overage female, I'm almost positive I can find some help for you."

Overage female? Was that what I'd been reduced to?

She chuckled at my indignation. "That term applies only to scholarship applicants. Here, you'll be designated as a nontraditional student, along with anybody else over twenty-five."

Better.

"And what is your life plan for after you graduate?" she asked me.

Life plan? Please.

I started to say *breathing,* but thought better of it.

I supposed I had to get used to the jargon. "I want to teach English in high school."

She nodded her approval. "Some systems will repay your student loans in exchange for teaching with them for two years." I knew enough teachers to know that those jobs were almost always at inner-city schools.

I was too old and too slow for combat conditions, so I shook my head in denial. "Ma'am, I am sixty years old. The last thing I need is debt of any kind. If I can't get a scholarship, I can't go to school. It's that simple."

She rose, offering her hand in dismissal. "Let's see what we can do, then. Take a few more of those FAFSA forms home with you. Fill one out to bring back with a copy of your last year's tax return." Sticking to the script, she went on with, "And your driver's license and a current passport, if you have one, or an official copy of your birth certificate. And we'll need transcripts from Sandford and your high school. Please have them sent directly to us. The address is on the application."

Noting my glazed expression as I stood to leave, she offered, "There's a checklist right below the FAFSA forms to help you remember what you need to bring."

She'd already told me twice: filled-out FAFSA, official birth certificate or passport, driver's license, tax return, and high school and college transcripts.

Thanks to Georgia's crackdown on voter fraud, even renewing a driver's license required all that documentation, plus two proofs of occupancy, like utility bills.

I nodded, amazed by the possibility that this might actually happen.

"Why don't we meet again in, say, three weeks?" she proposed. "That should give you time to get everything we need."

That would be at the end of the first week in August. "Three weeks sounds good to me."

It wasn't as if I had anything else to do. Besides visiting the General and helping Miss Mamie scour all five thousand square feet of the main house, but there was no deadline for that. I had already decided to leave the behemoth attic till cooler weather—assuming we got any.

Last winter had been so warm, we never got a good, hard freeze for more than a day or so, so the bugs were walking away with us all.

"The receptionist will make the appointment," Pam Brady told me. "And please accept my compliments on having the courage to come back to college. We rely on technology a lot more than we did when you last went, but with your intelligence, I'm sure you'll do very well."

What did she know about my intelligence? We'd just met.

Of course, I probably made a good impression compared to the pierced sluts who preceded me.

Judge not— Oh, shut up.

I wished I could be as sure of my success as Pam Brady was. "Thanks."

I picked up my FAFSA forms and documentation checklist on the way back to the front desk, then made my appointment for ten A.M. in three weeks.

Then I headed home to do battle with the records departments of Sandford College and Mimosa Branch City Schools. I'd lived long enough to know that getting my transcripts would take twice as long as it ought to. Once the transcripts were ordered, I'd fill out the FAFSA. Then I would drink wine and go to bed with my head under the covers.

Lord, I prayed from my bed that night, *please help with this, if it is Your will. If it's not, please show me* Your *life plan.*

The next morning when a call from my ex-broker Julia woke me up, God delivered, in spades.

Seven

Julia's voice crackled through my Walmart drop phone at eight A.M. "Lin, I know you said you were through with real estate, but your license is still active, and I have just one last customer I need you to take. He's new to town, and you're the only one I can trust him with."

I yawned. "Why don't you take him?" Much as I could use a commission, I knew Julia was almost as hard up as I was, except she owned her fancy house free and clear. "I'm helping Miss Mamie scour the big house, top to toe."

"This'll help her even more, if everything works out," she said cryptically.

I moaned. The last thing I needed was to haul some transplant around, only to have him decide he'd like to see everything on the market from one end of Metro Atlanta to the other, then buy a foreclosure or a fisbo (for sale by owner) behind my back. Been there, done that.

"I'm asking you as a special favor for me," Julia said, reminding me that I owed her, bigtime, for a lot more than hiring me after my divorce. A PK (preacher's kid), she'd been the total Goody Two-shoes of our graduating class, then gone off to college and turned into a flashy, anything-goes party girl. Three husbands later, she still was, dripping in real jewelry, without apology.

Working at her brokerage for the past decade, I had learned that she wouldn't let up till she got her way. "Oh, all right," I relented. "When do I meet him, and what's he looking for?"

"Day after tomorra," she all but crowed, "at nine in the morning, here at the office. And he's looking for a three-two in really good shape, here in town, under one twenty-five."

Thanks to the recession, there were plenty I could show him, but most were old, in varying degrees of disrepair.

"I've already pulled up what's available in the listings," Julia went on. "And by the time you take him around, I'll have shaken loose a few more."

Julia could tell you the financial, political, and medical condition of everybody within the old city limits. Plus every single person in the whole county who was in arrears on property taxes.

A lot of her deals were direct with sellers who needed to get rid of their houses, but didn't realize it till Julia brought them a buyer and laid out the numbers.

"Okay," I relented. "I'll come down tomorrow to get those listings and check them out."

"Oh, goodie." I could swear she was rubbing her hands together.

I frowned. "Julia, what have you got up your sleeve?"

"You'll see, day after tomorra," she gloated, then hung up.

I laid down my terrorist phone and sighed. Better get up and finish that FAFSA form, so I could go help Miss Mamie before I had to go back to work for this one, last customer.

And what a customer he turned out to be.

Eight

I tried my best to weasel the truth out of Julia the next day when I went to get the listings, but she refused to budge. Just smirked all over me and insisted I leave to preview the houses.

My completed FAFSA form and copies of my tax return and documents were in my car, to be dropped off at Ocee before I started checking out the listings. The transcripts were still pending.

No matter how it turned out, I felt better trying, at least, to start something new.

With that off my mind, I could concentrate on finding this customer a great house for the money. The first five listings I previewed were possibles, but the next four were too old and musty to snag even a male buyer. Of the remaining six, four had once been really nice, but abusive renters had seriously trashed them. Julia had said the customer wanted something move-in ready, so that eliminated a lot of the bargains in town.

Hot and frustrated, I went back to the real estate office and tried to find some more.

The problem living in town was, there were no guarantees about what you'd find next door. Tidy little bungalows with meticulous landscaping abutted rundown rentals or old-timer ramshackle places. Gracious homes of garden club members backed up to ancient shacks from the "black" section, as the old ladies called it.

Surely I could find one decent, attractive house for this guy.

Julia came in grinning like a mule eating briars. "You know that cute place next door to y'all that Jerry Ronson bought from the city for a dollar, then redid as an office space? Well, guess what? Since the bottom fell out of the commercial market, he's had it zoned back to residential and put in a kitchen, then converted the offices to two big bedrooms with two full baths." She handed me the keys. "He's carryin' a ton of properties, so he'd love to unload it. Asking only ninety-nine, five, completely redone. Probably what he has in it. Only thing missing is a laundry room, but there's a big closet in the back hallway where a buyer could put one in. Why don't you check it out?"

I took the key. "But it only has two bedrooms. He asked for three."

Julia dismissed that with a flutter of her scarlet manicure. "He can do with two."

Even though our thick, ancient camellia hedges blocked the house from Miss Mamie's first-floor windows, I didn't want a drug dealer or a cranky neighbor next door. Or another jerk like Grant Owens. "Here's hoping your guy's the kind of person we'd like to have as a next-door neighbor."

"Oh, he is, my dear," Julia crowed. "He is." She picked up her phone. "I'll call Jerry and have him spruce up the yard for tomorrow."

Julia was enjoying herself so much, I didn't question her further before I left.

I parked in our garage, then walked around to the front of the new listing. Once there, I unlocked the new insulated steel front door and stepped into a blessedly cool, simple space with neutral gray walls, white trim, dark hardwood floors, and new, energy-efficient doors and windows. Jerry had done away with the interior walls of the old living room, kitchen, den, and dining room, opening the smaller rooms into one big area with a shiny kitchen along the back wall, defined by a counter-height pale gray granite peninsula that offered lots of casual seating.

That should be plenty of kitchen for a single man. I'd once sold a run-down bungalow to a rabid recycler old bachelor who'd promptly torn out the rotted kitchen, then happily settled for a secondhand refrigerator, sink, and a microwave on a TV table in its place.

This bungalow, built for supervisors from the mill, used to have three small bedrooms, but Jerry had wisely split the space between two larger ones, each with generous closets back-to-back and a roomy bathroom with separate tub and shower for each one.

Great storage spaces in every available nook. Smart move.

And everything had that new-paint smell.

Perfect.

The only drawback (besides the missing bedroom) was, Jerry also owned a half-restored version of the same house on the other side, which might become an attractive nuisance if he couldn't afford to complete it for sale. In these times, abandoned houses quickly became drug hangouts.

I made a mental note to call and ask him his plans. Maybe I could nudge him into locking up the other place, at least.

Back home that night, I ate my frozen low-carb meal, then watched reruns of *NCIS,* but when ten rolled around, I wasn't sleepy.

The outside temperature had dropped to the mid-seventies, so I put on my pink seersucker robe, bombed myself with insect repellent, then took a quart glass of decaffeinated iced tea to the rocking chairs on Miss Mamie's porch. I eased into the second white rocker from the front door, then leaned back to savor the night.

I breathed in the smells of fresh-cut grass, granite dust, sweet autumn clematis, and creosoted railroad ties, an appropriate mix for a railway town like ours. In the "management" houses across the tracks, only a few small bathroom windows glowed yellow, just as they always had since I was young.

Apparently, people on what was now the good side of the tracks still went to bed at a decent hour.

High in the trees above me, July flies sang the summer songs of my childhood, accompanied by a chorus of frogs from the nearby branch (Southern for *small stream*) for which the town was named.

Serenaded by those ageless sounds, I closed my eyes, believing, just for a moment, that I was still in my prime, a woman who made men sit up and take notice. That I could still dance and sing and stay up really late to finish whatever I needed to do.

But I couldn't hold on to the illusion any more than I'd been able to hold on to my marriage, and the vision melted into the muggy darkness. An unexpected tear escaped the outer corner of my eye to run down in front of my ear, then another, and another.

Weary of losing the things I'd loved and having to fight my way back, I sank in the rocker.

Lord, I am too old to start over. Too tired. Too discouraged. I just don't think I can do this.

What about Sarah? my inner Puritan pointed out. *She was over ninety, and she had the good grace to laugh when she was told she would have a son. At least you're not pregnant.*

My stubborn self came back with *First, I haven't had a uterus since nineteen eighty-six, and you know it. And second, Sarah had a husband and servants to take care of her.*

A soggy cloud of self-pity settled inside me.

I should have brought my cell phone. I needed to talk to Tricia.

I was considering going to get it when Tommy came outside with a Diet Coke and plopped down beside me. He looked over and frowned. "You okay?"

"No." I had no intention of going into it. I'd sound as self-absorbed as I was. After all, I had plenty of food, a car, a safe place to live (for free), air-conditioning, and indoor plumbing. That put me head and shoulders above ninety-eight percent of the world's population.

Tommy didn't press. Instead, he took a long sip of his soda and rocked. Just having him there made the lump in my chest shrink.

Then he said quietly, "I felt rotten when I had to move back in. So I drank even more to compensate. But eventually, I realized I had to change, or die."

He rolled the cold, sweating can across his brow. "It took a long time to get my head on straight, but I've learned a lot." He finished the drink, placed the can on the painted floor beside his chair, then turned my way. "I learned to live in gratitude instead of anger and fear."

So had I, but I was fresh out of gratitude at the moment.

He went on, "There's joy to be had in every day, even if it's just rocking here with my big sister on the porch." The compliment was indirect, but welcome.

His voice softened. "There's still plenty of life in you, Lin. If you want to get a degree, get one. Don't let anything stop you, not even yourself."

I felt better hearing that and gave my brother's callused hand a brief squeeze where it rested on the arm of his rocker. "Thanks. But honestly, I'm not even sure I really want to, or if it was just the only other job I could think of that didn't make me want to put a gun to my head."

"Sounds like a good enough reason to do it." He smiled, looking out into the small-town darkness for a long time before he broke the silence with, "Sure I can't talk you into going fishing with me at five?"

I pulled myself up by the bootstraps and said, "Actually, I'm showing houses in the morning to some guy who wants to move into town."

"Thought you were through with that."

"I was, but you know Julia. She's bound and determined for me to show this guy around, so there you are. What Julia wants, Julia gets."

Tommy chuckled, followed by a salacious, "Oh, yes. Including me."

I tucked my chin and stared at him. "You don't mean to tell me that you and Julia . . . you know."

Tommy nodded with a smug smile. "Oh, yes, siree. Not recently, mind you. But for one spectacular summer when she was between husbands, she took me to places I had never been, for which I will be eternally grateful."

I covered my face with my hands. "TMI, TMI!" The thought of my brother and Julia doing the nasty . . . Please, mind, do not go there!

Tommy let out an exasperated sigh. "You are still such a prude."

"Yes, I am," I shot back, "and I'd like to keep it that way."

He sent me a smug sidelong glance as he got up to leave. "Just wait'll God sends you a man who rings your chimes, and talk to me then."

"I am done with all that, and good riddance," I said. Despite my failed marriage, I had very high standards, which had doomed the three relationships I'd tried since my divorce. Was it wrong of me to want a kind, intelligent, decent Christian man who wasn't totally self-absorbed or obsessed with alcohol or sex?

Tricia had said I wasn't being realistic, but I'd rather have no man than a bad one, so there you are.

Then I met Connor Allen.

Nine

I got up early, took a cool shower, then caught my chin-length blond hair back with combs and scrunched it well in back till it curled and dried, which didn't take long in the air-conditioning. I fluffed it into soft curls with an Afro pick, then dressed as nicely as I could, considering the thermometer. Customers and clients treated me with more respect when I dressed professionally, so I left the house in lightweight Chico's black travel pants, a white cotton camisole over an industrial-strength bra, a pink silk overshirt, and black sandals.

Pulling into the brokerage's parking lot at five till nine, I saw a gray Taurus with North Carolina plates parked next to Julia's Cadillac SUV.

Rats. He'd beaten me there.

I summoned my inner duchess, then sailed into the office.

Standing there beside Julia was one of the best-looking, kindest-looking older men I'd ever seen in my life.

He was tall and slim, just as I liked. His neatly cut hair was purest white, but his intense blue eyes and expression were young with the twinkle of a mischievous little boy.

He stared right back at me with unveiled assessment.

Then he broke into a million-dollar smile and offered me his hand. "Julia," he said, his eyes still on mine, "you didn't tell me my agent was going to be so beautiful."

His grip was firm and didn't let go, and that voice . . . low and smooth and cultured, but still Southern.

I blushed like a girl from the top of my camisole to my hairline. "And you didn't tell me our buyer was so good-looking," I said, then thought better of it. This was business, not a flirtation.

With my track record, he was probably the latest in a long line of jerks. But hubba hubba, was he a gorgeous one.

Chemistry. Serious chemistry.

What was I doing feeling chemistry at this stage of my life?

"Lin Scott, this is Connor Allen," Julia introduced. "Connor, Lin will be showing you the best of our local listings." Smug as a monk on a keg of wine, Julia revealed, "Connor has been called as the new pastor for Mimosa Branch First Baptist. He starts work in two weeks, so we need to get him into the perfect house right away."

I almost choked. A *minister,* and a Baptist one, at that?

Baptist ministers didn't date divorced women. Usually, they wouldn't go anywhere with a single woman unchaperoned, much less a grass widow like me.

My brain started cussing up a storm, but I managed to reduce it to *rats.* Just *rats!*

Frozen chosen Presbyterian or Episcopalian would have been fine, even Methodist, but why did he have to be a *Baptist?*

I could hear laughter echoing from heaven, and I didn't think it was funny. Not one bit.

God and I both knew perfectly well that I was nobody's idea of a proper companion for a Baptist minister. Mary Lou Perkins would go through the roof.

When I'd first moved home ten years ago, Grant Owens had told anybody who'd listen how I'd gotten high on weed (completely not my fault) and slept with him (which I hadn't, at the last minute, but I might as well have, because I'd planned to do it), making me notorious in Mimosa Branch forever.

God knew I hadn't followed through on the affair, thanks to a serious case of the giggles when we got into bed, but I don't think anybody else believed the truth. Except Tommy, God love him. So I'd been branded a loose woman without ever having tasted the sweet nectar of sin.

Wouldn't you know.

I cleared my throat. "Well, if you're ready," I told the AARP Adonis, "why don't we get started?" I held open the front door for him, letting in the waves of heat. "It will be simpler if I drive, because I know where the showings are."

He didn't make any of the usual man-noises that my male customers did about letting me drive. He simply said, "Great," then followed me to my car and got into the passenger seat.

"This is a really nice car," he said as we pulled out. "I used to have a minivan, too, but I had to give it up. Literally."

Curious, I asked without thinking, "What happened?"

He grinned and looked out the window. "My ex got it in the divorce."

I almost wrecked.

A *divorced* Baptist minister?

He was starting out with two strikes against him!

Times, they were a-changin' in Mimosa Branch, for sure, but even that didn't mean this man could be seen with me without causing a scandal. Never mind that over half the congregation had been divorced at one time or another.

When it came to divorce and remarriage, the convenient Baptist excuse was for the guilty parties to claim they weren't really saved when they were misbehaving and got divorced, but I don't buy that. Christians have the same choices non-Christians do, so they can sin like anybody else. And when it came to this guy, I didn't think that excuse would fly with his congregation. I'd seen him preaching on the big Christian cable channel as I'd surfed past.

Connor Allen looked at me with that same mischievous smile. "At least I didn't lose my job. She ran off with a much richer man who paid her a lot more attention than I ever did, so I had scriptural grounds for letting her go." His tone lightened. "Apparently, God hadn't called *her* to the ministry, only me. I gotta tell you, it broke my heart, and hurt even worse because I was the one who'd neglected her. I felt like such a failure, but my congregation didn't judge me. Very humbling."

Boy, was he forthcoming.

"I lost my husband to a stripper ten years ago," I confessed. "Well, to be perfectly accurate, I told him I wanted a divorce after he said he wanted to have us both. Was that scriptural grounds?"

Connor Allen chuckled. "Definitely."

"That's a relief."

Instead of preaching at me, he changed the subject to safer ground. "Julia said you grew up on Green Street. Where do you live?"

Seriously direct, but his lucent personality went a long way to allay whatever questions I might have raised about his motives.

"Actually, you'll see it when we visit the last listing. I recently lost my house, so for the moment, I live with my mother and my brother, right next door to the listing." I changed the subject back to business. "Will you be needing a financing contingency?"

"Not if we stay in budget. I owned my former house long enough to pay it off," he said. "Since most churches sold their pastoriums decades ago, we ministers have had the chance to build equity in our own places. The wife got half the proceeds, but that left me with my housing budget."

Must have been a really nice house. "You must have been at your last church for a long time, to pay off your mortgage."

"Too long, if you ask me." He watched the houses go by. "Our ministry grew so huge, I felt like I was riding a brontosaurus every day. The next thing I knew, our kids were grown and on their own. My workload was more than my wife could take. So she decided to quit trying to win me back from the church and found someone else who wanted her."

He shook his head. "Talk about a wake-up call. After she left, I decided to make way for a younger pastor and look for a smaller congregation that didn't need a big staff."

On the rebound?

"First Baptist has a great core congregation," I assured him. "And since the building boom crashed, they've stabilized at a reasonably intimate membership."

"So Ed Lumpkin told me."

I grinned. "Ah, yes. Ed." He'd been running the church for years, de facto. "It would be wise to make him your ally."

Connor Allen shot me a knowing look. "I appreciate the heads-up."

I really liked this man. But as usual, I jumped to rash conclusions immediately and assumed he was a teetotaling Bible-banger.

Drat. Drat, drat, drat!

I pulled into the driveway of the clapboard ranch house just a few blocks from the church. "Here we are."

The grass had been cut, but the house had no other plantings and looked neglected. Inside, it was bland and nondescript, clean but not redecorated since the sixties. "What's your impression?" I asked Connor Allen.

He didn't even ask the price. "It's a bit too . . . plain for my tastes. A traditional exterior is fine, but I'd really prefer something a bit more updated inside. With some character."

"Then I think you'll really like one I have scheduled for later. But I wanted you to see the bottom of the market for your qualifications, first. This one's only sixty-five thousand."

He shook his head with a smile. "As my history attests, being a minister doesn't leave me time to do much else, so I'd rather not see anything that needs work."

I mentally deleted all the other olde-towne listings but the one next door to Miss Mamie's. When we'd both gotten back in the van and buckled up, I decided to do something I'd never done before.

I mean, heck, he was my last customer. Might as well, right?

"Would you prefer to see more listings that don't exactly fit your preferences," I asked him, "to get a feel for what's available? There are more I can show you a few blocks farther out. Or would you rather I take you to the one close by I think you'll like best?"

Connor Allen laughed. "Good for you. I like someone who's honest and direct. I'm the same way." He leaned back in his seat. "Take me to the one I'll like."

I did, and when we passed First Baptist, then Miss Mamie's, I pointed them out.

"Wow," he said, scanning our house as we drove by. "You live in a mansion." He didn't even seem to notice the bathtub on our verandah, which was a definite plus.

"As you can see," I told him when we turned onto the crushed-granite driveway next door, "it's very convenient to the church. Just a few blocks' walk on our fancy new sidewalks."

In the short time since Julia had alerted Jerry, he'd gotten the grass cut and edged, and had had someone touch up the subtle blue exterior and white trim. The mature plantings in the yard had been trimmed, and the giant oak behind the house shaded it from the morning sun.

Connor Allen leaned forward and took it all in through the windshield as if he were looking at the original Ark of the Covenant.

"What do you think so far?" I asked.

"It's perfect," he said. "I like to garden a bit, so the yard is great. Not too big, not too small."

"It's on a third of an acre." I braked, then killed the engine. "The only downside is, the builder who redid it consolidated three small bedrooms into two larger ones with better closet space and two baths." I let that sink in. "Still interested?"

He nodded, getting out as I did, then followed me to the Chinese-red front door.

Connor Allen brightened as I put the key into the lock. "Energy-efficient doors and windows. I like."

"And new formaldehyde-free foam insulation," I added, turning the key. "It's all energy efficient, from the Euro hot water system with a proper baffle, to the appliances." I pushed open the door and stepped back. "Go in and check it out."

Connor Allen walked in as if he were entering a fairy tale. "Wow. This is exactly what I hoped for. Exactly." He shook his head, grinning. "Déjà vu all over again."

You had to like a man who quoted Yogi Berra.

Connor Allen just kept hugging the house with his gaze.

I followed him inside. "There's a large storage closet beyond the kitchen that can be easily converted to a laundry. I could have estimates for you in a couple of days from good local people."

He noted the built-in bookshelves that took up the whole north wall of the open living area, with a large space in the shelving for a big TV. "Plenty of room for my library and sermons."

He stepped into the office-turned-master bedroom. "Wow. Space for my big bed and a dresser." He opened the walk-in closet. "Wow. My stuff will get lost in here."

"There's a small attic, as well," I told him. "Fully insulated and vented."

He glanced into the roomy bathroom. "A separate tub that looks like I could actually fit into it, and a tall shower. Perfect."

I wouldn't mind having a tub like that, myself. Jerry had found an old, extra long and deep ball-and-claw-foot tub, then had it restored like new, with a shining chrome hand shower and taps that must have cost at least seven hundred, wholesale.

Connor Allen turned around and grinned like a kid on Christmas morning. "I'll take it."

I had to make sure this wasn't a whim he'd later regret. "You haven't even seen the other bedroom or asked how much it is."

"How much it is?" he shot back.

Witty. Another plus. "Ninety-nine, five."

"Twenty-five thousand under budget." He scrubbed his hands together. "Perfect. That will leave me plenty left over to get a new mattress and set up the laundry. And pay a yard service." He stuck out his hand, wiggling his fingers. "Give me a contract, quick, before somebody else snaps it up."

"We can do that back at the office. But I can nail this down with a phone call." I pulled out my terrorist phone and scrolled to Jerry's number, then hit the call button.

He answered right away. "Hey, there, chickadee. What you got me?"

"I sold your house next to Mama's. Asking price, cash, contingent only on inspection. What do you say?"

"Hot dang," he bellowed. "When do they want to close?"

I turned the phone to my shoulder and asked Connor Allen, "When would you like to close?"

"As soon as it passes inspection," Connor Allen said, still soaking in the details of his new house.

"As soon as the inspection clears," I told Jerry.

"Haw," he said in delight. "It'll clear, all right. I took that place back down to the studs. Fumigated it, remediated any mold, vented and damp-proofed the crawl space, repaired all the damage, then insulated the schmoo out of it. New wiring, new plumbing, new furnace, new roof, new AC, and appliances. It'll pass with flyin' colors."

"Good. We'll use Tyler Baskin for the inspection." Dreaded as a deal-buster by sellers, Tyler knew his stuff and rarely missed a thing.

"Bring it on," Jerry said, still in good humor. "Let me know when he's comin', and we'll schedule the closin' for the next day." As always, Jerry didn't waste any time beating around the bush.

"I'll let you know soon as I reach him," I promised.

Jerry went on, "You got you a deal, sugar, and for gittin' that off my hands so quick, I'm gonna pay you and Julia an eight percent commission."

With Jerry, we usually charged only five, but I was in no position to turn down any money. "That's very generous. Thank you. I'll bring the contract over this afternoon."

"You do that." As an afterthought, he added, "Who's yer buyer?"

"Connor Allen, the new minister of First Baptist."

"Married?" he asked, his tone sharpening.

"No," I answered.

Jerry burst out laughing. "Well, if that don't beat all. Single, and right next door. Way to go, Linnie."

I hated to be called Linnie. And I would have corrected his misconception, but he was the seller, so I let it pass. *Please don't let everybody else in town think the same thing,* I prayed, even though I knew they would. Mary Lou Perkins would see to it.

"Bye." I hung up, then turned to Connor Allen. "You've got yourself a house."

It would be all over town by midnight that I had sold the gorgeous, divorced new Baptist minister the house next to mine.

What would come of it remained to be seen.

Frankly, I liked the idea of having Connor Allen as my next-door neighbor.

If only he wasn't a *Baptist.*

Never mind that I had been a Baptist, too. That was only true because God has a wicked sense of humor.

Ten

The next morning at the diner, I found the place abuzz. A bunch of regulars up front waved and smiled as I came in. Some even congratulated me on the sale.

No privacy in this town, I swear.

The little person/midget at the lunch bar motioned me over to whisper, "Ya think there's any sin left in that new guy? 'Cause if there is, give him this." She tucked a business card with her name and phone number into my hand, then winked. "He won't be my first Baptist minister, and he won't be my last."

"I . . . I wouldn't know." Flustered, I tried to hand it back, but her stubby fingers closed around mine.

"You keep that, just in case," she whispered. "I'm real reasonable, and I know how to keep my mouth shut." She grinned and dismissed me with a pat. "Tell Tommy I miss him. He gets half price."

Whoa! She was a prostitute? And my *brother* had used her services?

Judge not that ye be not judged. Love the sinner, hate the sin, my Puritan reminded me.

But I mean, really? Mimosa Branch's local whore was a midget in Sheet-rockers' stilts? Please!

I guessed she'd appeal to those looking for some novelty, but *Tommy?* Gag me with a steam shovel!

And I'd spoken with her both times I'd come in, which I'm sure had set tongues a-wagging. I made a mental note to burn or flush her number at the first opportunity.

I escaped into the back room, and who should be sitting across from Ed Lumpkin and another deacon from First Baptist, but Connor Allen.

One look at the man, and my long-comatose libido leapt to full speed, making my whole face burst into flames.

No, no, no. This couldn't be happening.

Connor stood immediately. "Well, if it isn't the lovely lady who sold me my house." He drew out the chair beside him. "Would you care to join us, Lin?"

Remaining seated, Ed and the deacon shot me a stony look. Scalded by their disapproval, I deflected with a bald-faced lie. "Thanks, but my brother Tommy's meeting me in a few minutes. Y'all enjoy your breakfast."

I went to the last open table, in the far corner, doing my best to ignore the whispers and curious expressions among the regulars.

As subtly as I could, I called Tommy and asked him to come join me. To his credit, he didn't hesitate to say yes. "Why don't you bring the Mame?" I suggested.

"Only if you don't want me to get there for another hour. You know how she is."

Slow, and getting slower. "Never mind. Just come as soon as you can," I said between my hands cupped over the receiver, then hung up.

Waiting for him, I felt as if I were in one of those dreams where you're suddenly naked in public.

The same waitress as before came back with a setup and an indifferent, "What can I git ya?"

"Just coffee for now, please. I'm waiting for my brother. We'll order when he gets here."

She brightened. "Tommy?"

"One and the same."

"I'll git that coffee right away," she said with a wide smile, then left.

I wondered how she'd feel if she knew he frequented whores, especially that midget in Sheetrockers' stilts.

Oh, Lord, keep me from judgment, I prayed with fervor. *Help me focus on gratitude, instead. And forgive me for lying. I promise, I'll repent as soon as I can.*

I resolved then and there never to bring up my brother's relationship to the Sheetrockers'-stilts woman. How could I, when I had a plank in my own eye?

But I'd really appreciate it, Lord, I prayed again, *if you could keep me from knowing these things. That would help a lot.*

I could sense the Almighty shaking his head at me, as He so often did.

Speak of the devil, Tommy strode in, then stopped at Connor Allen's table. "Hi. I'm Tommy Breedlove. I hear we're going to be next-door neighbors," he said as Connor got up to shake his hand.

"Soon as the house passes inspection," Connor said.

"It'll pass," Tommy assured him. "I watched them redo the place, and they did it right."

Connor motioned to the empty chair beside him. "Would you care to join us?"

Tommy glanced my way. "Thanks, but I'm meeting my sister."

He waved, then came to my table and sat with his back to the room. "So *that's* the new Baptist minister," he said, his voice low. "Good-looking guy. No wonder you needed a beard. Ed never could stand you."

He nailed it. For once, my brother was where I needed, when I needed, and I was truly grateful. "Thanks for coming," I murmured back. "I would have left, but that would have caused even *more* gossip."

"Glad to be of help."

The waitress appeared with Tommy's setup and a cup of coffee. "Black, just like you like it," she said with moon-eyes, then got out her order pad. "What can I give you?" she asked seductively.

"The usual. How about you, sis?"

"Three over medium with the whites done and the yolks creamy but not runny, and bacon, flat and crisp." All legal on my basic Atkins regimen. I'd already dropped two of the five pounds I'd gained from Mama's welcome-home feast.

When the waitress left, I leaned closer to Tommy and said, "She's really got a case on you."

"She," Tommy said quietly, "is just a kid, and a party girl, at that. Definitely the last thing I need. But I don't want to hurt her feelings, so I let her flirt, but I don't encourage it."

"Very wise," I said. "And kind."

He nodded in appreciation, then took a sip of hot coffee. "Aaah, caffeine."

Connor Allen and the deacons stood to leave, and, even though I knew it was hopeless, I watched him go with the same expression the waitress had spent on Tommy.

"Uh-oh," my brother said. "I recognize that look."

"Why do we always want what we can't have?" I asked him, serious.

"Who says you can't have?" he challenged.

"All the deacons of First Baptist, I'm sure, and every gossip in the congregation, led by Mary Lou Perkins. Apparently, they didn't get the memo about forgiveness after repentance when it comes to the Grant thing."

Fortunately, Grant had sold the drugstore and left soon after our fiasco, but the damage was done. "Ten years later, and I'm still notorious for my checkered past, never mind the facts."

Tommy leaned closer. "Lin, everybody has a checkered past. God knows it, and so do I. And you certainly haven't done anything like that before or since."

His loyalty was one of the things that had helped me get through it.

Then he frowned and asked, "You haven't, have you?"

So much for loyalty. "No!" I whispered emphatically. Then my indignation evaporated. "But I might as well have slept with Grant. I planned the whole thing. Sinned in my imagination," I whispered, quoting Connor Allen's predecessor, whose pointed sermons about scarlet women had driven me to the Methodists. "Same thing."

"No it's not. You came to your senses and didn't go through with it, stuck to your own values. I really admired you for that. And for keeping your head held high in spite of the gossips."

I didn't want to talk about it anymore, so I changed the subject. "Ocee got my transcripts, so I'm going up there to make sure they're correct. Want to come with me?"

He shook his head. "I've got a meeting at ten."

The smitten waitress brought our food, perfectly cooked.

Tommy and I ate in silence, but there was still an elephant sitting at our table.

I had an irrational crush on the new Baptist minister.

Just like with Grant, only this time, the man might very well be worthy, but I refused to be the tainted woman who came between him and his new congregation.

My mind understood that the attraction I felt for Connor Allen was irrational, but that didn't discourage my body. I barely knew the man, and there I was, feeling like a fourteen-year-old in heat.

Fourteen wasn't one of my better years. Too much adolescent angst and emotion.

Was one good-looking, smart, kind, available Christian man all it took to rob me of all common sense?

Apparently, even though my inner Puritan scolded that it could never go anywhere.

Shoot.

What in blue blazes was I going to do? I was a sixty-year-old Christian woman, not some teenybopper drooling over Justin Bieber.

Just hell.

Sorry, Lord.

Eleven

As predicted, Connor Allen's new house passed the inspection with flying colors, and we closed one week after the sale, much to everyone's relief—mostly mine, for the thirty-nine hundred dollars in my bank account. (Julia gave me a fifty-fifty split as a farewell gift, instead of taking her usual sixty percent.)

The more I saw of Connor, even at the closing, the bigger crush I had, so I hid behind a mask of professional indifference, reciting inwardly, *Feelings aren't facts. Feelings aren't facts. Feelings aren't facts.*

This man was not for me. He needed a Debbie Boone of a woman, not a destitute blabbermouth with no filters and a bad reputation.

Oh, Lord, I was obsessing. *Please keep me from obsessing.*

Apparently, that wasn't in the plan, because I just got more obsessed as the days went on.

Practically the whole church turned out to "help Pastor move in" when his furniture arrived (translate: check out his things, down to his pants size and boxers or briefs), so my plate of deviled eggs got lost among the dozens of casseroles and desserts that bombarded him from every available woman over thirty in the congregation. He got so much food, he had to buy a small chest freezer to hold it.

(When I heard the delivery truck rumble in next door, I just happened to look through the glass pane in my apartment door and see them unload the freezer.)

Once Connor Allen was finally settled in and working at the church, I prayed that my adolescent emotions would wane. Miss Mamie and I had the whole of 1431 Green Street to disinfect, which should have provided an excellent distraction, but every time my mind wandered off course, it zeroed in on the gorgeous man next door.

So I scrubbed harder and sang good old, foot-stomping hymns to counteract it as Miss Mamie joined in.

Of all times to have my libido wake up! I'd never felt that way with my ex. But the feelings Connor Allen stirred still felt familiar, and very seductive.

Logic told me that everything I knew about Connor was surface. And as for his marriage, there were two sides to every story. For all I knew, he could be a saint one minute, then a monster the next. I'd met more than one minister who was awful to his wife and family.

Yet he seemed like a true holy man.

But trying to be logical about this didn't help.

The one thing I knew was that I was *not* the woman for that gorgeous man. That gorgeous, intelligent, honest, sexy man.

We won't even go into the obscene fanny tattoo I'd gotten during a drunken impulse on my honeymoon with the husband of my youth: two red cherries and "eat me" in script. I know. Vulgar to the max, but I was young and foolish. Marrying Phil was proof enough of that. And we won't go into the fact that it had gone a bit wrinkly when I'd lost my middle-aged spread, thanks to the divorce.

So the following night, I tried reading a few "sweet" historical romance novels at bedtime to ease the tension, but instead of transferring my crush to the heroes, all I could see was Connor Allen's face in the stories.

Which was definitely a sin, which only confirmed how wrong the whole situation was.

I took it up with God, but He just sat there, still and quiet, in silence. Not very nice, if you ask me.

I hated it when I was supposed to wait. I do not wait well at all.

I mean, couldn't the All-knowing share a way out of this? I'm just saying. *Lead us not into temptation,* remember?

Nothing.

Frankly, I think putting Connor Allen right next door was a pretty mean joke, but then again, I was the one who'd done it, so there you are.

I also hate irony when I'm the one who has to live it, which seems to happen all the time.

So when that still, small inner voice clammed up on me, I sought God's direction in scripture, focusing on the verses about holiness and purity, which just depressed me so much in my falling short that I had to quit that, too, or face major depression in spite of my antidepressants (loads of esci-talopram and trazodone, with a top-off of generic Wellbutrin).

My GP said that America was one big unsupervised study of the long-term effects of antidepressants, but I silenced her with, "Shut up and give me the prescriptions, or else."

Apparently, the threat of violence by the patient is enough medical justi-fication to continue them, because she quickly gave me the scrips. Ditto with my bioidentical estrogen.

By the middle of my third week back home, the Mame and I had fin-ished scrubbing down most of the roasting third floor with Windex, Clorox Clean-Up, or CitriSafe nontoxic mold killer and were working side by side on our kneeling pads in the hallway, doing the baseboards, when she leaned back and wagged her hand my way. "I don't know what you've been takin', daughter mine, but I sure do wish you'd give me some. You're wearing me out. This isn't a race, you know."

I couldn't stop the telltale flood of embarrassment that further reddened my chest and face. I leaned back, too, swiping a stray tendril from my eyes as I noted that Mama was sheened with sweat, just as I was. *Horses sweat. Men perspire,* my Granny Beth's voice scolded, *and ladies dew.* "I'm sorry. It just helps to distract me from . . . things."

Seeing that her knees were really red and swollen, I offered, "Maybe we should work in different places, so you can go at your pace and I can go at mine."

"Don't be silly," she said. "Then we couldn't do our hymns together. I just need you to slow down a bit so I'll have enough breath left to sing along." She waggled the scrub brush my way. "When we run out of songs we know, I've got my Grandmama Grainger's old hymn book in the library to remind us of more."

My Grainger great-grandmother had died when I was just two, but I remembered my paternal grandfather's second wife Granny Beth singing those old country hymns in the kitchen, early in the morning as she made our bread and biscuits for the day. Even all these years later, I still missed her dearly, yet her wisdom remained in my mind and heart, though I didn't always act on it. We'd been "cut out of the same bolt," as she always said.

My mother paused to study me. "I don't know who it is you've been trying to scrub away, but you can tell me, you know."

Only if I wanted it on the grapevine (aka the prayer chain—both Baptist and Methodist, so my mother didn't miss anything). I didn't spill the beans, deflecting with, "It's not somebody. It's my own stupidity and my stubborn, rebellious flesh."

Her left brow rose as she granted me a skeptical smile. "As bad as that?"

"Yep."

"Well," she said cheerfully, "you could always get a good dildo. There's nothing in the Bible that says you can't have a good dildo."

"Mama!" Had she really said that? "That's not what I was talking about." Though it might not be a bad idea. Or would it?

Shoot. There went my wayward brain again.

No wonder God had stopped speaking to me.

"Sorry," Miss Mamie said without apology.

Flustered, I heard my mouth engage before my mind. "I thought when I got old, I'd get better. Smarter. More mature. More in control of my emotions and my physical desires. But I'm still that same impulsive, contrary nit-head I was at puberty."

My mother peered at me till a light went on in her eyes. "Oooohhh. Our new neighbor." She sobered. "I was afraid of that."

Horrified, I splayed my hand over my heart. "Oh, no. Could you tell?" *Please don't let everybody in town know! Please-oh-please-oh-please.*

"Of course not." She patted my arm. "I just now figured it out. If I'd known, I wouldn't have asked you what was wrong."

Why didn't I believe that? Because it was the Mame. Her maternal compulsion to comfort Tommy and me always overrode such trivial inconveniences as the truth.

But I would never be able to show my face in Mimosa Branch again if she spread this around. "Mama, I know it's hard to keep things to yourself, but this one is a biggie. If anybody else even guesses this, I'd have to leave town and go to a shelter, and I'm not kidding. You and I both know perfectly well that nothing good can come from my crush on Connor, for him or me."

Miss Mamie sniffed, the simple gesture transmitting a blast of "Oh, yeah? Who says?"

"I mean it, Mama." I only called her Mama when things were drastic. "I have to nip this in the bud." My mind immediately conjured a bug-eyed Barney Fife hollering, "Nip it in the bud," but I stayed on topic. "I have no intention of acting on these ridiculous feelings, and it can't go any further than you and me." I grasped her rubber gloves in my own. "Please, this is *really* important. If you need to talk to anybody about it, talk to God. He sure hasn't been talking to me lately."

"Oh, sweetie." She leaned over and gave me an awkward hug, because getting up then back down was too much trouble for both of us. "I vow, this won't go any further than God."

I knew she meant it. I just didn't know if she could keep her promise, any more than I could stop cussing in my head.

Please, Lord, don't let this get out.

I went back to scrubbing, slowing my pace to the somber beat of "The Old Rugged Cross," one of Granny Beth's favorites, and mine. But no matter how hard I scrubbed or sang, my flesh wouldn't let go of thinking about Connor Allen.

Twelve

Three weeks after my first visit to Ocee State, I returned to the baking campus and waited to be called back to Pam What's-her-name's office.

Brady, I managed to remember as the receptionist (another student) led me back to see her.

Pam rose, as before. "Hi! We processed your registration and transcripts." She closed the door, then offered her hand.

I shook it. "Great. Any news?"

I waited till she sat to do the same, as mixed emotions warred over what she might say. She seemed happy—a good sign. A very good sign, as it turned out.

"Based on your finances and situation," she told me, "I am pleased to announce that you have qualified for a Pell Grant, which will cover both your classes and your textbooks, for winter/spring quarter."

I sat there, stunned, doing my best to stomp out the *Oh no*s and *You can't even keep up with what day it is! How do you expect to pass in college?* that erupted alongside my sense of accomplishment.

Holy crow! I was really going back to college.

Pam nodded to me, clearly expecting a reaction.

Closeting my fears, I found myself on my feet, pumping her hand. "Wow! Thanks. I don't know how to thank you. Thanks."

I still couldn't believe it had actually happened. A full ride! Wow.

Miracle of miracles. *Thank you, Lord!*

She grinned. "I think you're really going to like it here. Almost all of our nontraditional students do."

Still dazed, I subsided to my chair. "What's next?"

"You'll need to meet with your adviser." She handed me his card. "You can call and leave a message at his office for an appointment, but a student e-mail might do better." She paused. "Do you have any special needs?"

"Well, I can't filter voices when there's background noise. Is that a special need?"

She made a note on my file, then handed me a card that said "Cathy Wallace, Student Accommodations Office."

Too politically correct. Instead of saying *Disabilities Office,* they came up with a name that sounded like student housing—which they didn't even have.

She went on. "This is the number for our special needs office. You can schedule an appointment with them for evaluation, and they'll work with you on your accommodations."

"Thanks." Cool. When I'd gone to college in 1970, nobody gave a fig whether anybody needed special help.

She handed me an orientation packet. "Here's the information you'll need to get started. Your password for our Web site is your full birth date—two digits for both the month and date, and four for the year—then your mother's maiden name. Once you've registered for your classes, you can set up your student e-mail and get your ID and parking permit."

"How many credits transferred from my year at Sandford?" I wondered aloud.

She looked over the transcript, then said, "Five hours of art history."

Shoot! My mouth tugged down on one side. "That's all?"

She shrugged. "That's all."

I really was starting from scratch. "Then I need *everything*."

She lifted a finger. "I'd recommend your trying to CLEP out of some of your basic courses. We allow you to test out of up to thirty-five credit hours."

"Clep?"

"College Level Equivalency Program," she clarified. "Of course, if you qualify for special accommodations, you can register early in October, ahead of the other students, and Cathy can help you pick the professors who work best with limitations like yours." She showed me a printed blue sheet that listed the required courses, then she started checking off categories. "You'll need all of these core courses for an English degree, but you can select which ones you can CLEP from the link on our Web site."

There were an awful lot of checks.

Seeing my dismay, she smiled in sympathy. "Cathy will go over this in more detail if you qualify for special accommodations. Otherwise, your adviser can help you."

Based on past experiences, a question popped into my mind. "How long has my adviser been here?"

Pam made a brief face, then admitted, "This is his first year with us."

Talk about the blind leading the blind! "Well, I hope I qualify for accommodations, then."

Mouth, could you possibly be ruder? Shoot!

But Pam laughed, then leaned in for a confidential, "Me, too."

I tucked the cards in my purse, then rose along with her. "Thank you so much. And the grant committee. Thank everybody for me, please."

She nodded. "See you in January."

January, and it was already August. I had a lot to learn in a very short time if I was going to CLEP well.

My friends who'd gone back to school over the years had told me that it wasn't the courses that were so hard, it was learning how each school did things that made it difficult.

Frankly, my "life plan" had been more of an impulse than a calling. Yet there I was, all set to go to school for three years. Maybe less, if I could test out of a bunch of classes.

I could do that. I loved school.

Except math.

Shoot. I'd have to take math! Just one course, but still . . .

Passing that would take a Red Sea miracle.

But God had provided the scholarship, so I supposed He could provide the brains I needed to pass college algebra. Or a good tutor.

If not, I could always pay somebody to take it for me, online.

My inner Puritan flailed away on me with a hickory stick for even thinking such a thing.

Sorry, sorry, sorry. I was only kidding. I'd never cheated before, and had no intention of doing so.

Unless it was the absolute *only* way I could get my diploma.

I could sense God's shaking His head at me.

Thanks so much for the scholarship, I prayed again with conviction. *So much.*

More than even the money, getting that grant made me feel like I wasn't such a failure.

I decided to see the disabilities office and register as soon as I could, so I could get a basic algebra textbook and start reviewing, even though I knew perfectly well that all the bridges had been burned long ago when it came to math.

Thank goodness for grace and forgiveness, that's all I can say.

Thirteen

Back home, I parked in my spot beside Tommy's truck in the garage, then headed for the house.

You know, maybe poverty wasn't so bad if it made me eligible for a grant.

I wondered if I'd qualify for food stamps. Lord knew, I'd paid plenty of taxes in the past ten years, so I didn't mind trying to get some of it back.

By the time I got to the top of the stairs leading to the dining room from the verandah, I could barely breathe for the heat. It hadn't taken me a minute to get used to air-conditioning when I'd married, but getting used to our local version of global warming was taking forever.

I was panting by the time I reached the relative cool of the kitchen, where I found Tommy talking to the Mame under the gently whirring ceiling fans.

"Hey, Sissie-ma-noo-noo." (A nickname that came from an original episode of *The Dick Van Dyke Show*.) Tommy waved a glass of cold tea my way.

"Your decaf Splenda tea's in the icebox," my mother said. "In the tall, skinny pitcher, so I can keep 'em straight." She squinted at me in concern. "You look whipped."

"It's just the heat." I grabbed one of the quart glasses from the orderly cabinets, then loaded up on ice and tea. By the time I'd had a long sip and sat down, I could talk.

"Guess what?" I said, still unable to believe it fully myself.

Tommy frowned. "I hate when you do that. Why don't you just come out and tell us?"

The Mame patted his arm. "Oh, now Tommy, it's a girl thing. Just let it go." She turned to me in expectation. "What, sweetie?"

"I got accepted to Ocee State. On a full ride for winter/spring quarter. They're even paying for my books."

"Linwood Breedlove Scott," my mother crowed, shooting to her feet, arms wide. "I am *so* proud of you. Come here and let me give you a big old hug!"

I did.

Tommy's reaction was a lot quieter, but at least he was smiling. "I knew you could do it, Sissie-ma-noo-noo. When do you start?"

"January sixth. Which gives me some time to brush up on my algebra. I think I'll be okay in the language-based courses"—assuming I could still memorize and wasn't getting Alzheimer's—"but the math really scares me."

Tommy raised both palms to me, fingers splayed. "Don't look at me. I don't even remember what algebra *means*."

Miss Mamie chuckled. "Same here. Balancing our finances is as far as I go."

I needed to ask her about that, but this wasn't the time.

"You could always put off taking algebra to the last," Tommy suggested. "After you're back in the swing of things."

I considered that, but real estate had trained me to get the hardest things out of the way first. "I'd really like to go on and get it behind me." I sipped my tea, finally letting it all sink in. "Maybe I could try it, then drop it in time to schedule something else if it doesn't go well."

"It'll go well," Tommy said with more than a little edge on it. "School always went well for you."

"That was forty years ago, honey," I reminded him. "I haven't had to study since my real estate and appraisal exams, and trust me, those did not come easy."

The Mame got up and did what she always did when there was something to celebrate: she started cooking. "We'll have a special supper, then, for our coed. What would you like?"

I did my best to pick things that wouldn't leave me with five more pounds to carve off, like I had after her last feast. "I'd just love some baked chicken with plain broccoli and mashed cauliflower. And some of that cranberry sauce I made with Splenda."

Miss Mamie shook her head, even as she said, "Well, all right. If that's what you want, that's what you'll get. Though why you're so dead set on losing more weight is beyond me. If you get any skinnier, you'll look like a POW, and I'd die of mortification if anybody thought I wasn't feeding you."

Aha. There was the rub.

"Trust me, Mama," I reassured her. "Anybody who knows you will know you are *not* starving me."

Even though I was sixty, she still put me in a high chair. But the Mame was the Mame, and I wasn't about to be able to change her.

"Thanks for the tea. I really appreciate it." I stood, taking my tea with me. "I'm going home to take a cold shower and have a nap. When's supper?"

"How about eight?" she asked.

By then, I'd be ready for bed, but I would set my alarm for seven-thirty to accommodate my mother.

Fourteen

On my way back to the garage apartment the next afternoon after cleaning all day, a familiar voice accosted me from the hedge. "Lin?"

Oh, no. Not Connor Allen.

My hair was frizzed, my eyes and mouth were invisible because I didn't have on a lick of makeup, and I was wearing sweaty, grungy cleaning clothes that made me look a mile wide.

Shoot. Shoot, shoot, shoot!

I considered pretending I hadn't heard him, but by the time I got around to that, he was coming through the hedge, looking all spiffy in a navy golf shirt and khakis.

Seeing my obvious distress, he took a step back. "I'm sorry. If this isn't a good time, I can—"

"No, it's okay," I said. The damage had already been done. He'd seen me. I swiped at my frizzy hair. At least I'd left my rubber gloves at Miss Mamie's. "How are you?"

"Fine. Fine." As if to spare my ego, he didn't stare at me. "I just wanted to express my gratitude for your help with finding my house." Then he looked into my eyes, smiling like a shy young man. "I was wondering if you could come over for dinner tomorrow night. I have a wide selection of frozen casseroles, but it's sort of lonesome in a new place by myself."

I raised an eyebrow. "I figured you'd be eating with your deacons and congregation for at least a month. It's SOP for small towns like Mimosa Branch whenever there's a new minister."

He grinned. "I gained five pounds the first week, so I asked my congregation to hold off for a month or two, so I could get settled in."

I sized him up, my eyes narrowing. "You haven't already ticked them off, have you?"

He laughed, then said, "Boy, it's good to talk to somebody who speaks her mind, like I was a regular person. I have to be so careful with whatever I say, but you're a real breath of fresh air. And gorgeous, to boot."

Alarms went off inside my head, but looking into those crisp, sparkling blue eyes, I ignored them all. Of all times, and of all people for me to lust after.

Goofy from the chemistry that surged between us, I still managed to come up with an acceptable alternative. "Why don't you come over for dinner with us tomorrow, instead?" Chaperoned by my mother, our dinner would be totally respectable. But I was heading down the primrose path by encouraging him. "Miss Mamie is dying to meet you, and she considers it her highest calling to feed the clergy, regardless of denomination."

He brightened. "Perfect. When shall I come, and what shall I bring?"

Boy, did I love the educated Southern of his cultured accent. "I'll check with Miss Mamie about the time," I said, "but please don't bring anything. Just yourself."

Uh-oh. Did that sound as moony as I thought it did?

Connor nodded. "I finally got my phone. My number's 9342."

How did he know about that? Only the old-timers knew that giving the last four numbers meant the 222 exchange, which had long been Mimosa Branch's only one.

"I see you've learned a lot about us, already," I complimented.

"Small town is small town, the world around," he said, his gaze never leaving mine.

I faced him straight on and saw nothing but trouble, trouble, trouble.

My mind said I was too old and too wise to fall into this, but my body just wanted to jump his bones.

Not exactly spiritual.

God, this is cruel, and you know it. Please get me out of this before I do irreparable damage to both of us.

God just smiled, along with Connor Allen.

"You know I'm notorious, don't you?" I blurted out. "Not the sort of woman a man like you should be alone with."

His eyes narrowed in assessment. "I fail to believe that. I've heard wonderful things about you from several of the ladies in my congregation"—my mother's friends, no doubt—"and from Geneva and Donnie and Shelia."

"They're my pals, and they understand about forgiveness," I said. "But a lot of the so-called Good Christian Ladies of Mimosa Branch still hold it against me that I got stoned—completely unintentionally—and tried to have a fling with the new pharmacist—completely intentionally—ten years ago when I had to move back home after my divorce."

Clearly fascinated, Connor Allen actually laughed. "Nobody said a word about that." His grin lit up my world. "I can't wait to hear every detail. And I promise not to tape it and put it on YouTube."

A minister with a sense of humor. My crush deepened.

I shook my head at his naivety. "Boy, do you have a lot to learn about this town."

"Busted." His brows lifted. "Frankly, I was hoping you could help me with that. After I hear about the pot and the pharmacist."

"Not over dinner," I qualified. "My mother would die."

"How about on the porch, afterward?" he proposed. "Just the two of us, out in the open where anyone can see."

Just like Grant and me, ten years before.

But for all I knew, Connor might blab. I'd known several ministers who failed to keep pastoral privilege, including his predecessor.

As if he had read my mind, Connor sobered. "Lin, you can trust me with the truth. I'm not the kind of man who breaks a confidence."

When he said it, I believed him, even though I knew it was *not* a good idea—for so many reasons—to get involved. Yet my foolish crush answered before I could, "Okay. But it's your funeral."

"See you tomorrow, then. Be sure to bring that big brain of yours." Connor Allen backed toward the hedge from whence he had come. "And your sense of humor."

Nine-three-four-two. That was his phone number.

Mortified that I'd given in to my uncontrollable attraction, I hurried up the garage stairs without looking back.

Once inside, I wrote down his number, then looked in my living room mirror and let out a hoot of horror. I looked a thousand years old, with bad hair, to boot.

Shoot. Shoot, shoot, shoot.

And I'd said yes.

As a single, celibate Christian woman, I needed to practice my noes, not my yeses. And I needed this stupid crush like I needed a ten-speed racing bike: one slip, and I'd wreck the man's life. And my own.

Fifteen

"Ms. Wallace will see you now," the receptionist at the disabilities office said the next morning.

"Thanks." I didn't know why I was so nervous, but I was. Maybe it was the whole idea of "accommodations" and "disabilities."

A very nice-looking woman who looked about my age came out of the little corner office and welcomed me. "Hi. I'm Cathy Wallace. Please come in."

I was glad when she closed the door behind us before taking her seat. "I want you to know that what we discuss here is strictly personal and confidential. Only qualified staff have access to our records."

"Good." That was a relief. "I don't want any students on work grants nosing around in my deficiencies."

Cathy Wallace smiled, then changed the subject. "Congratulations on your Pell Grant."

I couldn't suppress a tight chortle. "Thanks. I'm so grateful for it. But, to tell the truth, that's kind of like having somebody say 'congratulations on your recent destitution.'"

Her gray eyes lit with intelligence as she laughed. "It is, isn't it?" Then she sobered. "I love your honesty. Do you always say what comes into your head?"

"Sorry," I told her, flushing with embarrassment. "I guess I don't really have many filters left, anymore, outside of work. Living alone, I got into the habit of talking to myself, so what comes up, comes out. I probably need to get a handle on that before January."

She nodded with good humor. "It would probably help in class, anyway." She looked at my file. "So, let's see what we can do to make your experience as smooth as possible, here."

I wondered whether or not to tell her about the words thing.

"It says here that you have trouble filtering voices during background noise."

I nodded. "Yes."

She smiled. "We can get permission for you to tape your lectures. That should make it a little easier."

"Great." Except that the tape would have the same background noises, but hey, why not?

She scribbled more in my file, then looked up. "Any other difficulties?"

She'd probably think I was nuts with a capital crazy, but I confided, "I have this weird word thing with reading."

She leaned closer, intent. "Can you tell me specifically?"

"Well, it happened after my divorce, which was very traumatic."

"And when was that?" she asked.

"Ten years ago," I told her, feeling foolish that I was still affected after so many years, "but this thing hasn't gotten any better. It happens when I try to read for pleasure, which I've done all my life."

She nodded. "What exactly happens?"

She would definitely write me off as a head case, but never mind. "I'll be reading along just fine, getting lost in the story, when all of a sudden, the individual words just jump out at me. I completely lose my train of thought. I have to reread several times before I can get back into the swing, and then, maybe after a page, or only a few paragraphs, there it goes again. I have no continuity reading for pleasure anymore." I lifted a finger. "But I can still write just fine."

Curiosity and professional concern warred in her expression. "That's fascinating. I've never heard of that before."

Figures.

She made notes in my file, then handed me a card from one of the holders on her desk. "I'd like to have you evaluated over at UGA in Athens, if that's all right with you. Normally it costs five hundred," she said. "But as a Pell Grant recipient, you'll only have to pay eighty-five dollars. Can you manage that?"

"Yes." Thanks to my commission for selling Connor Allen the house next door. Connor, who was coming to dinner at eight. I shivered briefly in anticipation. Mama was already cooking. "I can manage it."

"I'll notify Athens this afternoon. By tomorrow, you can call the number on that card and set up the appointment." She studied me with a clinical eye. "I'm very interested in what they find."

"Okay, then."

"Is there anything else?" she asked as if she hoped there were.

"Not that I can think of."

She rose to shake my hand. "I'll get back in touch as soon as we get the results. If you qualify, then we can register you for your classes."

Good. I'd get first crack at the good professors.

If I could find out who they were.

One of the checkout girls in the Kroger went to Ocee. Maybe she could tell me how to find the Web site that gave student evaluations for the professors. But even if I got the good ones, would I be up to starting over now that everything was done by computer?

Lost in a sucking vortex of self-doubt, I forgot I was standing there.

"Was there anything else?" Cathy Wallace gently nudged.

I came to with a start. "Sorry. No. Not at all." I managed a broken smile as I retreated to the reception area. "Thanks."

She waved as if she were watching a unicorn disappear into thin air.

Great. Just what I needed. Not only was I sixty, destitute, inappropriately horny, and a college freshman, but I was also a weirdo.

Nothing like starting off on the right foot.

I headed home through the heat to help Miss Mamie cook supper for Connor Allen, determined to convince her we had to eat in the kitchen.

Sixteen

It took half that afternoon, but I eventually convinced Mama it was more hospitable to eat in the kitchen with the air conditioning than to entertain our guest at one end of her table for twenty in the heat of our dark, stuffy, cavernous oak-paneled dining room.

The Mame consoled herself by breaking out her finest cutwork cloth and napkins, the best china, crystal, and sterling, and adorning it all with plenty of flowers from her cutting garden. The final table garnish was one of her award-winning triple-layer lemon cheese cakes (an old Southern favorite, which had no cheese, but dripped with tart, translucent lemon icing) elevated in a gorgeous crystal cake plate and dome.

I had to admit, Miss Mamie still set a mighty fine table, and I found it reassuring that some of the bygone customs of Southern hospitality still existed in my mother's heart and house.

Never one to lighten the fare when it came to company, Mama had made a boneless pork roast whose golden shine and rich aroma could summon angels, a Dutch oven full of her trademark pole beans (skinned by me down both sides with a potato peeler, lest anyone bite a string, God forbid), mashed peeled red potatoes whipped into stiff peaks, rich translucent pork gravy thickened with cornstarch, deviled eggs (my contribution), home-made pickled peaches so good they'd make you slap your best friend to get one, and summer squash with tons of butter and sautéed Vidalia onions, all washed down with plenty of iced tea: with caffeine and without, with sugar and without.

She'd started with the cake right after breakfast, but I'd only been help-ing since noon. A whole day of cooking and preparation, all for a mere hour of eating and some after-dinner conversation. (But there would be plenty of leftovers. Yum.)

In deference to Tommy's sobriety and Connor's being a Baptist, we left off the wine.

"Mama," I told her, looking at the feast, "this is amazing. How do you do it?"

She laughed like a girl. "I don't very often, anymore, but with your help, it wasn't so hard. It sure feels good to do it right every now and then."

Like all Southern ladies of her generation, Miss Mamie had her priori-ties straight, and those included offering her very best to her guests. Even when it meant ironing tablecloths and napkins in the heat, and polishing the silver.

"Connor Allen couldn't find food like this anywhere but on your table," I praised. "And he'll remember it."

She gave me an affectionate nudge. "Well, you helped. You know how to cook Southern as well as I do." Her eyes narrowed. "Don't forget: the way to a man's heart is still through his stomach." She took off her pinafore apron. "As long as men get good food, lots of sex, and plenty of sleep, they're happy."

What was with all this sex talk from my *mother*?

"I am not trying to catch Connor Allen." I didn't even attempt to address the fact that my ex had had great food, everything he'd wanted in the bed-room, and lots of sleep, but cheated on me anyway.

I flashed on my father and wondered if he had ever strayed. Knowing the General, he might well have, but he never would have let it get back to Miss Mamie. The old double standard had been alive and well in their generation, but I wouldn't embarrass my mother by asking.

Even if she knew he had, she'd never shame them both by admitting it.

The Mame touched my arm. "Why don't you go lie down for a little while in your air-conditioning, then shower and freshen up? We want you to look your best for your preacher friend."

"Miss Mamie, he's not my preacher. Or my friend."

She beamed, smug. "Uh-huh. And I didn't just fall off a turnip truck." She motioned for me to leave. "Shoo. Rest. Get ready."

"You rest," I retorted.

"I will." My mother waved me out with a satisfied lift of her still-strong chin.

Seventeen

As usual, I woke that evening just in time to put on my face and try to tame the curls I'd caught back, damp from the shower, with combs. The AC dried them out enough for me to fluff them into a passable attempt at a coiffure. Then I did my eyes, bronzed my cheeks, and donned my favorite pink silk slacks and matching unlined raised-collar jacket, with a white satin camisole underneath.

Cream flats, pearls, and my antique gold cross completed the outfit. I went to the big mirror in the living room for a final check.

If I squinted, I almost looked forty in the mirror. But Connor Allen wouldn't be squinting.

Nervous as a teenager on her first day in a new high school, I braced myself for the hot trip to the house.

I actually considered driving all the way around to the porte cochere so I wouldn't get all sweaty—correction, dewy—on the way, but rejected the idea as ridiculous, not to mention environmentally irresponsible.

Suddenly, I craved a cigarette.

What?

Forty years since I'd quit, and I was jonesing for a *cigarette*? Please!

Give the devil an inch, my inner Puritan scolded, *he'll take a mile.*

Can it, my inner hedonist retorted. *So you're attracted to the guy. It's not like you've done anything.*

Yet, my Puritan snapped.

Thinking cool thoughts, I glided out of my apartment and down the stairs, then up to the kitchen. By the time I got there, the lap of my slacks had creased from hip to hip like an accordion, but I did my best to ignore it and maintain my dignity.

The Mame had everything ready. "Oh, Lin," she said, "you look gorgeous."

"Thanks."

We both pulled chairs from the table and sat to wait.

"Do you think he'll be late?" my mother fretted.

"Nope," I answered, looking up to the old depot clock on the wall. "He still has three minutes."

Her immaculate nails tapped the cutwork cloth. "Where's your brother?"

"His truck's there," I offered. "He's probably getting ready."

The house was so well built, we couldn't hear the water flowing in the copper pipes or cast-iron drains.

The doorbell rang, bringing both of us up out of our seats like a fire alarm.

In unison, we shoved the chairs back into place. "You answer it," I whispered, the victim of cold feet.

"No. You need to introduce him to me," Mama whispered back, pushing me into the dining room. "It's proper form. So you answer it. Then introduce me. I'll be right behind you."

Shoot. Propelled by protocol, I opened the front door to find Connor haloed by the late evening sun. Blinking, I pushed open the screen. "Hi. Please come in."

When he did, I saw he was holding a pretty basket full of zucchini, the ubiquitous late-summer gift from anyone with a garden. Another gift from a single woman, no doubt.

"My, what lovely vegetables," my mother declared, the definite edge to her tone a reminder that I hadn't done my duty quickly enough.

"Miss Mamie," I hastened to comply, "please allow me to present our new next-door neighbor, Pastor Connor Allen. Connor, this is my mother."

My mother offered her hand like a queen. "Please call me Miss Mamie," she instructed. "I just know we're all going to love having you so close by."

Connor gently lifted her fingers with his own and briefly bowed above them. Then he bestowed that glorious smile on my mother. "Thank you, ma'am. I could say the same. I've heard so many wonderful things about your family already."

Underneath the mask of years, my mother sparkled like a debutante. "Please, please, come in." She motioned to the parlor. "Why don't you and Lin chat in the living room while I finish getting dinner on the table?" she instructed. "I'll ring when everything's ready."

As she left us, we went into the muggy parlor and sat at right angles, he in a chair and me on the far end of the white camelback sofa. For a moment, an awkward pause ensued, then we both started talking at once, which broke the tension.

Connor scanned the room. "This is quite a place," he ventured. "What was it like, growing up in such a wonderful house?"

"Hot in the summer and cold in the winter," I responded with a smile. "It's just a house, bigger than most, but I never thought much about that. What mattered was that my family and my grandmother were here. I adored my Granny Beth."

"Good grandparents are great for kids," he said. "Parents have to be the policemen, but grandparents can give unqualified love. Both are so important."

Generic preacher talk. Maybe it was the situation, but I wished for the easy honesty of our first conversations.

Another awkward lull set in, broken by the sound of Tommy's loud descent from the front stairs.

We looked his way with anticipation, and Connor rose.

Tommy strode across the parlor and broke the ice with a hearty handshake for our new neighbor. "Great to see you. I hope you'll come often." He leaned in confidentially. "I don't get to eat this way every day."

With that, the resonant little crystal bell from the kitchen announced dinner.

Eighteen

Tommy pushed open the swinging door from the dining room, then motioned me and Connor into the relative cool of the kitchen.

One look at the setting and the artfully plated food, and Connor all but salivated. "Wow. Miss Mamie, that's the prettiest table and the best-looking food I've ever seen." He crossed to seat her at the head of the table while Tommy followed suit for me next to the guest of honor's seat.

"Wait till you taste it," Mama said with pride. Then she ruined it by adding, "Lin's just as good a cook as I am, by the way, but she's always on some silly diet."

My jaw dropped behind flat lips as I struggled to keep from showing my embarrassment about her blatant hint to Connor.

Once we were all seated, she nodded to Connor. "Would you please bless this for us?"

Connor nodded, then closed his eyes. "Dear Lord in heaven, thank You for this wonderful food and the hands that prepared it. And thank You for the blessing of our homes, and for friendship. Open our eyes to the needs of others, that we might be Christ's hands and hearts in this world. Amen."

"Well said," Miss Mamie announced, then offered Connor the platter of sliced pork garnished with pickled peaches. No sooner had he helped himself to a few slices, than Miss Mamie followed up with mashed potatoes. Gravy would come next, then all the rest.

Tommy to the rescue. "So, how are things going with the church?" he asked Connor as we passed the food.

"Very well. They've been very receptive to my sermons about living a full Christian life." He looked over to me. "This Sunday, I'm teaching about unity and support within the body after a Christian has sinned, then repented. The scriptures are very clear that we should all support and forgive the repentant one."

Tommy chuckled. "That'll get their feathers up."

Connor nodded, unfazed. "The Lord's Prayer teaches that unforgiveness quenches the Holy Spirit, both in a believer and a congregation."

Tommy let out a low whistle, helping himself to the deviled eggs. "Good luck with that."

I would have loved to be there to hear it, but half the congregation was still mad at me for going over to the "heretic" Methodists who'd approved female clergy and homosexual unions. All sure signs to the hidebound that the apocalypse was soon upon us.

My views were traditional about what constituted marriage, but the last time I read the Bible, judgment was strictly God's business, not ours. So I'd left that to God and just loved folks, as my Granny Beth had always told me to do. Frankly, what went on behind closed doors was supposed to be private, anyway, no matter what a person's sexual orientation.

Behind closed doors with Connor Allen, my inner hedonist hissed salaciously.

My Puritan pounced on that immediately with *Do not go there! Danger. Danger. Lewd!*

I distracted myself by staring at my food and silently reciting the twenty-third Psalm, then the Lord's Prayer.

A skillful conversationalist, Connor soon had us all sharing our memories of Mimosa Branch. Mama told us about the Depression, when the Methodists and Baptists only had itinerant preachers every other week, so they'd banded together and met in the mill hall as one congregation, so the pulpit would always be filled. "Back then, you couldn't tell a lick of difference between us," Miss Mamie concluded with a wistful sigh. "Except that the Baptists couldn't go to the movies or dance or drink."

Connor said he wished we could have that kind of unity among believers again, and we could, as long as we kept the focus on Christ instead of our differences.

Miss Mamie's expression went wistful. "That's why I joined the women's club and garden club after the war"—World War II—"so I could keep up with the Presbyterians and Methodists."

The operative words being *keep up*.

Tommy put things on a happier note by reminiscing about his antics as a kid, and how he'd run away at twelve and tried to float down to Atlanta on the Hooch, only to have his inflatable raft snared by sharp branches, followed by his efforts to climb the banks for the long walk home. He'd arrived home scratched, remorseful, and covered with chiggers and mosquito bites.

He had all of us laughing.

By the time nine rolled around and we had done justice to the meal, we were all at ease over our decaf coffees and cake crumbs.

Connor rose. "Miss Mamie, why don't you stay seated and let me clean up?"

She bristled, standing. "No you don't. No dinner guest of mine has ever washed dishes, and I'm not about to let you be the first. I'd be mortified."

Connor looked askance at me, alarmed that he'd offended.

Once again, Tommy came to the rescue. "Tell you what, Mama. You and Lin cooked all day, so why don't I clean up? Ya'll go sit out on the porch with Connor. It's nice and cool, now."

A mere eighty degrees, a blessing for dusk in August after the sun had set.

Miss Mamie looked from me to Connor, then back to me. "Tell you what,

Tombo," she said in a sly tone. "Why don't I just sit here and keep you company? The kids can go to the porch to talk, if they want."

The kids. Ha!

A blatant setup.

Connor brightened. "Thanks. Sounds great. But you're sure you don't want me to help?"

My mother waved him out. "Don't you start that again, young man."

He winked at her. "As you wish." Connor offered his arm, then led me out of the kitchen, the door swinging shut behind us as we entered the dining room.

Boy, was I in for a shock.

Nineteen

I'm sorry," I whispered when we were safely out of earshot. "I had nothing to do with that. They set us up."

Connor mustered an enigmatic half smile, but his expression revealed a man at war with himself. About what, I couldn't begin to imagine, but with a face like that, he shouldn't ever play poker.

He took my hand and led me toward the porch, but halfway through the dim, oak-paneled foyer, he stopped, gently tightening his grip on my hand, and peered at me, his eyes sending so many mixed signals—conflict, resolution, temptation, wonder, shame—that I couldn't tell what it meant. But nothing prepared me for what happened next.

Proper Connor Allen, divorced Baptist minister, swung me into his arms and planted a dizzying, drop-dead, Times-Square-end-of-WWII-nurse-and-sailor kiss on me, his lean arms strong around me.

A simple kiss. No tongues. No pressing of bodies beyond respectability. Even so, it was the best, most amazing kiss of my long life.

My inner Puritan dropped like a fifty-foot poplar, on the spot.

Shoot! Shoot, shoot, shoot! I pulled free, reeling.

Grasping my upper arms to steady me, Connor let out a long, low whistle. He let go, and I almost staggered.

I struggled to regain my balance, my hand over my still-pulsing lips.

So *that* was how a kiss should feel.

Holy moley.

Connor tugged at his collar, his eyes darkening with remorse. "I am *so* sorry. I can't believe I just did that." He shook his head as if to clear it. "Yes I can," he confessed. "I've been dying to do that since the first minute I saw you."

"Oh, no." I steadied at last. "Me, too."

We held ourselves apart, as if lightning would strike if we touched again, even as the attraction pulsed between us like a giant generator.

His brows lowered in consternation. "I promise I've never done anything like this in my entire life. Never felt anything like this, either."

"Oh, *no,*" I repeated.

"Why 'oh, no'?"

"A man like you needs Debbie Boone, not a woman like me." How could I feel so wonderful and so wretched at the same time?

"Come." Connor held open the front door and screen for me. "We need to talk."

He helped me into the rocker to the left of the front door (the bathtub was to the right), then drew up the next rocker beside mine till they were only inches apart.

"I don't believe in coincidences," he said as he settled down to rock beside me, his perfect man-hands splayed to grip the wide, white wooden armrests. "And I don't believe it was a coincidence that we met. Or that we're attracted to each other."

He leaned forward, staring unfocused into the middle distance, his forearms braced on his thighs, revealing just the right amount of golden man-hair on his arms. His hands clasped, as if in prayer. "I'd like to court you, if that's all right."

I sat there, speechless.

Yes! Yes, yes, yes!

My Puritan resurrected. *No! Disaster. Think of someone else for a change. Don't do this to him!*

Or yourself! my practical self added. *Do you want to be a preacher's wife?*

Not! all my inner voices chorused.

· Common sense took hold. "Haven't you heard anything I said?" I asked Connor. "Half your congregation thinks I'm a scarlet woman, and the other half is mad at me for leaving and joining the Methodists after your predecessor kept looking straight at me and preaching about the woman at the wayside who lures men to destruction. For *years*."

Prodded, I'm sure, by Mary Lou Perkins.

Smiling indulgently, Connor clearly wasn't convinced. "You will note that the church fired him."

He just didn't get it. "I cannot be the woman you need. I've lived alone for ten years. I'm too self-centered, too irreverent, too set in my ways, too frank, and too independent. I say what I think, not what people want to hear. Really. Outside of work, I have no filters. And I've just started college."

Connor brightened. "A coed. I can't wait to tell my kids."

Kids. A perfect deflection. "So, tell me about your kids."

I could see that he knew I was being evasive, but he politely told me, "I have two girls. Rachel's thirty-two. Married. Has a great house in Richmond. Her husband's an emergency medicine MD. Corrie's twenty-nine. Still single and finding herself in the Big Apple."

Both far away.

"We talk on the phone occasionally," he said, "but ever since the divorce, things have been strained, even though it wasn't my idea to split."

Been there, done that. I nodded. "Same with my son David. He has a wonderful corporate job in Charlotte, and a great wife and the cutest little boy and girl you ever laid eyes on, but ever since he told me his dad was living in the Caribbean with his stripper, on money he stole from me and the IRS, David's dropped down to calling only once a week."

Connor nodded, compassion in his expression. "What his father did, and is still doing, is a heavy burden for David to bear. Maybe he hasn't dealt with it enough yet to get past it."

"Exactly what I thought," I said, "but that doesn't make it any easier. I miss the sound of his voice and knowing what my grandchildren are up to."

Connor sighed. "Ditto. But I call anyway."

"I tried that, but they see it's me and don't answer." Changing to the new number on my drop phone had helped at first, but once they'd memorized it, they just screened me out again.

Connor shook his head. "Sounds like they're as independent as my girls."

Affirmed, I confided, "Do you know the special ring tone they've assigned to my number? On both their phones? The *funeral march,* for goodness' sake."

Connor laughed. "Are you gloomy when you talk to them?"

"Of course not. I just ask what's up and how the kids are. I've never dumped my problems on my son." I had Tricia for that.

"Kids today," Connor said, then promptly repeated the question he'd asked me before. "Is it okay with you for me to court you?"

As stubborn as Julia, just a lot more polite.

As much as I wanted to say yes, I repeated, "I told you, seeing me could really cause a problem with your congregation."

Connor laughed, too. "I didn't ask you to marry me. Just to let me court you, strictly on the up-and-up, so we could find out if we're truly matched by God."

I resisted the powerful urge to grab him. Instead, I told the truth. "Connor, I can't do it. I can't get within ten feet of you without wanting to jump your bones."

He grinned, clearly complimented. "I have enough self-control for both of us."

I waggled a finger toward his face. "Oh, really? Then what was that kiss?" A shard of desire ran up through my body at the thought of it. "You can't just go dropping bombs like that on me."

He smiled like Dick Van Dyke. *That* was who he looked like, only Connor's nose was more classic. (Read: smaller.)

"We have a saying in the Baptist church," he said brightly. "Sometimes it's easier to ask forgiveness than to get permission." He waggled his brows. "Can you forgive me for kissing you that way?"

Flustered, I blurted out, "Well, of course." I straightened my clothes. "But please don't do it again without letting me know what's coming."

God was laughing. I could hear it echo in my soul.

No fair!

"Okay." He sobered. "If it will make you feel better, we can limit our dates to public places."

I must not let this get a foothold. "Connor, in addition to being the one woman in Mimosa Branch you don't want to be seen with"—well, except for the midget on Sheetrockers' stilts—"I have no intention of remarrying. My mother needs me, and so does my father."

"How convenient that I live right next door," he countered, smug.

"For how long?" I challenged. "Once the church sees us keeping company, they'll probably fire you."

He sobered for a quiet rebuke. "My congregation is made up of people like you and me. No better, no worse. Please don't write them off so easily. They just need guidance to shift their focus from other people's shortcomings to God's grace and forgiveness in Christ."

The compassion in his voice was real, which only made him more attractive.

I stood corrected. "Sorry. You're right."

There was that glint of little-boy mischief again, but his voice was dead serious when he told me, "I need this job, need to make it work. I need to prove to myself that God hasn't withdrawn His hand from my ministry. But as long as I don't break any of God's rules, who I date is my personal business. The Lord laid this church on my heart, so I mean to do what I can to help them, but I'm human, and it's better to marry than to burn."

All the more reason not to date me.

This was a true holy man. I could feel it. Far too holy for an impulsive, irreverent person like me.

I shivered at the mere thought of trying to be a minister's wife, covering my face with my hands. "This can never work."

Connor stood, then drew me to my feet. Facing the tracks, he put his arm around my shoulders. "Why don't we leave that to the Lord and take it one day at a time?"

Uh-oh. AA-speak. Was he a recovering alcoholic?

Oh, mind, shut up!

I needed to go to some convent somewhere to mortify the flesh. But I wasn't Catholic.

You are sixty years old, my inner Puritan chided. *Get a grip on yourself and run as far and as fast as you can from this man!*

My inner hedonist retorted, *Oooo, that kiss. Remember that kiss? You don't have to be married to kiss like that. What could it hurt to try a few dates?*

I let out a long sigh of surrender. I couldn't send Connor Allen packing.

But I could put on the brakes. "Okay, then. We can try dating. But not till Christmas, so you'll have some time to get to know your congregation first. If you're serious about this, you'll do as I ask."

Connor considered, his expression a bit wounded at first, then resolute. "Okay. I can wait. But may I have the honor of celebrating New Year's Eve with you at my church?"

Oh, yes. Yes, yes, yes.

But my Puritan commandeered my voice to say, "We'll see. If all goes well, ask me again on Christmas, but not before then."

His smile flattened and his brows drew together. "And what will you do till then?"

"Study algebra and try to CLEP as many classes as possible."

Connor stared into the night. "Nothing like math to distract a person."

I sincerely hoped so. "It's okay if you want to go out with other people till then," I lied. "Probably a good idea, really." True.

He said okay, but his head wagged *no.* "May I still come visit once in a while," he asked, "when your mother's there to chaperone?"

Oh, please. "I don't know," I blurted out. "It'll only make things harder."

"But if I avoid y'all completely," he reasoned, "people might think I'm shunning you."

Rats! He had a point.

"Okay," I conceded, "but not too often. I'm trying to do the right thing, here."

His expression softened. "I know, and I deeply admire you for it."

He's only interested because you're the one available woman in town who hasn't chased him! my Puritan scolded. *It's that guy thing, all over again. They want what they can't have till they find out you really won't have casual sex with them, then they drop you. And tell everybody you're a slut, like Grant did.*

A giant vise clamped down on my heart as I peered at Connor. "I think you'd better leave now."

Connor Allen took my hand and gave it a squeeze, sending a fine web of electricity up my arm. Then he let go. "As you wish. Please thank Miss Mamie again for the meal. It was the best I've ever eaten."

Tears of frustration and sadness welled behind my eyes. "I will."

But not tonight. Tonight, I would head straight for my bed for a good cry.

I hate being noble. Hate, hate, hate it.

Twenty

After twenty minutes of crying, off and on, I finally came up for air in my bed and called Tricia. I hadn't told her about my crush on Connor because I was too ashamed, but that paled now that he'd made his intentions known. I had to talk it through. Safely.

"Hey," I said when she answered.

"Uh-oh. You've been crying." She knew me so well. "What happened?"

"It's awful." I fought back fresh tears. "I have a horrible crush on the gorgeous man next door!"

Alarm sent her voice up high. "That divorced Baptist *minister*?" Tricia and I had celebrated long-distance about the sale and commission, but I hadn't told her about my crush, so this dropped like an atom bomb between us.

"Yes. And he has a crush on me, too. Asked if he could *court* me," I wailed. "And now, I'm so horny I can't see straight. So is he. This is a disaster."

"Whoa. This sure happened fast."

"Yep. That's one reason I don't trust it."

I could almost hear her shaking her head in consternation as she offered,

"I've been praying God would send you a good Christian man," she said, "but this is overkill." Having grown up in Mimosa Branch, she could appreciate fully what would happen if I dated the new divorced Baptist minister. "Poor baby, poor baby, poor baby, poor baby."

The maximum for non-life-threatening situations.

Too weary even to cry anymore, I let out a long sigh. "Absolutely."

After a pregnant pause, she asked, "What are you going to do about it?"

"I told him to date other people till Christmas."

"You *what*?" Tricia exclaimed.

How could I explain without breaking his confidence? "He's at a real turning point in his career and his spiritual life." Part of me wanted to tell her everything, but the better part of me kept Connor's confidences. "This job is very important to him," I told her. "I can't come between him and his congregation."

"Have you asked God for guidance about this?"

I shook my head no as if she could see me. "I told God this was a dirty trick, so now He's not speaking to me."

"Poor baby, poor baby."

"So I looked for direction in the scriptures. I'm so glad Jonah and that one whiny Psalm are in there."

"Hah," Tricia chided with a single word. "You'd probably do better if you stuck to the rest of the Psalms and made a gratitude list."

"I keep going back to the part about how a man who divorces his wife for any other reason than marital infidelity, then remarries, causes his second wife to commit adultery."

"You're reading that all wrong," Tricia, the Presbyterian, corrected. "That only applies if the people remarrying broke their original marriage vows. Why did he get divorced?"

"His wife left him for a rich man who paid more attention to her. And he admits it was his fault. He spent so much time with his church that he neglected her."

Uh-oh. I'd said too much. "Erase that. I shouldn't have told you."

"So the vows were broken by your spouses. You're both free, in God's eyes."

"I wish I could be sure of that." Something awful occurred to me. "What if this is a test?" It got worse. "For both of us?"

"I have no idea what to tell you."

That was one of the best things about our friendship. When we didn't know an answer, we said so.

Wrung out, I flopped back against my pillows. "Which puts me right back where I started."

"Poor baby, poor baby, poor baby, poor baby."

A huge yawn ambushed me. "Thanks, sweetie. 'Night." I hung up and sank into exhausted sleep, but my dreams were invaded by highly inappropriate fantasies about me and my minister.

I apologized to God in the dreams, but it didn't help.

I got up at three for my regular bathroom trip, feeling like my soul needed a good scrubbing, but still without a clue as to what to do.

As they say in my 12-step enabler's group, "When you don't have an answer, don't just do something, stand there."

So I went back to bed and dreamed of Connor Allen, over and over. And over.

Twenty-one

The next morning Miss Mamie woke me with a fresh cup of coffee in one hand and my copy of the *Gainesville Times* in the other.

I sat up abruptly, despite my sore muscles. How the heck had she gotten into my apartment without my hearing her?

How had she gotten in, period? I'd had the locks rekeyed a week before I moved back and not given her one, on purpose. I loved my mother, but I had to have at least *some* space to call my own.

At that moment, though, I was *way* too groggy for a confrontation. "Well, hey, Miss Mamie." I sat up and took the steaming mug, tasting a sip. Just right: half strength with two Splendas. "To what do I owe this?" I stopped short of saying *intrusion*.

"Well, sweetie, I figured after a kiss like that one last night, you might be dreaming of somebody special, but it's already ten-thirty. Time to get up and go for it."

That kiss? What the . . . I bowed up like a Chihuahua taking on a Great Dane. "You weren't supposed to see that! Y'all were in the kitchen!"

"We were," Miss Mamie said, all wide-eyed innocence. "Till we came out to make sure you were okay."

Ah, yes, the immortal mother-justification. "Okay, my fanny," I snapped. "Y'all were *spying* on me."

I'd scarcely gotten there, yet the walls already had eyes.

Help.

"I just wanted to make sure you didn't blow this one last chance." Miss Mamie patted my hand. "This man is a true catch. Don't let him get away. It's terrible to be alone when you're old."

Ah, the guilt card. If I didn't go along with her, I was guaranteeing a long and lonely demise. She'd pulled that one out so many times, it had totally lost its power.

"I'm not alone," I said, "I have you and Tommy and Tricia."

"I mean a *husband*," she insisted. "Even though your daddy's out of his mind, I know he's still here. That makes it easier for me to soldier on."

The martyr card. She'd also played that one too many times to be taken seriously. I wasn't buying it, so I counterattacked with a concerned, "Would you ever want to remarry if Daddy died?"

My mother waved the mere thought of that away with her perfectly manicured, buffed nails. "Good gracious, Lin, there's no comparison. I'm ninety years old! And I'll love your daddy till I die."

How, after all their fighting, escaped me.

"You're only sixty," Miss Mamie said. "The new forty. And you've never had a devoted husband. But you deserve one, and maybe God, not that real estate contract, put Connor Allen right next door just for you."

"Miss Mamie, I do not need another husband, good, bad, or indifferent," I said with decreasing conviction. "I'm going to college."

My mother clucked under her breath, then got sarcastic. "What? You want a football player?"

"Ocee doesn't even have a team, and you know it," I grumbled.

She rose from the edge of my bed. "You're no girl," she said frankly.

"And Connor Allen seems perfect. Don't waste this chance, Lins-a-pin. Remember the story about the boats and the helicopter." She headed for the door.

A devout man on his roof in a flood turns down two offers of rescue by boat, and the emergency helicopter, saying he's trusting God to keep him safe. When he wakes up in heaven, he says to God, "What happened? I was trusting You to save me!"

God shakes his head. "I sent two boats and a helicopter. What does it take?"

But I wasn't trapped on the roof in a flood.

Or was I?

I dared not tell Miss Mamie that Connor had asked to court me. "We've both agreed not to see each other till after Christmas, so he can concentrate on his church, and I can concentrate on testing out of some of my required classes."

Miss Mamie turned and rolled her eyes, then headed for the door, muttering, "Right in her lap, and she pushes him away."

"Please lock the door on your way out," I hollered after her. "And leave your key inside."

Not that she would.

Help, help, help.

I got up and went to nuke some precooked bacon, then put on a face because Connor Allen might see me on my way to or from the house.

Passing the bathroom mirror, I saw my fuzzy crop of curls and stopped to tame them into a reasonable shape with my fingers. Better.

Definitely needed some makeup.

Makeup, in the summer, just to go clean with the Mame.

I mean, really.

Seriously, renewed self-awareness at my age was a curse, not a blessing. Just when I'd made peace with my smile lines and sagging self.

I looked into the mirror again and the worst happened.

I saw myself as I really was, zeroing in on the once-proud bustline that hovered at my elbows.

Before The Kiss, I wouldn't have cared. But thanks to dadgummed Connor Allen, darn it, I decided I needed to jack up the girls with a bra under my cleaning T-shirt, just in case he saw me.

Shoot! Shoot, shoot, shoot.

A man in my life—even one on *hold*—meant *brassieres*.

My ideal bra quotient had dropped to three hours, max, yet there I was, going to clean for the rest of the day—in the heat—in a very expensive torture band.

Connor had better see me; that was all I could say.

Twenty-two

By noon the Mame and I started on the last room of the ninety-five-degree third floor—halleluiah, amen. Working together, we'd developed a system that started with my climbing the ten-foot stepladder to clean the overhead fans and lights and replace burned-out bulbs, then both of us sponge-mopped the high ceilings with Pine-Sol. Then I went back up the ladder to wipe down the crown molding. Then we used sponge mops and Pine-Sol on the walls, changing the rinse water often because of the dust of a decade. Next we vacuumed, moving everything, then cleaned the glass and mirrors with Windex, then sprayed the backs of the furniture with Citrisafe and polished the rest, then put everything back in place. Next, we put hypoallergenic encasements on the mattress and pillows, then changed the bed. And last, but not least, we WetJet-mopped ourselves out and closed the door, leaving the ceiling fan on to dry everything out.

When we were finished with the third floor—halleluiah—I dragged myself and the cleaning gear to the back stairs and collapsed on the top step, too hot and tired to get up.

"Poor baby."

I ducked as my mother passed me, gripping both rails for support.

She bloomed in the heat; said it warmed her old bones. "Come on, honey," she told me. "It's only eighty-five on the second floor. And there's plenty of cool in the kitchen, plus chicken salad and fresh sliced peaches in the fridge. Let's have lunch and regroup."

Ninety years old, and she lasted longer than I did.

I forced myself to my feet and followed after, clanking mops and cleaning supplies. Two more flights.

I left the cleaning supplies in the hall on the second floor, then headed down for a dose of cool air and homemade food, quoting Nietzsche in my mind for the twentieth time that day. *What does not kill me makes me stronger.*

Of course, Nietzsche died in an insane asylum, but left that quote for the rest of us peons in the world.

I couldn't stand the cinch of the bra band around my chest for one minute longer. I untucked my T-shirt so I could loose the hooks on my expensive shaped-foam bra with no underwires, but my silhouette didn't change, because the cups were formed to a 36 C, so nobody could tell my "girls" had immediately dropped back down to my elbows behind it.

I took my first deep breath in hours and thanked the Lord, then reached up under my shirt to rub the gouges the bandeau had left in my skin. Completely unself-conscious, I was still rubbing when I pushed into the kitchen.

Where Connor Allen sat beside Tommy at our table.

Seeing me, Connor smiled and jumped to his feet as I pulled my hands from my shirt in horror. Tommy took one look and barely managed to keep from laughing out loud.

"Lin, look who dropped by," Mama said brightly, her back turned to Connor so he couldn't see the horror in her eyes as she glared at my dishabille. "He brought flowers. Isn't that gallant? I insisted he join us for lunch."

Rats. Rats, rats, rats.

My bra's molded boobs had shifted when I'd rubbed the indentations and now pointed upward at an unnatural angle.

"How lovely." I spun around and fled to the dining room to put every-thing back where it belonged, which took longer than it used to, but adrena-line enabled me to fasten the hooks under the back of my tee on the third try. Then I leaned forward and pulled the girls back into place.

Why had I unhooked before I knew the coast was clear?

Phooey. Phooey, phooey, phooey!

I mean, I know I'd said I wanted Connor to see me, but not like *that*.

I tucked in my shirt, then turned to face the music, hearing my Granny Beth's voice from across the pale. *Never complain. Never explain.*

So I straightened my posture and glided back in like a duchess. "So glad you could have lunch with us," I told Connor, who stood as I'd left him, like the gentleman he was. "Please, sit," I instructed. "Mama, how may I help you?"

My mother arched a brow at my unnatural formality. "You've worked like a slave all morning," she dismissed. "Just sit down next to Connor and rest. I'll have our plates in a jif."

Awkward, I took the seat beside him.

Tommy was a study in repressed mirth.

I glared at him, telegraphing, *Don't you dare laugh.*

Then I stared at the gardenias and zinnias in the centerpiece, but it didn't help.

Kiss. Kiss, kiss, kiss, my inner hedonist reminded me.

It hummed in the air between Connor and me, but was almost drowned out by, *He saw you with loose boobs! Loose, loose, loose, behind the fake, fake, fake.*

"So, how is your day going?" I managed to ask Connor with reasonable calmness.

"I had a funeral at nine," he said, clearly feeling as awkward as I did. "Then I made an appearance at the reception afterward."

A funeral? The flowers he'd brought stood in a tall vase on the other counter. White glads with lots of greenery. Of course.

I couldn't suppress a chortle.

Connor went beet red, then stammered, "The family insisted I take these, but they wouldn't keep till Sunday, so I thought . . ."

"'Waste not, want not,'" I quoted with a smile, the tension gone. "Very resourceful."

He let out a short sigh of relief.

Mama arrived with our plates heaped with white-meat chicken salad covered in toasted almonds and mandarin orange sections, garnished to the nth degree with butter-crunch lettuce, sliced avocados, and her melt-in-your-mouth green tomato pickles. Quart glasses of iced tea completed the meal. "Yours is Splenda, Lin, like you like."

Only when we were all served did she serve herself and sit down. Mama looked at me. "Lin, would you please bless this for us?"

I knew she wanted me to audition for Connor, but I prayed the same way I always did when we bowed our heads. "Heavenly Father, thank You for all the wonderful things You have given us." Saying those words, I was instantly convicted of my complaints about having to move home. "Please bless this food and the hands that prepared it, and open our eyes and hearts to the needs of those around us. In Christ's name, amen."

Connor nodded his approval. "Well said." He waited to start till Miss Mamie spread her napkin and picked up her fork.

As soon as she began eating, he went straight for the green tomato pickles on his plate, and when he started to chew, a look of glory spread across his features. After that first, celestial bite, he turned to my mother and said, "Miss Mamie, I've been eating for a long time, but yours are the most amazing green tomato pickles I've ever tasted. And that's not just preacher talk. Heavenly. Just heavenly."

Mama preened. "I'll send you home with a couple of pints."

Connor beamed. "Now, that's a gift that money can't buy. I will cherish them."

The secret was in the proportion of alum to spring water, and how long she soaked the tomatoes before candying them with a touch more alum in the syrup. But when Mama had forced me to memorize her recipe, then help her make them, she'd made me swear on the Bible that I would never reveal her cooking secrets till time came for me to pass them on to the next generation of Breedlove descendants.

But David's wife Barb hadn't been interested. She didn't do sugar.

Maybe I could teach the grandkids when they were old enough not to tell on me.

Miss Mamie brightened. "It's nice to cook for a man again, now that the General can't be with us."

I looked to Tommy. What was he? Chopped liver?

He smiled back at me, shaking his head to indicate that it didn't bother him.

Miss Mamie leaned closer to Connor, her hand on his arm. "I've taught Lin how to make all my special recipes."

Could she be more shameless? Now it was my turn to color up. I felt the tide of heat spread up my chest to my neck and face.

Connor looked at me with wry appreciation for what was happening, clearly enjoying it. "Lin is a woman of many talents, I'm sure."

I blinked. Was that a double entendre?

I looked at Connor and saw that it was. Another brief pulse of desire went off inside me.

Kiss. Kiss, kiss, kiss.

No, my inner Puritan chided. *Lunch. Lunch, lunch, lunch!*

Kiss, kiss, kiss, my inner hedonist taunted, but I ignored her and focused on my food.

An awkward silence fell over our meal, one Miss Mamie seemed to be enjoying immensely.

When we were done, Tommy leapt up, empty plate in hand. "Great meal, Miss Mamie." He put his plate in the sink. "Sorry to eat and run, but I've got a meeting way down in Gwinnett." He nodded to Connor. "Good having you."

Connor picked up his own empty plate, then scooped up Miss Mamie's as he rose. "I won't take no for an answer, Miss Mamie. Today, I'm doing the dishes." When I started to rise, he shot me a commanding look. "That goes for you, too, Miss Lin. Both of you have been so welcoming to me"—a bald-faced lie in light of our agreement—"please allow me the privilege of serving you in return."

Without waiting for a response, he started washing away as if he'd always been part of the family.

For once, my mother sat back and let someone do for her.

When she was sure Connor was looking the other way, Miss Mamie motioned for me to go help him.

Unable to resist the prospect of being close to him, I joined him at the drainboard and started to dry with a bleached flour sack, my mother's favorite towel.

We worked in companionable silence till he said a quiet, "This feels nice. Very nice."

Darn him, it did. "Um-hm."

When the last dish and fork were clean and put away, he turned to look at me, well inside my typical American comfort space.

The promise and the peace in his eyes melted my insides.

Kiss. Kiss, kiss, kiss.

He kissed me, all right.

Hands on my shoulders, he gave me a peck on my forehead, then stepped back. "Thanks. I really appreciate it. Guess I'd better get back to my sermon."

"Don't forget your green tomatoes." The Mame got up and went to the pickle cabinet, then handed him two pints, as promised. "Don't be a stranger. There's plenty more where that came from," she said in a perfect Mae West imitation.

Connor laughed, bowed his thanks, then shot me a parting look that could have set a brick on fire.

He wasn't making this any easier.

Twenty-three

The next afternoon, Tommy and I pulled everything (half a truckload) out of the Mame's closet for her to peruse, then started going through the contents one by one, for her to rule on. We had four piles marked with butcher paper: keep, toss, give to me or David, and donate.

"A lot of these are really good clothes," Tommy said. "Once we get all the closets and cabinets purged, we should have an estate sale."

Miss Mamie bristled. "I will *not* allow the general public to haggle for my belongings on the front lawn! Touching all my things." She shuddered at the thought. "What I decide not to keep will be donated to a worthy charity, as is proper, and that is that."

"No need to get so riled up," Tommy told her. "I just figured you might need the money, with the General in the Home." Hint, hint.

Definitely hit a nerve. Miss Mamie's expression gelled into concrete. "I could make money as a cocaine dealer, too," she snapped, "but I wouldn't, because it's not proper. So there will be no more discussion of so-called estate sales." She glared at my brother. "And take off that hat."

He did, as an act of atonement.

Chastised, we went back to bringing out our mother's clothes in small batches.

What started as a chore ended up as a trip down memory lane with Miss Mamie as narrator. Every wrinkled dress had a memory attached, every age-curled shoe and smashed-up hat. Listening, we learned so much about our parents, and their parents before them.

Then we came upon a metal box of letters the General had sent Miss Mamie from the war (he was an aircraft mechanic in North Africa, then Italy).

Tommy opened one of the frail, thin international envelopes and unfolded to read the cramped writing in our father's usually expansive hand. "'My sweet little chickadee, how I miss you and our home. What I wouldn't give for some of your sweet kisses and good, long hugs. For a night of peace to hold you safe in my arms.'"

I couldn't imagine my father ever thinking so tenderly of Miss Mamie, much less writing it down, so I had to fight back tears.

Tommy's voice thickened as he read on. "'And for your wonderful cooking. The food here is brimming with garlic, which makes for some noisy nights in the barracks. One night it was so bad, I woke myself up! Just kidding.'"

Miss Mamie colored at the reference to passing gas. "Here, now. Give me that." She made a swipe for the letter, but Tommy dodged her, then resumed reading.

"'We are doing what we need to do here, and I pray every night that God will keep us both safe so I can come home to you. I don't know when, but I believe that day will come. I must. I hope you have enough to eat, with the rationing. Are my brothers putting too much of a burden on you? Bedford writes that he will join the navy as soon as he qualifies for officer's training at Tech. I wish he'd wait till he has graduated.'" He had. "'Waring doesn't write, but he never was much good with that.'"

"Too *drunk* for that," Miss Mamie corrected, her tone caustic.

"How old was Uncle Waring then?" I asked.

My mother didn't hesitate. "Nineteen, and already a sot. I swear, I don't think that boy ever did an honest day's work in his life. Wouldn't even cut our grass when he was living here."

Wow. I couldn't imagine being saddled with that, and Daddy away. At least Granny Beth had been there to help her with the load.

Tommy let out a fatalistic sigh, then read on. " 'Precious pumpkin, you are the only woman in the world I want. Even though we fight, we always make up, and I can't wait to make up with you when I get home. Your loving husband, Mr. Samba.' "

"Mr. Samba?" Tommy and I both asked our mother at once.

Miss Mamie's eyes were still dreamy from the end of his letter. "Your daddy was the best dancer in three counties. Hot-tempered, but oh, did we dance."

Then she blew her nose and motioned to the box. "Why don't you take that, Lin? I just cry when I read them, anyway. That's why I put them way in back, behind my dresses."

Why did she cry? For the tenderness lost? For the fact that Daddy had only appreciated her when he was half a world away, staring death in the face?

I would have asked my mother, but her expression warned me not to.

"Okay. I'll keep them." I turned to Tommy. "You can come over, and we'll read them together."

He nodded.

After that, we continued the trip from the nineteen-twenties to the twenty-first century reflected in Mama's clothes. I set aside a lovely little wool suit with raglan sleeves and a tiny waist.

Mama smiled when she saw it. "My mother made that for me in 1938. Did I tell you she was a tailor?"

Tommy said no at the same moment I said yes.

Miss Mamie went on. "I was so awful. I complained about my homemade clothes, but they were the smartest ones in our set. I wish I had thanked her."

I gave my mother's arm a consoling pat. "She made them because she loved you, and she knew you loved her." I noted the suit's classic tailoring. Old photos of Miss Mamie showed her as a slender little woman with the look of Edward's Mrs. Simpson. "May I keep this?"

"Of course. I'd like that."

Miss Mamie peered at me, then announced, "I don't want anything to go unsaid between us."

I expected her to make some sort of confession, but instead, she asked, "Is there anything you'd like to thank me for before I die?"

I didn't know whether to laugh or cry, but I was deeply moved. "Only for everything," I said. "Thank you for raising me right, and letting me make my own mistakes, and taking me in without saying 'I told you so' when Phil dumped me, and for taking me in again now that I'm homeless, and for singing hymns with me, and wanting the best for me."

My mother got up and bent between Tommy and me to hug our shoulders. "You and Tommy have always been the best things in my life, next to your daddy," she said, then arched a brow at my brother. "Even when you, sir, were out there actin' like an idjit. I still loved you."

I picked up a vintage fifties outfit to change the subject. "What about this?"

"I wore that to my first Service League tea," she explained, then launched into the charity work she'd done before I was born.

When we finally got through all her clothes in the closet and the gift of Miss Mamie's reminiscences, she sorted through the piles and threw away anything that was stained beyond salvaging or moth-eaten, which included a lot of her size six sweater sets and wool coats. Then she chose what to keep and what to donate to the Interdenominational Thrift Shop. That chore completed, Mama excused herself, clearly traumatized by having to part with the physical evidence that she was once tiny and the belle of the ball.

Tommy and I spread all the usable donations on the bed, photographed them, then inventoried them for the IRS. That accomplished, we carried them down to my minivan.

"Mama," I said as we came back inside, "you just gained three feet of closet rod and a clean floor for your shoes." Not to mention the empty shelves. "And a nice write-off."

She responded with a wistful smile. "Now comes the hard part."

Daddy's things. An emotional minefield.

Twenty-four

After a cold Coke Zero, the three of us went back upstairs and started hauling things out of Daddy's closet. All his clothes were classic styles from the best men's shops, because he loved to haggle with the owners, which he couldn't do at the department stores.

Tommy dusted off a snappy fedora, then put it on.

"You look like a skinny Indiana Jones," I complimented.

Miss Mamie scolded, "Thomas, remove that hat at once. You are in the presence of ladies, and indoors, to boot."

Helping himself to a British driving cap, he just grinned. "I won't tell if you won't." Then he went back to dragging out the closet's contents.

It didn't surprise me when we came up with four well-oiled shotguns, three large-caliber scoped hunting rifles, an assortment of handguns, our great-great-granddaddy's Confederate dress saber, and loads of ammo—from buckshot to hollow-points to copper shells. But the machine gun (oops: assault weapon) and long magazines of ammo came as a mild shock.

Seeing my expression, Miss Mamie sighed and shook her head. "He bought that for the coming rebellion, when the have-nots revolted against the haves, along with those undetectable tubes to bury his gold Krugerrands. Lord knows where those are, but they're undetectable, so there you are." Mama glanced at the arsenal. "I told him and told him, God has nothing to do with hate and fear, but he never listened."

Tommy and I exchanged pregnant looks. If only we could find Daddy's gold, he and Miss Mamie would be set for life.

Mama sighed. "But your father always imagined he was protecting us all from those crazy ravings he read about in those awful hate rags he subscribed to. Lord knows how much money he gave those people."

Miss Mamie shook her head. "All those Breedlove boys were paranoid about anybody but conservative WASPs, just like their daddy before them."

Which was a mystery, because the Breedlove men had opened the town and the mill to the blacks who were run out of Forsyth County so many decades ago. Despite their prejudices, they hadn't oppressed anyone. Quite the contrary. They'd given the refugees jobs. But like most Southerners of their generations, our forefathers were definitely men of stark contradictions.

She pulled out one of Daddy's nicest dark suits and flicked off some lint as she went on, holding it up to the light at the window. "What do you think about this one, for when he's called home?"

(Translate: dead.)

My stomach clenched, but I didn't overreact. "He always looked really nice in that one," I managed to get out in an even tone. "With his white pinpoint oxford shirt and that narrow red damask tie."

Help. I was using the past tense, already.

Mama closed her eyes as she sniffed the Old Spice embedded in the suit's collar. "It's selfish of me to want to keep your father alive. When God finally calls him home to heaven, he'll be healed of that hate and find peace at last."

We both believed that the cross was potent enough to atone for even bigots. Otherwise, we wouldn't be able to sleep at night.

Sadly, America didn't have a monopoly on hate. Look at the Balkans, the Middle East, and Africa.

Nobody was immune.

Look at Congress. I mean, really.

Tommy surveyed the General's arsenal, nothing but the finest. "What do you want us to do with all the firepower?" he asked the Mame.

She opened the drawer of her bedside table, then shut it briskly. "Just leave me a few boxes of ammo and magazines for my Glock."

Her *Glock?*

Whoa. Should we leave a ninety-year-old woman the means to blow somebody away? Maybe *us?*

Daddy's paranoia had obviously been contagious, so I knew she'd balk, bigtime, if we tried to take her gun.

Standing behind Miss Mamie, Tommy shot me a knowing glance and shook his head in denial.

He was right. We'd deal with the bedside-table drawer another day, after the purging was done.

Miss Mamie looked to me and asked, as if she were asking if I wanted one of her blouses or slips, "Anything there you'd like, Lin? These days, it's not a bad idea for a girl to have a gun or two."

I was too appalled by her casual attitude to respond.

She turned to Tommy. "Y'all help yourselves, then sell the rest. The sales slips are in there somewhere."

For everything but the *machine gun!*

Tommy nodded in agreement. "Thanks, Mama." An avid hunter, he laid aside two fine rifles and two shotguns with laser sights, then added a long-barreled Colt .45 for old time's sake. "I'll take care of the rest and make sure they don't get into the wrong hands."

He turned to me with a Glock across his palm. "Might not be a bad idea for you to have one of these for self-defense."

For an instant, I actually considered taking it, but common sense quickly intervened. "Nah. With my luck, I'd end up shooting myself or somebody else by accident." Which would *really* ruin my chances with Connor's congregation. I finished with, "I'm good with the golf club and baseball bat in my closet."

"Disarmed or not, God help anybody who tries to break in on you," Tommy said with a grin.

"Amen!" I seconded. Careful to avoid the firearms, I went back into the closet for another load of Daddy's clothes.

Twenty-five

Three hours later, the deed was done, and Miss Mamie had retreated to the kitchen to soothe her soul with baking.

The guns, Tommy would take care of. We'd itemized and photographed Daddy's castoffs, then loaded my minivan to the brim. I shut the back hatch. "The thrift shop's not open till tomorrow afternoon. I'll take these then. I want the Mame to have a little time to consider, in case she wants to take anything back."

Tommy rolled his eyes and grasped my upper arms. "Whatever you do, please do not offer her that option. It was hard enough on her, getting through this. Now it's done. Let her move on." He let me go.

He had a point. When he was sober, Tommy was always a lot better at thinking about how things affected others than I was.

"Okay, then," I conceded. "What next?"

"I seem to remember an ex–real estate agent telling me it's always best to do the hardest things first," he said, scowling at the right side of the house. "We've done the closets in Daddy and Mama's room. I've done mine. That leaves one more dragon to slay."

Uh-oh. I knew he wasn't talking about the attic. "The den of iniquity?"

Tommy nodded.

"I guess you're right," I begrudged. "Time to beard the dragon." The trouble was, my inner child felt wretched about invading our father's privacy, even though he wouldn't know.

But I wasn't a child anymore, and we needed to do this. I finally mustered up the courage to ask my brother, "Did you get the permanent incompetency statement from Daddy's gerontologist and file the guardianship agreement?" Mama had insisted that both Tommy and I serve as guardians. She didn't have it in her anymore to do it herself.

Tommy's expression flattened as he nodded yes. "The doctor asked me what took us so long." The pros at the Senior Mental Health Center down in Snellville had advised it months ago, when we first had Daddy committed. But Miss Mamie staunchly refused to sign Daddy over for life, saying she felt like Judas already for putting him away in the first place. To her, publicly filing those documents was the ultimate betrayal, equivalent to putting "our troubles" on the front of the *Gainesville Times*.

She didn't relent till Tommy explained that we needed to have access to all Daddy's records so we could straighten them out. Then he'd added that the IRS could put a lien on the house if Daddy hadn't paid his taxes. (Which was absolutely true.)

"What did Sumter say when you brought him the papers to put with the will?" I asked as we climbed the stairs to the kitchen. Daddy's lawyer was three years older than the General, but only half as crazy.

"He said he'd take care of things for no fee," Tommy said, "but I have no idea if he's still hittin' on all cylinders. Just to be safe, I recorded the certificate of incompetency, the legal guardianship, and the medical power of attorney at the courthouse, then got all three of us official copies."

A wise move. Sumter had been retired for ten years, and this was no time to have anything fall between the cracks.

Tommy went on. "I took the official copies to show the bank when I checked out the deposit box."

When he'd *what*?

I nudged him, annoyed that he'd done all that on his own without telling me. "Thanks for letting me know. I wanted to go, too." Not that I didn't trust him. I just didn't want to be left out.

"Most of what I found in the box was pretty routine," Tommy said. "No deeds or treasure maps. Just Granddaddy's gold watch, a list of names I hadn't ever heard of, ten gold Krugerrands, and a stack of hundred-dollar bills from before we went off the gold standard."

"How much?" I asked, realizing the minute the question was out of my mouth that it sounded sordid and greedy.

"Ten grand in bills," Tommy said. "More than enough for a respectable funeral."

My heart contracted, but I sloughed off the grim reminder with, "Every little bit helps."

"I have no idea what the Krugerrands are worth," he went on, "and I don't plan to find out till we've searched for the rest of them. Too depressing to know, if we can't find any."

Amen to that. *Pleeeeease, Lord, let us find enough to fix up the house and pay Daddy's bills.*

The one-hundred-and-thirty-four-year-old house needed a new slate roof, which was going to cost a fortune. The current "new" one was in its eighties and beginning to leak.

"I did find something interesting, though, in a small box." Tommy paused for dramatic effect, then revealed, "Fourteen deposit box keys from various local banks all over north Georgia."

Perfect. Not.

Ah-ah! No negatives. Just gratitude.

Well, at least we knew where to start looking for Daddy's missing gold. "Maybe we'll find some deeds or leases in those," I said. "If not, we could check the property records in those counties while we're there," I told him.

Fourteen, which left another hundred and fifty-five counties in the state, only some of which had computerized their records.

We looked at each other, flat-mouthed, then said in unison, "Road trip."

"But first," Tommy said, "the den of iniquity."

"Not today," I qualified. "Tomorrow."

Tommy frowned, clearly not as sore and tired as I was.

"To quote Lao Tsu," I said, "'every journey begins with a single step.'"

"Just can't resist showin' off, can you," my brother said affably.

Instead of bristling in self-justification, I laughed. "Apparently not."

It cleared the air immediately.

Tricia was always telling me to lighten up. Actually doing it was the problem, but as she'd predicted, it always worked.

The next morning after breakfast, we went to the pantry and rustled up a big roll of giant contractor's four-mil-thick disposal bags and some allergy masks, then ended up at the door to the General's study, bags open and in hand. Even through the masks, the smell of decaying paper, Old Spice, and cigar smoke stopped us both at the threshold.

Surveying the chaos of decades, I couldn't help asking, "Why in the world did he keep all this junk?"

Tommy shrugged. "Because he could. This was his man cave. Not even the Mame was allowed to touch anything."

Past tense. Now Tommy was using it. But he'd nailed our father.

"Maybe we ought to get a Dumpster," I suggested, hoping for a delay.

How do you eat Stone Mountain with a teaspoon? my Granny Beth whispered from my childhood. *One bite at a time, sweet girl. One bite at a time.*

"I think a commercial shredder would work better," Tommy said. "They'll come to the house with a giant one that processes whole bagsful, then spits out tiny pieces nobody could read into the back of their truck. Then they recycle it." He frowned at a heaping stack of *The Thunderbolt*. "I'd hate for anybody else to see Daddy's hate rags."

"I'm glad to hear you say that." I'd never been sure where Tommy stood on matters of race. He'd always avoided the subject. After he'd started drinking, our relationship had been so sketchy, I'd never dared to ask.

Seeing my expression, Tommy granted me a wry smile. "I learned a long time ago that any kind of hate turns inward and ruins a person. Look what it did to the General and Uncle Bedford. They were so great in so many ways, but that black cloud of prejudice was always hanging over them, feeding their fears."

I nodded, then changed the subject. "We'll have to go through every single newspaper, scribble, and book," I thought aloud. "There might be something about the Krugerrands in there. Or an offshore account somewhere."

"First things first," Tommy said, picking his way to the space beneath Daddy's enormous desk. He shoved the rolling office chair aside, knelt down, then disappeared behind the desk.

The safe. I'd forgotten.

I dodged my way to stand behind him as he rolled up the oriental carpet. "Do you know the combination?" I had once, but couldn't remember it to save my life.

"Yep." Tommy pressed a floorboard that dropped a section several boards wide, then slid it over to reveal the door and combination lock to the safe imbedded in the structure of the house. "He wrote it on the top in marker."

Sure enough, there were the numbers in Daddy's distinct handwriting.

Some security.

Tommy opened the safe, but to our disappointment, it contained only a few old loan satisfactions, articles of incorporation for his long-defunct business, and personal identification papers, including his birth certificate signed by his father as delivering physician.

I scanned the packed office. "Maybe we'll find something important buried in the rest of this junk."

Tommy nodded, but his face said, *We should be so lucky.*

After restoring the boards to their place, then putting back the rug, he picked up a thick heap of hate rags and plunked them beside a chair stacked with junk mail. Shoving the mail to the floor, he sat. "When we find out where Daddy has property, we can go over all the tracts with a good metal detector.

They make them with screens that show what they find, now. Saves a lot of digging."

"Mama said the tube for the Krugerrands was undetectable," I reminded him.

Tommy scowled at me. "Let's just pray it's not."

"Assuming the General didn't use a made-up company to buy the land." I wouldn't put it past our father. Even certified insane, he was still shrewd.

My brother shot me a brief glare. "Didn't I make it clear how much I appreciate *positive* input?"

"Sorry." There I went again, projecting the worst without engaging my brain.

I knew better, but under the circumstances, I'd reverted to my old ways.

Got to stop that!

I surveyed the office. "While we were cleaning upstairs, Mama and I checked for false panels and looked for money in all the books, so those rooms are clear."

At least I thought so. Daddy could be so blasted sly.

Tommy nodded. "After this, that just leaves us the basement, the garages, and the attic. I'll do the basement and garages if you'll do the attic."

Just the thought of how hot it would be up there almost made me fall out. "Let's just do this first, okay? I'll start with the desk." I waded through the piles, but didn't sit in Daddy's oak office chair, because it automatically tipped back to feet-on-the-desk position. Standing, I picked up a hefty pile of letters and advertisements from the desk.

Don't think about the attic and the basement, I scolded myself. Focus on this. Break it down into manageable bites, and eventually we'll end up somewhere, even if it isn't where we hope.

I worked my way to the door. At last, the Mame's fourteen-foot-long oaken Victorian monstrosity of a dining table would be put to good use. "I'm taking these into the dining room so I can start to organize things in piles," I told Tommy, who was riffling through copies of *The Thunderbolt* for money before tossing them into his trash bag.

An hour later, the huge dining table was covered in stacks of investment statements, bank records, bills and files from our father's construction business, old tax returns and receipts, court documents from the time he'd tried to declare everyone on welfare in the state of Georgia as a dependent, more court documents from the time he'd successfully challenged OSHA's right to enter his construction company without probable cause.

More records about insurance, bookkeeping, and countless other business and personal matters, plus one tall goodness-only-knows stack of things I was afraid to throw away, but had no idea what to do with.

Miss Mamie eventually came around and peeked in, but retreated in silence to the kitchen to cook, probably her personal penance for letting us dispose of Daddy's sacred stuff, objectionable though it may be.

In the four days it took Tommy and me to finish going through everything, drawer by drawer, page by page, panel by panel, never once did our mother mention what we were doing. She did, though, turn up fairly often with a spoonful of something for us "just to taste." At nine hundred calories a spoonful, I forced myself to decline, but Tommy always obliged.

Not that it was easy to resist. The air smelled like cakes, pies, and cookies the whole time.

After day two of aroma torture, I finally came up with a plan. "There are so many shut-ins from church," I reminded my mother after a breakfast of fried eggs and moist devil's food cupcakes with seven-minute icing, which she knew I couldn't resist. "Why don't you take these goodies to them?"

Miss Mamie brightened. "Excellent suggestion." She carried our plates to the sink with a fresh bounce in her step, then stopped and turned to qualify. "Not the ones who have the sugar." Southern for *diabetes*. "I'll do them some almond-meal cookies with Splenda and eggs and drawn butter. And baking powder, of course." A woman with a mission, she headed for the pantry humming "I'll Fly Away."

We went back to work. When Tommy and I finally finished with the den of iniquity two days after that, we'd found a lot, but not much of what we were looking for. Two deeds for vacant land were hiding under a false drawer bottom, but we didn't find any more.

What we'd really gotten was a picture of how gullible our father had been with any hyperconservative scammer who'd approached him for "investments" to make him safe from "the coming race war" or depression. He'd trusted these strangers with his hard-earned money, yet never trusted any of us.

How much of that was his illness, and how much was his stubborn, paranoid nature, we'd never know.

I felt as if we'd uncovered him, leaving him stark naked and exposed, and it didn't feel good.

He'd tried so hard to safeguard his treasure that we couldn't even find it.

No secret bank account records, on or offshore, materialized. All we found was a stack of receipts from coin dealers that valued Daddy's Krugerrands at over two hundred thousand when he'd first bought them, based on thirty-two dollars an ounce. Lord only knew what they would bring at current prices, but I didn't compute that for the same reason as Tommy.

The remainder of the den's nontoxic contents comprised seventeen Bibles of various translations—prompting Tommy to say that you have to read them and follow their teachings for them to count—two thousand dollars in crisp gold-standard hundred-dollar bills that had been stashed individually in various right-wing extremist books that we'd shredded with a satisfying growl from the giant commercial shredder; three glass jugs of high-quality (according to Tommy's nose) moonshine, which I poured into the toilet, wondering what effect it would have on the septic tank; four illegal boxes of hermetically sealed Cuban cigars; and five loaded handguns stashed away in hollowed-out pages of Daddy's radical Second Amendment books. But the kickers were two more assault rifles behind a spring-loaded door in the wainscoting that I just happened to bump up against.

Further investigation revealed no more secret panels in the desk, walls, or bookcases.

At least, not that we could find.

Once the room was emptied, we sent the faded rugs out to be cleaned, scoured every square inch of the place, then restored the floors to their former richness with Liquid Gold. But nothing was able to do away with the lingering hints of cigar smoke.

Frankly, I didn't mind. The den of iniquity wouldn't be right without it.

Surveying the revived colors of the oriental rugs when the cleaners brought them back, I said, "Man. The dust on those must have been half an inch thick."

Tommy scanned the wholesome remains of Daddy's library on the almost empty bookcases, then collapsed on the sagging leather couch that had once been butter-colored, but was now stained brown wherever Daddy had sat or lain over the decades. "You sure you don't want a Glock?" he asked me.

"Very." Why did he keep asking?

I flopped down at the other end of the sofa, only to encounter a resentful coil that popped up above the others. "This divan is shot, no good to anybody," I said as I tried to shift to a comfortable spot. "But we probably ought to check inside the cushions and under the upholstery before we toss it. "

Tommy sighed in resignation. "Prob'ly so."

We both sat there, not moving. My muscles had already seized up.

"But first," Tommy said, "Golden Corral. My treat."

Since Miss Mamie had been taking food to the shut-ins all over town, she'd stopped cooking anything for us but breakfast.

I looked at my watch. Two o'clock in the afternoon, already. The senior special was on till three: seven ninety-nine, plus tax, iced tea included. "You're on. But you'll have to help me up. I'm so sore and stiff, I can hardly move."

Tommy collected himself, then launched himself aright with a groan.

Offering me both hands, he braced his running shoes against mine. "Upsy-daisy."

I forced myself to stand. "Okay. Golden Corral it is."

"We'll talk about that road trip when we get back," he said. "I got a current Georgia map at the Welcome Station, then marked down where the deposit boxes are so we can plan our route, assuming the banks still exist." A very big assumption, lately. "Then I've got to catch up with some of my meetings."

"Amen to that." The last thing we needed was for him to fall off the wagon.

Ahead of us, Stone Mountain loomed afresh, times ten: the enormous task of trying to find the General's gold, investments, and bank accounts so we could pay the Home and take care of Miss Mamie and the house. But I could wait till after a good, healthy lunch and lots of artificially sweetened tea to face it.

Tommy headed for his ratty truck, pulling the keys from his pocket. "We'll need to check out the yard and the rest of the house with a metal detector before we start searching elsewhere."

"I'll research what's available secondhand on the Internet," I said as I followed, "and try to find a good deal on one." Stone Mountain got bigger. And bigger.

Then the road trip. Or two. Or ten.

The thing was, what if we just found tax liabilities? Heaven only knew when the General had stopped paying his property taxes. If he did have more property, some or all of it may have been auctioned on the courthouse steps already. If so, I doubted the new owners would let us prospect for those Krugerrands, much less keep them.

Getting into the passenger seat of Tommy's truck, I scolded myself. *Stop projecting the worst. Focus on the food. Be with Tommy in the moment.*

I thought about the butterbeans and baked chicken at the Corral, and was grateful.

But I still dreaded what remained for us to do.

The only good thing about it was, it took my mind off Connor.

Well. At least some.

Till we were invited to a political rally in the basement of the drugstore.

Twenty-six

While I was picking up Miss Mamie's and my prescriptions at the drugstore the next day, Shelia leaned forward and asked me, "We're having a rally downstairs at seven tonight. Can y'all come? Donnie's gonna be there, and we hope to find somebody to run for his job as mayor, now that he's leavin' to take that church up north."

I hesitated, remembering another meeting there ten years ago, when we'd drafted Donnie to run against our crooked mayor. Whoever succeeded Donnie would have some mighty big shoes to fill.

"I'll talk to Tommy and Miss Mamie," I deflected, leaving us an out, though my conscience urged me to come support Donnie in finding a candidate.

"We really need all our old-timers to come," she whispered, "so the transplants won't take over and put in somebody who doesn't know a thing about us."

Heaven forbid.

Still, I knew what she was talking about. It would serve us well if the next mayor had some sense of where we'd come from when he or she decided where we were going.

"I'll try," I told her.

What if Connor showed up?

I wasn't sure I could handle it.

But when I told Mama and Tommy about the meeting, they both said without hesitation that we should go.

"Donnie's done so much for this town," Tommy prodded. "It's the least we can do for him."

Miss Mamie nodded. "You're right. I'll bring a flag cake." She hurried to bake her famous U.S. flag sheet cake, with a moist white cake under a layer of sweetened, thawed strawberries, topped with Cool Whip icing and fresh sliced-strawberry stripes that complemented a fresh-blueberry square of "stars."

I'd have gone just for the cake, but I knew it was the right thing to do, Connor or not.

So I went.

This time, the warehouse under the pharmacy was in much better shape than it had been ten years before. The funeral home had provided chairs, and a couple of long folding tables offered tea, soft drinks, ice, and various homemade desserts.

When Tommy walked in with Miss Mamie's flag cake, a ripple of anticipation erupted among the people there, only a few of whom I knew. As Shelia had worried, the townies were far outnumbered by the transplants. But as the numbers grew, I spotted the last three of the coffee club members (from before the new owner closed the soda bar at the drugstore). And most of the members of Miss Mamie's garden club, aged husbands in tow. And at least half of her prayer chains and Bible study members.

Franklin Harris, who'd given us our famous local wildflower garden, arrived with a crowd of Donnie's African-American constituents. Franklin nodded a greeting, and I sent back a warm smile.

Such a wonderful man. He'd worked hard with Donnie to start a neighborhood improvement volunteer program and fund to help elderly homeowners all over Mimosa Branch spruce up their houses.

I was looking for Shelia when someone tapped me on the shoulder, and I turned to find Connor so close I could smell his subtle Jade East cologne. Talk about a blast from the past. Grant had worn the same cologne, but for some reason, it smelled a lot better on Connor.

Afraid I'd slip up and embarrass him and my entire family, I did my best to get rid of him. "Oh, hi, Connor. Glad you could come. If you'll excuse me, I need to find Shelia."

"She's gone to get some ice," he answered, clearly pleased that I no longer had an excuse to leave him. "She'll be back in a while."

Nostrils flaring in panic, I smiled as I backed away from him. "Good. Then I'll go keep Mama company."

"I'll go with you," he said evenly. "I'd like to thank her and Tommy for inviting me to the movie."

"Of course." Shoot! Shoot, shoot, shoot!

All those inappropriate feelings came rushing back, as if I'd never gotten a grip on myself in the first place.

On the way across the room, he commented, "Tommy tells me you won a full scholarship. Congratulations."

Rather than go into the details, I simply smiled, aloof, and said, "Thank you."

Why did he have to glom on to me? The room was full of his congregants.

As we approached Mama, who was talking amid the din of her prayer chain mavens, he cocked his head at me and asked, "Lin, are you angry with me about what I did in the foyer?" When I didn't answer, he went on. "Or have I insulted you somehow? Please tell me."

Not now. Not in public. Way too public!

"Of course not." *Kiss! Kiss, kiss, kiss!* "I was just thinking about our agreement."

He regarded me with open desire. "So have I. Every . . . single . . . day."

I realized I'd been holding my breath as he spoke.

Suddenly, the room seemed stuffy beyond endurance.

My reaction was so transparent, I might as well have ripped off my clothes and thrown myself into his arms. Anybody with the slightest knowledge of body language had us pegged, but when I looked around me, everyone else seemed to be engaged in private conversations.

There I went again: totally narcissistic. *You are not the center of the universe,* my inner critical parent scolded. *Focus on the big picture, not yourself.*

Was there no hope for me?

I sat down before I fell down from lack of air.

Connor frowned. "Let me get you some iced tea. Plain, with Splenda, right?"

I nodded. What I needed was a tub full of the stuff to jump into and cool off.

Fortunately, Donnie arrived with a huge group of his supporters, drawing all the attention to him.

He worked his way into the crowd, calling everyone by name. When he got as far as where I sat, he bent down and murmured, "You okay, Lin? You're white as granny's grits."

At which I promptly felt scalding embarrassment rise from my chest to the top of my head, my face throbbing. "I'm fine. Fine."

Connor arrived with the tea. "Here you go. Have a few sips of this."

Donnie looked from Connor to me, then back again, and broke into a huge grin. "Wow. Does the Lord have a sense of humor, or what?"

I glared at him. "Somehow, I'm not finding it so funny."

Donnie sobered. "Sorry. I'll pray for you."

Now, those were some prayers that would carry weight.

I turned to Connor. "Connor, have you met Donnie West, our mayor? He's one of my favorite people in the world."

Connor shook Donnie's hand. "Good to see you." Then he turned to me. "We have lunch every Wednesday together at the diner. With all the pastors in town who can make it."

My cheeks throbbed even harder, if that was possible. "Ah. How nice."

Donnie excused himself, leaving me with Connor, whom I did my best to ignore. Except when he brought us each a square of the flag cake. By the time we were finished, half an hour had passed.

Somebody thumped a portable mike, bringing everyone to attention, then I recognized Franklin Harris's voice say, "Folks, I want to thank you all for comin' out to help us find someone to succeed Donnie, here, as our mayor. And if you know somebody you can call to invite, please tell 'em there's still plenty of time to get here. We can lend you a cell phone if you don't have one. We need all the concerned citizens of Mimosa Branch here to help us."

Donnie went to the microphone.

"Ah, there he is," Franklin said. "Ladies and gentlemen, I give you our mayor, Donnie West." He handed the microphone to Donnie.

"Hey, y'all," Donnie said with a grin, his voice carrying out into the alley and beyond. "God bless each and every one of you for coming out tonight." He sobered. "As most of y'all know, I have considered it a great honor to serve each and every one of you as mayor for the past ten years. But my first work, and foremost, is to preach the good news of Jesus Christ to all I can. So when the Lord called me to Philadelphia, I had to say yes, much as I hate leaving you all."

A murmur of acceptance arose, then faded.

Donnie waited for silence, then went on. "But I know the Lord will bless Mimosa Branch for supporting my obedience to His call."

Amens erupted all over the room.

Again, he waited for silence, then said, "What you, the good citizens of Mimosa Branch, need to decide is who should be my successor." Silence stretched long this time, and expressions revealed a mix of anticipation, unwillingness, and confusion.

"Tell us who he is," Ottis Wilburn insisted, his voice thready with age.

Typically, he'd assumed it would be a male.

Donnie shook his head. "I've prayed about that long and hard, and the Lord's answer was that *y'all* should be the ones to call your new mayor, not me, because y'all will be the ones he serves. So I ask us all to bow our heads and pray for an answer. And if God gives you a name, be bold to speak it out." He dropped his head and closed his eyes. "May we pray silently, asking only God's will in this matter, and the courage to carry that out?"

We all bowed our heads.

Not a peep.

Shuffling of feet, squirming in seats.

The weight of the silence grew with every passing second, but no one spoke.

Sniffs. Soft clearing of throats. Toes tapping. Occasional coughs.

Lord, it would be really nice if You'd come up with a name. Everybody here wants what's best for our town. Please direct us.

Nothing.

I peeked at my watch. Only two minutes.

"We're counting on You, Lord," Donnie prayed with confidence. "Show us Your will, not because we are worthy, but because we belong to Christ, and when You look at us, You see His righteousness, not our sin."

More silence followed.

The Holy Ghost, He don't say nothin'.

The room got hotter, and you could sense the discomfort of the people as they breathed, but still, no word came.

Now granted, we have become an instant people in this country, but the Bible says that where two or more are gathered in His name, the Lord Jehovah, Creator of the Universe, is present, so I figured it only made sense to take Him at His word. *Please, God, show us the answer.*

At that very moment, Walter Lott and "Uncle" Delton Pirkle stood at the same time and said in unison, "Tommy Breedlove."

Talk about a lightning bolt!

The hairs stood on the back of my neck as everybody else, including Tommy, looked up in astonishment.

I thought Miss Mamie was going to fall out on the spot, but her prayer partners propped her up, murmuring soothing reassurance.

Donnie grinned. "I have a witness in my soul for that!" he said, pointing to Tommy. "A good man, Tommy, who appreciates the transforming power of God's grace the same way I do."

Donnie, too, had come from a background of drugs and alcohol. And worse. Compared to him, Tommy was squeaky clean. But Tommy had always kept his faith—and his recovery—to himself and his fellow AA members. And his AA fishing club, the Bassholes.

Tommy lifted his hands in a staying gesture. "I'm truly honored, y'all. Really I am. But it seems to me there are far better men than I who should take this job. And if God wanted me to do it, wouldn't He have told *me* about it?"

Donnie shook his head with a chuckle. "Brother, I told you I've been praying about this for weeks. And fasting. And the answer I got was that the people should choose my successor, and that's what just happened."

For a split second, my skeptical self wondered if Donnie had set this up. But he wasn't that kind of man. And Walter and Delton had seemed as shocked as everybody else.

I talked to God all the time and asked Him for things. Why was I always so amazed when He did as I'd asked?

But, I mean, really! *Tommy?*

Not that I didn't think he'd make a good mayor. He knew this town top to bottom, and back up again. And most of the people in it.

But *Tommy?*

The last thing he needed now was to be in the spotlight.

Tommy peered at me, his face communicating the same thought. And the spotlight would extend to me. And Connor. And us, if there was ever to be an us.

Oh, Lord, are You sure?

As if someone had flipped a switch, everyone rose from their chairs, clapping, then crowded around my brother, shaking his hand and telling him he'd make a great mayor.

Only Miss Mamie and I remained seated, both of us stunned.

Shelia approached Tommy with a broad grin. "Don't you worry, Tommy. I'm your campaign manager, and we already have plenty collected to get you elected. Donnie's been encouraging people to give for months. Just rely on me and be where I tell you, when I tell you."

Tommy frowned. "But I have to take care of some legal matters for my parents. I could be gone for weeks." His voice dropped to a murmur. "And I can't miss my meetings."

Oh, man. The road trip.

Shelia was undaunted. "We can work around all that. Why don't you come by tomorrow morning to do a game plan." She hugged his shoulders. "With Donnie's endorsement, not to mention his knowledge of city finances, you're a shoo-in."

And his past, an open book.

Tommy grabbed her upper arm and leaned close to speak to her. I read his lips. "I'm gonna have to talk to my sponsor about this."

She looked up at him with absolute confidence. "After what just happened, I have no doubt he'll approve."

Tommy scanned the crowd around him, then shot me a befuddled look.

If this really was God's will, everything would work out, no matter what we did or didn't find on our road trip. No matter what happened between Connor and me. No matter how crazy Daddy was.

Shelia was right.

I smiled and nodded. Tommy was the perfect candidate. Not to mention the fact that nobody else in town had even hinted at running.

It would be nice, God, if he ran unopposed. As long as it's okay with You, of course.

Tommy, mayor of Mimosa Branch. The more I thought about it, the better it sounded.

But the first Tuesday in October was weeks and weeks away, and Tommy and I had a treasure hunt to go on first.

Twenty-seven

For the next two weeks, Tommy met with his sponsor, went to lots of AA meetings, then finally officially accepted his call to run for mayor by qualifying on August fifth.

By then, Mama and I were both convinced he should run.

He and Shelia, with Donnie's invaluable input about the city budget, planned a great set of sensible, doable objectives for his term in office. Honesty, transparency, fairness, and fiscal responsibility were the watchwords of his campaign.

After he qualified, an out-of-the-blue transplant female CPA named Carla Simmons signed up to run against him as an independent. Then, when Shelia started booking Tommy for personal appearances that didn't conflict with his meetings, Carla's people promptly booked her for the same events.

Bad form!

Tommy was no debater, but when I went with him to the first booking with his opponent, he was extra courteous to her. Yet, thanks to Donnie, he had a wealth of knowledge about the bottom lines during the past ten years.

Carla proposed lots of new ideas, but Tommy politely asked how much each one would cost, then asked how she planned to pay for it. His suggestions came with explicit funding information. By the middle of September, they had appeared at Rotary, Kiwanis, Lions Club, the BPOE, and VFW. Also the men's and women's groups at various churches, plus the garden club and women's club.

And every time, Tommy politely asked Carla questions she couldn't really answer.

After the first few debates, he started coming home later and later, which worried Miss Mamie and me. We both knew alcoholism was a disease of recidivism, but neither of us mentioned it till he didn't come home all night.

Had taking on the campaign pushed him over the edge?

We were waiting for him at the breakfast table when he finally rolled in. He looked rumpled, but sober. Still, Miss Mamie asked him point-blank, "Tommy, have you been drinking again?"

He laughed with obvious amusement. "No, Mama. I haven't been drinking. Or drugging. But thanks for caring enough to ask." He poured himself a big mug of coffee, then sat down, the twinkle still in his eye.

"What *have* you been doing then?" my mouth asked without any participation from my brain.

Tommy smiled. "I am a grown man. As long as it isn't destructive to me or anyone else, what I do is my business." He nodded to me. "Think, Sissie-ma-noo-noo. A grown man stays out all night. You're smart enough to figure it out."

Again, my voice got ahead of me. "Oh, no. Not the midget in Sheetrockers' stilts!"

Tommy hooted, laughing till he cried, almost losing his breath before he finally settled down. "No. Definitely no."

"A midget in Sheetrockers' stilts?" Miss Mamie asked.

"It's just an inside joke, Mama," he said. "Don't give it a thought."

He had a point. He was a grown man, with a grown man's needs and emotions. Maybe he'd met someone at one of the campaign functions.

I'd already stepped over the line into Tommy's private life, so I didn't question him further.

Tommy got up, stretched, then told us, "If y'all will excuse me, I'm going to take a nap in the front guest room so I'll be fresh for the Knights of Columbus this evenin'."

Miss Mamie patted his arm. "Go right ahead. We'll try to be quiet."

We sat in silence until we heard his footsteps climb the stairs, whereupon my mother grabbed my arm and leaned in to demand in a stage whisper, "What is this joke about a midget in Sheetrockers' stilts?"

I thought fast, then answered, "We saw one at the diner, and she flirted with Tommy, so we've both joked about it. That's all."

Miss Mamie tucked her chin. "A midget in Sheetrockers' stilts." She went wary. "You're making that up."

"We're supposed to call them 'little people' now," I corrected, then raised the Girl Scout salute. "Hand to my heart, Miss Mamie, it's true."

Not the whole truth, but as much as she needed to know.

"Come on," I told her, carrying my dishes to the sink. "Let's get back to cleaning. But no hymns today. Tommy's sleeping."

The Mame joined me with the rest of the dishes. "Do you think Tommy was with a woman last night?"

I didn't remind her that he'd practically spelled it out. "I think that's a pretty good guess."

I expected concern, but she turned on the water with a grin of relief. "Thanks be to the Good Lord. I was beginning to wonder if he was still . . . you know, *normal,* now that he's sober."

As in not homosexual.

Different times. Different times. Miss Mamie was brought up believing homosexuality was an "abomination" that people came down with, like a virus.

I smiled. "If there is such a thing as normal in this family, I think Tommy definitely qualifies."

My mother started singing softly for joy as we did the dishes.

Can we say, double standard? If I'd stayed out all night, she'd be wailing about moral decay.

Once we were done with the dishes, we both made a trip to Jaemor Farms for a vanload of their Silver Queen corn and homegrown tomatoes and butter beans and crowder peas and bell peppers and eggplant and sweet, white Georgia Belle peaches to put up and freeze in the Mame's giant chest-freezer. We did the peaches first. Mama scalded the skins off, then cut up half of them into plastic bags for freezing, and used the rest in her famous homemade peach ice cream.

Honestly, she kept three ice-cream makers going from sunup to sundown for days.

While she was overseeing the ice cream, I stewed and froze the corn, then parboiled and put up the rest of the vegetables.

Meanwhile, Tommy roped up with his grapples and pulleys to clean the outsides of the windows and touch up the paint.

By the middle of September, we'd finished cleaning everything except the attic, the basement, and the garage.

I'd hoped the hot weather would cool down, but September was still blazing away, and we were worn slap out. One can only grub around in grime and heat for so long without needing a break.

So after we'd finally finished everything but the attic, then showered and cleaned up, Tommy escorted Miss Mamie and me—still wearing cool summer dresses—into the dusky front yard to survey the results.

Miss Mamie let out a satisfied sigh, not even seeing the bathtub anymore. "Looks just like it used to when I had a cook, two maids, and a yard man. And the General's whole crew to fix whatever needed fixing."

Another world, seen through rose-colored glasses.

As Albert Schweitzer said, happiness is nothing but good health and a bad memory.

Miss Mamie turned to me and Tommy. "Y'all are doing the work of all those people. Bless your hearts. And you, Tommy, runnin' for mayor. I don't see how you do it."

"It's the new economics," Tommy said. "Two people doing the work of ten. But none of us shows up on the unemployment statistics."

That was too depressing to address, so I turned my attention back to the house. "The place looks gorgeous," I complimented my brother. Then my evil twin said, "I wonder how long it will stay this way."

Tommy glared at me. "Could we just sit back and enjoy it, first? Be present, instead of projecting the negative?"

"You're right," I apologized.

Why did I *do* that? It didn't help anybody, least of all me.

"Hey, to celebrate," I offered, "why don't I treat us all to supper at Red Lobster?" It was Tuesday, a slow night, so we might not even have to stand in line. And thanks to my commission, I had enough money to pay for both of them, plus order the Ultimate Feast for me—lobster, shrimp, and Alaskan crab legs. Yum.

Mama nodded her assent, still gazing at the house in pride. "Good idea."

I dragged my stubborn self into the present. And into gratitude. We were there together, sober, clean, and in decent health, in this blessed moment of accomplishment. And Daddy was still alive. I sensed the spirit of the man he used to be there with us.

My mouth quivered with a mix of pride, grief, and resignation, and then the moment passed.

People with low blood pressure shouldn't stand stiff and look up for very long.

The heat pounced on me like a tiger, and my sugar took a nose-dive, along with my blood pressure. Suddenly swimmy-headed and feeling ten feet from my body, I promptly went boneless.

"Oh, Lord," Tommy sputtered as he grabbed my waist from behind to keep me from falling, which hiked my dress above my panties as I slid down. I felt the air when they were exposed, but was too dizzy to do anything about it.

Oh, no! I could see the headlines: MAYORAL CANDIDATE'S SISTER EXPOSES SELF ON FRONT LAWN.

Just when I thought things couldn't be any worse, Connor Allen drove by, a look of alarm on his face.

Oh, no! No, no, no!

Still reeling, I grabbed Miss Mamie's arm and struggled to regain my feet, jerking the hem of my dress back down. "Quick, let's go to dinner. Tommy can drive my car. I just need to eat."

Adrenaline came to the rescue as I rushed them to my car. "Wait here while I get my purse. And whatever you do, do not speak to Connor Allen. I'd die of mortification."

I snatched my bag from the apartment, then half tumbled down the stairs, tossing my keys to Tommy. "Go, go." I opened the driver's side slider, then hurled myself into the seat. "Go."

No sooner had Tommy backed out, then put my car into drive, than I looked through the rear window to see a bewildered Connor Allen push through the bushes and watch us go.

That panty thing was not nice, God, I scolded, but I could feel Him smiling.

I'd appreciate some help, here.

The smile was all I got.

Twenty-eight

By the time we reached the Red Lobster, my blood sugar had leveled out, but I was so upset about Connor Allen's seeing my underpants—and my *thighs*—that I scarfed down every scrap of my salad, cheese biscuits, and Ultimate Feast, then added insult to injury by having a triple-chocolate dessert. We are talking at least seven thousand calories.

Bloated, but still embarrassed, I got out when we reached home, then scrambled up the stairs to the garage apartment, praying Connor Allen wouldn't call or come over to see what had happened.

Like the gentleman he was, he didn't.

In the South, when anyone with good manners sees anyone else in an embarrassing but non-life-threatening situation, aid may be rendered when asked for or needed, but the subject is never brought up afterward. The embarrassee, likewise, doesn't make the situation worse by bringing it up, either. This is common courtesy, the opposite of the Jerry Springer and You-Tube degradations of our culture.

While Tommy went to meetings and stomped the campaign trail all over town, I spent the next few days finishing up the details in the house, and the nights online, finally finding us a "like new" metal detector you could push around on wheels, with a readout screen that worked on six AA batteries, for only $100 plus shipping. When I e-mailed the seller to find out if something was wrong with it, she told me it had belonged to her late husband, who had become so obsessive about it that he took the thing everywhere, embarrassing her. She was so eager to get rid of it that she said I could send her a check after I made sure it worked.

Sure enough, it arrived three days later by UPS.

I read the instruction booklet, loaded it with fresh batteries, then started scanning the yard in six-foot squares. Within minutes, I could understand why the guy was addicted. The possibility of a great find kept me going till Tommy came out and called me in for dinner.

He stopped on the verandah to shelter his eyes from the lowering sun so he could see me. "What's that?"

"Our metal detector, with a screen."

"Where'd you get it?" he asked.

"On the Internet. A widow sold it to me for only a hundred dollars, because it had a lot of bad memories from her recently deceased husband."

Tommy laughed. "So, you bought us a haunted metal detector." He started down the wide stairs. "Find anything?"

I turned it off and rolled the gizmo toward him. "Just the septic tank and the water line and the gas line. So far."

Tommy eyed it with alacrity. "Well, it's a big yard."

"You can try it out in the morning. The haul-away people left the Big Blue Bag under the attic window, so I plan to start cleaning up there at five in the morning, before it gets too hot."

It probably wouldn't hurt to scan the attic, too, but this model was way too big to get up all those stairs. I resolved to find another, smaller version for inside the house. Maybe I could borrow one from somebody Mama knew.

Buoyed by the prospect of finding Daddy's treasure close to home, I linked my arm with Tommy's and dragged him toward the house to wash up. "Down, boy. It's time to eat."

I was done in. We could deal with the metal detector tomorrow.

Tommy escaped my grasp to rescue the metal detector. "Better keep this thing inside, or somebody's liable to steal it."

He had a point. "Good idea." Mimosa Branch was still Mimosa Branch, but the days when we could safely leave any equipment unattended in the yard had passed away with the advent of cocaine and crystal meth.

Leaning it back, Tommy slowly pulled the machine up the stairs, one at a time.

I heard Miss Mamie's crystal bell ringing insistently from deep inside the house.

"We're coming!" I hollered, causing Tommy to flinch.

"Sheesh, Lin," he chided. "You know she can't hear you."

He was right. I was wrong. Again. "Sorry. I didn't think."

"That's one of our slogans in AA," he said benignly as he parked the detector beside the foyer fireplace. "Think."

Apparently, I hadn't been doing much of that since I came back. I just kept reacting on autopilot, despite the tools I'd been given by my enabler's recovery group. Why was I at my worst in my mother's domain?

I hadn't been to a meeting in weeks. Maybe I needed to get back to my program. Call my sponsor. Read my literature. I knew these things, but something inside me resisted.

That was the clincher: I definitely needed a meeting.

But not tonight. Tonight I needed food, then a long shower, then sleep.

On my way inside the house behind Tommy, I sent up an arrow prayer. *Lord, it would be really nice if we found the Krugerrands in the house or the yard. I mean, it would save us all a lot of time and expense.*

Again, I sensed God smile.

Sometimes it's not such a good thing when God smiles. You might just be in for a lesson.

Twenty-nine

At dinner, we told the Mame about the metal detector, and she wanted in on the new toy, too.

"Talk to Tommy," I said. "I'm starting on the attic at five A.M., and not quitting till it gets too hot. Then I'm taking a long, cool shower in Zaida's bathroom and heading back to bed."

Zaida had been our second mother and housekeeper till she retired at seventy to live with her daughter in California. She'd finally escaped this town, but I'd had to go back, a fact Zaida found hilarious. We kept up by e-mail, but I resolved to call her later from my apartment and tell her what was going on. She'd love to hear it.

"You've more than earned a long shower," Miss Mamie said, chipper, then turned back to my brother. "Ladies first, Tommy. As soon as we finish breakfast tomorrow, I want you to show me how to work that thing."

At five the next morning, I took a ten-pack of cold bottled water in a small, soft little cooler up the three flights to the attic, then put on my allergy mask and worked in bare-bulb, blessed silence till eight, when the air began to get hot and stuffy. So I turned on one of the General's giant construction fans that roared like a jet engine but put out a *lot* of air.

Box by box, broken toy by shattered chair, I sorted the trash of my heritage from the possible treasures, then threw what was definitely worthless (as in, twenty-seven cans of dried-up paint remnants, etc.) out the window and into the Big Blue Bag below.

My stomach went with it every time, but I couldn't help watching.

Once that was done, I started working through the ancient cardboard boxes, luggage, and military duffel bags that remained. Most of the boxes held aged-out paperwork or old toys, clothes, and junk that were beyond hope. But at least I managed to cull out the junk and organize the rest for further attention.

Please, Lord, help me find what we need to find. For Mama's sake.

I didn't find any Krugerrands or deeds, but I did find a lovely cameo between the floorboards and discovered an airtight strongbox crammed with ancient correspondence and documents reaching back to the late seventeen-hundreds, including an ancestor's citation for bravery in the Revolutionary War, signed by George Washington, and my great-great-grandfather's oath of loyalty to the Union after we lost the War Between the States. Miss Mamie would love going through those.

I found military uniforms from the mid-eighteen-hundreds to Vietnam. And in Tommy's duffel from his two years in that horrible war, I found a stash of what looked and faintly smelled like marijuana, so I took it down to Zaida's bathroom and flushed it, too.

Not only were the microbes in the septic tank drunk on moonshine, they were now high.

As for the holiday decorations, most were ruined and went into the big bag, but I did find the sturdy red, white, and, blue bunting Daddy had always put around the verandah's railings for the Fourth. The reds were darker now, but other than that, they seemed fine. Perfect for Tommy's election day!

I organized the salvageable things by type and era near the narrow stairs, to be gone through, cleaned, inventoried, then repacked in clear plastic bins.

Drinking bottled water in the heat, I made it till nine-thirty before I started seeing tiny meteors of light dance at the outer range of my vision, a signal that I needed to go downstairs.

Quittin' time!

I carefully negotiated the narrow stairs to the third floor, then took a cool shower in Zaida's renovated bathroom.

Only when I came out of Zaida's room, fresh and dry in the clean clothes I'd left there, did I hear the rattle of the metal detector in the yard. I stepped out onto the third-floor balcony and looked down to see Miss Mamie parading back and forth across the yard with the metal detector, her posture perfectly straight, as if she were modeling in the annual women's club fashion show, the wheels rumbling in the dried-out turf of our lawn.

I didn't see Tommy till he came down the front stairs and confronted our mother. "That's it, Miss Mamie," he said over the small racket of the metal detector's wheels. "Your arms and your forehead look like grilled salmon. You've got to come inside. I'll finish the rest."

I wasn't sure how much of that was genuine concern and how much Tom Sawyer's pal wanting to paint the fence, but the Mame poked a white imprint on her forearm and gasped, then hustled inside.

As my brother rattled on with the detector, I heard Mama slam the door on her way in and grumble up the stairs to her room. "Ninety years old," she scolded herself, "and you forget to put on sunscreen? Mamie, you are getting senile. That's all there is to it."

I could tell from her tone that she didn't really believe that.

I waited till she closed the door to her room to head for the kitchen and some eggs to top off the ones I'd had at five.

One glass of fresh-squeezed orange juice and four shiny scrambled eggs later, I was debating whether to give the attic another brief stab when my cell phone rang in the pocket of my cotton chef's apron (only a dollar each at the Dollar Tree).

"Hello?"

"Ms. Scott?"

"This is she."

Of course, Mama chose just that moment to enter the kitchen, ears perked. ··

I turned my back to my mother.

"Hi. This is Susan from the testing center at the university in Athens. We've had a cancellation. Would you be available to come in this coming Monday morning at eleven?"

Would I! Only three days away. I jumped at the chance to escape the attic.

The trip would take me almost two hours, half of it cross-country to access Highway 316, so the time was perfect. "Great. I'll see you this Monday morning at eleven in Athens."

I could sense my mother leaning closer, ears sharp.

"We'll e-mail the directions to your personal account," the girl said.

"Thanks." I'd need directions. The UGA campus in Athens was a maze of one-way streets and limited access.

When I hung up, I turned to find Miss Mamie perched like a turkey buzzard over a roadkill possum. "So. What was that all about?"

No way was I going to tell her about my weird deficiencies. "Just some final placement testing before I start school," I fibbed. "No big deal. But I have to go to Athens."

Skeptical, Mama went to open the refrigerator, then stood for a few seconds in the cold air before retrieving her sweet tea and mine with Splenda. "I want to hear all about it," she said as she put ice in two flagons, then served up the tea.

I took mine with gratitude. "Thanks." *Focus on the gratitude, not the annoyance,* my better self advised. *And set reasonable boundaries.*

So I simply didn't respond to her previous comment.

"So," Miss Mamie deflected. "What do you have on for this afternoon?"

"Tommy and I had talked about taking Daddy and Uncle Bedford over to Sonny's Barbecue after the lunch rush dies down. They keep talking about how much they miss good barbecue." I paused, then confessed, "We thought about bringing it to the Home, but decided they'd like going out a whole lot better."

Miss Mamie's eyes widened in alarm. "Lin, do you think that is wise?"

"Mama, it's little enough, if it makes them happy. And Sonny's is only a couple of blocks from the Home. If Daddy and Uncle B aren't doing well, we'll postpone, of course. But if they're having a decent day, we'll try it." With some backup medications, should they have one of their psychotic breaks.

Guilt ravaged my mother's expression. "Y'all shouldn't have to be the ones to do this. I know I should have gone to visit your father and Bedford, but I couldn't bear to see them there, caged and drugged like animals. I'd never get it out of my head."

"Mama, it's not your fault." How could I lift that terrible burden from her? "It's their disease. And their genes. We all knew there would come a day when we couldn't care for them at home."

Though her back remained ramrod straight, tears welled in Miss Mamie's eyes. "I know I should pray for God to take him, but I can't. It's so selfish of me."

Whoa. Time to lighten things up. "Trust me, Mama, it's a lot easier to love him now that he's not here. You hang on to the good memories. But he's still homicidal, and he's focused a lot of his anger onto you, which is really common, they tell me, so you're doing us all a favor by staying home."

She tightened her trembling lips into a determined line. "Really?"

"Absolutely."

The front door slammed, and Tommy strode in, red as a beet. "That's it for today. I'm done."

"So you didn't find anything," I declared, wet blanket that I am.

Tommy grinned in spite of me. "Yes I did. I found a lot of old construction debris about two feet down"—no wonder the lawn never did very well—"four cast-iron elbows, tons of minnie balls, and a broken plow that I left where they were, and a smushed pewter pitcher, which I dug up to have restored. I think it's Confederate."

Just what we needed: more broken treasures from the past. But I held my peace.

Tommy fixed and gulped down his own sweet tea, then headed for the back hall. "After my shower, we can go over to pick up Dad and Uncle B."

Maybe it wasn't prudent, but I wanted to try it, at least.

Thirty

Half an hour later, with the help of three aides, we loaded Daddy and my uncle into the minivan and buckled them up, then headed for Sonny's.

"Hah," Daddy said, poking Uncle B's shoulder. "We're gonna get us some Texas Toast and barbecue. And fries. And beans. And decent sweet tea."

"Barbecue," Uncle B said, wooden.

Once there, they got out with surprising ease and led the way inside like normal people. As I'd hoped, there were only a few customers inside.

Daddy flirted with the hostess. "Hey there, good-lookin'. We're starving. Put us in one of those big booths, and bring on the food."

He winked at Uncle B as she led us to a long booth. "Fine woman, that one," he blared behind her back as if she couldn't hear him.

I steered Daddy into the booth first, while Tommy did the same with Uncle B, the two of us saying almost in unison, "You go in first, so we can fetch you more food."

Conditioned by a lifetime of manners lectures from my mother, including booth etiquette (the lady goes in first), Daddy balked a little, but the promise of more food convinced him to go along.

The waitress came with her pad, winking at Daddy. "Hey there, honey. What're y'all drinkin'?"

"Three sweet teas, and one unsweet, no lemon," Tommy ordered. Sonny's served their excellent tea in quart glasses, just like Mama. "And we guys'll have three pulled-pork plates with beans, slaw, fries, and extra toast." He looked to me. "Lin, what'll you have?"

I restrained myself, hard though it was. "Smoked dark-meat chicken with tomato and cucumber salad. No other sides."

So far so good. Daddy started joking with Tommy like the old days, and Uncle B was at least behaving, albeit a shadow of his former self.

But he livened up when the food came, and so did Daddy. The two of them chowed down like a couple of teenaged boys.

Grateful for every uneventful moment that passed, Tommy and I watched them enjoy their food and their freedom.

Everything went perfectly till we were all finished and the waitress brought our check.

Who should walk in but Connor Allen, all by himself. He came over immediately. "Well, hey there, Lin. Tommy." He looked at Daddy and Uncle B. "And who are these fine gentlemen?"

Tommy stood, ticket in hand. "Let me introduce you. Daddy, this is our new next-door neighbor, Connor Allen. Connor, this is my father, Thomas Breedlove, but everybody calls him the General."

Daddy nodded, then pointed to Uncle B. "That's ma baby brother over there."

"My Uncle Bedford Breedlove," I added.

Connor finally noticed Tommy's grim expression, so he nodded and said, "It's an honor. Perhaps we'll have time to visit another day."

Uncle Bedford peered at him, as if trying to place him. "I know you!" he said with the first spark of recognition I'd seen in days. "Used to watch you preach on TV every Sunday evenin' from that place in . . . somewhere."

He didn't recognize his wife and daughters, but knew Connor from TV. I mean, really.

Connor smiled in acknowledgment.

Tommy counted out the cost of our dinner and tip from his wallet, then stood to say, "Come on, Daddy. Let's take a ride."

Uncle B let out a fierce, "Wait a minute! We can't leave yet." We all froze, including Connor.

Then, with everybody in the place watching—including the cooks—Uncle Bedford pulled out his uppers and *licked* them clean with a caved-in smile of satisfaction.

"Aggggh!" Everybody who saw it gagged, including Daddy.

"Whoa there, little brother," he warned, "that's not kosher in public."

It wasn't kosher *anywhere*.

Uncle Bedford bowed up and glared at Daddy. "You're not the boss of me!" He replaced his teeth, then shot an impressive left jab in Daddy's direction that, of course, didn't even reach halfway across the table.

Stupidly, I turned to Connor with, "He used to box at Tech and in the navy."

Perfect. Could I *be* more inane?

The General scrambled out of the booth loaded for a fight. I managed to get between him and Uncle B, but he pushed back with alarming strength.

Connor had the good sense to step out of the line of fire.

Uncle Bedford took another swing at Daddy, coming close that time.

Please, no! Dear Lord, please bring peace to these men. You made them feisty. I know You can soothe them, I prayed as I reached into my pocketbook for the Haldol injections, but they'd gone to the bottom, of course.

Desperately rummaging through sunglasses, cell phone, readers, lipsticks, calendar, pens, checkbooks, spare keys, frequent buyer cards, and Splenda packs, I finally found them just as Uncle Bedford let out a cackle worthy of the Wicked Witch of the West, then nudged me toward the door as if everything were just fine.

Thank You, Lord!

Suppressing laughter, Tommy motioned me to chill out. "Come on, Lin. Let's take these two fine gentlemen for a ride by the ballpark."

"Okay."

I glanced back to see that Connor had gone to a table in the far corner of the restaurant.

I do not appreciate this, God.

Mortified, I forced myself to focus on the positive. I put my arm around Daddy and gave him a hug as we left. "I love you, Daddy. Thanks for protecting us all these years."

He nodded in pride, his arm tightening across my shoulders. "It's my job. I'm your daddy."

"Well, you've done it well." Back outside in the heat, I helped Daddy into the seat behind mine. Tommy led Uncle B to the other sliding door, then helped him in, too.

While I was buckling Daddy in, he drifted away again, soft as a cherry blossom petal on a warm spring breeze that wafted over the thick, black wall of his dementia.

Uncle B retreated into delusion.

Neither of them had ever liked wearing seat belts. Maybe that was why they'd checked out.

There I went again, trying to make sense of insanity, just what I'd criticized Aunt Glory for doing.

Judge not, lest you be not judged, the spirit of my Granny Beth said inside me, adding a wry *sometimes for the very same thing.*

I prayed I wasn't going crazy, too. That was the last thing Tommy and Mama needed: one more nutcase to take care of.

Before I backed out of the handicapped space, I whispered to Tommy, "Were you serious about taking them to the ballpark? It's way down in Buford."

Tommy smiled. "No. But I had to get them back in the car before they started duking it out in front of Connor Allen."

The lies we tell to protect ourselves and those we love. And *from* those we love.

"Back to you-know-where, then?"

Tommy nodded. He notified the Home with his cell, so two aides were waiting with wheelchairs when we drove up.

I unlocked the doors, then opened both back sliders with a press of the buttons overhead. Sending up another arrow prayer that we could get them back to their room without incident, I unbuckled Daddy and helped him out. He was still absent but breathing.

"How'd it go?" Shalayne asked as she turned Daddy around so he could sit in the wheelchair.

"Really well, except for—" I started, but Tommy interrupted.

"It went great," he said. "They both ate a lot and seemed to enjoy it."

"Beans?" a wary Shalayne asked.

Tommy grinned. "Lots."

Shalayne and the other attendant exchanged pregnant glances. "Wal, I'm just glad I don't work the night shift tonight," she said. "If you git my drift."

As if on cue, Daddy let out a belch worthy of a grizzly bear, and just as foul.

I looked down my nose at Shalayne as I returned the unused syringes. "Please make sure the night shift is alert to their bathroom needs."

Tommy nodded. "If I get here at six tomorrow morning and find them in their own mess, I'll report it to the regulatory board."

The threat wasn't an idle one. He'd already sicced state inspectors on the place two times.

Not that the attendants cared. Shalayne responded to the threat with an indifferent, "I'll make sure to tell them."

Not that it would do any good.

On our way back to Miss Mamie's, I asked my brother, "Do you think we should move them? I've got a sneaking suspicion the night shift consists of one nurse napping, and one attendant with a flashlight doing bed checks from time to time."

"It wouldn't help to put them somewhere else," he said. "You'll find the same problems everywhere we can afford. We just have to stay on top of the staff. The squeaky wheel gets the oil."

For how long? I couldn't help wondering. Then I scolded myself for essentially wishing them dead with such a thought.

Guilty, I offered, "Maybe we'll find those Krugerrands so we can get them private nurses."

"Maybe," Tommy muttered without conviction.

Though it was only four P.M. when we pulled into the garage at 1431 Green Street, I told Tommy as we got out into the heat, "I am going upstairs to bed. Do you want me to tag along to the Home tomorrow morning at six?" Frankly, I'd rather go there than back to the attic.

Tommy shook his head. "Nope, but thanks. That's kind of our time together, now."

I nodded, too weary to speak. Then I summoned the strength to climb the narrow stairway to my hidey-hole apartment upstairs. Inside, I pulled the shades against the glaring light, then ran the thermostat down to sixty-eight, shucking off my clothes where I stood, mirror be damned.

Naked in my bed under nothing but the sheet, I thanked God for taking care of Daddy and Uncle B, but couldn't resist, *That Connor thing, though. That wasn't fair.*

The still, small voice asked me with authority, *Fair to whom?* (God doesn't make mistakes in grammar. Ever.)

I was too tired to argue. *I'm sorry. You're right. The ways of God are not the ways of a person.*

The next thing I knew, the alarm was going off at four-thirty A.M.

Shower. Coffee. Eggs. Attic.

I forced myself erect, found the shower, stood under a tepid spray, then came out to see myself in the mirror, dyed blond hair plastered to my head, giant circles under my eyes, and old.

Thank goodness there wasn't anybody there to see me that way.

With any luck, there wouldn't be.

At least till after Christmas, my inner hedonist whispered seductively.

Ignoring her, I pressed the button on the coffee maker, donned my pink seersucker robe, then went down the stairs to retrieve the *Gainesville Times* from the grass.

Four shiny scrambled eggs, the Jumble and crossword puzzle, and three mugs of coffee later, I drank a cold bottled water with my daily meds and vitamins, then dressed for the attic, not Connor Allen.

Maybe it was just as well that he'd seen how crazy my crazy relatives were.

I probably wouldn't be hearing from him again, which would help me disengage.

I made up my mind to focus on my family and the blessings we still had.

Monday was just around the corner, when I could go to Athens and maybe find out for sure whether or not I had the beginnings of Alzheimer's.

Thirty-one

The day of my testing, I slept till seven, ate some eggs and drank a pot of coffee, then put on a face and a bra and my one pair of dark skinny jeans with a white cotton camisole and an unlined emerald silk blazer. Satisfied that I wouldn't stick out like a sore thumb on campus, I headed cross-country, careful to slow down in the seven speed-trap microtowns between me and Highway 316.

It was blazing hot when I got to Athens, the air sodden with humidity and the sharp, microscopic haze of lingering summer. Fortunately, the campus was almost deserted (some kind of break), so I found a parking spot right next to the building I needed.

The catch was, I couldn't enter at the closest doorway. I had to hike all the way around the enormous brick structure, then do the whole metal-detector security thing. Sad, sad, sad.

Everybody inside, including security, looked like middle school kids to me.

By the time I got to the fourth floor and the proper office, I needed some water.

More baby professionals greeted me kindly and got me some cold water.

Then they took me to a tiny, cluttered office where a tall, thin young man introduced himself as Dr. Mitchell.

He asked me a lot of questions about my family's medical history, including Daddy's dementia, plus my childhood and school experiences before asking me to describe my weird word thing.

The whole time I was explaining the word thing, he peered at me as if I were some sort of specimen, his brows knotted and a look of intense concentration on his face. When I finished, he pursed his mouth, looked down, and bracketed his chin with slow strokes of his thumb and forefinger.

I took the opportunity to inspect the framed certificates on his wall and see that he had a doctorate in psychology, not a medical degree.

At last, he made eye contact and spoke. "Fascinating. I've been doing this for a long time, and I have never heard of what you just described."

Typical. Too weird. Again.

"My regular doctor said it could be PTSD," I offered. "I went through a really bad divorce." I motioned to the detailed medical history I'd printed out and brought with me, the first page taken up with my specialists and the ten prescriptions they'd given me—God bless my hormones and anti-depressants. "It's all in there."

Young Dr. Mitchell frowned. "So you can write and study, but not read for pleasure."

"I used to read all the time," I mourned. "Several books a week in all genres. I miss it terribly."

He rose. "Let's get you tested, so we can confirm or rule out PTSD and learning disabilities. Don't worry. By the end of the day, we'll know a lot more."

"Today?" Wow. Talk about fast.

He smiled. "It's all computerized now. I'll add my comments after the evaluation results come in, and you can go home with everything in a folder."

"Bring it on."

So the testing began. First came a hearing test, which confirmed I had moderate mid-range nerve deafness, but not enough to merit a hearing aid, thank goodness.

Next, they put me at a built-in desk in a tiny room with a big, sunny, tinted window behind me, and another glass window right in front of me that let me observe the testers in the cubicle beyond, and vice versa.

Then the written tests: ratios, spatial relationships, history, biology, some basic math (no algebra) and geometry (mostly "Which does not belong in this picture?"), and written passages followed by questions. The thing about the reading was, the selections were never more than a paragraph or two, so the word thing didn't crop up.

But this was a test, not a Calgon-take-me-away book, so maybe I used another part of my brain to process it.

By the end of the testing, it was two-thirty and my stomach growled so loud, it echoed in the little room.

The teenaged tester on the other side of the glass told me I could go get something to eat, and the results would be ready at four.

After trekking back to my car, I found a nice neighborhood grill downtown and enjoyed the simple food and funky patrons, lingering over an excellent flagon of iced tea.

I got lost on the way back (all those one-way streets), so by the time I returned to the testing office, it was four-thirty. The receptionist buzzed *Dr.* Mitchell, then said he'd be right out.

Sure enough, he leaned out of his door halfway down the hall and motioned for me to come in. "Everything's done."

Nervous, I went and sat in his lair to get the results.

Middle school Dr. Mitchell handed me a nice presentation folder with at least ten single-spaced pages with charts and graphs inside.

"I'll go over the scores with you in a minute. But I know you're probably eager to discuss our overall findings."

I sat up straighter. "Yes, please. You don't need to sugarcoat it. I want the truth."

He nodded. "We know now that you do not have a learning disability. If so, there would have been some indication in your school history or these tests, but there isn't, and you haven't had any strokes or head trauma, so we can rule that out. We've also ruled out post-traumatic stress; your test results don't fit the profile for that."

So much for that. I might as well ask the question I feared the most. "What about Alzheimer's?" He knew about Daddy, so I didn't have to explain myself.

Young Dr. Mitchell actually smiled. "No indication of that whatsoever."

Whew! Big relief. So far. "So what is it?"

"Frankly, looking at your medications, I'm inclined to think the phenomenon is a side effect of one or more of your prescriptions."

Shoot. Shoot, shoot, shoot!

Without my antidepressants and endorphin enhancers, I couldn't get out of bed. "So not being able to read for fun could be the cost of remaining sane and functional?" I challenged.

"Quite possibly. And you have been under a great deal of stress. That affects the brain, too. So I'll recommend accommodations."

"I don't know anybody who's not under a lot of stress lately," I grumbled.

I started to rise, but Dr. Mitchell stopped me with, "We still need to go through your results, but there's something else I'd like to discuss."

I subsided. "Okay. Shoot."

"Have you ever had an IQ test?"

I shrugged. "Way back in elementary school, but my mother never told me the results."

He showed me a sheet with a bold 140 in the results box. "This is your score. We rarely see individuals of your abilities here."

You have to have at least a 135 IQ to join Mensa; a friend had told me that. So I knew my score meant I was bright, at least.

My young doctor seemed to be expecting some sort of response, but what do you say to something like that?

Then I heard my voice blurt out, "If I'm so smart, how come I can't balance my checkbook or do college algebra?"

He actually laughed. "I can't answer that for you specifically, but many highly intelligent people have certain areas of difficulty."

I frowned. "So what does that number mean, really?"

"It means you are in the top one half of one percent in the population," he answered, "in intellectual capacity. One-forty puts you at entry level into the genius range."

My eyes narrowed in skepticism. If I was so smart, why had I married Phil? And gotten drunk on our honeymoon and gotten that wretched tattoo on my fanny? And tried to have a fling with Grant Owens? Or even *considered* dating and mating with a Baptist minister?

I shook my head in disbelief. "To be so smart, I've sure done a lot of dumb things in my life."

He smiled. "Emotional matters are another ball game, entirely."

One-forty IQ. I still had no idea what to do with that. So I was scraping the bottom of the genius pool. So what? I didn't have a lick of common sense, and I couldn't do algebra.

Seeing me deflate, he shifted to, "If you'll open your folder, we can go over the individual areas of testing and their significance."

When we were done, I rose and shook his hand. "Thank you. Should I take this to the disabilities office at—"

"No need. We already e-mailed everything over. Encrypted, of course."

"Well, thanks again." I paused. "And you're sure about the Alzheimer's?"

He nodded. "For now at least, you're in the clear."

I was happy with that.

So I took my folder and enjoyed my trip home, arriving just in time for dinner.

Thirty-two

I walked into my mother's kitchen and gained five pounds just from the heavenly aromas.

"How did it go?" Miss Mamie asked with obvious anticipation as I washed up to join them.

"Great. I scored really well." I sat down and covered my lap with my napkin, then accepted the meat loaf Tommy passed me.

"So what's 'really well'?" she prodded.

"I'll probably be able to CLEP out of a lot of required classes. But I'll still have to buy the prep quizzes and study. That comes to about a hundred fifteen a course, including the test fees." Thank goodness for that sales commission. "A lot cheaper than taking the actual courses."

Disappointment congealed Miss Mamie's expression. "And that's it?"

"Yep." I couldn't discuss the IQ thing in front of Tommy. And who knows? Maybe the test was wrong this time. "That's all."

Still, you could feel the unspoken thick in the air between us, opaque as a dawn fog in a mountain hollow.

"Oh," my mother said, clearly rebuffed.

In a gesture of conciliation, I added a glop of mashed potatoes to my plate. As long as I was climbing all those stairs and working in the attic, I could afford to comfort myself with mashed potatoes every once in a while.

"Well, there you go. Finally eating like a normal human, at last." Miss Mamie beamed with pride. "I told you, you're getting too thin."

Then she totally mixed her signals by handing me the low-carb catsup for my meat loaf. "Here."

Tommy had been observing us warily since I'd come in, but wisely remained silent.

I noticed he had on a new suit. And cologne.

Whoever she was, things must be heating up.

After dinner when he left for his meeting, I joined Miss Mamie at the sink to wash up. She washed and rinsed, and I dried.

Now it was safe to ask, "Mama, did I ever have an IQ test in school?" Not that she would necessarily remember.

"Yes. They gave them to all the children." She handed me a clean plate to dry.

I wiped it. "Do you remember what I made?"

"Yes." Nothing more.

She wasn't going to make this easy, but I was compelled to ask, "What was it, please?"

She forgot to rinse the next plate, handing it to me with suds dripping. "Why in the world would you want to know something like that at this late date in your life?"

I rinsed the plate under the tap, then started drying it. "I'm going back to school. I need to know."

She frowned as if I'd asked her when she lost her virginity. "Well, if you insist; it was a hundred forty."

Whoa. So the test was right.

And my mother hadn't told me. Ever. "Why didn't you tell me?"

She stopped washing and turned to face me. "Your daddy and I talked it over for a long time. We didn't tell you because we'd seen what happened to children who had that 'genius' label put on them. They never had a real childhood. Shipped off to little think tanks. Skipped grades. They were outcasts with the regular kids."

She patted my arm. "We didn't want that to happen to you. And we didn't want it to come between you and Tommy, so I swore the school people to secrecy. We let you have your childhood, and your high school years, like everybody else. We'd planned for you to go to college and come into your own, but then you ran off with Phil."

That still didn't explain why they hadn't told me when I was older.

But it was all water over the dam. What is, is, and what was, was. Nobody could change it, and it wouldn't do either of us any good for me to second-guess my parents' decision.

"Thanks for being honest," I said. Then my big mouth rebelled with, "It might have made a difference in my life if I'd known when I graduated."

"Baloney," my mother said, pointing a sudsy serving spoon my way for emphasis. "You still would have married that Phil. Your IQ had nothing to do with *that* decision. Hormones and adolescent rebellion trump intellect every time. You threw away your chance for a fine education to be a Buckhead housewife."

Yes, I had. And I'd enjoyed it immensely in clueless bliss till everything hit the fan. "You're right."

My mother went back to scrubbing the pots. "Darned tootin'."

To lighten the mood, I said, "I wonder if they have any tests for common sense."

Miss Mamie smiled. "If they did, you'd flunk, but you'd definitely outscore your daddy, Lord love him." She handed me the cast-iron skillet to dry, adding a peck on the cheek. "But I love you anyway."

"I'm glad somebody does." All that intellect, and not a lick of sense. Except what I'd absorbed from Granny Beth.

I realized God might have been tapping me on the shoulder with all this. Common sense and self-discipline were what I needed, especially when it came to Connor Allen.

I could think of him now without getting horny. Embarrassment over the faint-panty incident had supplanted my lustful urges.

"Common sense," I said aloud. "That will be my new goal."

Finished washing, Mama chuckled as she started putting things away. "Well, don't beat yourself up too much if it doesn't happen overnight."

I untied my apron, then helped her put things in their proper places. "Maybe I'll get some sense in college."

She let out a skeptical sigh. "Based on the college kids I've known, I seriously doubt it. But who can say? Maybe so." She closed the cabinet door and picked up a handful of silver to put into the drawer. "But don't go changing too much. I love you just the way you are."

For Miss Mamie, speaking those words went against the grain, but my inner child did cartwheels for joy. "I love you just the way you are, too."

Mama closed the drawer, but didn't turn around. When she spoke, emotion thickened her voice. "Why did it take so long for us to be able to say this to each other?"

I hugged her from behind. "Because we're both stubborn as a mule, and I knew how disappointed you were when I dropped out of college. I tried to be like you, I really did. You always seemed so strong, such a lady."

"Except for the wretched Phil thing, I've always been proud of you." She turned around, her eyes glistening with unshed tears. "I can hardly criticize you for marrying a difficult man. People who live in glass houses... But the difference was, I adore your daddy, warts and all." She studied my face. "Did you ever really love Phil?"

I exhaled, savoring our newfound intimacy even though she'd asked me the question I'd never allowed myself to ask. "Looking back, I don't know. Probably not. I was in lust with him, and desperate to get out of Mimosa Branch. And I knew he'd be a good provider. But I don't think I ever really loved him *that* way." Not like *kiss, kiss, kiss*.

Saying it out loud made something inside me come full circle, at last.

Miss Mamie patted my arm. "Poor baby. I've always prayed that you and Tommy could know what real love feels like." She drew me close and cupped my head to her shoulder. "Do you think Connor might be—"

I stiffened, pulling away. The idea of being a minister's wife still gave me chills. "Mama, do not go there. My life is complicated enough the way things are."

She arched an eyebrow that told me she had no intention of letting sleeping dogs lie.

I put the last clean dish into the cabinet and changed the subject with, "So what's on the agenda for now?"

Mama sighed. "After we finish with the house and you get back from your road trip with Tommy, we have the election. After that, Tommy will line up who he wants in his administration, you'll study algebra and your CLEP books, and I'll keep an eye on the house. The way I see it, besides the kitchen and bathrooms that have to be done every week, we can clean two unused rooms and one main one a week, in rotation. That shouldn't take us more than one day a week to stay on top of things."

A very doable goal. I had my apartment to keep up, but when you live in such a small space, you have to put everything where it belongs, or it's constant chaos. Dusting, disinfecting, and vacuuming only took me a few hours. "Sounds like a plan to me."

There went that eyebrow again. Mama nudged me toward the back hallway. "Off you go, Madam Genius. Tomorrow you can finish getting the cobwebs out of the attic, so you can get them out of your brain for school." She leaned forward for a taunting, "Genius, genius, genius."

Genius, indeed. I laughed all the way to my apartment.

Thirty-three

Miss Mamie was right: I finished cleaning out the attic the next afternoon and surveyed the large, clear plastic storage boxes with pride. I'd sorted, inventoried, and cleaned everything, then put them in logical groupings. Then I'd borrowed a small metal detector from one of the husbands of one of Miss Mamie's prayer chain friends and scoured the place for metal, but the only things it found were some old coat hangers and ten-penny nails underneath the floorboards.

Once the house was sparkling clean and funeral-ready, as we say in the South, we had sixteen days left till the election to go on our treasure hunt. Tommy asked Shelia to check in on Miss Mamie while we were gone "taking care of family business."

He had carefully planned our itinerary, then posted index cards all over the house with both of our cell phone numbers in bold print, just in case Miss Mamie needed anything. We planned to visit all the banks in one swell foop, as Daddy used to say.

Then, after a fabulous send-off breakfast by Miss Mamie at seven A.M.

on Monday morning, my brother and I started out on our road trip to fourteen different small banks.

Fortunately, Daddy hadn't gone farther from home than an hour or two in any direction, probably so he could be back by supper with none the wiser.

Hand to my heart, though, I never expected what we would find in all those banks.

The first one was up in Cleveland, the seat of White County and home of Babyland General and the Cabbage Patch dolls. Even though we'd left before eight, we didn't reach the bank till eleven because Tommy stopped at Office Depot in Gainesville to buy a heavy-duty nylon backpack in case we found anything bulky.

Once we got to Confidential Credit Union, we had to wait a while to meet in an office with the branch manager, who turned out to be a stout, balding man in a suit that seemed just a little too tight for him. We shook hands, then Tommy showed him notarized copies of the legal paperwork and Daddy's deposit box key.

It took another fifteen minutes for the manager to locate and check his directives on the computer so he could be sure of proper procedure in cases like ours. Clearly a very cautious person, he checked and rechecked everything, then finally rose. "Well, everything seems to be in order. Please allow me to escort you to the vault."

At last.

"This way please," he added.

Please let there be some deeds in the box. Tax-paid.

I knew the prayer sounded greedy, but I was thinking of Mama and that huge, money-hungry old house. Not to mention Daddy's bills for the Home, which I'd discovered were $3,500 a *month*.

We followed the manager across the lobby, then down a flight of polished black granite stairs to a black granite hallway where an armed guard opened a heavy, barred steel door, admitting us to a short corridor flanked by viewing alcoves and the open vault beyond.

As we passed through the corridor, the manager gestured to the two small mahogany desks with expensive lamps as we passed. "There's a viewing table in the vault, but if you'd rather have more privacy, feel free to use these."

Privacy? Hah. Can we say *surveillance*?

I looked up and saw at least ten dark-glass hemispheres in the ceiling. Eyes in the sky.

He motioned us into the vault ahead of him, then got out his key and turned it in the lock of the safety deposit box. To my surprise, the box wasn't very big.

The manager granted us an unctuous smile, clearly curious about what we'd find. "Would you like for me to remain, in case you have any problems?"

"No, thank you," Tommy and I said in unison. Tommy inserted his key, then opened the door to slide out the drawer just enough for the manager to retrieve his key.

"Very well." The manager straightened, smoothing the front of his tight serge jacket, then turned to the guard beyond the now-closed bars. "Paul, open." He looked condescendingly back to us. "If you need anything, just let Paul know."

He sailed out and didn't look back.

About to explode, I nudged Tommy and whispered, "Open that box. I'm dyin' to see what's in there."

"Calm down." Tommy leaned close to whisper through a fixed grin, "We're being recorded. For all we know, we might find evidence of some crime in there. Just smile and act as if you do this sort of thing every day."

I did my best, but I couldn't help looking for, and finding, even more small dark glass hemispheres in the vault ceiling.

Tommy slowly slid the drawer free of its niche. "Whoa," he murmured. "This is heavy."

"Box o' rocks," we said in unison, the way we had when we were asked to carry anything heavy as kids. The phrase had come from Daddy, of course, who'd sworn he'd hauled slabs of marble at a mine over in Tate when he was a boy.

I glanced at the narrow steel table in the middle of the vault, then whispered, "Think you can carry the drawer to the alcove?"

Tommy made a face and whispered back, "It's not *that* heavy."

He carried the box to the small desk in the hallway. I hovered over it, worried that it might really be a box o' rocks, but hoping for something better.

In the circle of soft light from the elegant lamp, Tommy said, "Well, here goes," then opened the long top. Most of the box was empty, except for a long, lumpy Tyvek envelope, sealed, taped closed, then rolled to fit inside the box.

"Let me," I said as he unfurled it on the desk.

Chuckling, he opened his pocketknife and handed it to me. "Be my guest."

I slit the top of the envelope, then bent to look inside.

I didn't mean to scream. Really, I didn't.

The guard turned abruptly to face us at the same moment that my brother smacked his hand over my mouth and hissed a giant, "Shhhhh!" into my ear.

"Is everything okay?" the guard hollered.

"Fine, fine!" Tommy reassured him, his hand still clamped firmly over my mouth. "I just stepped on my sister's sore toe. Sorry. Sorry. Everything's fine."

Humiliated, I managed to slither out of his grasp and step on *his* toe for real. I swiped my hair back into place. "Take a look in there and see how you do," I grumbled.

He did and stopped breathing altogether, his features contorted as he struggled to keep his famous serenity.

The envelope was half filled with gold coins, most marked "uncirculated" in clear, hinged plastic rolls, and at least a dozen in flat little presentation boxes marked "proof." Plus a nice, fat stack of Benjamin Franklins still in their original bank wrapper.

At last, Tommy breathed, reaching inside to free one of the coins from its roll, careful to keep it out of sight. "Krugerrands," he whispered in awe, then put the coin back. He reached inside again to bring the bills close enough to inspect, but not beyond the envelope. "Nineteen-seventy. A year before we went off the gold standard." Reaching deeper, he peered inside again, then told me, "And two deeds. One for thirty acres, and one for eighteen."

Lights flashed, bells rang, and the gates of heaven opened.

"C'mon," I prodded. "Let's get this out of here." We'd found a piece of Daddy's nest egg, but I felt like we'd robbed the bank.

"'Good plan, king.'" Tommy quoted Mr. Rogers from one of my son David's favorite kiddy shows.

Speaking of David, I hadn't heard from him in several weeks. I wondered why, fleetingly, then focused back on the treasure.

Tommy rolled the envelope closed and transferred it into his backpack, then slung it over his shoulder, shifting it several times till the weight was balanced. Then he took a deep, calming breath and returned the box to its place in the vault. "Think you can manage to look calm and collected?" he asked me quietly.

"Of course," I reassured him, as if I really could.

When we got to the barred door, the guard let us out.

"Sorry I worried you," Tommy said.

Skeptical, the man looked to me as we exited the door. "Are you sure you're all right, ma'am?"

Boy, was I ever. "I'm fine," I said with a convincing smile, because I was. Very fine, indeed.

Tommy offered him the deposit box key. "We won't be needing the box anymore. Should I give this to you, or turn it in upstairs?"

The guard nodded. "Upstairs. They'll give you a receipt and a written notice of termination."

Shoot. One more thing before we could escape with the loot. At least the bank wasn't crowded.

I plucked the box key from my brother's hand with a chipper, "I'll take care of that. Why don't you go get the truck and bring it around?"

"Good idea." He waved to the guard. "Thanks." Feeling as if I were in a movie, I followed my brother upstairs, then headed for the customer service desk while he carried the loot out the side door to the parking lot.

Ten minutes later, I climbed into his truck and buckled up, holding it together till we were safely away from cameras and listening ears.

As if anybody would notice or even care. But Tommy had warned me that what we found was our business, and nobody else's, till we could figure things out.

Several miles out of town on an otherwise empty two-lane road, we finally let loose and hollered for what seemed like five minutes, but was probably only two.

Then I asked Tommy, "What are we going to do with all this money and gold? Think it'll be safe under the mattress at the motel?"

Tommy shook his head no. "The only secure, discreet place for this is back home in Daddy's safe."

I frowned. It hadn't been locked when Tommy had found it empty. "But anybody who can read can open it."

"Don't worry," he reassured me. "I'm going to write the combination on my hip in permanent marker, where nobody else can see it. Then I'll black it out on the safe."

"Okay, then. Home we go."

Tommy shook his head, turning into a lay-by, then whipping a U. "If you don't mind, I'll drop you off back at the courthouse with the deeds, so you can look them up and find out if the taxes have been paid." He glanced at his watch. "It's only twelve-thirty. I'll be back in four hours to pick you up."

"Miss Mamie's bound to wonder why you came home."

"I'll deal with that when I get there." His stomach rumbled so loud I could hear it. "But first, let's grab some lunch."

"I saw a cute little diner near the courthouse."

"Good call."

Tommy had a huge cheeseburger while I ate my veggie plate (if you can call three starches and some green beans a vegetable plate, which they did), then he headed home and I headed for the deeds room and the tax commissioner's office.

At four forty-five, Tommy pulled up by the bench where I was sitting in front of the courthouse, enjoying a cool mountain breeze.

"Hey, good-lookin'," he called through the open passenger window. "Can I take you to supper?"

I stood. "That depends. Where?"

He lifted a brimming picnic basket from home. "At our elegant accommodations." The Best Eastern motel in the next town on our list.

"It's a date." I opened the door, then climbed in and buckled up. "How'd it go with Miss Mamie?"

"Great." He let off the brake, then headed for the next town, only twenty minutes away, carefully keeping to the speed limit. "She welcomed me home, asked how long I'd be there, then said she'd pack us some supper for me to take back. Didn't even mention the backpack or why I was there. Just went to the kitchen till I came to say good-bye, then kissed me and handed me the basket." His stomach growled, prompting him to reach under the clean tea towel atop the basket wedged between us and extract a fried chicken leg. "Sorry, but gold makes me hungry."

Shades of Midas.

My own stomach growled, too, so I helped myself. "Oh, goodie. All legs." Yuummm. Tommy's and my favorite.

"She sent her love."

After we'd finished our snack, Tommy shot me a sidelong glance. "So how was your afternoon?"

"Perfect. I was able to trace the lands' ownership back more than a hundred years. I even collected recent comparable sales. Not that there were many. The bottom's dropped out of this market, too. Then I found out the taxes had been paid a month before Daddy went to the Home. Won't be due again till December."

"That's a relief." He threaded his fingers through his hair. "Let's go hole up in our room, eat supper, and go to bed. I don't mind telling you, all this excitement has worn me slap out."

"Me, too."

Fortunately, the motel was just ahead. Once there, we washed up, then devoured our chicken, deviled eggs, broccoli slaw, and potato salad with plenty of decaf diet cola from the vending area.

We were both out like a light by nine.

The next morning while we grumbled about who would shower first, Tommy accused me of snoring like a chain saw. (True.)

I retaliated by informing him that he did, too. (True!)

Then we laughed, and he let me go first, because both of us knew I took really quick showers.

We had a very good breakfast at a morning place on the square, then headed for the bank.

Did we find deeds?

Yes. In all fourteen of the banks, for a total of nineteen, ranging from three to fifty acres.

Were the taxes paid?

All but two, which had been snapped up on the courthouse steps by the sheriff's son-in-law in one case, and a mayor in the other.

Was there gold?

Can we say *amen*? More of the same in every blessed Tyvek envelope, halleluiah!

And every afternoon, Tommy took what we'd found home while I researched titles, comparables, and taxes.

When the weekend came, we gratefully returned to our own beds in Mimosa Branch to rest, then set out again the next Monday morning.

And Miss Mamie, she don't ask nothin'.

Based on the sales slips we had found in Daddy's office, he'd bought the troy ounce Krugerrands for just a few dollars over the cost of their gold, which was only thirty-two dollars back then. Heaven only knew how much they were worth now that we'd found them. If they were genuine. As his mind failed, Daddy had trusted some real crooks.

But the gold pieces had to be real. I couldn't bear to think that we'd all been cheated along with him.

Twice, on banks nine and ten, Tommy was so tired of driving back and forth that he'd tried to lock the loot up in the motel safes, saying only that the contents of the envelopes were very valuable. But both of the motel managers said they could only be responsible for a maximum of five hundred dollars.

"If I hadn't had a program," Tommy confessed when he got back in the truck after the second try, "I'd have poked that guy in the nose. But I realized he was just doing his job and trying to make a living. Liability coverage has gone sky-high for everyone. I can't imagine what it must cost for a motel."

I cocked my head at him in admiration. "You really have grown up, haven't you?"

He nodded, his expression content. "I like being a grown-up and living in truth instead of self-serving lies." He let out a harsh chuckle. "I still have a lot of amends to make for taking advantage of Miss Mamie and the General. And you."

That didn't sound healthy, to me. "I forgive you, and I'm sure the Mame and Daddy do, too. Why do you have to keep on making amends?"

"I *want* to make them," he told me, and I thought of how he'd shaved Daddy almost every day and considered that time with him a gift.

He really *had* changed. If only I could be more like him. "Wow."

"It gives me a purpose," my brother added. "I can do the work at the house, and that makes me feel useful. Even if I get elected, I'll still take care of the house for Miss Mamie."

We'd never talked this way, and I wasn't sure how to respond. It seemed wonderful and dangerous at the same time. I didn't want to mess this up.

So I changed the subject. "What do you think we should do with the gold? I can see you're worn out."

"We'll stick with the plan." He let out a brief yawn.

"I can drive, too, you know. Why don't I take the stuff home, and you can search the records."

That hit a nerve. "Not. I'd drive to Miami and back before I'd face all those books and papers and know-it-alls. You do the research, I'll do the road."

I nodded. "Okay."

We ate a companionable lunch saturated with trans fats, then he dropped me at the courthouse and headed for Mimosa Branch.

As we went from one bank to the next, we had a lot of time to talk in the truck, mostly about what to do with the money from the coins. A new roof was priority one. And foam insulation in the attic.

And a private nurse for Daddy and Uncle B.

We decided that insulated windows would have to wait till we got some estimates, to see what that would cost. Fourteen-thirty-one Green Street had a *lot* of windows. Every time I tried to count them up, I lost track.

"And a maid for Miss Mamie," I added as we headed for bank number twelve. "No, make that a cleaning crew."

"Good luck with that," Tommy said. "I can hear the Mame already: 'I will not allow a herd of perfect strangers to poke around in my house or my things. They might steal. Or carry tales. No, it'll have to be somebody with references I know.'"

All of whom were either too decrepit or booked solid.

Discussing the money, we both laughed a lot, proposing wilder and wilder possibilities. We started by being practical with solar electricity, but ended up taking Daddy and Uncle B and the Mame to a spa in Bali.

It sure felt good to laugh in the midst of our search.

Somewhere in the course of our journey, we came to be friends. Enough so, that I felt free to tell Tommy about my physical obsession with Connor. "I'm afraid I'll end up being the scarlet woman for real. He turns me on so hard, I can't think straight."

"The guy's a grown man," Tommy responded, "perfectly capable of weighing the pros and cons on his own. Give him some credit, Sissie-ma-noo-noo.

He knows what he wants, and that's to date you so both of you can get to know each other better."

I glanced to the trees and fields we passed. "I want him, too. But that doesn't mean it's right." Pulled in both directions, I said, "Wanting isn't a decent criteria for a relationship."

"Hence, the dating," Tommy said.

As usual, my knee-jerk reaction was negative. "I just told you, I'm not sure I can control myself."

What was wrong with this picture? Ten years ago, I'd wanted to hop in the bed with Mr. Wrong. Now I was wanting to stay *out* of bed with Mr. Right. "Oh, Lord. I can't do this."

Tommy rolled his eyes. "I hereby officially butt out of this. You're secretly looking for a scapegoat, and I refuse to take the blame if things don't work out. From now on, what happens between you and Connor is your business, not mine."

Now, that sounded like the old Tommy.

"Say what you mean," I shot back, "but don't be mean when you say it." The slogan came from my enabler's group, probably stolen from AA.

I turned to look out the side window, my feelings ruffled. But the thing was, he could be right.

This time, it was Tommy who broke the silence. "That said, Connor seems to be what he appears to be: a decent, upright, intelligent, committed Christian. Who lives next door. Who's smitten with you." He finally shot me a sidelong grin. "Not that I'm pushing him on you. It's just that my instincts tell me he's an okay guy."

So much for butting out.

I nodded. "Instincts noted." After a pause, I couldn't help adding, "What about his congregation? You know how a lot of them feel about me."

Tommy let out a brief snort of exasperation. "If you're willing to give up someone like Connor because of what *some* people *might* think about you, then that's your decision. Just be honest with yourself about why the gossips' opinions mean more to you than Connor."

"It's not me I'm thinking about," I defended. "It's Connor. This job means a lot to him. I don't want to be responsible for jeopardizing that."

Tommy shook his head. "So that's what you're telling yourself, is it?"

My compulsion to be justified let loose a barrage of self-defensive reasons for why I was being noble.

My brother waited till I was done, then granted me a gentle smile. "Suppose you decided to go out with Connor. How does that make you feel?"

I thought a minute before I responded, my mind buzzing with inner voices inserting their pros and cons. I finally told Tommy what the voice that shouted loudest over the din was saying. "Terrified."

He nodded. "And why is that?"

"Because I might really cost him his job. And what if we broke up afterward, making it all in vain?"

"You sure are good at projecting dire consequences," he told me. "Have you ever considered just living in today? Being grateful for the good things in just this day, doing the next right thing, and leaving the future to God?"

My enabler's group stressed the same thing. It made a lot more sense than constantly worrying about what *might* go wrong. "Maybe I will."

"Forget maybe," he said. "Either you will, or you won't. But trust me, you don't have to be an alcoholic for it to work."

I knew that. "I don't want to be a minister's wife," I finally blurted out. "I can't. I don't play the piano, and little kids scare me to death. I talk too much without thinking first, and I'm too selfish, nobody's idea of a minister's wife."

"Except the minister's," Tommy corrected.

Aye, there's the rub.

"We have a lot to be grateful for," my brother coaxed. "All that gold and land and money. Rent-free accommodations. We can get out of bed every morning and walk and talk and see and hear."

Now he was getting corny.

"And we have Mama's cooking," he went on. "And both of our parents."

I skewed my mouth. "Well, we don't really have Daddy anymore."

Instead of being annoyed, Tommy grinned. "So we still have one and a half of our parents, then."

He always knew how to make me laugh.

"Okay. I give in. I'll try it one day at a time." I faced him. "But what about all those dark voices that go through my thoughts?"

"Just tell them they're liars, and to shut up. I swear, it works. Then do something useful to distract yourself."

Kiss! my inner hedonist called like a siren, Connor's arms and face and taste materializing in my brain. *Kiss, kiss, kiss.*

That's not what Tommy meant, my Puritan scolded.

I shook my head, but it didn't clear the din. "If you knew how many pieces of me were chattering away in my brain," I told my brother, "you might have *me* committed."

"Trust me," Tommy reassured me. "You are not crazy. After all these years in AA, not to mention Daddy and our uncles, I know crazy, and you're not it. A bit self-absorbed at times, but definitely not crazy."

"Thank you for the psych evaluation," I said with one brow arched in skepticism. "*Doctor* Breedlove."

We rode in awkward silence for the next mile or so till I couldn't stand the tension anymore. "With this one-day-at-a-time thing, am I allowed to ask about what we're doing tomorrow?"

Tommy chuckled. "Yes, you are. Plans are great, as long as we're flexible about what happens." He took a bank key out of the bare ashtray, then glanced at it. "Tomorrow is Gay First Federal in Meriwether County."

I frowned in confusion. Meriwether County was rural and conservative. "They have a gay bank in Meriwether County?"

Who says there are no stupid questions?

Tommy laughed. "No. The town is Gay, Georgia. Daddy's one aberration from stashing his stuff in county seats."

I broke up, envisioning sidewalks teeming with drag queens. "I can't wait to see it."

Tommy wasn't amused. "If we find more gold and deeds, I'll take you to Greenville to go through the records while I run the stuff back home."

The trip would take him two hours each way. "Tommy, you're exhausted. We can put it under the mattress while we sleep. Give yourself a break."

"No way. This gold is Miss Mamie's nest egg. I'm not risking it."

"I wonder if she has a stash of their money somewhere," I thought aloud. "Savings? CDs? Cash." My mind explored the possibilities. She hadn't let us go through her locked, fireproofed finance file box. "She's paying the nursing home out of something."

Three thousand five hundred a month for a smelly room, awful food, and not enough workers.

Tommy's brows lifted. "I think the time has come to talk turkey with Miss Mamie about money. Maybe what we've found will get her to open up. As Daddy's guardians, we have power of attorney and the right to see their finances, but I'd hate to use that on our own mother."

We gave each other a sidelong glance of dread.

"I should have tried harder to convince her to let me see how things stand," Tommy confessed. "But I couldn't bring myself to take away her last bit of privacy. Mentally, she's sound as Stone Mountain, so she'll probably tell us to mind our own business."

I chuckled. "Uh-oh. Now who's putting out the negative projections?"

That brought back Tommy's grin. "Touché."

I marveled at how well he kept his cool. "You really, really have grown up," I said.

He kept his eyes on the road ahead, a weary smile lifting the edges of his lips. "'Bout time."

If he could live his life one day at a time with such positive results, so could I. I needed some positive results, for sure.

Thirty-four

By the time we finished our road trip, Tommy had gone online at the local libraries of a few towns to research the value of the coins we'd found. Armed with what he'd learned, we detoured to Atlanta on our way home and stopped at two reputable coin dealers to inquire discreetly about what we could get for the Krugerrands.

The good news was, the rolls of uncirculated coins Daddy had bought for about forty dollars per coin were now worth at least sixteen hundred apiece. The great news was, the sets of proofs were worth even more, depending on their scarcity. We had several complete proof sets, but when we tried to get a definite price out of the dealers, they both waffled, probably because they wanted to buy them as cheaply as possible if we sold.

Tommy and I thanked them kindly, went back to his truck, then decided to find a reputable appraiser and go from there. I called Miss Mamie and told her we were an hour away.

"Good," she said. "See you then." Click, she hung up.

Buoyed by what we *had* found out about the coins, we were both more than ready to bring home the last of the loot when we finally rolled into the porte cochere at 1431 Green Street at one-thirty in the afternoon, two weeks before the election.

Miss Mamie was waiting for us inside in her apron, the kitchen set for a celebratory lunch.

"Home at last," Tommy rejoiced as he hugged our mother. "Halleluiah."

Miss Mamie held on for long seconds before she let go, then turned to embrace me, too. "Welcome home, my precious children. Take a seat in the kitchen. We'll eat first, then talk later."

Tommy and I exchanged pregnant glances.

After we'd eaten, the time would come to lay it all out and ask Mama about her funds and what she wanted to do with the gold. We still had to make sure the cash in the safe wouldn't trigger some kind of investigation, so those were off-limits for the present.

Lunch provided a welcome delay, and it was great: an orange and almond cranberry salad with homemade sweet-and-sour dressing, and lamb chops, broiled to perfection. Yum.

Miss Mamie didn't ask any questions till we'd all finished doing the dishes and putting everything away. Then she motioned us to the empty table. "Have a seat. We need to talk."

We sat side by side, facing her chair.

She sank into her place with a sigh of relief. "Feels good to sit down." Then she looked at Tommy. "I've been dying to ask, but didn't want to interrupt y'all. What did you find? I'm hoping it's spectacular, because this place has been dead lonely without you."

"We found deeds to nineteen undeveloped properties," Tommy told her. "Two had been sold off for nonpayment of taxes, but the other seventeen are current. The bad news is, we can't get much for them in this economy."

"Blasted recession," the Mame spat out. "The General always said this country would go bankrupt if we went off the gold standard, and he was right." She straightened like Mrs. Miniver, chin lifted. "What are the taxes on them?"

I answered. "Altogether, we need to pay about ten thousand a year to hold on to them till prices get better."

Daddy had always been big into owning raw land, risky though it was.

"I'll have to look into that and make a decision," the Mame deflected. "How much do you think the land would sell for right now?"

"I checked recent comparable sales at the courthouses," I told her, "so this is just an informed estimate: at best, maybe a hundred thousand for everything. Half of them don't even have utilities."

Mama arched a brow as she nodded. "I see." She turned back to Tommy. "And what have you been bringing home every afternoon?"

At last, he got to tell her that her financial troubles were over. Tommy smiled wide. "Forty thousand in old bills, and a passel of gold Krugerrands. Proofs and uncirculated. But only half of what's missing, according to the receipts we found in Daddy's office."

Mama lit up like a two-hundred-fifty-watt incandescent bulb. "Thank You, Jesus! Never mind what you *didn't* find. How much are these worth?"

"The General bought the coins right after we went off the gold standard in seventy-one," Tommy explained, deliberately drawing out the bottom line. "The receipts then were for over a hundred thousand—cash—when gold was thirty-two dollars an ounce."

Back when our mother was home clipping coupons and trying to save every dime. I was grateful to Daddy and furious, at the same time.

Tommy went on. "I need to bring in a reputable appraiser to look everything over before we'll know exactly what you can get for them. Then you can decide if you want to sell any of them."

"Of course we'll sell them." Mama gloated. "But not all at once. Why bother the IRS? Your daddy bought them with post-tax dollars."

She leaned forward. "You didn't answer my question," she said politely. "How many uncirculated coins did you find, and what are they going for today?"

Tommy answered immediately. "Five hundred fifty rolled uncirculated coins, plus a hundred and fifty proofs still in their boxes." Tommy had counted and recounted, so he'd know if any were missing. "As of this morning, the rolled coins are about sixteen hundred each, conservatively. The proofs vary, but they're all more than that."

Mama nodded, her bookkeeper's mind clearly whirring away. "So for five hundred fifty coins, that's . . ." She shot to her feet. "More than eight hundred thousand dollars! Not even counting the proofs!" She dropped to her knees like someone had lopped off her lower legs, then started sobbing.

Tommy leapt over the table as I scrambled to see if we'd given her a stroke or a heart attack. We found her on her knees, curled toward the floor with her hands clasped, repeating, "Thank You, God. Thank You, Jesus," through her tears.

We both asked in unison, "Mama, are you okay?"

She looked heavenward, her face aglow despite her tears. "Thank You, God. I knew You'd come through, but we sure cut it close, didn't we?"

Laughing and crying at the same time, she took our forearms and rose with the grace of a dancer. "I was down to a thousand dollars in the bank and didn't know how I'd pay the Home." Grinning, she swiped the tears from her face. "It's like Corrie Ten Boom said, 'you don't need the ticket till the train pulls into the station.' I trust God, but I must confess, my faith began to waver when I got that last bank statement."

I hugged her, tight. "Thanks be to God, and to Daddy."

Mama's expression shifted to one of wonder. "The General always told me we were well provided for. Then when he lost his business and his mind, I asked him about our nest egg, but every time, he just patted my shoulder and said, 'Don't you worry, Mame. We have all we'll ever need.'"

She shook her head, wistful. "Once he was at the Home, I couldn't let myself think about what might be out there that we would never find. Too depressing."

She brightened. "Then y'all found it. God and your daddy provided, right when we got to the bottom of the barrel."

Kind of cruel of God to wait so long, if you asked me, but I sent up my own prayer of heartfelt gratitude anyway.

I looked to Tommy, who was obviously relieved that we hadn't jolted our mother into kingdom come. "So much for asking Mama about her finances."

Miss Mamie sobered abruptly. "Quick, Tommy. Get somebody up here to value that stuff, then start selling it off."

"Whoa, whoa, whoa," he said gently. "We have all those bills."

Canny, Mama shook her head. "Those would attract too much attention," she said, "rare as they are."

She had a point.

Mama's eyes lost focus briefly as she considered the situation, then they cleared. "Since your daddy's officially incompetent, and Georgia is a community property state by adjudication, let's just say that the half y'all found is mine. What sort of tax exposure do I face when we sell it?"

I chuckled. "I thought you didn't want to bother the IRS."

"I was only kiddin'." She made a flat-mouthed Stan Laurel face. "'Christians, pay your taxes,'" she quoted scripture. "No gettin' around that. I just don't want to pay any more than we have to."

"I think it'll be a capital gain," Tommy said. "I've got a buddy in the program who's a tax lawyer. I'll call him right away and find out how we should do this, and see who he recommends as an appraiser."

Tommy pulled out his cell phone, scrolled down, then hit the call button. After a silence, he said, "Paul, this is Tom B with a 911. I've got an urgent question concerning some liquid assets I found. Please call back ASAP. Thanks."

His brows drew together as he hung up. "Message."

Miss Mamie frowned. "I'm already late with the payment to the Home. We need some funds right away."

Tommy thought for a minute, then said, "I'll offer to pay the coin appraiser a Krugerrand if he'll come up right away. Once he's given us the values, I'll give him the chance to buy a few. That would take care of us for right now. Otherwise, I'm sure I can find some cash customers within a day or two."

I don't know why, but the enormity of what we'd just given back to our mother—and Daddy—finally sank in, and I needed to sit down. *Thank You, thank You, thank You, thank You, God. And Daddy.*

"I'd like to keep all this as confidential as possible," Tommy said. "Daddy already paid the taxes for the money he used to buy this, but if we dump everything at once, there'll be a huge tax exposure, I'm sure. I don't want to red-flag the IRS."

"Bloodsucking bastards," our proper mother purred.

"Amen to that." When Phil had skipped the country back in 2002, they'd auctioned our house and all that was left (except some clothes and furniture I'd been able to hide with friends). Never mind that Phil had duped me as much as he'd duped them; I'd taken the hit.

Tommy got up. "I'll call my friend again from the study. By suppertime, we should have a reliable appraisal, at least."

The Mame nodded. "Come on, Lin. Let's break out the peach ice cream while Tommy figures this all out."

"Hey!" he protested on his way to the den of iniquity. "What about me?"

Miss Mamie hollered right back. "There's plenty of peach ice cream, but you need to get us out of the hole first, so I can pay the Home."

She lowered her voice and wrapped an arm around my shoulders, leaning her head against mine. "We'll have ours with some of your daddy's ancient brandy." She moved us toward the freezer. "I made plenty of extra peach this summer because your brother loves it so much. But no brandy for him."

I considered, then whispered, "I thought you got rid of all the booze in the house when Tommy got sober." Except for the moonshine Daddy had squirreled away.

Looking like herself again, now that the weight of the world wasn't on her shoulders, Mama shook her head. She glanced toward the den, then whispered, "You don't just get rid of hundred-year-old brandy. I've kept it in a big ole Kotex box in my bathroom linen closet for situations just like this one."

The one place my brother would never go near. Brilliant. "Come on, Mama," I whispered back. "You get the ice cream, and I'll get the Kotex, and we'll both celebrate in my apartment." For a much happier reason than the last time I moved home.

"Great idea," she said. "Tommy will take care of the financial end of things. He's very good at that."

Not the old Tommy, but he wasn't the old Tommy anymore.

She leaned out of the door to the back hallway to issue a melodious, "Ohh, Tommmmy! We're going to the apartment. Let us know when you're all done!"

Tommy's voice yelled back, mimicking her intonations, "Re*mem*ber. Save me a lot of that *ice* cream."

"Ooooh-kaay," she sang back.

Like fleeing felons, we grabbed the goods and hurried to my apartment.

By four-thirty, my ninety-year-old mother and sixty-year-old self had gone through all my picture albums and were both high on sugar and brandy, feeling no pain, and dancing to my golden oldie Beatles and Motown CDs.

Tommy probably knocked before he came in, but we didn't hear him. He just appeared, a grim expression on his face that caused Mama and me to freeze.

"Whassa matter?" I heard myself ask.

Uh-oh. If I'd had enough brandy to mess up my speech, heaven only knew how many calories of ice cream I must have consumed.

Tommy scowled. "Nothing."

Maybe we'd offended him. "Oh, Tommy, I'm sooo sorry. I didn' mean to offend you by gettin' tipsy. We were both jus so *releeeved* that we—"

Tommy lifted his left hand, his right behind his back. "Your choices are not my business. Unless you make a habit of it."

"Well, if thaas true," our lady-mother enunciated, pointing the almighty finger of judgment at him, "why are you so mad?"

Tommy broke up laughing. "I'm not mad. I'm jus' so *releeved*," he imitated, then smiled.

"Okay, then," the Mame said. "Whass the verdict?"

"My lawyer friend said Mama could gift us each fourteen thousand a year, tax-free to us, or we could divide the proceeds three ways and pay the capital gain up front. He also recommended that we ask for cash when we sold anything, and deposit no more than nine thousand, nine hundred, and ninety-nine dollars on any given day. Then he gave me the number for the most respected coin appraiser in Atlanta."

He really *was* good at this.

"When I told the appraiser we'd pay him one of the Krugerrands for an official appraisal, he dropped everything and came. After he checked out the coins and said they were genuine, he showed me comparable sales from the international coin dealers' official Web site, then conservatively valued the collection at one million, four hundred fifty thousand. Wholesale, which is what we'd get for selling the collection."

Wow. I might end up one third of a millionaire. But the money was really Miss Mamie's, so the ownership didn't count.

Ownership doesn't count for anything, Daddy used to say, *it's control that matters.*

Tommy went on. "He did the written appraisal on the spot from his laptop, then printed it out on a black gizmo the size of a box of tinfoil."

He paused a minute to let that sink in, but we were so amazed (and swacked), Mama and I just stared at him, agape. Miss Mamie plopped down abruptly onto my sofa behind her.

My brother peered at both of us, waving a hand before our eyes. "Earth to Lin and Miss Mamie. Did you hear what I just said?"

We nodded in unison, struck dumb.

Tommy brought his right hand from behind his back and showed us the thick, well-worn stack of fifty-dollar bills he was holding. "Look. The appraiser bought six of the coins for himself. Cash."

Whoa! I grabbed his hand and riffled the bills. Nonsequential. "Holy crow! How much?"

"Nine thousand, nine hundred, and fifty dollars."

Just under the ten thousand a day that had to be reported to the feds.

Lord, please strengthen our hearts to do this legally. Meanwhile, my inner hedonist was seeing dollar signs and scheming to go black market with every single cent. But that still, small voice silenced her with, *It's all right. Even after tithe and taxes, you'll all be fine.*

How soon we forget the miracle. God had given Miss Mamie this treasure when she needed it, yet there I was, dishonoring the gift by wanting to evade the taxes. I gave myself a mental head-slap worthy of Leroy Jethro Gibbs.

"Tommy," I asked with a mixture of dread and anticipation, "what did your lawyer friend say about the taxes?"

"He said to call him with the appraisal, and we'd figure things out with Miss Mamie from there," Tommy said. "We have an appointment tomorrow at one. You're welcome to come."

"Any idea how you'd like to handle this?" I asked them both.

The Mame answered immediately. "Frankly, I'd rather split it up and get everything settled right away. Unless it's too costly. But it sure would be nice to have everything all settled."

"My instincts are the same," Tommy confessed. "But we'll have to see what the tax lawyer says." He focused on my worried frown. "Don't worry, Sissie-ma-noo-noo. We'll do this right. I have no intention of risking my serenity over money."

Thank You, Lord.

Then I realized we'd get to tithe the money, and a brilliant idea came to me. "Can we tithe to Connor's church?" I asked them.

Tommy laughed. "If we split this up, I'd like to donate my ten percent to AA."

Mama arched a brow. "And my tithe will go to our Methodist missionaries."

"Sounds like a plan to me," I said. I'd forgotten how good it felt to be able to *give* again.

Tommy handed Miss Mamie the stack of fifties. "Come on, Miss Mamie. Let's get this deposited into your account before the bank closes."

I glanced at the clock. It was already after five, but the branch in the Walmart was open till six.

My mother extracted three of the fifty-dollar bills from the stack, then handed them to me, folding my fingers over the money with a quick squeeze. "Here. Get a mani-pedi. Have your hair done. Go to a show with one of your friends. Anything that's just for you."

Things I used to take for granted when I was married to Phil, but never would again. "Thanks, Mama. I will."

Tommy put his arm around our mother's shoulders and shepherded her toward the door. "After we deposit the money, we can go by the Home and pay the bill so you won't have that hanging over you anymore."

The Mame hesitated, clearly still phobic about seeing Daddy locked in the Home. "I'll let you take it in, if you don't mind."

"Fine with me." Tommy opened the door for her. "Did I ever tell you how proud I am of how you've handled all of this with Daddy?"

She looked at him with bare-naked gratitude. "Only all the time. But I never get tired of hearing it."

Tommy shot me a wink, then closed the door behind them.

A day of miracles.

Content for the first time in a long time, I made sure the freezer door of my ancient fridge was closed tight so the remaining peach ice cream wouldn't melt, then brushed my teeth and went straight to bed.

The last thing I remember before falling into oblivion was the image of Connor in my mind, and how pleased he'd be when he got the news of my anonymous donation.

Happy. It made me very, very happy to think of it.

If only I could have stayed that way.

Thirty-five

Once we had all the facts, Miss Mamie decided to split everything three ways, pay the taxes up front, and go on with our lives. When Tommy and I told her that all the money was really hers, she hugged us and said she'd only use our shares if she must, to take care of Daddy.

Then we all agreed to order a new roof for the garage and house, and have the house insulated with formaldehyde-free foam. Thank goodness Daddy had replaced the plumbing with new cast iron and copper years ago, and redone the electrical with premium copper wiring and ample circuit breakers before he lost his marbles and the business, so at least those issues were addressed. Tommy planned to have the ductwork cleaned, then fitted with remote-controlled duct routers when we replaced the furnace and AC with high-efficiency models, so our childhood home would finally be comfortable and up-to-date.

Except for the windows. Those would have to wait. For all we knew, Daddy could live another decade, especially since we'd hired a strong, pretty young LPN to take care of him and Uncle B, much to their delight.

Before we knew it, the second Tuesday in October (our local election day) was only a few days away. Miss Mamie and I joined the volunteers calling voters and asking them to turn out for the election. We also asked who needed a ride, then made a list of those who did, to pass on to the volunteer drivers. Then we set up the victory party at our house, enlisting cakes and casseroles from Miss Mamie's prayer chain friends.

I got out the cloth buntings Daddy used to put up for the Fourth, then tacked them just below the railings of the verandah. Inside, I finished everything off with flags and red, white, and blue crepe paper streamers. And if I do say so myself, the place looked great.

Even if Tommy lost to that transplant woman, we'd still have a great party. Five guys from the Bluegrass Barn in Suwanee had volunteered to provide the music (on the porch).

When election day dawned cool and clear, Tommy and I both got to the kitchen early and made the coffee.

"So," I asked my brother after the caffeine had had time to soak in. "How do you feel?"

Tommy stretched, yawning, then said, "Actually, I feel fine. Either way it goes, I'm good."

I couldn't resist, "So what about this new woman in your life? Judging from the overnighters, you two must be getting serious. When are you going to tell us about her?"

Tommy's expression congealed. "In good time. I've had my plate full, and so has she. So we've agreed to keep our private business to ourselves."

I groaned in frustration. "Can't you just give me a little hint?"

Tommy smiled. "Telegraph, telephone, tell a Lin."

I frowned. "That is not true. I have kept all your confidences, even when you didn't keep mine."

Typically male, Tommy avoided answering by doing something totally unrelated. He got up and retrieved a carton of eggs from the fridge. "Scrambled or fried?"

Could he cook? I had no idea, because Miss Mamie always cooked for us.

Speaking of Miss Mamie . . . "Mama's never this late getting up," I said, a tingle of worry in my fingertips. "I think I'll go up and check on her."

Tommy nodded with a frown. "Good idea."

I took the back stairs, then approached Mama's bedroom door. Placing my ear against its oaken panel, I didn't hear a sound.

Nobody lives forever, an insidious inner voice hissed. *She's over ninety. Oh, shut up and leave me alone!* I shot back.

Gently, I turned the handle, not wanting to wake her if she was still sleeping. Then I slowly cracked the door open.

My mother was lying propped up against the pillows, her mouth wide open and a book across her chest.

I didn't see her breathing. Alarmed, I hurried over and touched her, which sent her bolt upright in alarm. "What? What happened?"

"Oh, Mama, I'm so sorry. I didn't mean to scare you. I just wanted to make sure you're okay."

She shook her head side to side to clear it, then patted my forearm. "I couldn't get to sleep till four this morning," she said, her voice hoarse, "praying for you and Tommy and the election."

I hugged her. "I'm sorry we worried you, but everything's going to be okay, I promise."

She narrowed her eyes at me. "Now how in the world can you be so sure of that?"

"Because no matter what happens, Tommy and I will be okay."

Her arched eyebrow betrayed her skepticism. "Um-hmm."

She started to get up, but I stopped her. "Why don't you stay in bed and rest. Tommy's making breakfast, and we'll bring you a tray."

Mama's eyes went wide. "Tommy, cooking?" She swung her legs off the bed. "Quick, hand me my slippers before he sets off the fire alarm."

She grabbed her robe from the foot of her bed and launched herself into action. "Go downstairs and stop him, whatever he's doing. I'll be there directly."

"Okay," I muttered, heading for the hall, where I detected the unpleasant smell of burned egg whites. That was enough to hitch up my get-along.

I arrived to a faint miasma by the stove. Tommy made a face, then turned over the frying pan he'd been using. The eggs didn't fall out. "Oops."

"That is so male," I scolded, taking the pan to the sink and running cold water in it. "Offer to do something, then do it so badly, somebody comes along and does it for you."

He smiled. "It worked, didn't it?"

Grrr. "In case you'd like to know, Mama didn't get to sleep till four, worrying about both of us. That's why she didn't wake at six."

We heard her coming down the back stairs.

"I can smell it," she announced. "Burned the eggs again, didn't you?"

She bustled in and gave each of us a peck. "At least you didn't set off the fire alarms," she told Tommy. "They'd have sent three companies, if you had. The fire inspector told me this place was a tinderbox just waiting for a spark."

Tommy showed genuine remorse. "Sorry, Miss Mamie. I just had it in my mind that I could at least make some eggs."

"Darlin'," she responded, "you have me for that. And if you don't have me, you have Lin. She's a great cook."

Consigned to the kitchen to cook for my brother? That was not my idea of a plan. "There's always the diner," I reminded him.

I heard the local paper hit the porch floor. "I'll get it."

Tommy's Gwinnett paper was there beside Miss Mamie's and my copies of the *Gainesville Times*. Maybe they'd put mine up front in honor of the election. I pulled it from its blue plastic sleeve, then opened it to see Tommy's photo beside Carla Simmons's taking up the top half of the page, and a condensed version of their platforms underneath. To my relief, Tommy's was accurate and compelling. And his opponent's, bless her heart, was rather fuzzy.

Still reading, I took them back to the kitchen and found breakfast well on its way, Mama humming happily at the stove and sipping on a cup of coffee in her left hand.

"You made the front page." I handed Tommy the first section and the sports, then his Gwinnett paper. Then I settled with my coffee to do the Jumble and the crossword in the Our Region section.

"Must have been a slow news day." Tommy read the front page, then turned to the end of the articles on the editorial page. "Miracle of miracles, they got most of it right."

Miss Mamie looked over. "What did they get wrong?"

"Just a few minor points. They mixed a few of the details from my platform with my opponent's, but at least it wasn't anything major." He picked up the Gwinnett paper. "It's a law, you know, that the media have to get something wrong in every story."

He turned the pages, then opened the slim second section. "We didn't even make the front page of the B section in Gwinnett. We're on page four. And they really scrambled the facts. But there's no time to do corrections, so there you are."

I would have been livid, but Tommy took it in stride. "No sense complaining. It'll only make them mad. If I'm meant to win, I will. Then, I'll need their support."

He had a point. Definitely not the hothead he used to be.

After we finished breakfast, we all put on our Sunday best to go to the polls. We voted nearby in the fire station by the elementary school, so we decided to walk and enjoy the cool morning.

People who knew us honked and waved as they passed, some shouting well wishes, which sent Miss Mamie and me out of our skins the first few times, but we got used to it well before halfway.

The rustle of dried-out poplars combined with the cool breeze to make it feel like fall, which usually lasted only a few weeks before the first Canadian Clipper brought raw weather ahead of it.

Enjoying the smooth new sidewalks, I took my time and didn't rush Miss Mamie, who seemed to be savoring every drop of Tommy's fame.

By the time we reached the campaign limit at the firehouse, the two of us sat down on the new metal bench on the sidewalk while Tommy shook some hands and greeted folks. I wondered if he knew them from AA, or something else. By the time Tommy came over to escort us inside, Mama and I were beginning to squirm on the cold, curved metal slats of the bench.

"This is it," he said.

"Will you be awfully disappointed if you don't win?" I asked, then realized how negative that sounded.

Tommy shook his head with a wry smile. "Frankly, I'd be relieved. But if this is the job for me, then I'll do it."

With that, the three of us went into the garage where the fire trucks usually resided. On election days, they were parked outside, and tables and voting booths took their places.

Once I showed my driver's license and filled out the form to get my plastic voting card, I took the first open booth and shoved the card into the machine, then selected my way to the mayor's race on the screen, the only choice besides a referendum about trash collection days.

There it was. Mayor's race. Thomas Breedlove on the left, Carla Simmons on the right, both independents.

I touched the screen beside Tommy's name, then went on to the referendum, which sounded reasonable to me, so I voted for that, too. Then I touched "completed," and the card popped back out.

Who in a million years would have guessed that my wayward brother, the drunk, would end up on a ballot, and I would gladly vote for him? I stood there, contemplating how momentous that was and how far he'd come, till someone came close behind me.

"Excuse me, please," she said nicely. "Are you having trouble with the machine?"

The polls worker. I snapped out of it, embarrassed. "No. It's just that I voted for my brother."

She nodded, leaning close to whisper. "So did I."

Then she pointed to the basket by one of Miss Mamie's friends from Women's Club who was handing out flag stickers with I VOTED on them. "You can put the card in that basket, then get your sticker."

If everything went the way it usually did, the results would be available well before the eleven o'clock news.

I dropped my card into the basket and proudly stuck on my sticker as I headed outside.

Miss Mamie came up behind me and took my arm just as I stepped into the sunlight. "What a glorious day," she said proudly. "I just voted for my son. How about that?"

I closed my hand over hers. "Tommy says he's fine whatever happens, but I want him to *win*."

Mama smiled. "Me, too."

Tommy caught up with us. "Okay, ladies. Let's get back home and have us a party."

No liquor would be served, but that wouldn't matter. We would have good friends and good food and music.

Thirty-six

By the time the polls closed at seven, the house was packed with a generous cross-section of our town.

Tommy held court out on the front porch, while Mama and I helped keep the food and iced tea coming.

Her friends had done themselves proud, bringing everything from fried corn to pole beans to chicken legs, barbecue, and pot roast. Plus desserts by the raft, from sugar-free to decadent.

I brought Tommy a fresh Diet Coke on the porch. "Where are Carla's people gathering?" I asked him between constituents.

"At the Presbyterian fellowship hall," he said.

"So what happens when the results come in?"

His brows lifted. "Either I'll go congratulate her, or she'll come congratulate me."

No nerves for this boy.

"Can I bring you a plate?" I offered.

He shook his head.

Well, maybe a little hint of nerves. Tommy rarely turned down food.

Then another of his friends came out to sit beside him, so I left them in peace.

I stood just inside the front door, listening to the bluegrass band tune up outside.

Four hours from closing till the results. I sure wished I had something more than food to distract me.

Be careful what you wish for.

Connor Allen walked up the front stairs, and I hightailed it for the kitchen.

Thirty-seven

I managed to avoid Connor till the news van arrived at ten and set up their lights on the verandah to tape Tommy's reaction to the final results.

Everyone gravitated toward the lights, crowding around to find out the results. Fortunately, Connor kept his distance.

Then a car drove in and parked behind the news trucks, and out came the election supervisor with a sealed envelope in his hand.

I watched him work his way through the crowd, then approach Tommy. All the TV lights flashed on, briefly blinding my brother. Everybody fell silent as the elections supervisor handed the envelope to Tommy. Then he saluted and wished my brother well before stepping out of camera range.

Tommy looked at the envelope, his lips rolled in, then looked to me. "Lin, would you please do the honors?"

Suddenly dry-mouthed, I hustled over and took the envelope. Blinking rapidly from the glaring lights, I turned to the crowd and opened the envelope. Then I unfolded the letter to see two names and two totals in the center. Somebody handed me a cordless mike and I read, " 'For the office of mayor of Mimosa Branch, Thomas Breedlove, fifteen thousand, seven hundred, and eight. Carla Simmons, twelve thousand, three hundred, and fifty-two.'"

The crowd exploded after they heard *twelve thousand*. Everybody hugged everybody else, the bluegrass band struck up a lively number, and I shared a proud look with my brother, the mayor, then handed him the mike.

Geneva came up and put her arm around me. "Told ya. God does some good picking, doesn't He?"

"With your help as his campaign manager," I said.

"I just put the icing on the cake." She beamed. "This was meant to be."

She turned so the cameras couldn't see her yell, "Speech! Speech!"

The little red lights atop the cameras lit up again.

My brother stood with a humble smile, then said, "I am so grateful to all of you who helped me get elected, vote by vote. Citizen by citizen, every one of you in Mimosa Branch deserves a *fair* administration—"

Applause and cheers erupted.

"A fiscally responsible administration," he said over the din, which just escalated the noise.

He ate the mike for a firm, "And an open, honest administration."

More cheers.

"Like we had with my beloved predecessor, Donnie West. So thank you all for entrusting our city to my care for the next five years. With God's help, I promise to live up to your trust." He dropped the mike and waved to the cheering crowd.

Then who should walk up but Carla Simmons, looking like a million bucks. A path cleared between her and Tommy, and we all watched in anticipation as she approached the victor.

With a genuine grin, she put out her hand, and Tommy took it. A chorus of "Shhhh!" and "Quiet!" calmed the crowd.

Carla Simmons didn't need a microphone. Her cultured voice projected to the back of the onlookers when she turned toward the camera lights and said, "Please accept my congratulations. And I'd hereby like to pledge my support for what I know will be a wonderful administration under Tommy Breedlove's leadership."

Then, to everyone's shock, she pulled Tommy over and kissed the daylights out of him just the way Connor had kissed me.

Laughter exploded, and it was all caught on camera.

His cheeks flaming, Tommy raised the microphone and said, "Well, I've always considered my business life and my personal life to be separate, and I'd thought we'd wait a while to announce this. But after what she just did, I think I'd better introduce y'all to my fiancée, Carla Simmons, who has agreed to marry me next June. Why she said yes, I couldn't begin to tell you, but I sure am glad."

The mystery girlfriend was his *opponent*? A CPA and lawyer?

Mama and I looked at each other with a mixture of happiness, worry, and shock.

The crowd went wild.

Loosely hugging Carla, Tommy tried not to blink when half the crowd lifted their cell phones for photos as a battery of media flash cameras went off.

"Isn't that illegal?" somebody hollered.

Carla fielded that one. "No, sir, it is not. We have thoroughly checked the statutes and regulations. Our personal lives never affected our political lives, and we both plan to keep it that way."

Tommy drew her toward the house, waving. "And with that, we'll bid you all good night."

Framed by the lights inside the screen door, Tommy kissed Carla back with steaming intensity, then they both laughed and headed for the den of iniquity to hide.

Abruptly, the lights went out and the camera crews loaded up their vans.

The party went on, but my mother and I headed for the relative quiet of the kitchen. Once there, she sank to a chair and started bawling.

"Mama?" I sat beside her, my hand on her back. "What's the matter?"

"Nothing," she wailed. "I'm just so *happy*. Tommy finally fell in love for real, and she's a *wonderful* woman." She wiped her nose with her lace-trimmed hanky. "I know, because I talked to her after several of the debates."

"That's *one* prayer answered," I soothed, fighting my own sense of emptiness that threatened to shadow my happiness for my brother.

The door from the back hall swung open, and Tommy brought a grinning Carla in. "Mama, we have something to ask you," he said gently, "if you don't mind."

Miss Mamie dried her tears with her sodden hanky, then straightened like a queen. "Of course I don't mind. And congratulations, Tommy."

Carla held back, suddenly shy, while Tommy seated her next to Miss Mamie, then joined her. He didn't mince words. "I was wondering if you would be okay with our moving in here after the wedding."

Mama's eyes widened, her mouth dropping open, but not in shock. "Okay? I'd be delighted." She beamed. "Thank you both so much. Thank you."

I gave myself a mental head slap. Of course! She'd thought Tommy would leave her when he married.

"Tell Miss Mamie what happened," Tommy urged his bride-to-be.

Carla leaned over. "I first saw this house when I was riding Amtrak on my way from D.C. to Atlanta for a meeting, and y'all waved to us from your verandah. It was magic, love at first sight, your house and your hospitality. Everything that my driven, workaholic life was not. So I found out about the town and started dreaming. And when I finally faced how miserable I was as a corporate financial lawyer, I sold my town house in D.C. and moved here."

Tommy hugged her shoulders, a proud smile on his face. "Tell them the rest."

"Every time I passed by, I wished I could live in this house. Then I ran into Tommy at an AA meeting and realized he'd been the one who'd waved to me."

Tommy regarded her with admiration. "Seventeen years, clean and sober. I fell for the way she worked her program before I fell for her." He smiled our way. "We have a lot more in common than you'd think."

Both in AA. That could be great or awful, depending. But for now, it was great.

Carla grinned. "I flirted with him all the time, but he never asked me out."

His plate was full taking care of our parents, but Tommy never complained.

"We really, truly love each other," he said. "I know our time together seems short, but there are no secrets between us, and we still love each other."

Carla nodded. "And *like* each other."

"What are your plans after the wedding?" I asked her.

"I'm going to do bookkeeping and a few tax returns part-time from home," she said.

Glory be! An in-house accountant. And an honest one.

Mama shook her head, opening her arms and gathering Carla to her. "Welcome to the family, precious girl."

After they'd hugged, Carla drew back. "I hear you're a fabulous cook. I can't even boil water; I've always been too busy to learn to cook. Tommy said you could teach me, if that's okay."

Perfect. It was perfect.

Mama could pass on the family recipes to an eager student, so she wouldn't be alone while I went to class and Tommy went to City Hall.

Miss Mamie leaned close to Carla to whisper, "Why don't you two go to the justice of the peace in Gainesville and get hitched right away? You don't have to tell anybody, so you can still have a church wedding. That way, you could move right in."

Carla's expression lit with a sparkle of mischief. "Couldn't I just come anyway?"

Uh-oh. Tommy's expression looked like he'd just stepped on a rattlesnake.

Miss Mamie didn't miss a beat. "Oh, no, precious girl. I refuse to let my son's bride sell herself so cheaply. You need a ring on that finger before you cohabit with my son in this house."

Carla looked to Tommy, her face asking what he thought.

He shrugged. "We could get the blood tests up there, I guess." He looked into Carla's eyes. "What do you think?"

"I think it makes perfect sense," she told him.

"But what about the big wedding?" he prodded.

Carla scanned the room, her expression clearing. "Obviously, your mother feels very strongly about this. So, as a gift to her, I have just decided that the most important thing is *being* married, not how we get there."

Bald lust limned my brother's face. "Tomorrow it is."

"Would y'all like to come?" Carla asked.

Perfect, perfect, perfect. "Yes!" Miss Mamie and I answered.

There's no such thing as perfect in this world, my still, small voice reminded me.

Okay, okay. But it's great enough.

So the next day, Miss Mamie and I stood witness as my brother married his true love. Halleluiah, amen.

Thirty-eight

Tommy and Carla pulled a fast one to complete the final item on our immediate plan for the house: while Carla took Miss Mamie down to Atlanta to the museum, then to the Swan Coach House for lunch, Tommy supervised a highly recommended cleaning service that gave the whole house a thorough going-over, right down to the grout and the refrigerator. In five hours, the place looked and smelled as good as it had after our big clean.

When the Mame and Carla got back that evening, my mother inhaled one breath after stepping inside, shot me a knowing glance, shifted a candy dish in the foyer a half inch, back into its original place, then proceeded as if nothing had happened.

So the four of us went back to our regular routines, me with my studies (I CLEPed out of seven English, lit, and history courses, but still struggled with the algebra textbook). Carla and Mama cleaned the kitchen and bathrooms every Wednesday, she and Tommy went to their meetings, and he and I visited Uncle B and Daddy at the Home.

You'd think I'd feel displaced by Carla, but I didn't. I was grateful, grateful, grateful for how she studied cooking with Miss Mamie and made my mother feel she had a purpose again.

Tommy told me later that he hadn't said anything about the nest egg to Carla, in case Miss Mamie needed our shares. When I asked him if that was wise, he shrugged.

"Do you think she's a gold digger?" I challenged.

"Of course not," he blustered. "She has more money than I'll earn in a lifetime. She retired at thirty-seven to come here. Showed me her entire portfolio and bank statements."

My brows lifted. "And you've kept this from her? Not a good start, Tommy. I'm just saying."

He nodded, clearly seeing how he'd messed up. "So what now?"

I couldn't believe he had to ask.

"Tell her the truth," I advised. "All of it. If you don't, it means you don't trust her."

He nodded. "You're right." He threw his arm around my neck and gave me a noogie. "I hereby appoint you my consultant on women. If you see me making a mistake, or getting ready to, please pull me aside in private and help me out."

Carte blanche? Surely he couldn't be serious.

But then again, he *was* a frog, not a prince. "You've got yourself a good woman," I told him. "Don't screw it up."

He sent me an ironic glance. "I could say the same to you."

I sighed. "I can't be a minister's wife. End of story."

Tommy grinned. "Talk to me about that in six months."

Then he went upstairs to join his wife in assassinating the headboard for yet another night.

Miss Mamie said it made her giggle every time, because they just might be making a grandchild—a possibility, since Carla was so much younger than Tommy.

But Mama already had a grandchild! What was my David, chopped liver? And the Mame's two great-grands.

Grumpy, I left the house for the apartment.

Maybe I ought to get a dildo, after all.

Thirty-nine

My newfound wealth made me ineligible for the Pell Grant, so I pre-paid my tuition, bought my books (talk about expensive, even for used!), and worked out my Tuesday–Thursday class schedule with Cathy at the disabilities office. Then I started studying algebra in earnest.

But even with that as a distraction—and quite a distraction it was—I still obsessed about Connor. Instead of rejoicing that an amazing man like him wanted me, I whined at God over and over: *Why did he have to be a Baptist minister?*

The more I whined, the more I admitted to myself that I did *not* want to be a Baptist minister's wife, any more than Connor's deacons wanted me to.

Not funny, God.

Yet I still looked forward to Christmas—and to Connor.

Unless he'd found someone else.

Blast! Blast, blast, blast.

Maybe going back to school would help me concentrate on something besides him. I've always loved learning and done well in class, but I'd been away from it for so long, my anticipation was laced with fear. Did I have enough gray cells left to pass?

Forget IQ. Could I still memorize and study?

If algebra was any indication, the answer was no. But I refused to give up and slogged my way through, page by page, even though it gave me headaches.

Christmas and Connor were coming. I longed for the day, yet dreaded it with equal intensity.

The next Sunday afternoon, my phone rang at precisely three o'clock. David, right on schedule, after more than a month without explanation.

"Hello?" I resolved not to bring it up. Focus on the present.

"Hi, Mama." He seemed chipper. "How about that, Uncle Tommy winning the election and getting married?"

"Things have been pretty exciting here, lately."

"Isn't Aunt Carla great? We talked for a really long time when they called to tell us."

Oh, great. He'd talked to Carla for a really long time. What about his mother?

"Mama? Are you there?"

"Yep. How are the kids?"

"Kids. You know. Runny noses, vaccinations, and plenty of energy. How are you?"

Tired. Conflicted about Connor. Feeling like a moron in algebra. Scared about school. But I knew better than to tell him the truth. He'd clam up emotionally and hang up.

"Mama?" This time, his voice was tinged with concern.

"Sorry. I'm just a little tired and down."

"You're not supposed to be the one who's down," he said. "You're the one who cheers everybody up."

"Not today, sweetie."

Now it was his turn to fall silent, but I let the silence be.

"I'm sorry I didn't call you for a while," he finally said. "We've been taking the kids to fall soccer and football games on Sundays."

So he *was* aware. "I figured no news was good news."

Never mind that I was afraid something had happened to one of you. Or how forsaken I felt when you didn't call. But I didn't give my self-pity a voice.

He was my son, my only child, and I loved him. *Expectations are premeditated resentments.*

So I took responsibility for my own happiness. "That's okay, honey, but I really miss hearing your voice and finding out what y'all are doing. Is there a more convenient time for you to call?"

I heard surprise in his voice when he said, "Actually, yes. How about Monday at nine, after we get the kids to bed?"

"Sure." I could do that. "I don't want to interfere with your life. I just want to be in the loop."

"Fair enough." He paused. "And Mama . . ."

No expectations, I reminded myself. "What, honey?"

"I'm proud of you."

My smile returned in earnest. "Thank you, sweetie. I love you."

"Love you. Talk to you at nine tomorrow."

"Great. Bye." I was still smiling when we hung up. I'd been honest (well, partially), but he hadn't run screaming into the woods. It was a start.

Wondering what he'd think about me and Connor, I couldn't suppress a dry chuckle.

Forty

Sooner than I would have guessed, Halloween arrived. Instead of trick-or-treating, First Baptist and several of the other churches had fall festivals, where the children could dress up as nonoccult objects, animals, or characters and play games for candy. I'd always enjoyed helping, but this time I didn't. I couldn't bear seeing Connor without touching or speaking to him.

The week after that crawled by. Then the next.

I kept checking my e-mail for word from school, but found nothing. By the week before Thanksgiving, I called Cathy in the disabilities office and found out they'd been sending all the e-mails to my student account on the college network.

The *student* account.

Perfect. Talk about feeling stupid. I'd completely forgotten about that. Giant head smack.

With her help, I finally got onto the school Web site (writing each step and my password down for future reference) and found my schedule and a slew of messages. It took me half a day to get through them, and I'd already missed orientation.

Not a good start.

Maybe I shouldn't have done this. At my age, half my brain was full, and the other half was dead.

But I persevered. (I am, above all things, stubborn by nature.) So the days of getting to know Carla, going to the Home, studying, and checking my *student* e-mails slipped into comforting routine.

Before I knew it, Thanksgiving arrived. As usual, David and Barb were spending it with her family in Charlotte, saying it was too hard on the kids to bring them to us.

So I felt even emptier without Connor, especially since Tommy and Carla were there, totally smitten with each other.

I wasn't jealous of them. I was glad to see them both so happy.

It just made me feel more alone than ever. I missed Connor so much, I almost cried.

Sensing my sadness as we all cleaned up after we finished, Tommy proposed, "Why don't we invite Connor to see the latest Shrek installment at the Imax this afternoon? Carla and I have enjoyed that series."

Was I that transparent?

Miss Mamie brightened. "I'd like to see that one, myself."

Carla had the good sense to butt out, for which I loved her even more.

Tempted though I was, I shook my head no. "Y'all can go without me."

"Okay. Martyr if you want to," Tommy said. "I'm asking him."

"Go right ahead," I told him. "I'm going to bed."

Mama scowled. "Suit yourself, Lin, but I'm going."

"Great," I said sincerely. "I hope y'all have a wonderful time." Before they could pressure me further, I wrapped my loneliness around myself and headed for the apartment. "Fabulous feast, ladies," I called back as I left the room. "It may take me two days to sleep it off."

Then I went home and martyred myself nonstop for two hours, one on the phone with Tricia, but to no avail.

Then David topped the day off by calling to tell me his company had given them and the kids a two-week Christmas cruise as a bonus. Great for them, rotten for me.

Forty-one

One day at a time, Tommy's words reminded me. *Be in the present. Stop projecting.*

I tried, and every time I tried, it got a little easier. But I kept reverting to my old ways.

Still, I took my schedule to the campus near the end of fall quarter in December and found my way (with much help) to all my classes. The biggest trek would be from my morning classes in the Humanities Building to the Science Building all the way across campus for algebra.

For once, I was glad my bad knees merited a handicapped parking permit, because there was always a free spot right beside Humanities. But walking across campus twice a day would be good for me, even if it hurt.

And unlike the students, who wore as little as possible regardless of the weather, I planned to dress warmly and use an umbrella. And drag my textbooks in a stout rolling briefcase behind me. So call me a nerd. So what? At sixty, I didn't give a rip.

Actually, I was no longer afraid of school. I looked forward to it, because that gave me something to be excited about besides Connor.

Forty-two

Early Christmas morning, I got up at six and put on my face and did my hair, just in case Connor showed up. Then the family met at the giant Christmas tree in the family room at seven. Miss Mamie never let anybody sleep late on Christmas.

We'd long since given up trying to buy each other presents. Instead, each of us picked out something we wanted that cost less than a hundred dollars, wrapped it up and put it under the tree, and donated an equal amount to our favorite good cause. On Christmas morning, we showed each other what we'd bought before we went in to breakfast. Worked for me.

Tommy got a little chain saw on the end of a long fiberglass pole, which would make trimming our ancient bushes a lot easier. (He always bought himself tools.)

Carla had bought herself a bunch of old Southern cookbooks, which Miss Mamie asked to look over after we'd eaten.

Miss Mamie opened a large Kindle *and* a Nook electronic reader, beaming as she did. When she saw our surprise, she went coy. "A girl's got to keep up with the times. I've already loaded both of them with Deborah

Smith, Patti Callahan Henry, and half a dozen more of my favorites." She hugged them to her. "I can't wait to try them."

She had definitely blown the price ceiling, but neither Tommy nor I pointed that out. Let her splurge. She deserved it.

Last in line, I started unwrapping my treat: a new makeup mirror with powerful LED SWAT-team lighting to help me get those nasty white whiskers on my upper lip and under my chin. Of course, I didn't share my reasons for needing a new one with the others.

Then we all went in and helped Miss Mamie finish her annual Christmas breakfast blowout: fresh biscuits, made-from-scratch blueberry pancakes, eggs, grits, country ham and redeye gravy, bacon, fresh ambrosia, homemade cinnamon rolls, and cherry turnovers.

By the time we all sat to eat and blessed it, my stomach was roaring, so I chowed down as if I hadn't eaten in a week.

"These biscuits are so tender and light," I complimented my mother.

Miss Mamie beamed at Carla. "I didn't make 'em. Carla did."

Obviously having heard about my notoriously bad biscuits, Carla had the good grace to look down and blush.

A tang of resentment tried to rise up, but I stomped it flat. "They're fabulous. Now I can give up trying and eat yours."

Then the doorbell rang, and Mama shot to her feet like a volunteer fireman answering the siren, a smug gleam in her eye. "I wonder who that could be?" She motioned us to stay seated. "Y'all keep eating," she said as she glided out of the room like Theda Bara in an ancient Broadway drama.

My heart suddenly beat fast. Connor? *Please, oh please, oh please. Let it be Connor.*

I knew he was off. Unless Christmas fell on Sunday, the Baptists canceled services.

Sure enough, there he came with Mama.

"Isn't this nice, now?" Miss Mamie gloated. "Look who's come a-calling."

Suddenly I was as awkward as a seventh-grade girl in ballroom dance class, waiting for a boy to take me onto the floor and terrified that no one would.

"Hi," I said, looking into Connor's gorgeous face with patent relief.

His answering *hi* was just as pregnant as mine with the unspoken things that had come between us, but then he grinned, and I basked in its warmth.

Miss Mamie brought him a place setting and laid it beside mine. "I was hoping you'd come, so I had this ready. Now, you dig in."

Connor regarded her with affection. "Wow. What a spread. Tommy, could you please pass me those sweet rolls?"

Tommy and Carla watched us like spectators in the final game at Wimbledon.

My hedonist whispered, *Man, could I sweet roll with him.*

Shut up, I countered, per Tommy's advice, but it didn't work.

Kiss, my inner wanton seduced, bringing back the hunger as if Connor had just pulled away from me that first time. *Oooh, kiss, kiss, kiss. Bodies. Bodies, bodies, bodies.*

"I've been thinking a lot since the summer," Connor told me, blessedly interrupting my downward spiral. "And praying."

His expression was very serious, so I braced myself.

"Maybe we shouldn't date too long before we get married," he said. "Would that be okay with you?"

My better instincts had disappeared with his arrival, so I barely managed to keep from suggesting we fly to Maryland, on the spot.

What was it he'd asked me? Oh, dating.

"The shorter the better," I said, breathless.

Tommy and Miss Mamie beamed at me in approval.

"Would y'all like to take in a matinee this afternoon?" Connor asked. "The latest *Star Trek* installment opens at one."

Miss Mamie smiled. "Y'all will have to go without me. I'll be getting Christmas dinner ready. Carla and Tommy can help me with that."

In on the conspiracy, Tommy nodded.

That left just Connor and me at the movies.

Miss Mamie nodded to Connor. "You'll join us for dinner, I hope."

"I can't think of anything I'd like better," he answered.

"Then I'll be expecting you both back by eight to eat turkey with candied cranberries and my homemade biscuit-and-cornbread dressing," Miss Mamie concluded.

Connor grinned. "Of course."

We settled in to breakfast while Connor filled us in on the work he was doing with the church and how an anonymous donation had allowed them to repair the spire and reroof the sanctuary.

He didn't look at me as he said it, but I had a strong sense he suspected the truth.

I did my best to remain calm, but colored up like a ripe summer tomato anyway, feeling the heat from my neckline up, cheeks throbbing.

Connor turned his attention to Miss Mamie. "I'm happy to see that you've been able to make some improvements lately, too."

Mama peered down her nose at him with a frosty smile. "Amazing, how everyone's business is everyone else's business in this town."

Not that any of us had thought for a second that word of our good fortune wouldn't get out.

Connor wasn't daunted. He turned to me. "I've met your new sitter at the Home. She's making things so much better for Mr. Breedlove and your uncle." Then he leaned in toward Miss Mamie. "I think they have a crush on her."

To my surprise, my mother broke out laughing, covering her mouth with her napkin as she let out a strangled, "Better her than me!"

The rest of us hooted with delight.

That began the best week of my life.

Connor and I went to the movie at the Imax, and we both loved it. On the way home, he told me that he'd prayed and prayed, and the Lord had shown him that we were made for each other. If I'd have him, he wanted to marry me, but I could take my time making up my mind.

The idea of being a preacher's wife still put me on the inhale, but who was I to wrestle with God? What if Connor was right?

So I let go and lived each wonderful day of that week with Connor to the fullest, my lust receding as I accepted our growing friendship and spiritual concurrence.

We told each other our life stories, his in the hand of God since college, and mine a series of missteps and corrections, but he didn't judge me. Instead, he comforted me and assured me of God's grace and mercy.

Never having been in a whole, healthy relationship, I drew closer and closer to him and the charismatic glow of God's spirit within him every day.

Not only did I love this man—yes, I finally admitted it—and lust after him, I liked him immensely and deeply respected his honesty and strong religious calling.

Then, two days before the New Year, we sat rocking in our coats on Miss Mamie's porch, the air perfumed by the waning aroma of live pine garland with sprays of magnolia leaves that festooned the railing as it had every Christmas since I was little.

After a long, comfortable lull, Connor drew his rocker closer and turned to ask me, "Would you come to our New Year's Eve prayer service with me? I'd really like for you to hear the message God has laid on my heart."

Gulp.

Message, schmessage. Time to pay the piper.

Soon. It was too soon.

I'd been so happy, just the two of us in our own little world. I knew I loved him, had loved him from that first day I saw him. But, as much as I wished we could go on in a vacuum indefinitely, I'd realized, deep down, that the time would come when the two of us would have to face his congregation, and all that came with it.

I sucked in a steadying breath, then let it out in a long, slow exhale that betrayed my fear. Still, I nodded, eyes downcast. "I guess it's time." In spite of my efforts to the contrary, my mouth trembled as tears sheeted onto my cheeks.

Connor got up and drew me to him for a comforting embrace. "There, there," he whispered, gently rocking me back and forth. "It's going to be all right. Just wait and see. It's all going to work out, I promise."

I relaxed into his arms, grateful beyond words for the strength and encouragement he offered.

Phil had never held me that way. Ever, even when we were courting. His touch came with an expectation of sex, and always had, and once he was satisfied, he drew back into his closed, tangential world, leaving me on the outside again.

This was so different. So healing, yet terrifying.

Why couldn't I just accept what came with Connor and face it together? I wanted to. But evil still deviled me with what-ifs.

For the second time in six months, Connor Allen kissed me, but this was a very different kiss. It came with no demands or expectations, and lingered only long enough to tighten the connection between us. Then he cupped my head and rocked me to him. "It's going to be all right."

Like every woman in the world, I needed to hear that. Not solutions. Not plans. Just the assurance of a good man that he would stand between me and whatever might hurt me, and make things right.

To my horror, I heard my voice wail into his shoulder, "Would you marry me?"

He laughed, then hugged me tighter. "Of course. When?"

The weighty baggage of my past dropped instantly from my shoulders. "Tonight?" I half joked.

I drew back to weigh his expression, and he stroked the tendrils away from my forehead, shaking his head in denial. "Not in secret. You're too special for that. I want to marry you in my church, for all to see. With plenty of notice, so everyone will know what a blessing God has sent me in you."

"I was thinking more of a justice of the peace in Ringgold," I blurted out, not sure whether it was the truth, or just an attempt to lighten things up.

Connor chuckled, the warm sound of it resonating through me, then reared back to look at me. "How about we make our plans over dinner at my house on New Year's Day? I'll provide the turnip greens and black-eyed peas."

I hated turnip greens, but didn't want to hurt his feelings. "That can be my reward for facing your congregation," I said, more serious than joking. "But only if you promise to be my first-foot on New Year's morning."

He frowned. "First foot?"

"It's an old Southern superstition, supposed to bring good luck if the first visitor of the new year who crosses the threshold is a man. Totally sexist, of course, but that's our heritage."

He drew me close for a deeper, more lingering kiss, gently wakening my libido, then pulled free. "I'd be glad to be your first-foot, even though I don't believe in superstitions," he promised, then started back to his house. He waved. "Remember, we're driving up to Lake Clare in the morning."

In the cold. But the drive up would be nice, and we planned to lunch at the Dillard House, where we'd be just another doting couple in the presence of strangers.

The next day, we had a wonderful time, as usual.

For the rest of the time leading up to the New Year's Eve service, I cherished every instant we were together, but finally on New Year's Eve, supper was over, and I dressed for church in my most conservative outfit, usually reserved for funerals.

I checked myself in the mirror. Waaay too dark and serious. Definitely not me.

Defiant, I changed into my favorite church outfit: black knit travel slacks, a white mock turtleneck, and my favorite red jacket, a find from the Goodwill. I tied a long, abstract silk scarf in red, white, and black around my waist as a sash, then looked at my reflection again.

Now, that was more like it. Take it or leave it, I loved bright colors, went to R-rated movies, talked too much, laughed too loud, and sometimes (well, maybe more than sometimes) stuck my foot in my mouth. But still and all, Connor loved me, and everything would be all right.

Uplifted by that hope, I put away the knowledge that everybody in town knew we were courting and had an opinion about it. I reminded myself that the only opinion that mattered was God's.

I put on my most comfortable Life Stride flats, got out the mink coat I'd hidden from the IRS, then set out, standing tall and proud despite my quaking fear underneath, and paving the sidewalk with prayers for grace and strength in the four blocks to First Baptist.

As I approached the church, I read the lighted marquee: WELCOME TO A NEW YEAR. WELCOME TO THE FREEDOM OF FORGIVENESS.

A tiny frisson of anticipation ran up my spine. Now, that was a lesson I'd like to hear.

I smiled warmly and took a bulletin when I was greeted, then strode confidently down to the first row and took the aisle seat on the left (usually reserved for the preacher's family), passing a visibly appalled Mary Lou Perkins. At least on the first row, I wouldn't have to see her or anyone else talking behind their hands about me. Then I laid my coat across the back of the seat beside me, which was cause enough for trouble all by itself.

Putting on airs.

It seemed like eons before the church filled and Connor took the dais, granting me a reassuring grin, but I felt as if I were leaning against a glacier of condemnation from the pews behind me.

Talk about being egocentric. Here I was in church to welcome a new year, and all I could think about was what the people behind me were thinking about *me*.

This was why I could never be a selfless preacher's wife.

God, I'm sorry, really I am. I'm trying to focus, but I have this brain You gave me, and it won't shut up. Please help me focus on You.

Forty-three

Nice try, but my prayer didn't work. By then, I felt like I was sitting there buck naked. I'd dreaded this moment since the minute I'd found out what Connor did for a living.

Unexpectedly, the still, small voice inside me responded with, *So you're human. Just relax and listen.*

I looked up to see Connor quiet the murmuring in the pews by throwing wide his hands and projecting his warm baritone to the very back of the church. "Welcome to a new year in the community of Christ! Welcome to forgiveness, and the precious gifts it brings!" His words radiated joy and affection.

I'd known he had to be a dynamic preacher to have pastored such a huge church before he came here, but seeing him speak in person was more than impressive. Unlike his predecessor, there was no judgment in his presence, no condemnation.

So I sat back and listened, my inner voices silenced at last.

The choir director led us in "Amazing Grace" (my favorite), then we sat back down and Connor finally gripped the pulpit to speak. "Please open your Bibles to the sixth chapter of the Gospel of Matthew, beginning with verse five. These teachings are part of Jesus' famous Sermon on the Mount. In verses five through fifteen, Jesus teaches us how to pray and reveals an amazing source of power and unity for all of us who live in him. First, he cautions us not to repeat ritualized prayers in public, because they're just empty words."

He spoke simply, like a best friend over coffee, but with the confirmation of scripture.

"The clear message here," he went on with gentle authority, "is that prayer should be a private, intimate thing between a person and Jehovah God, not an empty recital before others. Even so, Jesus then gives us a model prayer, which we call the Lord's Prayer."

He paused, smiling softly but with sorrow in his eyes. "The sad thing is, we've probably said it so often that it, too, has become a vain repetition. Tonight, I'd like to challenge each of you, as we welcome the beginning of a new year of grace, to repeat the Lord's Prayer with me, this time thinking about the meaning of each passage and how it applies specifically to each of us, individually, and our relationship with God and the other members of this church."

He stepped from behind the pulpit and moved to the front of the platform. "What standards does it set for us? What comes first? Does one part matter more than the others?" He paused. "Are there any conditions that apply to us as Christians?" He returned to the large open Bible on the pulpit. "Think about those questions as we bow our heads and say together, 'Our Father who art in heaven—'" The congregation joined in with a low swell of voices as we recited the prayer together, but when he got to the part about forgiveness, Connor's voice rose with emphasis. "'And forgive us our sins'"—he slowed, pronouncing each word deliberately—"'as we forgive those who sin against us. And lead us not into temptation, but deliver us from evil. For Yours is the kingdom and the power and the glory, forever. Amen.'

"Please be seated. Thank you," Connor said as we all settled back into the padded pews. "But we shouldn't quit there, because after Jesus finishes showing us how to pray, He goes on to say, 'For if you forgive those who sin against you, your heavenly Father will also forgive you. But if you don't forgive those people their sins, your Father will not forgive your sins.'"

Connor's brows lifted in awe. "Wow. Does that mean we're not saved?"

I could feel the question hovering among us.

"No. For we believe that we are sealed by the Holy Spirit till the final day of redemption. But if I'm washed clean tonight, does that mean I won't get dirty the next day?" He smiled and shook his head. "Of course I'll get dirty, because I'm not perfect. I'm human, just like all of us here. That was the whole point of the Sermon on the Mount, to show Israel, and us, that we *cannot* keep the law of God. Jesus was showing why He came, and why He willingly gave His life for us, so we can be forgiven."

Connor closed the Bible and came to the edge of the platform to face us directly. "We're still human. We make mistakes, willingly and without even knowing."

He lifted his eyes toward heaven. "Forgiveness. That is our gift from God in Christ. But once we become His people, we are called to forgive those who hurt us. Not with resentment, but with *agapeo,* the unqualified love God showed us in the person of Jesus. And if we don't?"

He scanned the faces of his people with sympathy. "In the sixth chapter of his letter to the Ephesians, Saint Paul doesn't mince words. 'Do not grieve the Holy Spirit of God who seals you for the day of redemption. Get rid of all bitterness, rage, and anger.'"

Connor sucked in a breath, then let out a soft, low whistle. "*Some* of the bitterness and anger?" He shook his head in denial, then resumed quoting from memory. "'*All* bitterness, rage, and anger, brawling and slander, along with every form of malice. Be kind and compassionate to one another, forgiving each other just as Christ forgave you.'"

He tucked his chin. "Wow. First, Jesus tells us that as long as we are here on earth, *we* set the standard of our own forgiveness by forgiving others. If we don't, it puts a barrier between us and the power of the Holy Spirit to heal and forgive. God doesn't put the barrier there. We do."

The congregation was absolutely silent. Not so much as a wiggle or a cry from a fretting child.

"I don't know why it took me so long to understand the full importance of this concept," Connor admitted, "but I had to share it with all of you. Like so many of God's instructions, it goes against everything the world teaches us, but it works. It goes against our feelings. Our pride. Our excuses. But it works."

Connor spoke with authority. "I'd like to ask you all to put this key concept of our faith to work now by doing a very important exercise with me. First, please close your eyes."

I did, but could have bet that a lot of those behind me wouldn't, especially Mary Lou Perkins.

"Now," Connor intoned, "I'd like you to think of someone you resent—with or without reason."

Mary Lou Perkins came to mind. I'd forgiven Grant and Phil years ago, even though the feelings weren't there yet.

He paused again. "Now, I want you to mentally tell that person off."

Another pause, in which I envisioned Mary Lou Perkins scolding me before the whole congregation, to which I counterattacked, exposing her two-faced, destructive gossip and the trail of victims she'd left behind.

"Whose voice do you hear in your own condemnation of another?" he asked with compassion. "The father who told you you'd never amount to anything? The husband or wife who constantly criticizes? The mother who tried to scare you away from sin with dire predictions and put-downs?"

My voices were many. Miss Mamie, verbally brawling with Daddy; all my so-called friends in Buckhead who'd disappeared along with my ex. My son, who didn't want to talk to me.

Connor asked, "Now I want you to forgive the one who put that pain or criticism into your heart. You may not feel it at first, but feelings aren't facts. Make your forgiveness an act of sacrifice in obedience to God, and keep on forgiving. One day, you'll have the feelings to go with it."

He leaned back, eyes sparkling, with that irresistible grin. "My challenge to you for the new year is to practice forgiving those who have hurt you or your family. I dare you."

Then the warmth returned to his voice. "Will it be easy? Not if you've hidden resentments in your heart for a long time. Will it feel good? It may not feel anything but awkward and insincere at first. But every time you will it and speak it and pray it into being, your soul will grow stronger. And one day when you speak or pray your specific forgiveness, your heart and emotions will finally get on board.

"We have been forgiven, but as we live this life, we can put barriers between us and God, slowing the flow of His healing forgiveness." He paused for effect. "God doesn't put the barriers there, we do. Look at verse twelve. If we fail to forgive, our resentment becomes a barrier to God's ongoing forgiveness."

Connor paced briefly behind the pulpit, wringing his hands, then returned like a man facing sentence in a courtroom. "It took me a long time to forgive my wife for leaving me, but when God finally opened my eyes to how my own shortcomings had helped destroy my marriage, I started speaking forgiveness for her every time she came to mind. For a long time, my emotions didn't go along. But then, one day, I finally felt that forgiveness in my heart."

Light and joy suffused him. "And guess what happened? I finally began to be free from that awful experience. I still struggle to forgive myself for how I took her for granted, but that's a part of the process, too. I failed. I made destructive decisions, using God's kingdom as an excuse. So, since my divorce, I have begun and ended every day praying for my ex-wife's happiness and forgiving her, along with everyone in my life who causes me pain, because that is the model of grace that Christ teaches."

Dead silence.

I'd done that with Phil and Grant, but still the feelings hadn't come.

As if he'd read my mind, Connor said, "I'm not asking you to forgive and forget. That's not in the Bible. We can't erase the things and people who have hurt us. But we can make a deliberate sacrifice of forgiveness for each and every one of the people who despitefully use us. Love our enemies, Jesus tells us. The ones who don't deserve our pity. The ones who scarred our souls and hearts, who trampled on our dreams. And when we do that, what happens?"

He scanned the waiting faces, earnest, then stepped back, erect, arms spread. "We are set free. *We* are set free. The power of the Holy Spirit flows strong again in our lives. Forgiveness doesn't erase the past; it releases us from hurt and anger, the enemies of peace."

I could sense the congregation's swell of approval.

"But there's more good news for us as a body of believers!" Connor declared. "If we practice forgiveness, first in our families, then with our congregation, then with the world, our lives become witnesses of grace for all to see."

He exhaled slowly, then resumed. "The Bible tells us that we, the church, the bride of Christ, will be known by the love—the unconditional love that we see in Christ for each of us—we show to one another."

True, but I'd seen precious little of that in Mimosa Branch in the past ten years. Of course, I hadn't been focusing on the good people at church, only the ones who judged me. What's wrong with this picture?

Connor shifted the subject. "So then, I ask you, what happens when someone in our church fails, commits a sin, then repents. Are we supposed to judge them?"

Bingo.

Oh, Lord, please don't let him use me as an example. I'd croak of mortification.

"The scriptures tell us that there's a process for dealing with someone who continues to sin, even in the face of counseling from his or her brothers and sisters in faith. But that's not what I'm talking about. I'm talking about a fellow believer who messes up, sometimes royally, but sees the error of his or her ways and repents, turning back to God. How are we to respond?" He cupped his ear and leaned toward the congregation. "Anyone?"

I sat mum, waiting to see what happened.

"Forgive them," Ed Lumpkin's familiar voice grudgingly admitted.

Connor feigned confusion. "Did he say talk about them behind their back?"

An uneasy chuckle spattered the congregation.

Connor leaned in, ear cupped again. "Did he say, judge and criticize them?"

An unwed teen mother stood defiantly to her feet, baby in arms, and called out, "No. The Bible says the church should forgive them, then rejoice and welcome them back into the fellowship."

Connor brightened, pointing to her. "That's what I'm talking about. Thank you, good lady."

Her back still stiff, the girl subsided to the pew.

Connor addressed the congregation again. "So forgiveness and love without condition is our gift from God, and we are called as believers to extend that same love and forgiveness to each other. First in our families. Next, in our church. And then, to the world around us."

The truth hung like a golden haze in the air around Connor. This was no run-of-the-mill minister; he truly was a holy man.

Awed and repelled in equal measure, I finally admitted to myself that I deeply, truly wasn't cut out to be the wife of a holy man. I'd be a constant disappointment to everyone around him.

Connor's tone shifted to one of wonder when he said, "What do you think would happen if we obeyed this teaching?" He smiled.

The question was rhetorical, because he picked up immediately with, "For one thing, we'd be free of that anger and resentment. Free of judging others. Free to live in joy, in spite of the circumstances."

He waited, then proposed, "Will you join me in making forgiveness our word for this coming year?"

Connor motioned to the carpeted steps leading up to the platform where most preachers called people forth to kneel in penitence. "I'm not asking you to do this publicly, but intimately, between you and God. In your heart. In your bed before you go to sleep, and before you rise. As you go about your way. God will help you."

I could sense a fresh commitment welling up from Connor's people.

"But there's another side of this," Connor said. "The Bible tells us that when we go to make a sacrifice, and *anyone* has *anything* against us, we are to go make peace with them. It doesn't say when we are guilty. It says to make peace, no matter what. So we are called to apologize for our own part in ill will. That doesn't mean we trot out our excuses and rationalizations. It means we say we're sorry and ask for forgiveness."

Me, apologize to *Mary Lou Perkins* and ask for peace between us?

Connor paced the dais, scanning the faces of his congregation. "Is there anyone here you'd like to ask for forgiveness?"

I turned and looked to Mary Lou, whose face was in her hands, and I realized that I'd been every bit as judgmental of her as she had been of me.

I bowed my head. *Please, Lord, erase the bad feelings and my own judgmentalness. Help me to see what you see in every single person I meet.*

Then my prayer was interrupted by a soft touch on my shoulder. I looked up to see Mary Lou standing beside me, tears covering her cheeks. "When I thought of you and my fears for Connor," she said as she sat beside me. "I heard my mother's voice, scolding, telling me I had to be perfect, and punishing me when I wasn't."

Her mouth trembled. "And then I realized that I've been doing the same thing. Judging you for things long past." She grasped my hands. "I don't want to be my mother. It's only made me angry and sad. I'm so sorry for how I judged you. Can you forgive me?"

"Only if you can forgive me for doing the same thing to you." I leaned closer. "Can there be peace between us, no matter what happens?"

She sighed, a small smile on her lips. "Peace. I'd love that." Then she added, "My mother never had a day's peace till she died. She was too busy criticizing everybody else to look at herself. I don't want to be like that anymore."

I couldn't help hugging her, and the contact sealed the bond of forgiveness between us.

When I looked back to the congregation, I saw Christian brother approach brother, sister approach sister, and wives and husbands meet in a cleansing ritual of reconciliation that lasted for almost fifteen minutes.

Surely, the Spirit of God was in that place.

Mary Lou gave me a parting squeeze, then headed back to her seat.

When all of them had returned to their seats, Connor beamed. "I am *so* proud of you. More important, *God* is proud of you. Forgiveness brings unity to the body, despite our differences, and frees the Holy Spirit to work among us and through us. Give yourselves a hand in praise."

Applause broke out everywhere, swelled to a wave of release, then subsided.

"For all of you, I plead, practice forgiveness, for your own sake, if nothing else," Connor urged softly. "Test God. I can promise you, He will not fail to help you. Learn to forgive, and be free. When you feel yourself being drawn back into those old, angry ways, fill that dark place with joy and light instead. It's up to you."

After a protracted silence, Connor bowed his head and asked, "Brother Lumpkin, will you dismiss us in prayer?"

Ed rattled off his usual closing prayer, but as he reached the end, he faltered, then went off script with a broken, "And Lord, help us all to forgive. The anger feels too heavy in my heart, and I want to be free." He regained his composure. "And now, let us go into the world as beacons of love and light. Amen."

I picked up my coat, then turned to face the congregation as a positive rumble of conversation rose among them. Many were wiping tears from their eyes. Even more headed straight for Connor, surrounding him, but every few seconds, his eyes searched for mine, asking if he'd done well.

I nodded. All too well.

This was bad. Very bad. I lusted after a holy man. A man I now revered. What was I supposed to do with that?

Shrugging into my coat, I quietly made my way to the side exit and escaped.

I had to think. And maybe drink.

I'm sorry, God, but this requires ice cream. And brandy.

Forty-four

Mama and Tommy and Carla were still at the AA social when I got home, so I served myself up a big bowl of frozen and liquid therapy, then bundled up with a warm quilt over my fur coat on the second rocker on the porch. It seemed like a long time before Connor's car approached from the left, then pulled into his driveway, but it was probably less than half an hour.

What would I say to him? I couldn't even think straight, much less figure all this out.

But I heard his footsteps on the gravel, then made out his silhouette as he approached.

He didn't say anything. Just took the chair beside me and began to rock.

We'd planned to watch in the new year at Miss Mamie's, but I suddenly felt too weary to rise.

I forgive You, God, for putting me in the middle of this. But I don't know what You want me to do. I can't figure it out. Help.

Be careful what you pray for.

At last, when I'd finished the whole bowl of peach ice cream, I set it aside and tried to speak, but my tongue was frozen, so I came out sounding like I was totally snockered, which in this case was an exaggeration. "You were a true pipeline from God in that pulpit."

"That's my goal," he said quietly.

"It scares me to death," I confessed, unexpected tears escaping. I swiped them away, knowing that my mascara probably made me look like a raccoon.

Connor didn't try to get closer. He just gave me my space, asking a simple, pregnant, "Why?"

"Because you're a holy man," I accused, propelled by residual anger at God despite my efforts to forgive Him for doing this to me.

Connor shook his head, gripping the wide, white arms of the chair. "I'm just a man who loves God and was called to preach. No more, no less. I fart under the sheet, just like everybody else."

The uncharacteristically coarse comment made me laugh in spite of myself, but it came out truncated from my tear-swollen nose and sinuses. Then I sobered, letting out a long sigh. "How can you be so sure that I'm the one God wants for you?"

"I just know. I've prayed about it, and I know."

"Well, I sure wish He had told me." Too tired to discuss it anymore, I gathered Mama's quilt around me and managed to find my feet. "And on that note, let us retire to the family room to watch the big ball drop in Times Square."

At last, he circled my shoulders with one arm and led me inside. "Big ball, it is," he said with affection.

Do not go there, my inner Puritan scolded from the closet I'd locked her in.

I turned to look up into his face. "Happy New Year, Connor," I said with a blast of brandy breath. "God help me, I love you beyond all sanity."

He continued guiding me to the family room beyond the kitchen. "I love you, too. All of you, just the way you are."

The liquor spoke before I could intervene. "I wish I could say the same. You scare me, you holy man, you."

Connor chuckled and recited, "'For our God hath not given us a spirit of fear, but of power, and of love, and of a sound mind.'"

A ridiculous giggle escaped me as I plopped onto the sofa facing our new big-screen TV. "Second Timothy one, verse seven," I cited. "I used to claim that verse every day after my divorce, for the fear. Now I claim it for the sound mind, but I'm not convinced it's working." Another giggle escaped.

Connor sat beside me, then picked up the remote and turned on the TV.

Chilled from the inside out and outside in, I shivered, curling tighter in the quilt as I laid my head on his thigh to watch.

I sighed, content to be just as we were, in the moment. "Fabulous sermon. Need to hear that one every week."

"We recorded it on CD. I'll bring it to you first thing in the morning."

"Mmmm." I closed my eyes. So cozy. Wish we could stay that way forever. "First-foot," I mumbled as the world began to fade away.

Connor bent to kiss my hair. "First-foot."

"I forgive Phil," I murmured. "I do. I really do. And Mary Lou."

The next thing I knew, it was morning, a sunny, unseasonably warm New Year's Day, and I was still laid out on the sofa, but Connor was gone. The strong aroma of coffee drew my eyes to my brother as he approached.

He put the steaming cup on the coffee table. "Happy New Year, Sissie-ma-noo-noo."

I sat up, catching a glimpse of myself in the mirror across the room, and hooted. My hair was slabbed up on one side, my eyes ringed with tear-smudged mascara. Tears had erased tracks of my foundation and blush, so my cheeks were striped, and I had no lips.

Dear heaven, did I look this way when Connor was there? *Please, please, no.*

Instead of teasing me, Tommy frowned in concern. "We found you here alone when we got back last night. Is everything okay?"

"Connor wasn't here?" Alone with a drunken me, my head on his thigh.

Miss Mamie stopped rattling pots in the kitchen, eavesdropping, no doubt.

"Nope," Tommy said.

"'Abstain from the appearance of evil,'" I quoted. "First Thessalonians, five, twenty-two." I never cared much for that one, but Connor couldn't afford to ignore it.

I stretched, then swung my legs to the floor, raking at my hair. "He must have left when I fell asleep."

"I smell you had help going to sleep," Tommy observed. "Is this becoming your knee-jerk reaction to stress? I'm starting to get worried."

"No," I lied deliberately. If I had married Connor, I would have given up alcohol altogether for his sake, but not till then.

I put my palm in front of my nose and exhaled a sour gust of death-breath, still tainted by the odor of peaches and stale brandy. "Gross."

I stood. "Gotta run get a shower and brush my teeth before Connor's our first-foot."

Speak of the devil, the doorbell chimed "Auld Lang Syne."

Shoot! "What time is it?"

Tommy cocked his head. "About ten."

Shoot, shoot, shoot! "Why didn't y'all wake me sooner?" I headed for the basement stairs, snatching one of Miss Mamie's Hermès scarves from the hooks by the basement door. I tied it over my hair, then ran down the stairs to escape. "I'll be back as soon as I'm human." I safely escaped out the back while he came in the front.

Forty-five

Twenty minutes later, I entered the kitchen in jeans and a pink cotton sweater, my damp curls caught up with combs on either side, and my face as natural as I dared. (Eye makeup, concealer, lipstick, and bronzer.)

Miss Mamie surveyed me with approval, as did Connor, who immediately stood and pulled back the chair beside him. "Wow." The compliment was soft, but more than sufficient.

"Hi, Connor" came out with surprising calm.

Blind horny despite my sensible self's escalating warnings, I sat beside him. As it had since the beginning, attraction pulsed between us like a quasar.

Connor's smile strained a bit; he shifted in his seat and looked away. "Ah, could you please pass me the muffins, Miss Mamie?"

Obviously, this was mutual.

Smug, my mother handed him the basket, then the butter. "Take as many as you like, young man. I think of you as part of the family."

Can we say, obvious?

Minister, I scolded myself. *Holy man, holy man, holy man.*

It didn't do any good.

Tommy glanced at me and murmured, "One day at a time."

My churning emotions grabbed hold of that. Just think of now. Be here. Be grateful.

I started mentally reciting my blessings: my relationship with God, my warm bed, my apartment, Tommy and Carla, Miss Mamie, Daddy, even as he was, poor Uncle B, David and his family. The Home, my car, gas in the tank. The cash and Krugerrands. Very grateful for those. Hot baths. Good health.

As I went on, the intensity of my attraction eased, but only a little.

"Lin, honey, are you okay?" Miss Mamie's voice intruded. "Aren't you going to eat?"

I lurched back to reality, the table coming into focus to reveal that all four of them were peering at me in concern. Embarrassment throbbed in my neck and face. "Sorry. Just spaced out for a second. Food. Yes. Please pass the muffins."

I took a sip of the coffee Mama had served me. Perfect. Half-strength, with Splenda. Had to have that caffeine.

Connor's expression brightened. "Miss Mamie," he said with deference, "I'd like your permission to court your daughter with the intention of marriage."

Mama snorted, shooting him a surprisingly sharp look. "My daughter, sir, is a sixty-year-old woman, in case you hadn't noticed. If you want to marry her, quit beating around the bush and *ask* her, for heaven's sake."

Connor tucked his chin. "I stand corrected." Then he turned to me. "Will you still let me court you?"

Wrong question.

Say no! No! my inner Puritan pleaded. *Do not do this!*

"Yes," came out, instead, in unison with my brother and mother.

"But just to make sure we're right for each other," I qualified. "In God's eyes, not our own."

Connor nodded with assurance. "Of course."

Tommy and Mama leaned back in relief.

But I still couldn't stomach the idea of being a minister's wife. I'd spent a lot of years twelve-stepping myself into somebody I liked, and I couldn't turn my back on her. People had certain expectations of ministers' wives, especially Baptists, and I didn't fit the bill.

Still, I couldn't resist Connor, so I was willing to take this one day at a time.

Connor nodded, then asked, "There's a new *Star Wars* movie at the mall. Would you like to see a matinee?"

Just for today. "Sure."

Connor brightened. "It's a date." Happy, he dug back into the pile of grits, bacon, scalloped apples, and fried eggs on his plate.

Just for today, I could enjoy his company and go to the movie we'd both been looking forward to. Be in the moment. Take what comes. Stop beating myself up.

I sighed, letting loose of the mental melee that had been going on inside me since Connor had declared himself. Just for today, I could savor Mama's muffin with my coffee while I watched him eat.

Like my mother and grandmothers before me, I loved to see a man enjoy his food.

Truly content for the first time in a long time, I relaxed and put it all in God's hands.

Just for today.

Then the doorbell rang again, and what was on the other side made me take everything back.

Forty-six

"Y'all go on," Tommy said as he rose. "I'll get it."

Probably one of Mama's friends come a-calling. For years, they'd swapped homemade treats on New Year's. Mama rose, untying her apron, then checked her hair in her mirrored reflection on a glass cabinet door.

But the low voices that filtered back through the kitchen door didn't sound like Mama's friends.

When more time passed, Miss Mamie started for the door to see what was up, but just as she approached it, the paneled oak swung in on her, revealing a red-faced, steaming Tommy.

"Tommy, what's wrong?" Carla asked as he steadied the Mame.

"Here, Mama." He drew Miss Mamie back to her seat. "Lin's got company. Why don't we all keep Connor entertained till she's back." He glared at me. "Very quickly, I would hope."

Connor's gaze darted from one of us to the other, then settled on me. "Go ahead, Lin. I'll be here when you're done."

Tommy rolled his eyes. "Let's hope so."

Wary, I got up and headed for the foyer. As I approached, I made out a suit-clad man looking out the front window, his figure silhouetted by the sun, a huge bouquet of flowers wrapped in pink paper tucked into his arm.

Then he turned and spoke, and I almost keeled over. "Hi, Lin. It's me. I've come to apologize and beg you to take me back."

"Phil?"

No! Not now! Not today. Not ever!

My wayward ex approached me, proffering what I could now see were red tulips, my very favorite. Until that moment.

"I had a conversion," Phil said. "I'm not the man I was. And I want you to take me back."

God had just dropped the A-bomb.

I faced Phil, my doubts about Connor evaporating as if they'd never existed. The two men didn't even function in the same dimension.

"Let me be the man you deserve," he said with clear sincerity. "We made a vow to God that I broke, but I want to make it right."

He'd never humbled himself for anyone, let alone me, yet there he was. I stood there, wanting to run, wanting to scream. But the husband of my youth had just come back, supposedly transformed, and asking my forgiveness.

Where was my forgiveness now? All I felt was panic and anger. "What about your mistress?" the worst in me spat out. "How does *she* feel about this?"

Phil's mouth tightened into a line, then he told me, "She left me. That was part of my conversion. When that happened, I finally understood what I'd done to you."

Because his *mistress* had dumped him? Please!

Outrage exploded inside me and I felt my expression harden with rage. Conversion, hah! A snake is a snake is a snake. "Get out."

"Please give me a chance to make it up to you," he kept on pleading. "To be the man you deserve. Lin, you were the best thing that ever happened to me, but I was an idiot and took it all for granted. I threw us away with both hands."

"Along with all our money, and then some," I retorted. "Leaving me destitute."

"You have every right to hate me," he said with convincing contrition. "If I could take it all back, I would, but that's not possible. But I swear, I'm not the man I was. I've been changed, and I want you back more than anything. Please give me a chance to show you." Tears welled in his eyes. "I'm the husband of your youth. We belong together."

No! No, no, no! God, how can You let this happen? You know I love Connor.

My inner Puritan whispered, *But weren't willing to take on what comes with him.*

Was that what this was about? Penance, because I didn't want to be a holy man's wife?

Cruel. Cruel, cruel, cruel.

Phil dropped to his knees before me. "I beg you, Lin. Give me another chance. Just a chance to prove myself."

He'd already done that. Dumped by his mistress, indeed.

"I'm seeing someone," I heard my voice mince out.

Clearly astounded, Phil scrambled to his feet. "Really? Who?"

Once again, he revealed himself. Shocked that anybody would want to date *me.*

"If you must know, he's a Baptist minister."

Phil actually laughed, just as I would have if anybody had said I'd date a Baptist minister before I'd met Connor. "And he doesn't care that you're divorced?" Phil challenged, showing his stripes.

"No." I didn't want to elaborate, but my compulsion to justify myself kept talking. "He's divorced, too."

Phil shook his head. "Goodness. The Baptists have changed."

Then, as if he were slipping a mask back on, he went humble again. "What's his name? I'd like to talk to him, if that's okay."

"His name is Connor," Miss Mamie's voice declared from the dining room.

Traitor! "Miss Mamie!" Why in heaven's name was she butting in? "This is a private conversation!" Alas, no more.

"Where does this Connor live?" Phil pried, a spark of the old darkness in his eyes.

"Next door," Miss Mamie called back, accompanied by the sound of a scuffle. Tommy, no doubt, trying to drag her back into the kitchen. Fainter than before, she sent one final parting shot. "He's in the kitchen!" The last word was muffled midway.

"So he's here." Phil started stepping backward into the dining room. "Why don't we see what he has to say about this?"

The last thing in this God's green earth I wanted was a confrontation between my ex-husband and the man I loved. Especially with Phil claiming to have been converted—noticeably without mentioning Jesus.

"Lin," he said as he backed toward the door, "I broke our vows, but I want to make it right."

Before he reached the door, it swung open and Tommy shoved Connor out of the kitchen.

Connor recovered his dignity while Phil looked him over like a hungry lion spotting a lame gazelle. He stuck out his hand, taking Connor's, then clasping Connor's forearm as they shook, a clear dominance gesture. "So you're Connor," he purred. "I'm Lin's husband, Phil."

"Ex-husband," I corrected, my arms still filled with tulips.

Visibly shaken, Connor looked to me. "What's this all about, Lin?"

Phil answered before I could. "I've been converted, seen the light," Phil declared, "and I want to make it up to Lin. She's the wife of my youth, and I want to marry her again, but this time, as the husband God wants me to be."

Connor went deadly still.

I rushed over to take his hand. "I explained to Phil that we're seeing each other."

Connor's hand was cold as ice in my warm one, but he returned my grip with equal strength, binding us together. Then he let go and stepped back.

No! No.

I didn't know which was worse, having to deal with Phil, or Connor's desertion.

Phil straightened, a few inches taller than Connor, and faced him squarely. "As Jesus said in Matthew five, thirty-two: 'Anyone who divorces his wife except for unfaithfulness, causes her to become an adulteress, and anyone who marries the divorced woman commits adultery,'" Phil recited with deceptive gentleness. He cocked his head at Connor. "Is that what you want for Lin, or yourself?"

I shuddered, watching Phil use scripture as a weapon.

Connor let out a harsh sigh, then looked down. When he looked back up at Phil, his expression radiated pain and confusion. "I'll have to pray about this."

I grasped his upper arms. "But we have a date. Today. Please, Connor, don't let Phil ruin this. He's already ruined my life once. Don't let him do it again. Help me. We love each other."

Connor gazed long into my face with infinite compassion. "You are the wife of his youth. He has repented."

Phil stood back, smug in his silence. The damage had been done.

"No," I argued. "He says so, but what if he's lying? What if this is all some self-serving ploy?"

Connor smoothed back the hair from my forehead, then wiped the tears from my cheek with his thumb. "What if he's telling the truth?"

I curled against Connor, willing him to put his arms around me to protect me from Phil. "He's lying. He always lies." I wept into his shoulder.

Connor exhaled heavily, his arms still at his sides. "Before things go any further between us, we both need to know the answer." He stepped away from me. "I have to pray about this, and so do you." He shot a look at Phil. "God's will be done." Then he left.

Wimp! Why wouldn't he fight for me?

Phil came closer, as if claiming me as his prize, but before he got too close,

I shoved the flowers into his arms, then hauled off and slapped the molasses out of him.

Major ouch! I waggled my hand to ease the sting.

But instead of reacting with anger, as I expected, he laid down the flowers, then stepped back, his hand to his cheek. "I deserved that, and more. Get it out of your system, Lin. I can take it. But I'm not going away. I can't. We belong together." He started for the door. "I'll call you, after you've had some time to think this over."

He stood in the open doorway, letting in a cool breeze. "I love you, Lin. Just the way you are. I was a fool ever to have betrayed that."

Then he left, getting into a very expensive Mercedes convertible and driving away.

Ruined. He'd ruined everything.

I sank to my knees and sobbed.

Then, in the fog of pain and disappointment, a single question formed, clear and distinct, in Connor's voice: *What if Phil was telling the truth?*

Everything inside me rebelled at the possibility, but my soul told me I needed to know God's will in this, not my own.

Phil had challenged me with the one thing I couldn't deny. We had promised God to stay together till death parted us, and when I'd divorced, I had broken that vow, too. Hadn't I?

Forgive, and be free, Connor's voice echoed in my head.

God, I can't. Help. Help me. Help!

What was I supposed to do now?

When no answer came, I forced myself erect, then went out the front door and headed for my apartment. Once there, I locked the door, pulled off my jeans, then crawled into bed, planning to stay there forever.

No brandy this time. No ice cream. Just denial.

Forty-seven

This time, I lasted five days. The good news was, I lost eight pounds. The bad news was, my classes started on the sixth.

So on the morning of the fifth, I took my minivan to the office supply store near the mall and bought a rolling briefcase big enough to hold my books. Then I set about rehabilitating myself: the works at Flora's, then a mani-pedi. Then I found some black, slim-leg Levi's stretch jeans on sale for twenty-five dollars a pair at JC Penney, and a cute jacket on sale at Chico's. Which led to a sassy new pair of comfortable Life Stride flats at Shoes R Us.

Armored to face academia, I laid out my clothes for the next morning, then nuked my supper. The bell went off just as a knock sounded at my door.

Connor?

I rose, heart pounding.

But it wasn't Connor. Tommy stood on the tiny stoop, dwarfed by a glass cylinder packed with tulips, purple this time. He barely had room to let me open the screen door.

Inside, he plunked the vase on the counter. "We're running out of room. He sends 'em twice a day. Must cost a fortune."

I groaned, then stepped on the garbage can pedal to open the lid, and dropped the whole thing inside, slamming the top over stems and blooms alike.

Tommy nodded. "I get that, oh, yes, I do."

Then he motioned for me to sit, moving behind me to get my supposedly healthy dinner out of the microwave. "Here. Eat. You look scrawny."

"Scrawny?" I protested. "I'll have you know, I fit comfortably into a size twelve pair of jeans today. I couldn't wear a size twelve when I was twelve."

"You've got big bones," he said.

True.

He reached into the refrigerator for a couple of bottles of cold spring water. Handing me one, he sat facing me at the little table, then took a long swig of his own. "So. Are you excited about tomorrow?"

I looked down, toying with my fake mashed potatoes. "Phil pretty much took the wind out of my sails about anything."

"I hear that," he said with sympathy. "But you're making a new beginning tomorrow. Nobody can take that away from you, not if you choose otherwise."

I nodded, wishing I could muster up some enthusiasm, but still feeling dead inside. "Actually, I'm looking forward to the distraction."

Tommy took another swig of cold water. "Good stuff."

Then he told me what he'd come to say. "Miss Mamie's really sorry for butting in. I tried to stop her, but she had the notion that Connor would stand up for you and send Phil packing."

An elephant sat on my sternum. "Unfortunately, Phil used scripture to do the opposite."

"I heard," Tommy admitted. "Made me want to puke."

And Connor hadn't stood up to him.

Tears welled at the backs of my eyes, surprising me. I'd thought I'd cried them all away. "Can we not talk about this?"

"Sorry." Tommy patted my hand. "The Mame has decided to make it up to you by having a maid two days a week, so you can study and Carla can work."

"Wow." I'd already forgiven her. It was God and Phil I was having trouble with. And Connor. "That's really putting her money where her mouth is."

"Actually, I brought in a friend of mine who's a male nurse. Straight. Thirty. Tall. Good-looking. Works four ten-hour days at the hospital, then picks up extra cash cleaning houses, so he can buy his own place with cash before he's forty. He does really well, because he actually follows instructions." He waggled his brows. "And treats old ladies like queens. He had the Mame in the palm of his hand from the moment he cleaned the sink just the way she told him to."

I couldn't help smiling at the picture that evoked. "Good for him. And her."

"So you'll be free to study," he concluded.

"All I want to do is study. Not think. Not pray. Just study and learn."

"Sounds like a plan to me."

I stood, then bent to hug my brother's shoulders from behind. "I sure am glad you're here."

Tommy patted my arms. "You, too, Sissie-ma-noo-noo." He faced me. "The world's a bigger place than your skin, Lin. And it doesn't start and stop on this block. There's lots waiting for you out there."

I wanted to believe that, but I was still a prisoner of my emotions. "I'll try to look out, not in," I promised.

Forgive and be free.

Right. I couldn't even forgive Connor for letting a single piece of scripture drive him away.

So I couldn't forgive. Yet.

But I could go back to college.

So on the very next morning, I did just that, and boy, did I learn a lot. Not so much in the lectures as between them.

Boy, had college changed.

Forty-eight

I left forty minutes early for campus, and good thing, because the parking lots were almost full when I got there at seven-thirty. After a half hour of searching, I finally found a spot in the lot beside the Humanities Building and hurried to make my first class in time.

Along the way, I sized up every student and professor I saw. Apparently, being back on academic turf was all it took to activate my long-buried adolescent self-consciousness and judgmentalness.

I evaluated and criticized every student I passed, then criticized myself for doing it.

First Connor, now this.

Don't think about Connor!

Only the older students—nontraditional, I corrected—wore coats against the wind and cold. The rest had on drab hoodies with jeans so tight, they looked sprayed on, many of them deliberately ragged.

I really couldn't tell much about my fellow students beyond that, with their heads covered and hands dug deeply into the front pockets of their hoodies.

By the time I got to the entrance, I realized that the only people with rolling briefcases appeared to be professors. The others all toted backpacks.

I took the elevator to the third floor for my Communications class. When I got there, all the seats against the far wall and back were filled with semicomatose students, so I claimed the first seat in the next-to-farthest row, parking my rolly thing in front of me, then pulling out my pen and legal pad.

I was the only one present wearing nice clothes, so I stuck out like a pink-iced cupcake in a platter of brownies. Since my daily uniform was black travel pants, cotton knit tops that varied with the season, and colorful jackets or long sweaters, I had plenty of nice yet comfortable clothes, but very few jeans. And my jeans were dark, not ripped and faded like the others'. Not that I'd be caught dead in ripped, faded denim.

A snicker sounded from behind me, but when I looked around, nobody made eye contact.

Then I realized they all had laptops or computer tablets.

Embarrassed, but mad at myself for being so, I turned back to peer at the lectern.

So I was a dodo. Big deal.

A laptop or tablet computer wouldn't do me any good. I'd tried again and again to learn to type without looking, but my brain was too stubborn to do it, and wasn't likely to change now. I had to see and hear things, then write them down, to memorize.

Embarrassed nonetheless, I turned around and waited for class to start.

A cute little blond girl in the row beside me, her computer plugged into the wall, introduced herself. "Hi, I'm Meredith. This is my first day."

I turned and smiled, whispering back, "Me, too."

She nodded, clearly grateful to find a friendly face. "I have to sit by the outlet because my battery conked out for good."

"If I get here first, I'll save your seat," I told her.

Dimples appeared in her cheeks. "Thanks. I take care of my mama, so I can't work. So money's really tight."

Such ingenuous lucidity stirred my sympathy.

"I just lost my house and had to move back in with my mother," I confided, wondering if the girl's mother was ill, or a drunk. I didn't mention that I had chosen to stay with Mama of my own free will when we'd found Daddy's treasure.

We both nodded, then she went back to her computer.

The room might have been in any high school, the chalkboards replaced by dry-marker whiteboards, except the teacher didn't have a desk, just a hypermodern rolling podium with a long electrical cord plugged into an outlet, and a tall swivel stool behind it.

Almost all the seats were filled when a tall, sandy-haired middle-aged man with glasses strode in. He had on a baggy wool sport coat over a gray pullover sweater, from which peeked a subdued plaid, button-down collar. Baggy, faded jeans and black running shoes completed his outfit, making him almost indistinguishable from his students, except for his jacket and absence of rips in his jeans.

Once he settled on the stool, he opened his notebook (a real one, not electronic), and commenced. "Okay. Please choose the seats you wish to stay in, because I'm going to put your names on the grid, here, and call roll for the first and last time. After that, I can tell who's missing from the chart. And believe me, your absences will be noted."

He glanced up, seeing that we'd all stayed where we were. "Change if you want to, or forever hold your peace."

Nobody moved a whit except the boys against the back wall, who planted their feet in a territorial gesture to claim their places.

Must be Baptists. They love the back row.

Don't say Baptist, my inner self chided. I shoved the thought of Connor back into its tiny closet and slammed the door.

"Breedlove," the professor called out, and my hand was halfway up before the girl next to me answered.

Breedlove! Why had I done that? I wasn't a Breedlove anymore. Hadn't been for forty-one years. I was Lin Scott.

By the time the professor got to the *ss*, half the class was dozing in the warm classroom.

"Scott," he called out.

"Here." Nobody registered my answer but the teacher.

I was hoping to ace the course. I'd done lots of speaking for charity events, so I prayed it wouldn't be hard.

"As you can see from your schedules," he said, "I am Dr. Ellis. I have twenty-five years' experience teaching creative writing in Ohio, but because my doctorate is in communications, the powers that be in this institution have insisted I teach only communications. As an *adjunct*," he emphasized, clearly unhappy over the whole thing.

Uh-oh. He had a Ph.D. and twenty-five years of teaching experience, and he couldn't get a full-time job with benefits in a community college?

So much for any aspirations I had about working there someday. High school, it would have to be.

Our instructor handed out copies of the course syllabus, and I was dismayed to see three lessons—back-to-back just after midterms—that set off alarm bells: PowerPoint Basic, Intermediate, and Advanced. All of it, in less than two weeks!

Aaaaggggh!

I struggled to remain outwardly calm, because nobody else seemed to be upset.

Maybe I could find somebody to give me a crash course, so I could practice, first.

That was the thing about trying to master new skills at my age: I needed time and a tutor to distill the instructions, so I could write each important step down to remember it.

Ask Cathy about a tutor for PowerPoint, I wrote in the top margin, above the date, page, and class name I'd already put on the first ten pages so I wouldn't have to do it while I was taking notes.

Dr. Ellis hit a button on the lectern, projecting an overview of the syllabus to the whiteboard. "As you can see, you will be responsible for giving three presentations, the last of which is integrated with PowerPoint visuals."

Definitely needed that tutor. And while I was at it, maybe I could find somebody to take me through the ins and outs of the student Web site. I kept forgetting to go there to check my student e-mail, and when I did, I still couldn't find half the stuff I was looking for.

Class time was only half done when Dr. Ellis finished the syllabus. "My e-mail address is at the top of your syllabus. If something truly dire happens—like the flu, or a sick child, or a death in your immediate family, contact me by e-mail so we can work something out. My objective is for you to learn how to state your case clearly, with good evidence, before an audience, not to punish you when life intervenes. But *do not* call me. I don't ever answer my phone messages."

Do not call him! E-mail on school Web site, I wrote in caps at the top of the page.

He looked at the class. "Lucky you. Class dismissed."

As I gathered my things, he looked up from the lectern and asked, "What brings a woman like you here?"

Caught off guard, I sputtered, "I want to get my degree."

He frowned. "In what?"

Please. Bug off!

But he was the teacher, so I answered with a defensive, "English."

He shook his head. "Haven't you heard all the jokes about people with English majors driving cabs and mowing lawns and—"

"I want to teach English in high school," I said, summoning my inner duchess. "Preferably in Mimosa Branch."

Again, he shook his head at my naivety. "Did you check to see if they might have any openings by the time you finish?" he challenged.

Of course not, but I wasn't about to tell him. "You'll find," I said, my tone icy, "that I always do my homework."

He broke into a grin. "I like how you went all aloof when I pried. Very good." With that, he headed for the door. "See you on Thursday."

Relieved that he'd left, I gave him a long head start, then hiked over to the student center for some coffee in my unexpected break. Inside the eating area, small groups of matching kids took up most of the tables: geeks, goths, rednecks, Hispanics, Vietnamese, popular girls and guys, wall-flowers, loners, et cetera, based on their appearance. Since I didn't fit into any of those categories, I found a two-top near the wall and settled in to watch.

On one end of the cafeteria, a game room offered a maze of computer stations, lit to varying degrees, that allowed the students to play Internet games or do research. Whenever the door opened, the sound of electronic bombs and gunfire escaped. Based on the screens I could see, only a couple of Asians were actually doing assignments.

When I finished my coffee, I headed down the wide hallway that led to Registration. On the right, all the special-use rooms had glass walls onto the corridor. Opposite the student bookstore, one room was reserved for "multicultural" students, even though all the seats were taken by African Americans, which didn't seem very multicultural to me. Next to that, a room marked NONTRADITIONAL STUDENTS provided an island of calm for people like me. Checking it out, I found six women inside, all but one of them using the computers hooked up to the school's network, with several small tables and chairs at the back, and a long one in the center covered by the spread-out papers and books of a *very* heavy woman who looked about forty and didn't make eye contact, bless her heart.

I sat at a computer on the shelf against the wall and slowly managed to access my student e-mail. Fortunately, nothing had come in since the night before.

Satisfied that I'd managed it without any help, I signed off, then started for my next class with fifteen minutes to spare.

Smile, I had to remind myself. *Be friendly, no matter what they think of you.*

Easier said than done. I felt like a walking anachronism, which I was.

On the way back to the quad, I discovered that the handicapped exit buttons didn't work, so I had to back into both doors, bumping some of the incoming students, to get my briefcase outside.

Report broken doors to maintenance, I made a mental note, even though I knew I'd forget it the minute I got to class.

Then I headed for American Government, which turned out to be very different from the whitewashed version of history I'd learned in high school. Though the curriculum was clearly designed to drop a shipload of guilt on every white founding father and current white student, I liked my woman professor a lot. She was down-to-earth and succinct, which I deeply appreciated.

As for my fellow students, they were so clueless, I felt sorry for them. I mentally checked Government off my worry list. If they wanted political correctness, I could give it to them, even though I silently refused to take the rap for my racist ancestors, Daddy included.

I mean, really. I've never been a racist. My whole life, I'd considered people, people, end of story.

Then I headed for French.

Forty-nine

NOTE: This is my recollection, so the French is probably mangled, but that's my fault, not my teacher's.

"Bonjour mesdemoiselles, mesdames, messieurs," my tall, elegant French teacher greeted. *"Je m'appelle Madame Fouchet. Asseyez-vous, s'il vous plaît."* She strolled closer, down the single aisle between the tables and chairs that faced the board in rows. *"Aujourd'hui, et tout les cours avec moi, nous parlerons seulement français ici."* She paused. *"Comprenez-vous?"*

She said it all so fast, my ears couldn't keep up.

Okay. Think. Hello, girls, ladies, men. Please sit down. I am Madame Fouchet. Today, and all your lessons with me, we will speak only French here. Understand?

Non! By the time I'd translated, she was rattling off a bunch more French.

Oh, heaven help me. I should have taken Spanish. That way, we'd have started off with the basics.

But I'd aced two years of French in high school, so I'd CLEPed out of

Basic French, thinking I'd save time and money by taking Intermediate and Advanced French.

Can we say, *wrong*? In English, please.

The teacher rattled away while I developed flop sweat.

I copied down the homework on the board, then got out my huge textbook and turned to page 200 in the middle of the book, not because I understood the teacher, but because the cute little brunette beside me told me where they were.

At least the textbook was in English. Maybe I could manage by doing the assignments.

I tried to relax and get the gist of what the professor was saying, but the more I attempted to force it, the more nervous, confused, and worried I became.

Suddenly there was a pregnant pause, and I looked up to see everyone staring at me. *"Et vous madame,"* (and you, ma'am) the teacher said to me. *"Comment vous appelez-vous?"* (What's your name?)

"Je suis Lin Breedlove," I shot back, then realized my error.

My first day, and I couldn't even get my *name* right? Or my reply.

"Pardon, madame," I hastily corrected. (Sorry.) *"Je m'appelle Lin Scott."* (My name is Lin Scott.)

As it had when I'd gone to Paris with Phil on our twentieth anniversary, my good accent brought on an onslaught of even faster French, so I waited till she stopped for breath, then trotted out my favorite phrase: *"Je vous en prie, madame, parlez plus lentement et distinctement. Je suis sourde comme un pot."* (I pray you, ma'am, please speak a little more slowly and distinctly. I'm deaf as a post.)

At least, that's what I thought I said.

The teacher burst out laughing, but nobody else got it.

"C'est vrai," I deadpanned. (It's true.)

She arched a perfectly shaped brunette brow and pronounced slowly, *"C'est à voir."* (We'll see.)

Now that, I could understand.

Then she went right back to talking a mile a minute. The rest of the class was a blur of trying to pick out the instructions hiding in her barrage of French and failing abysmally.

At the end, she took pity on us and gave out the assignment in English, then explained we'd have to do at least three exercises a week in the language lab.

Assuming I could find the language lab, I decided to get that over with right after my classes on Tuesdays.

Boy, did I have a lot of catching up to do, especially with my grammar and irregular verbs.

After that, I found the classroom for my survey course on world history and was happy to discover that my professor was young, kind, and spoke clearly. Best of all, he said that if we took good notes, we really didn't need to use the textbook, which had a lot of extraneous material.

It was so nice to hear someone casually use the word *extraneous*.

I loved history, which had changed drastically since I'd studied it in high school thanks to recent finds and DNA analysis, plus the politically correct filter applied to the facts. Still, this professor seemed like a winner, so I checked that class off my worry list and took copious notes about a politically correct (but decidedly unscriptural) interpretation of prehistoric man.

After that came English, with another kind, flexible young professor, who started off discussing the "magic realism" novel we would all read and analyze, about four contemporary Native American characters who struggle with leaving their reservation for good.

In all my previous years as an avid reader, I'd never heard of magic realism, but he explained it perfectly.

I just hoped I could manage to read the book without having my weirdness kick in.

Then came math.

Fifty

College algebra. I shiver now, just thinking about it.

When Cathy registered my classes in October, I'd told her it didn't matter that I'd tested out of remedial algebra, because I'd done it by eliminating the two clearly wrong answers, then eeny-meeny-miney-moing the two choices that remained, which turned out to be right in too many cases. I'd insisted that I needed a review class (noncredit) before I tackled college algebra, but she'd insisted right back that I at least give the regular algebra a try. Then she'd reassured me that I could always drop it if I found myself over my head, and take something else.

It didn't take me but three minutes in that math classroom to know I was over my head. My female professor began by asking who could define and explain quadratic equations.

Shoot! Shoot, shoot, shoot.

Hands went up all over the room.

I had no clue what the question or the student's answer meant.

My brain seized.

Shoot, shoot, shoot! Shoot, shoot, shoot, shoot, shoot, shoot—

Oh, quit griping, my practical self scolded, *and focus on what she's saying! You might understand* something.

The teacher activated the white "smartboard" that provided an unending list of equations, which she solved at record speed, rattling off a stream of mathspeak as she did.

Shades of French!

My inner child promptly had a hissy fit.

Mildly hysterical beneath my frozen exterior, I managed to keep from running screaming from the classroom while the instructor continued to race through dozens of equations on the "smartboard."

When the teacher dismissed us half an hour early, I waited till almost everyone else had left to approach her. "Excuse me, ma'am, but I'm afraid this class is *way* over my head."

She faced me squarely, matter-of-fact. "I appreciate your telling me right away. You can register for another class, making room for someone who might want to get into this one."

Apparently, gone were the days of "Let's see how we can help you manage this."

Feeling totally inadequate, I nodded, then headed for Cathy's office. I had forty-five minutes before anthropology, so I hoped she could get me into another Tuesday-Thursday core course in that time slot.

I had to wait for twenty minutes before she was free, but when Cathy talked it over with me, she checked availability against my required courses, and informed me that human biology had an opening in that time slot.

Not even thinking there might be a reason the class wasn't filled, I sagged in relief. "Oh, good. I'm great with body stuff."

"The only thing is," Cathy said, "some people have trouble understanding the professor. She's from Nigeria. But it's the only core science class open that fits your current schedule."

The comment about not understanding went in one ear and out the other, but not the "it's the only core science class that fits." Next she said,

"You'll have to do lab once a week. I'll see if I can find one that's open after your last class."

As it turned out, there was an opening for lab with the same biology instructor on Thursdays, so I hadn't missed the first one.

Again, it didn't occur to me that there might be a reason why her lab wasn't full.

"I'll notify your new professor," Cathy said. "Fortunately, you've only missed the first lecture."

"Thanks so much." At my age, I couldn't afford to drag my classes out. I needed to take a full load, and then some. And make at least a C average, preferably a B.

Whether I could manage it remained to be seen. So far, I was doubtful, since I couldn't even get my own name right.

Anthropology was next. Though the windowless classroom was crammed with decaying cardboard boxes of specimens, the professor was a hoot. He assigned each table as a team, which didn't work out so well for me, because a passive-aggressive girl from my government class ended up on my team.

But the prof was so excited about what he was teaching that I couldn't help liking him, even though he refused to admit even the *possibility* that Homo sapiens might have evolved from its own distinct ancestor. But he didn't treat me like an idiot for asking, so I liked him.

Science was always so adamantly sure of its prevailing theories, when, in fact, the entire system was only a series of wrong conclusions working toward the truth.

I mean, if I'd told him ten years before that I could prove every person on the planet came from a single sub-Saharan African mother, would he have even entertained the possibility?

I think not. But all in all, I liked the class.

When it was finished, late in the afternoon, I decided to do my language lab assignments, since I had biology lab on Thursdays.

As it turned out, there was so much ambient noise in the language lab that my mid-range nerve deafness made it almost impossible for me to hear the voices on the verbal French exercises. I turned the volume up all the way, but it was still so soft and distant that I was stumped. So I finally gave up and resolved to have Cathy work out a way for me to do them in the quiet rooms.

Fifty-one

When I turned in at our driveway at seven that evening, Miss Mamie and Carla and Tommy were waiting for me in the light from the dining room by the porte cochere.

Worn out, I parked under the cover, then joined them on the porch.

"So, how'd it go?" Tommy asked with a smile when I got out, his breath clouding in the cold.

Frankly, I was too tired and hollow to talk about it, but I didn't want to hurt his feelings, so I said, "Scary. And hard. I had to switch math for human biology." Embarrassed—why, I couldn't tell you—I curled my lips inward, then I admitted, "You were right. I need to study some more before I tackle algebra. Maybe summer quarter. Or next fall."

He nodded. "Sounds like a plan."

The Mame bustled over and pulled my coat closed, then put her arm around my shoulders. "You look exhausted. Come inside, and we'll all have vegetable soup and cornbread to warm us up. Then you can tell us all about it."

Maybe I'd have the energy to go through it all after I'd eaten. "Soup sounds perfect." Miss Mamie's "vegetable" soup had shredded white-meat chicken and homemade chicken stock, canned Roma tomatoes, Silver Queen corn that she'd frozen herself, butter peas, fried bacon, and plenty of chopped Vidalias. No okra, no peppers to override the flavors. And her cornbread was moist and buttery, a perfect base for homemade blackberry jam.

After we'd all eaten and cleaned up, Miss Mamie took off her apron and sat facing me. "Okay, tell us all about it."

I couldn't deny her a blow-by-blow account, since her gold had paid my tuition. So I gave her my day and my new beginning, with plenty of humor salted in. We laughed a lot. Then I headed for bed, dragging my loaded briefcase up the stairs behind me.

I would study hard the next day, but that night, I wanted to sleep.

Nodding off in my soft, warm bed, my last conscious thought was that I'd only thought of Connor twice all day. Not counting thinking about thinking about him.

But then, blast it, I dreamed about him all night.

Just rats.

Fifty-two

The next morning I woke up grumpy from my mind's refusal to let go of Connor. I brushed my teeth, raked an Afro pick through my curls, then threw on a warm pair of sweats and headed for the big house for some company, picking up my copy of the *Gainesville Times* on the way.

Dadgum Connor. I'd been fine on my own for years till he came around. Now, thanks to him, I no longer found myself good company.

It didn't help much having Miss Mamie and Carla and Tommy sip their coffee in silence as Mama read her *Gainesville Times* and he, his Gwinnett paper. Carla entertained herself with a book of sudoku.

I'd rather take a beating than try to do another sudoku. One was enough for a lifetime with me.

Feeling anything but energized, I snapped to when the front doorbell rang.

Connor?

Tommy jumped to his feet. "I'll get it."

"No." I was standing, too. "Please let me."

Tommy shrugged. "Suit yourself."

Miss Mamie, she don't say nothin'; just eyed us over her coffee.

I saw the florist's van through the front door, and somebody I didn't recognize holding a huge glass globe overflowing with purple tulips.

Not Connor. My spirits fell.

Drat. Drat, drat, drat.

When I opened the door, the deliveryman asked me where I'd like him to put them.

I pointed toward the long table behind me. "On the dining room table. Let me get your tip."

I went to my purse on the shelf of our Victorian hat rack, coat hanger, and umbrella stand in the foyer, then opened my wallet. No ones, just a single five.

"Here." I gave it to him. "Thanks."

Pleased by my generosity, he offered a little salute, then left.

On my way back to the kitchen, I eyed the enclosure card with dread, wishing it wasn't from Phil, but knowing it was.

Tulips, this time of year. A needless extravagance. But Phil had always expressed his feelings for me (assuming he'd ever had any) with expensive gifts that felt like bribes.

Obviously, he had no idea what other flowers I liked (there were plenty) so he'd stuck with the tulips like a needle caught in a scratch on a record, and just as annoying.

The enclosed note confirmed my fear. "I know you," he wrote. "What you like. What you love. What you need. Please let me love you the way I should have all along. I'm not the same, selfish man. Your true husband, Phil."

I started to soften a bit, then remembered he'd only come back because *Bambi* had dumped *him*.

"Well, I know you, too." I wadded up the card and threw it into the gas flames in the foyer fireplace. "So the answer is definitely no."

All his words were right, except for the conspicuous omission of *Christ* or *Jesus*.

My sensible self told me Phil was nobody's fool, then asked what he was up to.

The still, small voice chimed in with *he wants something.* But it didn't tell me what.

I fought the urge to call Connor and ask him if he'd felt the same thing, but didn't dare. He'd asked for time to pray over our relationship, so I had to respect that.

That left my family. So I took the flowers into the kitchen and plonked them on the table.

"Mercy," Miss Mamie exclaimed. "Please tell me those are from Connor."

"I wish," I said, reclaiming my seat. "Unfortunately, they're from Phil."

"Well, shoot," Miss Mamie spat out, the exclamation as close to cussing as she went.

Discreet as always, Carla quietly left us, giving Tommy's shoulder a squeeze as she passed behind him.

"I need advice," I told Miss Mamie, then looked to my brother. "From you, too."

"Mama, pack our bags for heaven," Tommy responded in his best televangelist imitation. "The end is nigh. Lin just asked for my advice."

I gave him a good-natured shove on the arm, then sobered. "What should I do here? I want to do the right thing, but God's not telling me what I need to know. Past experience tells me Phil's up to no good. And as for his conversion, he never once mentioned Jesus." Then I turned against myself. "But what if he's really accepted Christ?" This was giving me a headache. "What if he really has changed? Do I owe him another chance?"

"Do you *want* to give him another chance?" Miss Mamie asked.

I shook my head in denial. "What I *want* is Connor, but maybe that's just lust talking. *Lust,* at my age." I shook my head. "Intellectually, I want to do what's best for Connor, but humanly ... things don't feel complete without him anymore."

Tommy and Miss Mamie exchanged pregnant glances that said, "Uh-oh."

Uh-oh was right.

"We have a slogan in the program," Tommy said. "When you don't know what you should do, don't just do something; stand there."

We all knew how terrible I was at waiting.

Miss Mamie nodded. "I think Tommy's right, honey. There's a lot you don't know about either of those men. What harm could it do to wait and see what happens?" She didn't leave time for me to answer, just forged on with, "Focus on your own life. Thank God for taking care of this, then study, study, study." She lifted her chin with pride. "Don't give either of them power over you. Just put them out of your mind. And every time they come back, put them out again."

"Easy to say," I groaned out. "Hard to do." Anger rose like bile inside me. "I'm so furious with Phil for messing up everything with Connor. And even more furious with Connor for letting him."

"So use my punching bag in the garage." Tommy pointed to where my biceps used to be. "Those arms will tighten right up."

"My luck," I retorted, "I'd dislocate my shoulder on the first punch."

Tommy gave my back a consoling pat. "You can get through this. Let go and let God."

Normally, I love platitudes, but this time, I bristled. "That's what I've been doing, and it hasn't worked."

"Yet," Tommy said in a superior tone.

I sighed heavily. "I do not need this drama. I need to focus, so I can study."

"That's what I'm talkin' about," he said.

I peered at my brother. "What do your instincts tell you about Phil and Connor? I really want to know."

He looked away, then up. "Well, AA is all about second chances, so I wouldn't say Phil *can't* change. But I question why he would want to get you back after what he did, much less why he's pressing you so hard. You didn't get any alimony, so that's not it."

He left you destitute, my stubborn self reminded me. *You'd be a fool to buy into his act.*

Then Connor's voice asked again, *What if he's telling the truth?*

Tommy regarded me with sympathy. "I'd just say be careful and keep your eyes wide open with Phil."

"And Connor?" I asked.

"My impression is that he's a really good guy, but I'm disappointed that all Phil had to do was hurl a couple of Bible verses at him to get Connor to let you go. Who knows?" He stared off toward Connor's house. "Maybe he's not what he seems. People don't get divorced for no reason."

"He told me about that," I defended. "He said his wife and family always ended up with the short end of the stick, that he paid more attention to his ministry than his marriage, so she finally had enough and left him for a man who appreciated her. Connor blamed himself completely, said that was why he gave up his megachurch and took a smaller one here."

"And promptly shot himself in the foot by falling for *you*," Tommy said. "You've gotta wonder what's with that."

I bristled. "Is it so incredible that a man like Connor might be in love with me?"

Tommy colored. "Heck, no. It's just, well, we both know you're nobody's idea of a Baptist minister's wife."

I agreed with him, but hearing him say it hurt my feelings. "How would you know? You haven't darkened the doors of a church for seven years, much less First Baptist."

Tommy's eyes narrowed as his mouth flattened into a straight line. "Watch out, Sissie-ma-noo-noo. Judge not, lest ye be judged."

He had a point.

Miss Mamie said nothing, but her expression matched Tommy's.

I fought down the urge to defend myself and said, "Sorry. You're right."

"Mama, pack our bags!" he said for the second time. "The end is upon us! Lin just said I was right."

"Enough, already."

What I'd *really* lost in my divorce were my illusions about Phil. That had broken my heart, but he'd never asked me to imagine him as more than he was. "I imagined Phil as a better man. He didn't ask me to. I just did, all by myself."

I wiped a contradictory tear from my eye. "When I finally understood that the man I loved never had existed, I was able to let go. Who he is now, I couldn't tell you. But I definitely don't want him back."

My Granny Beth's long-ago words echoed in my brain: *There's no such thing as Prince Charming. All the men out there are frogs. Just pick the very best frog you can find.*

Even after she'd warned me repeatedly, I'd still eloped with Phil, then spent the next thirty years trying to be the perfect Christian corporate wife for the prince I'd dreamed up, despite all evidence to the contrary.

You'd think I would have learned my lesson. Yet there I sat, convinced that *Connor* was a prince.

The trouble was, as frogs go, Connor definitely seemed to be the best one in the pond. Why did he have to turn out to be a wuss?

Tommy was right. I could wait to see how things shook out.

Thank goodness for school. At least I was starting something new.

Thinking of school, I couldn't stifle a chuckle.

"What's so funny?" Tommy asked with a smile.

"Me, a college freshman."

He grinned. "Smokin', and I don't mean cigarettes."

"Oh, right," I challenged.

"What?" he asked. "I know this Phil thing threw Connor for a loop, but he still wants you. And so does Phil the fish." An apt allusion: my ex was definitely slimy. "I call that hot, missy."

My heart lightened. "The only thing hot about me is those ThermaCare patches I put on my knees at night."

With that, I got up and gave them each a hug. "Thanks for listening. I'm going to the apartment to study."

"We won't bother you," Mama said.

"Thanks."

Me, a college freshman, with two men competing for my attention.

I laughed about that all the way to my apartment. Never mind the note of hysteria that shaded it. A laugh is a laugh is a laugh, and I needed one.

I started my homework and didn't even come up for air till my stomach demanded food. After eating, I worked till my eyes wouldn't stay open, then crawled into bed at one-thirty in the morning. I set the alarm, closed my eyes, and three seconds later (actually, five hours), the alarm sounded for ten minutes before I swam up to consciousness.

Thank heaven for coffee, that's all I can say. And Miss Mamie's breakfasts.

Fifty-three

Two weeks after Connor had left me hanging, my cell phone finally rang at nine on Tuesday evening and showed his number. Heart pounding, I grabbed the phone and raced to the little window in the apartment's front door, peering through the hedge at his house. "Hello?"

My first word sounded breathless, because it was. I suddenly missed him so much—or the man I hoped he was—that I could barely speak.

"Lin?" His tone was grave.

Fear caused my heart to shrink. "Connor?" All my hopes resonated in his name.

A long pause followed.

"I wish I knew what to tell you," he finally said. "I've prayed and prayed, but I'm still not getting any answers. So I've focused on the Lord's work, and there's a lot of work to be done with my congregation. But I still can't get you out of my mind, or my heart."

Yes! Thank You, Lord!

"It's the same with me," I confessed. When he didn't respond, I hastily filled the silence with, "I started school. I'm taking seven courses on Tuesdays and Thursdays. Makes for long days and lots of studying." Still no response. "Daddy always wanted me to finish school."

I caught myself. "There I go again," I blurted out, "referring to Daddy in the past tense, when he's still very much present in body, if not in mind."

"Don't beat yourself up about that," Connor said in a softer tone. "The father you knew *is* gone."

"No he's not," I countered. "He's magnified times ten; the bad parts, anyway."

"But that's not the man he was," Connor comforted. "We're all a mixture of good and bad, of sinner and saint. Your father just can't control the balance anymore. It's his dementia, not him."

I knew that, but it didn't help when I had to deal, week in and week out, with the consequences of Daddy's paranoia.

Then a huge pulse of grief shifted my heart back to Connor. "I can't stop thinking about you," I said, knowing I shouldn't. "Missing you."

"I miss you, too," he said, then clearly regretted it. "I'm sorry I said that. I don't want to lead you on. I didn't mean—"

"It's okay," I lied, anything but okay.

He changed the subject. "Have you heard from your ex?"

That. Ouch.

"He sends tulips every day, and he's called a few times from a blocked number. Then, out of the blue, he shows up to take me out to dinner and some plays, but I still don't trust him."

Connor took the bull by the horns. "Lin, why did you marry him?"

I sighed. "At the time, I thought it was love. I waited on him hand and foot, made sure he got everything he wanted at home. But after the divorce, I went into counseling and realized that Phil was my way of escaping my parents and Mimosa Branch. He was steady. Respectable. Sexy. At least, that's what I thought then. I had nobody to compare him to."

I paused, waiting for Connor to laugh, but he didn't. "He had a good job and great prospects, and I wanted respectability, anonymity, and a house in Buckhead."

Still, Connor didn't respond.

My reasons probably sounded too mercenary for a man like him.

But I went on, unable to bear the silence between us. "Looking back, I feel sorry for him. Ours was no love match. No wonder he dumped me for someone else."

Connor's next question was gingerly stated. "Did you ever love him?"

I searched my soul about those long-gone years. "I took care of him. Tried to be the perfect Christian wife. The perfect corporate wife."

Perfection. Was I fantasizing about Connor with that same expectation?

"We were a partnership, more than a marriage," I admitted. "But I don't think I even knew what love really was. Not what it should be between a man and a woman."

"Do you now?" he asked quietly.

I weighed my response, then opted for honesty. "Unfortunately, I think I do."

Connor groaned.

"Enough for me to want the best for you," I went on, "even if it means I can't have you."

Liar, liar, pants on fire! my Puritan blared with the finger of judgment pointed in my direction.

I can be noble, I argued back.

My sensible self joined the conversation with, *Martyr, martyr, martyr!*

Rats. Would all my parts *please* just shut up?

Above the clamor, I heard my voice ask Connor, "Why did you marry your wife?"

I sensed his surprise in the long pause that followed. Then he admitted, "Because it was time for me to take a wife, and there was a huge physical attraction between us."

Just like the one we felt for each other now?

Connor inhaled slowly, then let it out. "She was a wonderful, devout Christian woman, and she wanted to marry me." He let out a brief, dry chuckle. "I don't even remember asking her. She probably gave me an ultimatum. I was so wrapped up in seminary, I couldn't tell you." Another pregnant pause. "First school, then my doctorate, then the girls and my first churches. I didn't realize I was taking my family for granted, but I did. I failed miserably as a husband and a father, blinded by my pride about my work."

He paused again. To collect himself?

"I blew it again and again for years," he confessed, "like the tap of a chisel on alabaster. I took Helen for granted, chiseling away at her heart till there was nothing soft left. No wonder she left me for someone who paid attention to her and made her feel loved."

Had he really learned his lesson, or was he unconsciously repeating what he'd done before, but with me, a very different woman, telling himself everything would work this time?

Was that why he didn't stand up for me? Or was it because I was so inappropriate, forbidden fruit?

I sighed heavily, barely escaping the tidal wave of *what ifs* that slammed down on me.

The two of us sat in silent commiseration for almost a minute.

"It's not going to happen for us, is it?" I finally asked.

"I don't know," he said. "I honestly don't know. But for now, we have to stay apart. I said I had enough self-control for both of us, but that's not true. If I'm going to sort out this thing spiritually, I have to stay away."

My inner Puritan understood completely, but my hedonist shouted, *Fight for him, the way you want him to fight for you! Show him how it's done.* She finished with a seductive, *Kiss kiss, kiss,* that sent me straight back into heat.

Maybe it was time for me to give up my HRT at last and be neutered.

"Can we still talk to each other on the phone?" I asked him.

Pain permeated his answer. "Not yet. Not now."

He was right, of course.

I finally knew what it felt like to lose someone I truly loved—or was Connor just another fantasy I'd concocted?

What difference did it make? I still felt it, and the anguish of my divorce paled in comparison.

Fighting back tears, I managed to choke out, "Bye," before hanging up.

Immediately, the phone rang again, making me jump. But the screen only said *wireless*. The last thing I wanted was to talk to some salesman, but my finger automatically pressed the talk button. My voice soggy with sheets of silent tears, I managed to answer, "Hello?"

"Lin, what's the matter?" Phil responded with concern. "Why are you crying?"

Even after all these years, he could still tell from a single word.

"Because I didn't even know what love was when I married you, and that wasn't fair to either one of us." Why was I telling *him*?

"Aw, honey," he said with compassion he'd never shown before. "Nobody knows what they're doing when they marry young. I didn't, either."

Clearly, he'd changed his responses, at least. He'd never been sympathetic before, just offered solutions, then left.

"I never appreciated you the way I should have," he soothed. "I was an idiot for leaving you."

I willed away my sadness over Connor so I could be in the present with Phil. "No," I told him. "You had good reason to leave me, because I never really loved you."

I waited to see how he'd respond, but he didn't, so I went on, baring it all. "You deserve to be with someone who loves you for who you are. And so do I."

"But I want *you*," he said. "I love you. I *need* you."

All about Phil, as usual, my skeptical self declared. *And not even original.*

Old, fat Elvis had done it better.

"Can't we try again?" he pleaded. "If it doesn't work out, I swear, I'll give you a divorce, this time with alimony." When I didn't answer, he sweetened the pot. "We can even put it in writing. I'll have it drawn up today. I swear on my mother's grave."

Why was he pushing so hard, in such a hurry?

Do not swear . . . Let your yea be yea, and your nay be nay.

I felt a check in my spirit, warning me that he was lying, but I couldn't say why.

Monty Python and the Holy Grail, flashed into my brain, the knights crying, "Run away! Run away!"

Enough. "Phil, I can't talk anymore. Please, just leave me alone for a while. I need to study. I'm taking seven courses, and I have two papers due day after tomorrow. I have to focus on that."

"Please, baby," he pleaded with surprising urgency. "Let me see you."

My sympathy evaporated with a *poof.* I hated it when he called me baby.

"Just give it a try," he coaxed. "You won't be sorry, I swear."

Phil had sworn a lot of things to me over the years, but rarely kept his word, casually brushing off his broken promises with a merry apology, as if he'd just eaten the last cookie in the package instead of ruining my plans and my trust.

"Phil, I'm hanging up now," I told him. "If you care about me, leave me alone. I need time to think."

"I'm not giving up!" he hollered as I hit the off button.

I set the phone down. "I am." Then I went to bed and pulled the covers over my head, crying for what seemed like hours, till I finally fell asleep from exhaustion. My last waking thought was, *I can't do this, God. I can't fix it. Uncle. Just take me home to heaven.*

But He didn't take me home to heaven.

I woke up at ten the next morning with a red nose, swollen eyes, and blocked nosels. I called Miss Mamie and pleaded a cold, which she believed.

"I'm not surprised," she said. "Going back to school with all those kids who don't know enough to stay home when they're sick."

That was true, too.

"I'll bring you some homemade organic chicken soup within the hour," she said. "No antibiotics. Just a little salt. You'll feel better right away."

I balanced the risk of her seeing me against the promise of hearty chicken broth. I could always put an ice pack over my eyes for a while. "Okay. Thanks. I'll leave the door unlocked."

"Needn't bother," she shot back. "I have a key."

Finally presented with the opportunity to broach the subject, I reared up. "And where, pray tell, did it come from?"

"The locksmith, of course, silly. You didn't think he was going to leave me without one, now, did you? After all, this is still my house."

The Mame had just sprayed the garage apartment like a tomcat marking his territory.

I gave up. "Of course it is. I'd just like to know when you're coming inside, especially when I'm not here. Or when I am."

"Sure. I promise," she said, her dismissive tone telling me she had no more intention of keeping that promise than Phil had of keeping his.

Miss Mamie shifted gears. "Do you feel well enough to come to breakfast? I'll make French toast. Tommy and Carla were . . . *up* till the wee hours. Then she left at six-thirty this morning to meet a client. Tommy'll probably sleep in."

Miss Mamie's French toast. My favorite. The ultimate comfort food, even with low-calorie syrup. "I can come down. I'll probably feel better on my feet."

"Good. Take your time," she said. "I'll be ready when you get here. You can study in the den of iniquity afterward, if you want to."

Frankly, the idea of a big, clean desk and its comfortable new executive chair appealed to me.

So I put ice on my eyes for ten minutes, then dressed in stretch jeans and a mock turtleneck under my sable jacket (another remnant of my past life), and dragged my book briefcase down the stairs, across to the big house, and back up to the family room.

It was all worth it when I walked into the warm, cozy kitchen of my childhood. I shoved Connor and Phil behind a steel door in my mind, then slammed it. Focus on the present. Don't project the worst.

After a gloriously fattening breakfast, I retreated to the study. Now spotless, the room was a haven of quiet and light. I started writing my paper on my new notebook computer, and before I knew it, Miss Mamie called me to lunch.

After we ate our chicken soup and salads, I was back in Daddy's study working when the doorbell rang and Miss Mamie answered it.

"Flowers for Miz Lin," the deliveryman said. "Agin."

"Thank you." I heard my mother close the door without tipping. "Lin," she called.

"I'm in here!" I rose just as she walked in with yet another big bowl of red tulips.

Summoned by the ruckus, Tommy finally emerged from upstairs, disheveled, and followed Miss Mamie into the office.

The Mame frowned as she set the tulips on the den's new coffee table in front of the new leather couch I'd found at The Dump. "They're from Phil," Miss Mamie announced with open disapproval. Brows lifted, she stared down at me. "The card says 'Marry me.' What's that all about?"

About your reading my personal messages, I wanted to say, but didn't. "I told you: Phil claims he's been born again and wants to remarry me," I said.

I'd mentioned the marrying part to her before, hadn't I?

"Why on earth would he want to do that?" she and Tommy asked almost in unison.

Apparently, I'd left that out.

I shrugged. "He claims I'm the wife of his youth, and he wants to do right by me now."

Tommy's eyes narrowed. "Surely you're not considering *marrying* him."

Miss Mamie's spine went rod-straight. "Remarriage, indeed. As if you could overlook what he's done to you." She glared at me. "Mark my words, Phil's up to no good, as usual."

Tommy peered at me with sympathy. "The trouble is, he struck a nerve with Connor." He frowned. "I have a few friends in law enforcement. Is it okay if I try to find out what's really going on with Phil?"

"Knock yourself out," I told him. "I've given up. On him *and* Connor," I said, realizing that it was true as the words came out. "I'm through wanting what I can't have, and not wanting what I can. From now on, I'll just go to college and stay here to look after y'all. And Daddy."

Tommy and the Mame exchanged pregnant glances that said they weren't buying my resignation for a second, but I didn't care.

"Now, I need to get back to my homework."

The two of them moved reluctantly toward the kitchen.

After the kitchen's swinging door closed behind them, I heard a muffled hosanna of "French toast!" from my brother.

Smiling, I settled back to work.

Once the paper was finished, I had a big human biology assignment. I was doing very well in that class, despite the fact that my Nigerian lady professor was barely intelligible in English, although I'd managed to decode some of her lectures as the weeks passed. (I found out later that all the lecture notes had been available somewhere in the maze of our campus network.)

I stood up, stretched, cracked my knuckles, then looked for my mother. I found her in the family room that opened onto the kitchen, sitting on the sofa and listening to *Focus on the Family* on the radio while she stitched yet another kneeler for the Methodists.

"Mama, do you have any more of that chicken broth? I could use a mugful."

"There's plenty." Miss Mamie laid down her needlework, her expression wily. "It certainly cleared up that cold in a jiffy, didn't it?"

If only it could do the same for me. "I wish it could heal my heart."

Tommy snuck up behind me and affectionately hooked his arm around my neck. "Okay, Sissie-ma-noo-noo. No more about Connor and Phil. Back to the books for you."

I let him drag me back to the desk, then sat down.

Miss Mamie arrived with a fresh mug of chicken soup. "Good for what ails you." Then she herded Tommy out and closed the door behind them.

You cannot lose what you never had, I told myself for the thousandth time. My dream of Connor might never have materialized, but how it hurt to let it go.

Just get me through this day, Lord, and then the next. Help me to be present in every moment.

I prayed it. And prayed it. And prayed it.

If only I could feel it.

Fifty-four

Phil kept sending me presents with cards asking me to marry him, but I never responded and blocked his number.

But at night, whenever I was tired or discouraged, mourning washed over me, flooding my soul till I cried myself to sleep, which only made me more disgusted.

I'd never been a blubberhead. Why was I crying so much?

Was it possible to go through puberty again? I hadn't been so emotional since I was twelve, and now my face kept breaking out.

The real question was, how many tears would it take to wash Connor Allen out of my life?

Fifty-five

On Tommy's and my regular Friday morning visit to the Home on March first, we walked in to find Aunt Glory and my cousins Laura and Susan huddling in the foyer, Aunt Glory's lace handkerchief dabbing away at her eyes.

I halted in my tracks. *Uncle Bedford.*

I closed my eyes and tried to prolong the moment when it still felt as if he were in the world.

Laura burst into tears and headed straight for me, her arms extended. "Ooooh, Lin," she sobbed out, collapsing over me to hug the smithereens out of me. "It's Daddy."

Poor Uncle B. Poor Daddy.

And it *would* happen on the nurse's morning off.

I mustered myself to help. Like all Southern women, I knew my role with funerals, our time-honored Southern transition from life to the here-after. "I'm so sorry, honey."

Still wearing my cousin around my neck, I reached out and took Aunt Glory's hand. "I know you must be devastated."

My aunt gave my hand a brief squeeze, clearly satisfied that I'd said the right thing, regardless of the relief she must be feeling. We were ladies, after all. Out of respect for the departed, none of us would officially acknowledge that relief. Ever.

After a while, we'd be able to say, "He's gone to a better place," but only after Aunt Glory said it first.

Cousin Susan came over and gave me a pat on the shoulder. "We know you loved him, too."

Finally, Laura let go of me. "The hearse is on its way," she murmured. "Mama insisted on calling Finnegan's because it's so close."

"Would y'all like us to have the reception at our house," I volunteered, then stupidly added, "or are you going to have the services in Atlanta?"

Aunt Glory said, "Here," at the same moment her daughters said, "Spring Hill."

Spring Hill? Where Atlanta's nobility were put to rest? Talk about pricey.

I hugged my aunt, leaning close to her ear to whisper, "You're the widow, sweetie. It's your call, not theirs. I'm sure you can work this out." I pulled back and said in a normal tone, "Do you mind if we go make sure Daddy's okay?"

Aunt Glory nodded. "Y'all go. But please come back. I need to ask you about the family plot up here and all."

"Don't worry," Tommy soothed. "This won't take long."

I petted my cousins on the way past, then we headed for the Alzheimer's wing. The staff were busy getting Uncle Bedford onto a stretcher when we walked in, but Daddy wouldn't let go of his brother's hand.

Unshaven, the weight of the world in his face, Daddy told us, "He went without me. Just left, without even telling me he was going." Tears overflowed his red-rimmed eyes. "How am I going to manage without him? I don't even know who I am, without him here to remind me."

Tommy wrapped Daddy in a fierce hug. "You're going to be okay," he said through his own tears for our father. "Lin and I are here. We'll take care of you."

Daddy went limp, pulling away but still gripping his little brother's cold hand. "Not always. And you don't know," he stated flatly.

"Don't know what, Daddy?" I sat beside him and gently pried his fingers from Uncle Bedford's cold, waxy yellow ones, replacing my uncle's lifeless hand with mine.

Daddy was inconsolable. "What our life was like after Mama died. How I protected Bedford and Waring when Daddy got drunk. The boy I was then. The good things I did. The man I was with your mama in the beginning." His mouth crumpled. "She loved me then. Before the women. She loved me then."

So there had been other women. Hardly a shock. "It's okay, Daddy. We love you, too. And so does Miss Mamie. She just told me so."

I stroked his arm as Tommy let go and faced him. "It's gonna be okay, General. I swear it. I'll come every morning, and you can tell me anything, no matter what, and I'll love you."

"We both will," I added.

But Daddy turned his face to the wall as if we'd both just disappeared. "You don't know. Nobody does. He was the last one."

All our father's brothers had left him here, at the mercy of his fears and decaying mind.

Junior Finnegan and the undertakers arrived outside the door and transferred Uncle Bedford to the long body bag on their stretcher. When he was all zipped in, they added a furry blanket with the funeral home's logo at the center to cover the bag, then rattled off down the hall.

Daddy didn't seem to notice. He just sat there, frozen and unseeing. I wondered if he was catatonic from the shock.

Tommy took the electric razor from its charger by the sink. "Come on, Daddy. Let's get you all spiffed up for the day."

Daddy didn't say anything, just sat there, totally passive, while Tommy lovingly shaved him, then wiped his face with a warm, damp towel. "That's the ticket," my brother told him. "Now you're the man." He wiped Daddy's hands, now limp.

I tried to rouse him. "Would you like me to get you a Blizzard, Daddy?" Sane or crazy, he never turned down a Blizzard from the DQ. Until this time.

He didn't respond.

Then, quick as lightning, he snatched my brother's wrist. "I want to go," he snarled. "Do you hear me? I want to go!"

Tommy pried at Daddy's fingers in alarm. "Ouch, that hurts! General! Ten, hut!"

The fury in our father's face remained. "I want to go!"

"Go where, honey?" I begged, praying he'd let go of Tommy before he broke something. "Where do you want to go?"

He turned his anger on me. "You know. You all do, but you won't let me! I have to get out of here." He went canny. "I have to have words with my wife. She's the one who put me here. I'll kill her, that's what I'll do. Knock her in the head."

I stuck my head out into the hall and hollered, "Help! Haldol! Stat! Help!"

For once, the nurse was at her station. She unlocked a syringe from the meds cart, then double-timed it down the hall. I pulled her into the room. "He just went psychotic, won't let go of Tommy's arm."

She nodded, then thrust the syringe into Daddy's thigh.

He sputtered for a few seconds, then went limp, his eyes as dead as his brother's.

Tommy reclaimed his wrist as the nurse and I laid Daddy onto the bed, then raised the sides.

"That'll put him out for the day," she told me.

I hated having to drug him into oblivion. Hated, hated, hated it. But what other choice did we have?

I turned to Tommy, who was massaging his wrist. "Let me take you to the urgent care to make sure that's not broken."

"No. It's okay. Everything works fine."

I looked at Daddy, understanding what he'd said and why, which was disturbing, in itself. I knew what had sucked him back into madness. "He wants to die, too, and I can't blame him. Somewhere in there, he knows what he's become." I exhaled heavily to stem the tears that collected in the back of my eyes. "Why didn't God take them both?"

Why *is the devil's trap,* Granny Beth whispered in my mind.

She must have been whispering to Tommy, too, because he tapped his skull and quoted her. "If you could put God in a box this big, He wouldn't be much of a God, now, would He?"

Seeing my distress, he shook his head. "Tearing yourself up about this will only make you crazy. What is, is. All we can do is deal with that."

I nodded, aching inside, then went to the head of Daddy's bed to kiss his forehead. "I love you, Daddy," I murmured into his ear. "So does Miss Mamie. And Tommy. We're all praying for God's mercy for you."

Then I rose and hugged my brother, careful of his wrist. "Let's go home and tell Miss Mamie about Uncle B."

Tommy nodded, hugging me back. "She was like a mother to him. She'll take it hard."

"Not as hard as she will when we lose Daddy." I had no idea what she'd do then.

We left to talk to Aunt Glory, then deliver the bad news to our mother.

Fifty-six

When we told Miss Mamie about Uncle Bedford, she stiffened, said it was a blessing for everyone, particularly him, then turned and went to her room.

I started after her, but Tommy grasped my elbow to hold me back. "Give her some time. Uncle B was like a son to her. We need to respect her privacy. When she's ready to talk about it, she will."

I nodded. Once again, his wisdom surprised me. "You're right."

That afternoon, we called Junior, who told us Aunt Glory had won out about burying Uncle B in the family plot by reminding her girls that he'd always wanted to be buried beside his long-dead mother. When that didn't convince them, she'd promised—in writing—that Patterson's Spring Hill could bury her in Atlanta when her time came. That sealed the deal with my status-conscious cousins.

So Uncle Bedford would be viewed (to avoid speculation about how he'd *really* died), then properly funeralized at Junior's, then finally laid to rest beside his beloved mother in the Breedlove burial section of Mimosa

Branch Cemetery, along with our departed forebears from the past hundred seventy-five years.

Somehow, Daddy found out Junior was doing the funeral, then insisted on going to visitation, so we took a chance and brought him (heavily sedated) with us. Miss Mamie had been there since the doors were opened, sitting next to Aunt Glory and the girls while most of Mimosa Branch's old guard came to pay their respects, including both of the Mame's prayer chains and her garden club, along with a delegation from the Athletic Board of Georgia Tech and another from the Podiatry Association.

I'd worried what Daddy would do when he saw Miss Mamie, and sure enough, he took one look at her and wrenched free of us with superhuman strength, then strode over to her and grabbed her up from her seat before we could stop him.

Everybody in the room but us froze.

Fearing the worst, Tommy and I raced after him. But the moment our mother gained her feet, Daddy started singing softly in his wonderful baritone and dancing with her.

Before our eyes, the decades fell away.

Miss Mamie laid her head on his shoulder and followed his lead, calling him Mr. Samba, which made him smile. Across the room and back, he led her.

Then abruptly, he halted, confused. "Where's my wife?" The anger returned. "I need to have a word with her."

I whisked Miss Mamie out into the hall and asked her to stay out of sight till we took him back to the Home. Then I went back in to help Tommy, who'd taken Daddy to the open casket to distract him.

Looking down at Uncle Bedford, Tommy said what most people say. "They did a good job with him, General, didn't they? He looks real natural."

In a moment of lucidity, Daddy covered his brother's crossed hands with his own and said, "I wish I was in there with him." Then he turned to the room and bellowed, "This is my baby brother."

Everyone present tensed, but Daddy went on. "We used to blow up straw hats with firecrackers at the barber shop. And steal moonshine from Scruffy Gober's still, sweet as the corn it was made from. And run wild in the woods like little boys should. And hide together when our father came home drunk and mean. I loved Bedford like my own son. He made me proud. Five-letter man at Tech. Officer in the navy. Top of his class in podiatry school. And now he's gotten out of that hellhole before me."

Daddy bent over, bracing his hands on his knees, and wept. "Gone, without me."

My father, who never bent. My father, who never cried.

Everybody present looked away, except Miss Mamie.

From the hallway, she stared straight through Daddy, as if she could erase what was happening by ignoring it, but that didn't work. I could still see the shame and pity in her stoic expression.

Then I realized things could take a turn for the worse at any second. So I signaled Tommy, and the two of us all but dragged our father out of the other end of the room, slowly progressing toward the parking lot.

"Come on, Daddy," Tommy soothed. "I'll take you home."

"No you won't," Daddy moaned. "You'll take me back to that place, that hell. I'll be alone." He shook his head like a dog that needed to be put down. "How much longer do I have to stay there paying for my sins before I get to go to heaven?"

Tommy and I both almost fell apart, then and there.

We'd become the enemy. Dear Lord, we *were* the enemy.

But what choice did we have? We couldn't control him anymore. He was dangerous.

I hugged Daddy as we made our way toward my minivan. "It's going to be okay," I lied. "It's going to be okay."

The lines of grief in his face shifted to sly anger in the blink of an eye. Daddy demanded with hostility, "I want to come to the funeral. I have a right. He's my brother." His muscles hardened. "Promise me I can come to the funeral, all of it, or I'll knock you both in the head."

By now we were in the parking lot, closing in on my minivan.

"Promise me!" Daddy growled, his resistance firming.

I hit the key remote and unlocked the doors, then pressed the button to open the passenger-side sliding door.

The General balked. "I have to be at the funeral!"

"We can try, Daddy," Tommy said, struggling to get Daddy into the backseat, then buckled up. "I promise, we'll try."

Never mind that he was certifiably insane and homicidal. There were rules about funerals in the South. Uncle B was Daddy's brother, so he had a sacred right to be there (as long as he wasn't armed).

It would take more Haldol, but maybe we could manage it.

Fifty-seven

After what happened at visitation, Miss Mamie decided not to go to the funeral. She said she'd rather stay home and supervise the caterers the girls had hired for the reception at our house, but Tommy and I both knew she was doing it for Daddy, to make sure he didn't go off again when he saw her.

Uncle Bedford's girls didn't want Daddy anywhere near the funeral, but Aunt Glory put her foot down, hard, this time. She told them how the General had paid Uncle Bedford's tuition for Georgia Tech and podiatrists' school, then bought a lot for them to build their first house in Hanover West. She reminded her daughters that Daddy had been like a father to Bedford when their own started drinking, and how proud the General had been of his baby brother's accomplishments.

So, grudgingly, the girls agreed to let him come, but only if the General was zonked, which was a reasonable request under the circumstances.

We worked it out with the nursing home, and when we came to pick Daddy up the next morning, he was dressed and clean-shaven, but moved like a zombie when we helped him out of the wheelchair at the front of the Home.

The nurse motioned for me to stay behind as Tommy seated Daddy in the minivan in slow motion.

She handed me what looked like a pencil box. "Take this with you, in case he has another break. The syringe is all loaded and ready to go. It works like an EpiPen. Just jab it into his backside or his thigh, and he'll be out in no time."

More Haldol? "He's already out of it," I protested. How much could he take? "We don't want to kill him, even though I know he'd thank us for it."

The nurse shook her head. "It won't kill him. It'll just knock him out. But bring him back right away if you have to use it, so we can monitor his breathing."

Please, Lord, don't let Daddy have another break. Have mercy. Give him peace.

I tucked the emergency sedative into my bag, then hurried to the driver's seat as Tommy closed the slider where Daddy sat like a zombie.

Wishing, wishing, wishing that things were different, but steeling myself for whatever happened.

Might as well accept things as they are, my Granny Beth used to say. *Banging your head against it won't change things. It'll just give you a headache.*

I surrendered the whole situation to God, then promptly picked it up again.

Lord, I bow to You, who makes a way where there is no way. Please let there be peace and comfort for Uncle Bedford's family, and ours. Have mercy on Daddy.

By God's good grace, the funeral went off without a hitch. One of the pastors from the Anglican church Aunt Glory and Uncle B had attended in Buckhead conducted the brief service from the 1928 Book of Common Prayer.

Neither of my cousins had brought their children, which made me wonder if those kids would grow up without the rituals that made death a part of life, instead of a sudden disappearance with no good-byes.

Daddy actually seemed to come to his senses enough to know what was going on, but he didn't get angry. He just tightened his grip on my hand and watched through silent tears. Seeing him that way, I cried, too. Of all times for him to realize what was happening. Too cruel, too cruel.

Then Tommy reached behind Daddy's shoulders to pat mine. I looked across our father to see my brother's features clouded with concern for me. It was a gift I very much needed, one that held me up and kept me strong.

After the service, we went to the graveside. It wasn't easy for Daddy to navigate the uneven ground, but between the two of us, Tommy and I managed to get him under the tent and into one of the navy blue faux-fur-covered folding chairs behind Aunt Glory and the girls and their husbands. For safety's sake, Tommy and I sat on either side of the General.

The interment service was mercifully brief.

When everything was over and the last of those present had offered their parting condolences to Aunt Glory and the girls, Junior told them they could go to the reception, then come back afterward to see the grave when everything was in place. So they got back into the limo and rode away.

But Daddy remained in his chair and refused to get up. He just sat there, staring at the lift that slowly lowered the casket into the vault below.

I couldn't help wondering what was going through his mind. Was he remembering better times? Or the spectacular arguments that marked his and Uncle Bedford's volatile relationship? Or his pride in Uncle Bedford's hard-fought accomplishments?

Or was he merely blank, his memories stolen by the sedatives or his disease?

I didn't ask him, because I couldn't handle what he might say.

We let him sit there for thirty minutes, then gently pulled him to his feet.

"Daddy, you did so well," I said clearly. "We're proud of you."

He sighed. "I'm proud of you both. Please, please don't die before me. I'd go crazy."

"We won't, Daddy," Tommy promised, ignoring the irony of what Daddy had said.

It took us almost another half hour to get him back to the Home and into his bed. Then we put in a brief appearance at the reception, after which I holed up in my apartment and cried and cried and cried. Not because Uncle Bedford was gone, finally free of his fears and illness, but because my daddy had lost himself and lived in the hell we'd put him in.

Fifty-eight

It was well past ten when I woke in the dark, stuffy-nosed and logy, to the sound of slow, heavy steps climbing the stair to my garage apartment.

Who in the world?

A chill ran down my spine. *Please, Lord, not Phil.*

I forced myself out of bed, into my robe, then across the tiny living area to the single pane at eye level in the door. Shrouding the house, a cold, heavy fog turned the streetlights at the sidewalk into haloed pricks of light.

I turned on the porch light, stepped to the side, and looked askance down the stairs so I could see who it was.

Major relief. I unlocked and opened the door. "Mama?"

What was she doing here in the middle of the night?

Then I saw the big, round plastic container she used for her homemade ice cream.

Salivating, I helped her in.

"Thank you, honey," she panted out. "I just couldn't stand it another minute alone in our bedroom. Every time I closed my eyes, I saw your daddy in that coffin instead of Bedford." She pulled a small wine bottle from the deep pocket of her blue seersucker robe. "Here. Ice wine, for the ice cream."

I took the bottle, locked the door behind her, then turned on the inside lights and went to the kitchenette for some bowls and spoons. And aperitif glasses.

Mama plunked heavily into the chair at my little table, then put down the frosty canister with a thunk. "This is from the final batch I made this year, a particularly good one. I try to avoid sweets, but this is an emergency."

I returned with bowls, spoons, and my ice cream scoop. I handed Miss Mamie the bowls and scoop. "Bombs away," I said, pouring the ice wine into the tiny goblets.

Mama served us both heaping portions of ice cream, then took a sip of her ice wine. She rolled her lips together, then opened them with an audible smack. "Aah. Nothing like sweets to soothe the soul. Especially ones with spirits."

Waiting for her to take the conversational lead, I dove into the peach ice cream. "Whoa," I said with my mouth full. "This *is* exceptional."

For the first time ever, she didn't correct me for talking with my mouth full.

We went through two whole bowlfuls apiece and two aperitifs before Mama looked at me and said, "I loved Bedford, too, even though I had to get tough with him near the end. Do you think he knew I still loved him, anyway?"

"Of course he did." My mouth was frozen, my tongue thickened. "'Now that he's with the Lord, he can only remember the good things,'" I quoted Granny Beth. "'Or it wouldn't be heaven.'"

Mama peered morosely into her bowl. "It made everything so real, seeing him in that coffin. It made me see the boy he was when he came to us. Then all I could see was the General, lying there in his place. Too real. Too real." She let out a heavy sigh. "I'm not sure I can bear up when your father's time

comes. Despite the way we fought, there were so many precious memories."
I noted her use of the past tense, but remained mute.

"The General did the best he could with no mother to teach him the
softer things," she went on. "He made it possible for Bedford to do things
and be the man your father never could."

She rarely spoke about that time, so I couldn't keep from asking, "Were
they close, really?"

Mama nodded. "In that man-way of theirs, of course. They talked about
politics"—to the right of Attila the Hun, I was sure—"and sports. Hot-
tempered, the both of them, so they had plenty of arguments, but they always came around. Did chores together or worked on your uncle's hot rod.
You know how men are."

Actually, I didn't. Even as a kid, Tommy had always avoided me, much
less confided in me. And Phil, an only child, never socialized except for
corporate or professional events. As far as I knew, he had no close men
friends, just a handful of other CPAs who played golf or tennis with him.

Phil certainly wasn't present in David's life. I was the one who went to
all our son's games and pageants and parent-teacher conferences. Phil was
always unavailable.

I thought back about all those times he hadn't come home from the office till almost midnight and wondered if he'd been cheating even then.

Not that I cared about what he did anymore. I'd finally detached from
him, and our past. There was a blessed blank spot where Phil had been,
and I wanted to keep it that way.

If he would just leave me alone.

Miss Mamie cocked her head. "Penny for your thoughts."

I forced myself to focus. "I'm so sorry, Mama. My mind wandered." A
yawn escaped me as I rose to make room for the remaining ice cream in my
small refrigerator freezer. When I finally got the freezer door closed, I took
Mama's hand and pulled her up. "Come on. Let's pile up in my bed. You'll
do better staying with me tonight."

She nodded in gratitude, then followed. "I think you're right."

"You'll love this mattress," I said. "And you have your own control for the electric blanket."

Mama perked up, following me into the bedroom, then took the opposite side of the bed. "You know, I've never slept under an electric blanket before."

My jaw dropped. "Never?"

"Nope." Mama pulled the covers up to her chin. "Your father said they were a Communist plot, that the electrical fields would ruin our brains. But you don't seem to have suffered for it, so I'm willing to give it a try."

I got up and adjusted her control to a medium setting. "This one's warmer down at the feet," I told her, then showed her how to adjust it. "The little light stays on, so you can see the numbers if you need to change it in the night."

I went to brush my teeth and relieve myself, then brought back a new, unopened toothbrush for Mama to use. "Here. This is brand-new, and there's plenty of toothpaste. The bathroom's all yours."

Mama regarded it with disdain, then snuggled even deeper under the electric blanket. "I don't need the bathroom yet, and I think I'll skip brushing my teeth for tonight."

I tucked my chin. Uncle Bedford's death really *had* hit her hard. "Egad! The world's turned upside down. Miss Mamie, going to bed without brushing her teeth?"

"It won't hurt, just this once. And anyway, your daddy's not here to fuss at me about it."

Shaking my head at hearing such talk, I crawled into my side of the bed and curled onto my side, my back to my mother.

Miss Mamie did the same, then put her freezing feet against my calves. "Oh, good," she murmured. "You sleep hot, just like your daddy."

Five minutes later, she was snoring as loud as my daddy ever thought about doing.

Good thing I didn't have classes the next morning.

To my surprise, I grew drowsy right away despite the noise. I'd forgotten how nice it was to have someone breathing on the other side of the bed. Even my mother. Even though she snored.

I just didn't want her to get used to it.

Fifty-nine

Every time I went to see Daddy between class days, he seemed a little worse, not just mentally, but physically.

Thank goodness for school. It took all my thought and energy to keep up with so many classes. After midterms in March, I had a ninety-eight average in history, a ninety-nine in Communications and English (I used contractions in my first lit paper, or I would have aced it), an A in Anthropology (my professor was a generalist who only gave letter grades), and a ninety-six in human biology with a ninety-one in lab.

My only B was in French, but I counted myself lucky there. My teacher still rattled off everything in French, but my ears were gradually catching up, and the textbook made the assignments clear, so I tested well.

The language lab was another matter. When I found out what a big deal it would be to have the lessons in the disabilities quiet room, I decided to tough it out in the regular lab. I had to replay the exercises over and over before I could understand. But eventually, I managed.

There were no noisy distractions in human biology or lab, but I still couldn't understand my Nigerian bio lab teacher's lectures about genetic traits, so I made an appointment with her to figure it out. After I'd told her I didn't understand, she explained it again for twenty minutes, leaving me more confused than ever. So I informed her of my grades in my other classes, then quoted *Cool Hand Luke:* "What we have here is a failure to communicate."

Bless her heart, she tried again, with no better luck. Definitely a language barrier, there.

It occurred to me to ask her to do the genetic charts with me, and when she did, suddenly all became clear. I had been adding an extra step to the analysis. Presto, I got it.

But what if I hadn't thought of getting her to do the steps?

I didn't care what gender, race, religion, or nationality my professors were. I just thought they should be able to speak English well enough to be understood. I'm just sayin'.

Thanks to my heavy schedule, I gradually thought about Connor less and less.

But Phil refused to let up. Flowers, letters, e-mails, and cards (with no return address) came almost every day, begging me to see him, but never saying when.

I asked Tommy if he'd heard anything from his friend, but he said no.

Easter came in April, and on the tenth, my phone rang.

Seeing *unknown* in the little readout on the phone, I answered anyway. "Hello?"

I never screen my calls. If they're sales calls, I always start off by asking if they know Jesus as their personal Lord and savior. So far, all of them had hung up immediately. But maybe someday, I'd get to share my testimony. You never know.

Connor's voice surprised me. "Lin, I'm calling to ask you to come to our Easter service on the twentieth."

Hope bloomed, warm and golden inside me, despite my vow to give up on him. "Does this mean you've gotten your answer?"

After a daunting pause, he said, "It means I would really like you to be there."

Still a wuss!!

Shoot! Shoot, shoot, shoot.

A searing stab of disappointment plunged into my heart.

As always, just the sound of his voice was all it took to take me right back to that first, fabulous kiss. And the fun conversations we'd had. And the movies we'd seen, hand in hand. And my longing for safety in his arms.

But he hadn't gotten his answer, or he would have said so.

I groaned inside. *Honest, Lord, I've tried to trust and be patient, but You see what he does to me. And You keep letting him call or show up. What's with that?*

Maybe I could go to the service and put an end to our relationship at last. But if that didn't work, I decided I'd knock his socks off.

The dress! *The* dress.

"Are you there?" Connor prodded gently.

"I'm here," I said. "I'll come." Boy, would I ever! "It'll give me a chance to wear my big, beautiful Easter bonnet."

I had a wonderful white, finely woven straw picture hat with gorgeous, convincing magnolia blossoms at the base of the crown. And a flattering white cutwork dress, long and slim, to go with it. Miss Mamie had said I looked like an angel in it.

Let Connor put that in his pipe and smoke it.

Connor laughed, a warm, consoling sound. "Just get there early so you won't be blocking anybody's view."

"Okay. What's early?"

"Nine. The service starts at nine-thirty, but it's Easter, so we're jammed, and folks come early to get a good seat."

"Nine it is." Fed up with his dragging his feet, I said a quick, "Bye," then hung up, already scolding myself for agreeing to go when it might only make me miserable.

Sixty

That one phone call, and the anticipation of seeing Connor again rattled me so that I almost blew two major assignments. But somehow, I managed to suck it up.

Finals were only a month away.

English would be a take-home essay, which made things easy. Anthropology was open book in the classroom, divided up into teams, so my notes would come in handy.

Human biology was multiple choice—a big help as a memory jogger—and lab would be easy, because the instructions for each experiment would be written out.

American government was multiple choice, too.

Speaking of the government class, I'd gotten into trouble when we were studying opinion polls, and the teacher put us in groups and asked us to come up with an unbiased question, then a weighted question on a variety of assigned topics. Unluckily for me, the passive-aggressive girl from anthropology was in the group. So when we came to the public health topic,

I suggested for the biased question, Should illegitimate children qualify for Medicaid?

That plump little nineteen-year-old bowed up and huffed, "My sister has two babies with no daddy."

I resisted the urge to ask, "And how's that working out for her?"

Instead I just shrugged and said, "See? The question made you mad, didn't it? That's what the teacher wants us to see, how wording can play on people's emotions and affect their answers."

Clearly, she didn't make the connection, because she scowled at me thereafter.

We won't even discuss the abortion questions. God forbid you be a right-to-lifer in college these days.

I'd come to the conclusion that the only people you could safely ridicule in college were white people (especially the founding fathers) and Evangelical Christians.

Who knows? Maybe prejudice against the Christians was cumulative retaliation for all those rudely unannounced weeknight "visitations."

I mean, if God can soften a person's heart to the Gospel, He can do it when you're polite and call first, wouldn't you think?

But I have to admit, it didn't feel good being branded a bigot and a hypocrite simply because I held traditional views about marriage and sexuality. Not that I tried to force them on anyone else. I'd really been working to leave the judging to God. Every time I slipped, I remembered *forgive.*

And every time I thought of Mary Lou Perkins, I thanked God and prayed that He would give her peace.

The main point is, my midterm exams and assignment grades erased my fears about incipient Alzheimer's, but strained my brain so much, I wasn't any good at keeping up with the rest of my life. So I buried my head in the books and pretended nothing was wrong.

But life has this annoying way of jerking me back to reality.

Sixty-one

On Thursday night the week before Easter, while I was working late on a chapter report for English, I heard heavy footsteps coming up my stairs.

I finished my sentence on the keyboard before I hit save, then got up to see who it was.

I looked out the little pane in my front door, but didn't see anyone.

Oh, gosh. What if it was Miss Mamie, and she'd fallen?

I took off the chain lock and turned the bolt, then opened the door and stepped across the landing to look down the stairs. Nobody there, thank goodness.

Then I turned around and almost had a heart attack. Phil stood inside with a big picnic hamper. He must have been hiding against the wall and snuck in behind me.

"Lord, Lin, don't faint on me," he said as I staggered inside and collapsed into a chair. "I only wanted to surprise you, not scare you."

Right. I glared at him, but didn't speak.

As if the place were his instead of mine, Phil plopped down in the club chair across the coffee table and placed the basket between us, then opened it, sending heavenly aromas into the room.

"Terra di Luna," I breathed out. One of my favorite restaurants in Buckhead. Even after eleven years, I could still recognize the aroma.

In my case, the way to my heart can very well be through my stomach.

Phil grinned, an expression he'd rarely used when we were together. "I hope you still like it."

Like it? I still dreamed about it.

He pulled out a bottle of rosé covered with condensation. "Cold and sweet, just like you like it."

And he hated it.

Then he took out a shiny food carton with the restaurant's logo, then another and another and another, identifying their contents as he did. "Chopped salad for two. Chicken piccata over capellini for you, lasagna for me, and grilled eggplant." He finally got to the bottom and gingerly extracted a plastic cake dome that protected two six-layer slices of Terra di Luna's famous zabaglione cake with Italian creme icing, and fresh berries and custard between the light, tender white layers. Orgasm on a fork.

Putting aside my reservations about Phil's sneaky "surprise," I rose slowly so my blood pressure wouldn't take a nosedive, then went for plates and utensils, my better instincts overwhelmed by gluttony.

Phil knew me, all right.

While he served up our dinners, he asked about Uncle Bedford and the funeral, then Daddy and Miss Mamie and Tommy. And, miracle of miracles, he actually paid attention when I answered.

By the time we were done, I had a slight buzz on and decided to rinse the dishes and leave them in the sink till morning. I didn't sense Phil's coming up behind me till his hands slid gently down my upper arms. "Now, that's a change," he purred into my ear, moving closer to reveal his desire for me. "You never left a dish unwashed before."

To my horror, my body responded. "I'm not the person I was then, anymore," I told him as disjointed flashes of our sex life attacked me. Our physical relationship had been the one good thing in our marriage.

Part of me wanted to run, but a small glimmer guilted me into giving him a chance.

Phil turned me around, then cupped my face and kissed me, gently at first, then deeper.

Nothing. No *kiss, kiss, kiss.*

Nothing like the way Connor kissed me.

With that, Phil and I became a threesome, with Connor in the middle.

I stepped back. "I think you'd better go."

He seemed genuinely crushed. "Lin, I ask you again, and I won't give up till you say yes: please marry me. We can go tonight."

Oh, right! Can we say, clueless?

And if he were sincere, he'd have left, as I'd asked.

"Give me a chance to prove to you I've changed," he repeated for the jillionth time.

"I just did." I looked down, then met his troubled gaze with one of resolution. "It's over, Phil. I don't know how things with Connor will work out in the end, but the one thing I'm sure of is that you and I are done. Have been for years."

"That isn't true! It can't be." He drew me to him, pinning my body against the counter, his kiss demanding, his hands possessively roaming over my body.

I tried to pull my mouth from his, but his hands closed, hard, around my skull, preventing it. I screamed, but it was lost inside him.

Lord, please don't let him rape me, I prayed as my knee shot up between Phil's legs with a wisdom of its own.

At last, he released me to double up and bellow in pain.

"Help!" I shouted, racing for the door. I managed to get it open for one more plea before he grabbed me and pulled me back inside kicking and calling for help.

"Lin, please," he said, his calm belying the force of his arms around me.

"We were happy together once. We can be again. I just want a chance to love you. Not to force you. You mean so much to me, now that I've understood what I did to you, how awful it was. Please calm down, before you scare Miss Mamie."

No lights came on in the big house.

Calm down, my sensible self commanded. *Pretend to forgive him, so he'll let go of you.*

But the still, small voice overrode my survival instincts with, *Forgive him,* reminding me of Connor's sermon. *Forgive and be free,* the memory of his voice echoed.

I went stone-still in Phil's grasp.

That stopped him.

"What?" he said, clearly perplexed.

"I forgive you." The amazing thing was, I meant it.

A weight lifted, and all fear went with it. "I forgive you," I repeated, reveling in the peace it gave me.

His expression made me think he was going to slap my head off, but instead, he let me go and took a step backward, toward the door. This time, his voice was vulnerable. "What?"

"I forgive you," I said softly, almost overcome by a wave of sympathy. "For everything, even this." Poor sad, misguided Phil, trying so hard to find happiness in sex and money and putting things over on us all.

I thanked God heartily that I wasn't like him, or still bound to him in any way.

Phil backed to the door, then grasped the knob behind him and turned it. "Why?"

"Because I love you. Not like a wife, but as a person. Just as you are. God commands it."

Struggling not to lose control, Phil stepped forward, but only to open the door. As a cold breeze swept past him, he turned to glare at me, backing onto the little landing. Then we both heard hard, pounding footsteps ascending the stairs and looked toward them.

Connor!

"No," I cried as he vaulted toward Phil, grabbing him by the shirt and shoving him hard against the flimsy railing.

"What did you do to her?" Connor demanded. "I heard her scream."

I grabbed his wrists and tugged. "Connor, it's okay. Let him go!"

He turned as if seeing me for the first time, but he didn't let go of Phil.

They'd both go through the railing if he didn't back off.

"It's okay," I repeated. "He scared me, but it's okay now."

"What did he do to you?" Connor demanded.

I cupped his cheek. "That doesn't matter. I forgave him, just like you told me to in your sermon."

As if he were scalded, Connor let go of Phil.

When I saw the guilt in Connor's expression, I stepped between them and put my arms around the man who had come to my rescue. I could feel his heart beating fast and strong against his chest, and his muscles roped for combat. No way could I physically restrain him. "Let him go, Connor," I pleaded. "It's over."

He did. But his body was still primed for a fight, so I pushed him inside, then turned to close the door. I said to Phil through the crack, "Go, before he comes after you."

"Whatever happened to turning the other cheek?" Phil accused.

Forgive him.

I did, but I still slammed and locked the door. I mean, I'm not an idiot.

I turned to find Connor with his arms stiff, braced on the counter, his brow against the cabinet, eyes closed, panting from adrenaline.

Sixty-two

Lord help me, I couldn't stop myself from going to him and drawing him close again.

At that very moment, my fight-or-flight reaction fizzled. "I'm glad you're here," I said into his chest as he hugged me back so hard I could barely breathe.

"What did he do to you?" he asked, his voice dead. "I have to know."

"No you don't," I told him. "What happened doesn't matter. I forgive him. End of story."

A flame of anger ignited inside me. Did Connor think he could blast back into my life that way, ask me such a question, only to leave me hanging again?

He stared into my eyes, then kissed me fiercely, possessively, too much like the way Phil had kissed me.

No!

Before I could pull free, he wrenched his mouth from mine. "If anything had happened to you . . ."

Though what had happened was my business, and mine alone, I relented and said, "He arrived unannounced with dinner from my favorite restaurant, then kissed me, and nothing happened. So I told him it was over."

A flash of jealousy crossed Connor's face.

I'd have thought that having Connor come to my rescue and care enough to be jealous would make me feel like a fairy-tale princess, but it didn't. I just felt rotten about the whole thing. Except for the forgiveness part, the devil had been well served by the whole incident. And I'd given in to the compulsion to grab on to Connor twice without a second thought.

I eased out of his arms and gently pushed him away.

He meant it for evil, but God meant it for good, my still, small inner voice said about Phil.

Right. Well, I was sick and tired of waiting for a sinner and a saint to determine what I'd do with the rest of my life. There wasn't that much of it left.

Then I saw the fear in Connor's expression and relented. I exhaled heavily, then said, "I've been telling Phil it's over since he turned up on New Year's, but he won't listen."

I straightened to face the man who'd said God had made us for each other, only to abandon me. "I'm tired of waiting for you two to make up your minds. Phil says he's changed and showers me with gifts, then disappears for weeks at a time. He knows where I am, but I have no idea where he is. So I can't begin to tell if he's truly turned his life around."

Connor's left eyebrow lifted in premature confidence.

"And you," I scolded, "you leave me sitting on the fence for all these weeks. Is that really because you're waiting for God, or because of your own fear about legitimizing our relationship, and what that would mean for both of us?"

There. I'd finally asked him.

Connor scowled, his posture defensive. "I can't believe you asked me that question."

Just like a politician. Don't answer the question. Attack the asker, instead.

I felt as if someone had poked a hole in me and my confidence was draining away. "Connor, please go away and leave me alone. I can't deal with your indecision anymore."

That much was true, indeed.

When he didn't respond, I continued. "I'm going to try to make a life without either you or Phil. Just me and God and my family. We managed before I met you, and we'll manage again."

Not that I believed it, but I hoped it.

Connor's face hardened.

Men. I mean, really.

Granny Beth's voice scolded gently from the depths of my heart, *The best man in the world is still just a man.* Especially *preachers.*

"I appreciate your coming to my rescue," I told Connor, "but I had the situation under control. God showed me what to do, and it worked."

He tensed. "God doesn't want anybody to hurt anybody, yet because we have free will, horrible things happen to good people all the time. Phil's still out there. Still determined to have you." The muscles in his jaw flexed. "He could knock that door in with one swift kick, bolt and all. You aren't safe alone."

"I'm not alone," I told him, then quoted, "'If God is with us, who can be against us?'"

Connor came closer, but didn't intrude into my space or touch me. "I believe that with all my heart," he said, "but when I heard you scream and saw the car parked on the side street, everything went out of my head but protecting you."

Even though I was handling everything already, by God's direction. "You took his attention away from me. I'm grateful for that. But he was already on his way out."

Connor peered into my eyes. "And . . . ?"

"And now I'll miss you more than ever." It took all my self-control not to return to his arms, but this time I managed to stay strong. "Until you're ready to put a ring on my finger, leave me alone. I'll be living my life without you."

Oh, help! I'd just given him the ultimatum, like his ex. Was I subconsciously playing into the scenario?

As for Connor, I might as well have shot him in the heart. Shock and anger replaced his calm demeanor. "If that's what you really want . . ."

No it wasn't.

"It is," I lied. What I really wanted was for Connor to fight for me. To marry me, no matter what. I was finally ready to do that for him. But Phil had blasted an abyss between us that Connor refused to cross.

He quaked, then turned away. "Please come to Easter service. It's all I ask."

It was little enough. I wasn't ready to burn *all* the bridges. "All right. I'll be there at nine." Looking my very best.

He left without looking back, just unlocked the door, strode out, then slammed it behind him, leaving a gaping emptiness where he had been.

Drat! Drat, drat, drat!

My own company and independence had always been enough till Connor happened. Now even my cozy little refuge seemed bereft without him.

Weary and aching to my soul, I leaned my forehead against the door, beyond tears.

God, I don't know how much more of this I can take. Please tell me what You want before I do something stupid.

I felt His presence, but the still, small voice had once again fallen silent.

I locked the chain, then turned the dead bolt, frustrated beyond description.

All I had left was my favorite desperation prayer. *Thank You, God, for my life just as it is.*

If only I could mean it; yet I prayed it anyway, despite my heavy heart.

As Granny Beth had said, at least it made the devil mad.

I faced my apartment with a sigh. Life goes on, and I had homework.

Scanning the textbooks and notes spread all over my bed, I shook my head. How in the world was I supposed to finish my assignments now?

Sixty-three

Easter eve, I set my clock for five forty-five A.M. then woke, groggy, to the first hint of light when it went off.

Connor. I'll see him today.

And First Baptist will see me, in my best Easter finery. Determined to jog them all—Connor included—off their duffs, I sat up and put my feet to the cold floor.

As usual, April had been unpredictable after a very warm March, and the lows lingered in the high thirties.

I stepped into my fuzzy slippers and pulled on my robe, then went to my kitchenette to turn on the coffee maker before I answered nature's call.

By the time I'd taken care of that, washed up, then brushed my teeth and combed my hair, the aroma of caffeine arrived from the kitchen, drawing me like an invisible hand.

I poured myself a clear glass mugful, added three Splendas, then cupped its warmth as I opened the door to the first pale light of dawn. If I hurried, I could make it on time to the service at the chapel on the lake.

First Baptist was for everybody else, but the sunrise service was just for me, in jeans and no makeup except for lipstick. (I had to wear lipstick, lest anybody think *I'd* just risen from the dead.)

A light went on in Miss Mamie's kitchen, and I saw her beginning to make her usual Easter luncheon feast, as she had every year since Daddy had come back from the war. My stomach growled in anticipation of home-made biscuits and cinnamon rolls, sliced melons, Georgia Belle peaches, cheese-egg soufflé, strawberry flan, tons of crisp bacon, sliced ham, sawmill *and* redeye gravy, and grits that melted in your mouth. But that wouldn't be ready till one, after church.

So I dressed warmly in jeans, winter boots, and a heavy white cotton sweater under my purple windbreaker, then poured myself a second mug-ful of coffee for the trip and set out for the lake, doing my best to absorb the peace of this special morning.

I was only the fifth person to arrive at the simple pavilion on the little hill overlooking the marina, but the view from there was gorgeous: the ma-rina, then the lake, dotted with islands, then the black, lacy silhouettes of trees against the now-crimson horizon.

As the minutes passed, thirty more people came in from the marina on foot, and a few more in cars, but there was no sign of a minister. So we all watched the sun rise together with a quiet sense of reverence.

I thanked God for pouring as much of Himself into a human body as it could hold, then walking among us as the Christ, and I praised the beauty and intricacy of His creation.

Particularly in space. When I got to heaven, where there is no time, I planned to ask God if I could take an eon or so to cruise the universe and witness all the wonders of His hand, then come back and serve Him for-ever. I'm convinced He'll let me.

Fifteen minutes late, the young minister arrived, his plastic nametag identifying him as Bob, associate pastor at a splinter denomination's huge church in Oakwood.

His flustered apologies seemed loud and raucous after the cooperative silence, so I prayed for him to relax and focus.

Then I sat on a bench to hear his Easter message, but Connor had spoiled me. I expected something wonderful and hopeful and inspiring, but got only recited Bible readings about the Resurrection. No application, bless his heart. Clearly, this young man of God was nervous standing before us.

I prayed again for God's peace on him, then did my best to take something from hearing the familiar words of Christ's Resurrection in the King James version. But I couldn't help thinking about Connor and what he would say at First Baptist.

Then I brought myself up short. Holy cow. I was being just as judgmental about that poor young minister as the old biddies in Connor's church were about me.

Judge not that ye be not judged, in spades.

I hadn't made it to seven before I'd messed up. *Sorry, God. I don't want to think like that. Help me mind my own little red wagon and keep my eyes on You.*

He, more than anyone, knew I couldn't do it on my own.

I sensed an affectionate shake of the Godhead.

After the brief service dismissed, I shook the young minister's hand and thanked him for volunteering, then headed home for breakfast.

Mama must have seen me coming, because she'd laid out two plates on the kitchen table, with soft-scrambled eggs, crisp bacon, buttery grits with just the right texture (not dry, not runny), and two fresh biscuits with a side of homemade blackberry jam. And coffee with semisweet chocolate morsels added to the grounds. I could smell the faint hint of chocolaty sweetness rising from the pot.

"Wow, Mama. That looks perfect, as usual."

She plopped down beside me with a satisfied sigh. "Tommy's asked three people to lunch, so I decided to make fresh dinner rolls. They're rising now."

Yum. An appropriate choice, considering the day.

Sitting there, I decided it might do Connor some good to stew a bit. "Will you help hook me into that cutwork dress when I change for the eleven o'clock service?" I asked Miss Mamie. "You won't have to leave the kitchen. I'll come over here."

"I thought you were going to the nine-thirty," she responded.

"I changed my mind," I told her with my best duchess face. "Let him wonder where I am for a change."

Mama got it immediately. "Great idea. Won't hurt to have him see what that feels like." She dabbed her mouth with her damask napkin. "I think that white dress will be perfect. I told you when you bought it, you look gorgeous in it. Just like an angel."

Back in 1980 when I'd seen *Somewhere in Time* with my ALTA tennis group in Buckhead, I'd looked for the closest thing I could find to Jane Seymour's white dress in the movie, right down to the white stockings, hat, and shoes, because Phil and I had been invited to a high tea and croquet party given by one of his wealthy clients.

When I'd modeled the outfit for Phil ahead of time, he'd frowned and said I looked ridiculous, then ordered me to take it off and find something more conventional. "The nail that sticks up always gets hit," he'd chided (one of his favorite Japanese sayings). So I'd worn a pale pink silk suit and white silk camisole, instead.

But I'd kept the *Somewhere in Time* dress and hat for all these years, knowing that the day would come when I'd have the perfect occasion to wear it, and this was the day.

I indulged as much as I dared in breakfast, then rolled from my seat to go put on my face and my fancy white dress and hat for the eleven o'clock service at First Baptist.

I even rummaged up my skin-colored body shaper and French bra for underneath.

This time when I walked into that church, I wanted to attract attention. I wanted to look like an angel for Connor, no matter what the congregation thought. Let him put that in his pipe and smoke it.

Sixty-four

My arrival at First Baptist stirred a flutter of whispers behind hands and overt stares as the nine-thirty congregation came down the front stairs on their way to the parking lot.

Before, I'd have been mortified, but not today. Today was my turn to start over and rise from the ashes of my past, and the more who knew it, the better.

I smiled and nodded to everyone.

A little girl broke loose from her mother and ran to touch my skirt. "Are you real?" she asked with the candor of her age. "Because Mama says people aren't angels, but you sure look like one."

I crouched to her level and gave her a hug. "Mama's right. I'm not an angel, but I sure do like this dress."

"Is a dress a getup, because that's what Mama called it," she told me as her red-faced mother caught up with us.

I rose and extended my hand. "Hi. I'm Linwood Scott. You sure have a darling daughter, here. She remembers every word you say."

The woman colored even deeper as she shook my hand. "I'm so sorry. I didn't mean—"

Forgive and be free.

I smiled. "It's okay."

At the top of the stairs, I kept smiling and nodded to the slightly frozen greeter, then accepted the service bulletin. After only a brief arrow prayer, I braved the sanctuary, where more whispers and stares greeted me. Wherever I made eye contact, I smiled and nodded, remembering that Christ's people were still just people, with all the same flaws and weaknesses I shared.

Forgive us our sins as we forgive those who sin against us.

I still needed plenty of forgiveness, so how could I refuse to forgive them?

Something huge and humble broke loose inside me, and I began to see them as Connor did when he looked at his congregation. And suddenly, I wasn't afraid to be a minister's wife anymore.

Assuming I'd ever get the chance, which was a big assumption.

As I had on New Year's Eve, I went down to the first row, left, and took the first seat from the aisle, staking my claim.

The low hum of conversation behind me swelled, then cut short as the organist signaled the start of the service when Connor and the minister of music mounted the front platform.

The minister of music greeted everyone, then asked us to stand as Connor took his place beside the altar, facing the congregation. And me.

I thought his eyes would pop out of his head. He peered at me as if I were a dream of Glory.

Yes, yes, yes. Even though I was an old woman, my dress and hat had done their job. Along with my underpinnings. Halleluiah!

We all started singing "Christ Our Lord Is Risen Today" (one of my favorites), but Connor remained transfixed. Then the choir sang a beautiful Easter special about being renewed.

While they did, Connor bowed his head, and I could see from his expression, he was struggling to shift his concentration to the upcoming message.

When we'd all finished the praise choruses, the minister of music motioned for us to sit, and Connor came to the pulpit, his eyes filled with compassion for those who faced him. "Praise be to God, for on the first Easter Day, our Lord and Savior defeated death and rose again."

Applause and amens erupted behind me.

"So what do we do with this gift?" he challenged. "We who have given our hearts to Him so that we may take our cares directly to the holy God who made us? Do we use it as a license to sin? Paul said no, in most emphatic terms. Yet many of us do. We judge others instead of forgiving. We sin and fall short. We fail to forgive ourselves when we see the error of our ways. Yet Christ has covered all our sins with His sacrifice."

I could see he was homed in on his message, and what a message it was.

"The best part of being a Christian is that we can start every day anew, as if we, too, have risen from the dead, as long as we sincerely repent our shortcomings and want to grow closer to God."

He smiled. "Sometimes I make it till nine A.M. before I need to repent. Sometimes, my feet don't hit the floor before I have to say, 'Oops, God. Sorry about that,' and start over.

"But the message of this day is that those of us who have given our lives and hearts to Christ *can* start over, as many times as it takes, without having to drag the guilt of our past shortcomings with us."

He scanned the rows. "As Dickens depicted with Marley's chains in *A Christmas Carol,* our past mistakes can be a heavy burden till we release them to God through Christ. Once we sincerely turn away from our wrongs—no matter how many times it takes—we no longer have to bear the weight of those chains."

The choir—to a person—listened, intent. As for the rest of the congregation, I was glad I was sitting in the first row, or I'd have been tempted to look around to see how they were taking this gentle admonition. God knew that I needed to hear it as much as anyone.

"So criticism about past failures," Connor went on, "our own or other people's, has no place in the Christian life. We don't have to beat ourselves up for failures that are over and done with.

"Turn from them? Yes.

"Learn from them? Yes.

"Use them to remind us of a better way? Yes.

"Our own shortcomings *and* those of fellow Christians." He leaned forward, cupping his ear to the congregation as a signal that he expected a response. "Does it say anywhere in scripture that we're allowed to stuff our resentments into a grudge box and nurse them?"

The congregation responded with a halfhearted, "No."

"No!" he echoed with zeal. "What are we to do when someone—Christian or not—despitefully uses us?"

He waited, but no one responded at first. So he waited some more.

At last, one of the deacons said, "Pray for them!"

Connor cupped his ear again. "We all pray for those who love us. But how often do we pray for those who do us wrong? Praying for the people we have every right to hate, my brothers and sisters, is the mark of a Christian."

He looked over the congregation with affection. "Can you let go of your grudges and surrender them to God so you can rise anew every morning without dragging those with you?"

I didn't think I had any grudges. Except for Connor. And Phil. And my human biology teacher.

So I'm human, all right? I'll pray for them, I promise.

Connor went on, telling us how we could turn away from our shortcomings and start clean every day, confirming every step with scripture. By the end of the sermon, a fresh energy and resolve pulsed through the congregation.

As always when I heard a wonderful sermon, I thought, *God, maybe between the two of us, we can do this.*

Connor paused, then said, "The ushers are now going to pass among you for the offering. If you are visiting and have been blessed this day, we invite you to come back. Our arms and our hearts are always open to those who seek God."

While the choir sang and the ushers passed the plates, I pondered Connor's message, and chewed on the idea that I really could leave the past behind and start anew every day. Even without Connor.

When the collection special was done, Connor returned to the pulpit to give the altar call, during which I pondered again.

But I came to abruptly when I heard him say my name.

"A blessed Christian woman whose friendship"—uh-oh, friendship?—"I cherish, and whose faith leaves me in awe," Connor said, eyes on me. "I hope you will all welcome her back and cherish her as I have."

A spark of mischief flashed in his eyes. "Lin, would you please come down front to allow us to welcome you back after the service?"

Had he lost his freaking mind?

The shock on my face twisted to an outraged glare witnessed only by the choir, some of whom smiled with glee.

What nerve! I hadn't told him I was going to come back to the Baptists!

Anger set my face on fire.

Pray for those who despitefully use you.

Okay. *God, please open the skies and show that man what he just did to me.*

Connor's ambush was every bit as bad as what the old preacher had done: singled me out as a prodigal.

Behind me, the biddies muttered, shushed by Mary Lou, God bless her, but I was strong enough now to know that their problems with me were theirs, not mine.

God, I know I'm supposed to forgive him for this, but this stunt is going to take some serious time. I'm just being honest, here. And while we're being honest, I cannot fathom why You would let this happen.

God held His peace.

A quote from Corrie ten Boom came to mind: "Every experience God gives us, every person He puts into our lives, is the perfect preparation for a future only He can see."

Okay, then. I forgive him, I grudgingly prayed as an act of obedience, but my humanity wanted to haul off and kayo Connor Allen in front of the whole congregation.

Not a good idea, the still, small voice said. *Let it go.*

As if!

He'd used me, without even asking.

God's thought-voice in my head spoke with authority. *Let it go. I know the plans I have for you. Let it go.*

Still boiling, I had no choice but to obey, so I started reciting Bible verses in my head to clear the anger while the deacons welcomed six people who'd come down the aisle. All of them beaming about their decisions, they turned to face the congregation as we sang the final hymn, "Arise My Soul, Arise."

Connor said the benediction, then came straight for me, taking my hand and drawing me toward the four men and two women who'd professed their faith in Christ.

Fortunately, I'd managed in the meantime to hide my fury behind my inner duchess.

As the congregation rose and lined up to greet us all, Connor whispered softly, "You are the bravest woman I've ever met to do this. Looking like an angel, I might add."

I leaned close to his ear. "When I get you alone," I said through a fixed smile, "I am going to *kill* your ass."

Connor pulled back in surprise. "Why?"

Idiot man. He *was* just a man, as Granny had warned me.

"If you have to ask, you are too clueless to live," I murmured through my smile.

Flummoxed, Connor turned his attention to greeting each congregant by name. When the reluctant biddies came through, he gently asked each of them to welcome me. If they remained stiff, he prodded with a grin, "Now, is that the best you can do?"

Of their group, only Mary Lou embraced me with kindness, prompting some of the others to relent. But more remained erect and said that it *was* the best they could do, then stomped off.

Happily, though, the great majority of the congregation was warm in welcoming me.

At least I knew that most of them were glad to see me. But I still wanted to do mayhem about what Connor had done.

After everyone had come through the line, Connor removed his plain black robe and offered his hand. "May I walk back with you? Tommy invited me to your mother's famous Easter brunch."

Seeing him reach for my hand, a few stragglers zeroed in on me, so I continued the outward charade of calm, ignoring his gesture. "Sure," I murmured, "as long as you do not touch me in any way."

Again, he frowned at my hostility. "Why are you so angry?"

"Because you are so unaware of how you just used me." I sailed out, down the steps, then onto the sidewalk with him scrambling to catch up.

Strolling ahead of Connor, I greeted all I saw, then nodded and smiled at the cars that passed us and waved.

By the time we neared my house, I had calmed down enough to wonder who else Tommy had invited. Probably someone from the program who didn't have any family here. He often invited those.

Whoever it was, I was glad. I could talk to them instead of Connor.

We reached 1431 Green Street, now adorned by red tulips in the wretched bathtub, tons of daffodils in the lawn, and budding azaleas.

Before we stepped onto the graveled drive, Connor stopped and took it all in. "What a beautiful home you grew up in."

Trying to see it with new eyes, I admired it myself. "Yep."

When I started forward, Connor remained on the sidewalk, as if he didn't want to go in.

I turned to face him squarely with a hostile, "What?"

He glanced at his feet, then back to me with apology on his face. "You deserve an answer from me, one way or the other, but I still don't have one."

So what else was new? I started for the house, prompting him to catch up and walk beside me.

"You said God had made us for each other," I challenged as we headed for the front stairs. "Do you think He's changed His mind?"

Connor exhaled sharply. "I don't know what to think anymore."

I wasn't impressed. "Whatever."

As we climbed the stairs, his expression went grim. "I need to know what I've done wrong," he said as he opened the screen.

"Don't worry," I said. "You'll find out in heaven, where all things are known."

That shut him up, good and proper. Stiff, he followed me to the kitchen where God's answer to our prayers awaited.

Sixty-five

There, in Daddy's chair, sat my ex-husband, and Miss Mamie was waiting on him like royalty, refilling his iced tea. Carla busied herself with the buffet.

"Now you're sure," she cooed, "you wouldn't rather start off with a nice hot cup of coffee?"

Phil looked up at Connor with visible resentment as he rose. "Lin." He nodded to me in deference, then scowled. "What's he doing here?"

"Tommy invited me," Connor said before I could answer, his voice firm. "What are you doing here?"

Phil plopped back down into Daddy's chair, his hands claiming the polished arms as he leaned back to cross his leg at the knee. "Tommy invited me, too."

What the heck had my brother been thinking?

Miss Mamie straightened, showing her steel. "This is my home," she said to them quietly, "and I won't have you two acting like two tomcats in the same sandbox." She brightened. "Carla and I have prepared a wonderful meal, and I expect all of us to enjoy it together. Civilly."

Not much civility there, but I knew better than to disobey Miss Mamie at her table, and so, apparently, did Connor and Phil.

Connor eased. "You're right, Miss Mamie. I can't wait to eat when Tommy gets here."

She waved her hand in dismissal. "If we wait for him, everything's liable to get cold. That's why I set up that buffet line on the counter. Y'all get your plates and dig in."

"Connor," I interrupted, "would you please bless this for us?"

He nodded, bending his head but keeping his eyes on my ex. "Lord, we thank You for the many blessings You have given us, including Miss Mamie and this wonderful meal she prepared for us, and for the presence of each person at this table, including Phil. May we be humble in Your sight and do Your will this day. Amen."

Clearly skeptical, Phil took up his plate and headed for the food, then remembered himself and motioned Miss Mamie, Carla, and me ahead of him. "Ladies first."

Mama actually batted her lashes at him. "Now Phil, dear, have you forgotten? I always go last."

Connor quirked a smile. "The last shall be first."

What must he be thinking?

What was *Phil* thinking?

And why was Mama being so nice to him?

Carla quietly started through the line.

Thoroughly confused, I started helping myself to the feast.

When we all had sat back down, Miss Mamie spread her napkin in her lap, then took up her fork and started, so we all chowed down, even though you could have frozen molten steel with the iciness between Connor and my ex.

Miss Mamie leaned over to Phil. "Now eat up, honey. I want to be sure you're well filled before you leave this house. It's the least I can do."

What was that about?

We'd been eating for about fifteen minutes when we all heard Tommy's truck arrive and stop in the porte cochere.

I knew something was up the minute he and his guest entered the room. "Sorry we're late. John here had some last-minute paperwork to finish." He introduced John Mason to Mama, then they both sat down, John next to Phil.

"John, you've met my wife Carla," Tommy went on. "And this is my sister Lin, and Connor Allen, pastor of First Baptist, and sitting next to you is Lin's ex-husband, Phil Scott."

John leaned across the table to shake hands with all of us, then settled back down.

"All right, you two," Mama said. "It's already blessed. Take your plates over and eat up. I don't want any leftovers."

"Thank you, ma'am. This sure smells great," John said as he rose.

Mama grinned with pride. "It tastes great, too. Not many folks besides our Carla want to take the time anymore to cook true Southern the way I do."

John focused an enigmatic glance at Phil, then headed for the buffet with Tommy.

Once we were all eating, I looked to John and asked, "How do you and Tommy know each other?"

"Through a mutual friend," they both said at once.

That was a common AA answer, so I changed the subject. "What line of work are you in, John?"

An odd expression flitted across his face. "I'm an accountant for the biggest employer in the country."

The hint went right over my head. "Ah. Then you and Phil will have plenty in common. He used to be a CPA."

"Still am," Phil grumbled.

Tommy peered from one to another of us as if we were all in a movie. Clearly, he expected something to happen. But what?

Meanwhile, Miss Mamie got up and refilled iced teas, then passed her yeast rolls and sweet rolls, then the sliced melons.

I felt like the only kid in the class who didn't know what was going on, but Connor's expression told me he didn't know, either.

We were all stuffed when John rose. "Miss Mamie, that is the best brunch I have ever eaten in my life. Thanks so much. Now, if you'll excuse me, I have to go to work."

"But it's a holiday," she protested mildly.

Tommy rose, too, and stepped between me and Phil.

John reached inside his suit jacket and retrieved a gold badge and a pair of handcuffs, then hoisted Phil to his feet. "Philip David Scott, as an officer of the Treasury Department, I hereby place you under arrest for thirteen counts of tax evasion and three of deliberate underpayment, in addition to evading arrest, felony perjury, and eighty-three counts of electronic mail fraud."

Stunned, Phil glared at him.

As John read him his rights, Phil turned a vicious look on me. "This is all your fault. If you'd just married me, none of this would have happened. But no, I had to *woo* you. Do you have any idea what that ended up costing me? Now look what's happened, you stupid bitch."

I smiled and said, "So you weren't really born again. I can't believe I was stupid enough to think you might be."

The man I'd been married to for thirty years responded with a hiss of hate.

Once Phil was well secured between Tommy and John, John handed me a paper from the inner pocket of his jacket. "Ms. Linwood Breedlove Scott, this is a summons for you to appear as a material witness at Mr. Scott's trial. We have a lot of questions about your marital property. As you two are now divorced, you may speak freely."

So *that* was it. I turned on Phil. "You wanted me to marry you so I couldn't testify against you." I had to laugh. "Wives can testify against their husbands if they want to. They do it all the time. They just can't be *forced* to testify against them."

Phil spat my way, then called me a word so vulgar I cannot repeat it, upon which my mother stood up and slapped the bejeebers out of him, then blithely returned to her seat.

"I do not tolerate insults and vulgar language at my table," she said sweetly.

I looked to my brother with infinite gratitude. "Thank you, Tommy. Thank you *so* much." Then I turned to John, "And you, working on the holiday. God bless you."

"Ma'am, believe me when I say I was glad to do it. We've been trying to catch Mr. Scott for years," John said, "but he always evaded us with fake passports. When Tommy contacted me with what he knew, we were able to locate where Mr. Scott had been hiding out with his ex-girlfriend. We tracked her down, and she rolled on him in exchange for a reduced sentence. Her testimony and yours will put Mr. Scott away for a very long time."

"So there is justice, after all," I breathed.

Tommy shot me a grin as he and the T-man hustled Phil away to meet the consequences of his crimes.

I stood there long after they were gone, wondering how I could have been gullible enough even to consider taking Phil at his word. As Aesop showed us, a scorpion is a scorpion is a scorpion.

Then I heard a sound behind me that brought my attention back to the table.

Connor had put his face into his hands and sat there bent over and shaking. At first, I thought he was crying, but he wasn't. He was laughing.

He looked at me in amazement, then jumped up and pulled Miss Mamie into a polka, singing "When the Roll Is Called Up Yonder," while my mother joined him at the top of her voice.

A Baptist minister, dancing. Good for him.

It sank in, deep, that I didn't have to give up who I was to be with him, clueless though he might be. I had college to keep me busy, my own life and interests. I didn't have to be an extension of Connor or his ministry, sitting home and trying to fit some ridiculous stereotype.

He'd said he loved *me,* just as I was.

The stone that had been crushing my hopes rolled away.

I sat watching till they both collapsed back into their chairs. Brows lifted, I asked Connor, "Was that enough of an answer about you and me, or what?"

Still breathing hard through his grin, Connor got up, then went to one knee before me, taking my hands. "Linwood Breedlove Scott, will you do me the honor of becoming my wife Saturday after next at our church?"

I looked into Connor's eyes and said, "No. I will not."

Stunned, he shot to his feet. "What?"

"I cannot marry a man who uses God as an excuse to leave me hanging." I glanced into my lap. "I want a man who will fight for me, protect me, even from his own children, and go to the chair for me if I rob a Seven-Eleven, as Christ died for his bride, the church. That's the husband Ephesians teaches. Not a man who would put his work above our relationship, no matter how wonderful that work might be."

I thought of Helen with renewed sympathy.

Connor raked his fingers through his white hair, smoothing away the deep worry lines across his forehead. "Dear Lord, I did it again."

I nodded, seeing the truth sink in with maximum impact.

With that, he drew me from my seat and embraced me. "Lin, I am *so* sorry. I was so busy trying to discern God's will that I didn't see what it was costing you. Is there any hope for me?"

"Maybe," I said, nestling close. "I might be able to help."

He smiled with wonder. "I think you could. Please, will you be my help-mate?"

I had one last reservation. "Connor, I'm so weary of losing the things I love and having to fight my way back alone. I can only marry you if you promise to protect me, sometimes even from myself. Even from the demands of your work. Even from our children."

His gaze searched mine, the promise of ages in his eyes. "I will."

"Then I will marry you Saturday after next at our church." I was taking a chance, but he was worth it.

Instantly, the tension evaporated from the room. Miss Mamie clapped with glee.

Connor was definitely a frog, but all in all, a darned good one. "Boy, do you need me," I told him. "The next time you want to pull a stunt like you did today in church, run it by me first, before you shoot yourself in the foot."

It finally dawned on him what he'd done, and he had enough sense not to try to justify it. He whacked his brow. "I should have asked you first."

"Bingo."

He shook his head in shame. "I just wanted to surprise you, welcome you back." Then he brightened, blue eyes sparkling. "I *do* need you."

His lips grazed my ear as he murmured, "And your bodddy."

Bang, zoom! Chemistry.

It was my turn to laugh with joy. "Mama, do you mind if I move next door?"

Miss Mamie grinned. "Go ahead, as long as you leave me that electric blanket. And still come to breakfast."

"Done."

Connor stood and drew me into his arms for another of those Times Square kisses while Miss Mamie looked on with approval.

"Now, *that's* how a man should kiss a woman," she declared.

I curled into his arms afterward, and my inner child, my practical self, my hedonist, and my wild side—even my inner Puritan—joined in a group hug with a unanimous chorus of praise.

The Queen Bee of Mimosa Branch had found true love at last.

Now, if I could only pass math.

Sixty-six

Two weeks later, on a glorious day in May, I walked to the old Presbyterian/new Baptist church in my *Somewhere in Time* dress and hat, accompanied by my brother and his wife, and Miss Mamie. Never has there been a happier procession. Because Phil and I had eloped, this was my first real wedding, so I walked very slowly to prolong the anticipation.

When we got to the church, the parking lot was full, and the iron railings were swagged with fresh daisies and white tulle, a gift from the local florist in gratitude for Phil's tulip orders.

Inside, Mary Lou was waiting and gave me and Miss Mamie a hug, then headed back to her seat, closing the doors behind her. But not before I caught a glimpse of Noel Austeen waiting on the dais to marry us.

Noel Austeen! Pastor of the largest evangelical church in America! And Connor hadn't told me.

I *loved* Noel Austeen's preaching!

You marry a holy man, I guess you rate another high holy man to do it.

Fighting butterflies, I kissed Miss Mamie, then sent her off to be seated.

Tommy escorted her and Carla down the aisle, closing the door behind them. Then he came back for me.

We waited till the Bridal March cued our entrance, then we opened wide the doors and processed toward Connor, who was winking and grinning toward two young women in the first row of the groom's side.

Then I looked toward Mama and saw David with his whole family, beaming proudly at me from the first row. Two-year-old Barrett stood up and hollered, "Hey, GoGo!" much to his four-year-old sister's embarrassment.

I blew him a kiss while Barb snatched him into her lap.

An indulgent rumble of laughter rolled through the congregation

Tommy and I both waved.

Then I turned to Connor's daughters and gave each a hug and a whispered, "I'm *so* glad y'all could be here. It means so much to your daddy and me. Thank you."

Only then did I focus on my radiant groom, resplendent in a white seersucker suit.

Okay, God, here we go. If this isn't what You want for us, speak now or forever hold Your peace.

The still, small voice remained silent, thank goodness.

I was taking a chance marrying Connor, but he was worth the risk. In the last week, we'd been inseparable until we'd gone our separate ways to sleep. Tonight, we wouldn't have to separate.

A shiver of anticipation shot through me. This was the way it was supposed to be.

Tommy laid my hand atop Connor's, then took his place beside Mama.

I leaned close to whisper, "This is it. Last chance to escape." Not that I thought he would.

He clasped my hands with a radiant smile. "Noel, let's get this show on the road."

Fortunately, Noel's marriage ceremony was far briefer than his wonderful sermons. I especially liked it when, after we'd said our *I do*s, Noel had us turn to the congregation, then asked their promise to help and encourage us in our marriage.

To my deep gratitude, they answered as one with, "We do!"

Then Noel looked across the sea of faces and said a firm, "Those whom God hath joined together, let not *anyone* put asunder."

Then he turned to us and said, "You may now kiss the bride."

Connor's kiss was brief and gentle, then he turned back to the congregation to announce at the top of his lungs, "We're having a party in the fellowship hall downstairs, with homemade ice cream and cake, and you're all invited. May the Lord go with you, amen."

Everyone crowded down to congratulate us and get a closer look at Noel, but I turned my attention to Connor's daughters, who were more than cordial. When I asked about their mother, they seemed mildly suspicious, but I eased their fears with, "I know how hard the divorce must have been on all of you. Especially on your mother. I so hope she's happy in her new relationship."

The elder of the two brightened. "She is."

I nodded. "That's good. I'll never ask you to choose between us. She's welcome at anything and everything. She's your mother, God bless her, and Connor and I both wish her well."

She peered at me with guarded approval.

Good. At least it was a start.

I patted her arm, then said, "If you'll excuse me, I need to speak to my son and my mother."

She and her sister nodded, then headed for Connor while I went straight for Barrett and Callista, who were inspecting Miss Mamie with little fingers and eyes.

"Look, GoGo," Callista chirped, "Bam's got lots of love lines."

Miss Mamie submitted to their inspection with a smile. "It sure feels good to have the little ones around again." She gave them both a squeeze.

David looked over them to ask, "Are you as happy as you look, Mama? I sure hope so."

I nodded. "Ecstatic. Especially about tonight."

Miss Mamie chortled while my son and his wife reddened. But David wasn't daunted. "I wish you all the happiness in the world. Especially since Dad's gotten his comeuppance."

I laid my hand on his arm. "Oh, sweetheart. Your dad is who he is. Nobody's all bad or all good. I hope you two can find some common ground to maintain a relationship. He needs you now. I promise, you'll never be sorry."

He peered at me, considering. "I need to talk to you more often."

I beamed. "That's what I've been tellin' you. Now come on." I picked Barrett up and headed for the fellowship hall. "Let's celebrate with ice cream and cake."

Connor came over and introduced himself to my son and his wife, then Callista.

Enchanted, Callista practically climbed up into his arms. "Who are you?"

"I'm your new granddaddy. What would you like to call me?"

She considered, frowning. "I don't know."

Connor gave her a reassuring smile. "How about I give you some names to choose from, and you can pick your favorite?"

Barrett chose that moment to intervene. He pointed to me, then Connor. "GoGo, Dodo."

Callista clapped. "That's it. GoGo and Dodo."

I couldn't help laughing. "That's what you get when you let a four-year-old choose your name."

Connor rolled his eyes. "Very humbling, but I accept. I reserve the right, though, to encourage them to change it."

David chuckled. "Good luck with that one."

Then we all went to the party. It was hard work, laying the groundwork for good relationships in the congregation, listening to their concerns and encouraging them, so by the time everyone else had left, I was worn out.

Connor put his arm around me. "I saw what you did. It was wonderful."

"I'll never learn all their names," I admitted.

He gave me a sidelong squeeze. "You have me for that."

We soaked in the silence, then Connor got out his key to the church. "Come on, Mrs. Allen. Let's lock up, then go home and go to bed."

Yes! Sex. Sex, sex, sex!

So we strolled home, hand in hand, the chemistry building with every step. Then we had a very interesting shower together, after which we rolled all over that big old bed and acted like we were twenty-five again. And again. And again.

Nothing like what I'd known before. This was like fireworks compared to an ember.

Heaven. It was heaven.

Halleluiah, amen!

Who cared if I passed math? I mean, really.